A Little Luck

USA TODAY BESTSELLING AUTHOR
TIA LOUISE

This book is a work of fiction. Names, characters, places, and incidents are products of the author's imagination or are used fictitiously. Any resemblance to actual events or locales or persons, living or dead, is entirely coincidental.

A Little Luck
Copyright © TLM Productions LLC, 2023
Printed in the United States of America.

Cover design byY'all that Graphic.

All rights reserved. No part of this publication can be reproduced, stored in a retrieval system, or transmitted in any form or by any means—electronic, photocopying, mechanical, or otherwise—without prior permission of the publisher and author.

Playlist

See You Again - Tyler, The Creator, Kali Uchis

Banana Republics - Jimmy Buffett

Not Strong Enough - boygenius

And So It Goes - Billy Joel

Don't Think Twice, It's All Right - Bob Dylan

I Did Something Bad - Taylor Swift

The Thing That Wrecks You - Tenille Townes, Bryan Adams

…Margaret - Lana Del Rey, Bleachers

Beautiful Boy - John Lennon

Karma - Taylor Swift

I'm Goin' Down - Bruce Springsteen

It's All Coming Back to Me Now - Céline Dion

Love Story - Taylor Swift

"I'll make up for all the years I was supposed to be kissing you…"
—Leo Christopher

"Be bold and mighty forces will come to your aid."
—Goethe

For my readers and Mr. TL, Love never fails.

Reader Note

This book contains references to past domestic violence. It is my hope I have handled this topic with the care it deserves.

Prologue

Piper

That night...

"**P**IPER ANN, STAY WITH ME!"

Searing pain twists my abdomen, and I'm rethinking Taco Tuesday for dinner.

"It hurts so bad," I gasp, gripping the dash and holding the base of my stomach as my mother squeals tires, coming to an abrupt stop in front of the glass double doors of the small, community hospital in Ridgeland.

"We made it!" My mother's eyes are wide as she jams the truck into park.

Slamming the door, she runs around the front, waving her hands and screaming at the two men in scrubs leaning on the counter on the other side of the entrance. "Can we get some help out here? We've got a baby on the way!"

I'm too distracted by the cramps snarling my insides to care that my crazy mother looks even crazier right now.

For nine months I've been mentally preparing for the chaos of labor, but I didn't expect to be so out of control—or for my mother, the queen of suspicion and hiding, to have the reins.

I'd been feeling off all day, so after dinner, I decided to take a walk to Mom's. Our town of Eureka, South Carolina, is small enough that the walk from my ancient house behind the tiny newspaper office where I work to my mom's even ancient-er house on the street behind the church takes less than ten minutes.

I had just made it to the edge of her driveway when my water broke—and all hell broke loose with it.

Opening the door of the step-side, she reaches for my hand. "Are you able to climb down?"

"I'm afraid he's going to fall out." I do my best to deadpan.

A therapist once told me laughter was my trauma response.

"Oh, God!" Mom actually drops to one knee as I climb out of the vehicle.

"I was joking," I manage through a hiss.

A beefy man appears beside her, reaching for my arms while his friend holds a wheelchair. "Easy there, we've got you."

I'm lowered into a different sitting position as uncomfortable as the first one, and they wheel me to the entrance of the hospital.

The man at my arm motions to a stocky woman sitting behind a desk. "We'll just get you checked in, and then we can get you to a room."

"We don't have time for that!" Mom is in the guy's face. "This baby has been coming for almost an hour! We drove here from Eureka!"

His dark brow lowers, and he glances at his partner.

The woman at the desk waves us along. "Take her to a room and get her hooked up to the monitors. Ma'am, you're going to have to move that truck."

A strong hand grasps my wrist. "I'll be right back." My mother's tone is conspiratorial as she eyes each of the staff members. "Don't worry—I won't let either of you out of my sight."

I'm only worried I'm about to barf refried beans into my lap. This pain is like the worst stomach cramps multiplied by a thousand, and I didn't take any natural childbirth classes. I'm on my fucking own right now, and I have no idea what to do. I should've at least prepared for the chance I might not get pain meds. I've heard of it happening.

"What was I thinking?" A sheen of sweat is on my forehead and upper lip, and I'm hurting so bad, I'm trembling.

"If I had a nickel for every time I heard that one." The deadpan voice rivals my own, and I glance up to see a nurse in pink scrubs striding in my direction. "Let me guess, the father's not in the picture?"

My lips part over gritted teeth, and I shake my head as another contraction hits me hard. "He's dead." It comes out as a grunt.

Her demeanor changes at once. "Shit, I'm sorry. Me and my big mouth. I'm always sticking my foot in it."

Holding up a hand, I shake my head harder as if that'll help me get through this long, long contraction. Tears flood my eyes as it knots lower in my stomach, and I try to breathe. Even if I didn't take the classes, I've seen enough movies to know they're always telling women to breathe. It's harder than it looks.

"Can I get the drugs now?" I quickly read her name tag. "Sally?"

"Anesthesiologist is working with another patient at the moment. Your doctor is on the way to check you." She helps me onto the bed and starts peeling paper off the backs of little round leads. "Let's get you hooked up so we can hear what's happening."

She affixes them to my stomach and chest. Then she holds my wrist and rubs a numbing gel on my skin before sticking me with the IV port, as if that needle stick holds a candle to the pain that hits me every three to five minutes.

Still, I'm grateful for the little things.

All at once, the room is flooded with persistent beeping noises. Green lines trace up and down across the stacked monitors to my left, telling us what's what.

"Looks like a healthy heartbeat for both of you, if a bit elevated." She gives me a wink as another contraction hits.

It's the hardest yet. My hand shoots out to grip the side of the bed, and I try to breathe. It's not enough. My hand flies to my mouth just as Sally snatches a plastic bin from somewhere and puts it under my chin. Taco Tuesday is back.

"Why hasn't she gotten the epidural?" Mom's voice echoes in the room. "Oh, my girl, my poor Piper Ann."

My damp eyes are closed as Sally does her best to clean the vomit off my face and chin. She sweeps the pan away as a doctor enters the room.

"Let's see where you are now." This is not my doctor, but barfing has taken the wind out of my sails. I'm too miserable to fight.

I'm arranged on the bed, my feet in the stirrups, and a cool breeze wafts around my bare lower half. My body tenses at what he's going to see on my inner thighs. I'm not prepared to answer questions or endure pointed looks. Miraculously, he doesn't seem to notice.

"It's time! Nurse, put the bed together! *Stat!*"

"She wanted an epidural—" Sally tries to argue, but the doctor cuts her off.

"It's too late for that. This baby is coming now."

"Just my luck," I grunt as another, harder contraction grinds through me.

I'm not sure how much more of this I can take. I'm pretty sure my hips are about to pop out of their sockets, and they have me lying on my back when everything in me wants to stand and pace the room.

"I'm here." Mom's voice is quietly urgent at my side, and

everything seems to slip into a slow-moving tunnel. "Work with your body. Do what it's telling you…"

The swirl of voices and beeps and busyness blends into a dull roar in my ears. Pain has me tight in its fist, and I howl like a wounded animal. Sally holds my legs, and the doctor guides something warm and wet between them. They tell me to push again, and just when I think my strength is gone, relief comes.

A mirror is at the foot of the bed, and a dark brown bundle pushes through my thighs. I'm crying again, only this time they're tears of relief, joy, *disbelief…*

Another push, and his entire body shoots out. The doctor lifts him, and the shrillest, sweetest wail echoes through the room. Fresh tears flood my eyes, and I'm not the only one crying. Looking to the side, I see Mom sobbing. Even Sally's apple cheeks, lifted by her broad smile, are damp.

After that, it all wraps up quickly. The placenta passes, my son is cleaned and weighed, then he's in my arms snuggled at my breast and nursing like he hasn't eaten in weeks.

"He has a perfect latch." The lactation consultant at my bedside preens.

I'm so exhausted, I only nod, holding him closer as the blankets wrap tighter around us. Everything about him is perfect, from his tiny button nose to his thick black hair, and his giant, dark blue eyes.

My mom stands guard at my side, keeping her eyes on everyone.

Sally walks up with a clipboard and a smile. "If you have a name in mind, I can get the birth certificate filed."

"First name, Ryan…" I've been in love with that name since I was a girl. It always reminds me of the sun rising over the hills. "Phillip…"

"Last name?"

"Barlow." My mother says fast.

"Jackson!" I glare at her.

"But that's—"

"I want him to have *my* last name."

Sally hesitates, looking from her to me, and my mother's lips purse. Before we can answer, my best friends Britt and Cass rush into the room followed closely by Britt's mother Gwen.

"Piper! Oh, my gosh, we got here as fast as we could." Britt makes a beeline to my bedside with Cass right behind her.

Gwen goes to stand beside my mother, and I don't miss the two of them exchanging concerned looks.

"Mom insisted on driving as slow as molasses in January," Britt complains.

"I drove the speed limit," Gwen speaks over her daughter.

"We missed the whole thing."

"Ohh… But he's so adorable!" Cass coos, leaning down to trace her finger over my son's dark hair. "Sweet baby Ryan. You're the most precious little boy in the whole world, and we're just going to spoil you rotten!"

Cass is talking baby talk, and Britt is at my side. I can relax.

Shifting to the side, I allow my best friend to take my son, who's finished nursing and is now looking at all of us with round eyes.

"You're exhausted." Britt smooths her hand over my forehead. "Just sleep. We're not going anywhere."

Nodding, my eyes are so heavy, and a wave of gratitude hits me. I blink back tears, holding her hand to my cheek. "I'm so glad you're here."

"Oh, honey." Britt leans her forehead against the top of my head. "We'll always be here."

My chin bobs up and down, and she hands me a tissue.

Sleep is a heavy weight, and I guess I've been holding on for them to arrive. "I'm just going to rest a few minutes."

"Okay," my friend laughs softly. "You do that."

When I open my eyes again, the room is dark and quiet—except for the nonstop beeping of the monitors. Ryan is asleep in a clear plastic bin at my bedside, and as I blink slowly, I see he's wrapped tight like a little burrito. Standing beside his crib is a man whose presence warms me to my soul.

Adam Stone.

He's dressed casually in a navy tee and loose, faded jeans. A dark blue ball cap is turned backwards over his longish, light-brown hair. Short sleeves reveal tanned, muscular arms, and I know from so many summers spent in bathing suits at the beach, his legs are equally muscular.

His body is perfect.

Naughty blue eyes now brim with affection, and a smile curls his full lips as he traces a finger over Ryan's dark head.

"Beautiful boy." His voice is low and rich. "You look just like her."

My breath hitches, and my eyes close. He's here. He came for me.

We've been close since we were tweens—we were all close friends, but as we got older, as we all started thinking about love and sex, it was his best friend Rex Barlow who asked me out and wanted more.

At the time, I wasn't sure. I liked them both, but when Rex made the first move, Adam pulled away. We were only ever friends after that, and as Rex's perfect mask fell away and I learned who my boyfriend really was, the shame set in and the walls around my heart began to grow taller.

Tonight, in this dim-lit room with everything changed, I hold my breath and wish…

I wish for a different life—one without secrets and where I have no fear. Where shame and broken trust don't haunt me. Where I'm not a prisoner of the past, and when I reach for him, he pulls me close. He promises to keep me safe and never let me go.

My baby stretches, turning his little head to the side and opening his mouth in that funny, birdlike way that means he's hungry.

Adam's smile loosens, and he shoves his hair behind his ears.

The ends are touched with caramel from long days spent on a surfboard. He lives on a surfboard, carefree and open.

Only, since Rex died nine months ago, I've watched him slowly grow less carefree and more careless. A silent gulf stretched between us, and the more pregnant I became, the further he withdrew into drinking or drugs.

I have no right to question his choices, but I don't like them. I'm not the only one.

The baby sneezes, and Adam's eyebrows lift. "Bless you," he laughs, and I shift in the bed, sitting up slowly, drawing his attention.

"He's probably hungry." My voice is hoarse from all the yelling earlier when I was in labor.

Adam's blue eyes land on mine, and the change in them is striking. Tonight the distance is gone, and heat has taken its place. It burns in my stomach, reviving a longing so close to the surface, I have to look away.

"Stay there, Piper Ann." A teasing note is in his tone as he lifts the tiny infant in his hands, carrying him like a football across the space from the crib to me.

"Only my mom calls me that." I take my swaddled little boy, moving him under my hospital gown and pulling the blanket over me. I turn to the side, self-conscious at the state of my body, all out of sorts, damaged and misshapen.

"I know." He watches us quietly before lifting a white paper bag. "I brought you something."

My brows rise, and I press my lips into a smile. "What is it?"

"A push present."

"Oh, really?" I laugh softly. "You didn't have to…"

I don't want to finish that sentence.

Reaching inside, he slides an oversized, elaborately decorated cupcake from the bag. It's dark-brown chocolate with tan frosting and tiny Oreos on top. "Your favorite."

"Chocolate peanut butter Oreo!"

"Not too much peanut butter to overpower the chocolate."

"Just how I like it." My voice fades into a whisper, and my hormones must be wrecked, because more tears try to sneak out of my eyes. "You're too sweet to me."

"No." Swaying closer, he places the small cake on my bedside table before reaching out to cup the top of Ryan's little head. Only he doesn't quite make it, rocking back on his heels before moving forward again, so close I think he'll try to kiss me. "He's sweet."

That's when a slice of pain, the pain of loss moves through my chest. My heart becomes quiet, and the intense longing stills.

The baby boy in my arms moves to the front of my attention, and I realize I've changed in a way I can't control. At some point, during the searing pain of labor or the soothing calm of nursing, a new force rose inside me.

It's stronger than my heart, and it has no more tolerance for bad behavior.

"Are you high?" My voice is quiet.

At first, I'm not even sure he heard me, but he did.

Guilty blue eyes meet mine, and the hope I had evaporates like smoke. His pretty eyes are bloodshot and tired, and that sliver of pain in my chest hurts so much. He was too far away before, or I was too blinded by lust or sweetness to see it.

"I'm not *that* high." He winks, attempting the bad-boy grin that melts most girls' panties.

Ryan stretches in my arms, finished nursing, and I move him onto my chest. Adam steps closer, and I catch the scent of whiskey. He's not just high. He's been drinking.

"You can't keep doing this." It's not a scold—it's a simple statement of fact.

"Piper..." He reaches out to wipe the tears from my cheeks, but I turn away.

"Don't."

"Why are you crying? It was just a little celebration."

"Every day's a celebration." I look up at him. "How long before you're dead, too?"

A wince, and he leans down as if he'll pull me into his arms—what I've always dreamed he'd do, only now it leaves me cold. Now it makes me wonder if I'll always be this way, falling in love with men who aren't who they seem to be.

Or who I need them to be.

"You can't be around my son like this." I swallow the knot at the base of my throat. "Or me."

"What are you saying?" He tries to smile, but his dark brow furrows.

"You have to go."

Our eyes meet again, and I'm afraid when I see the pain in his. But I have to be strong… for my son.

"Don't come back until you're clean."

His hand holding mine drops, and he turns, leaving the room as quietly as he entered it, breaking my heart as easily as he stole it all those years ago.

Adam

My forehead is pressed against the steering wheel. I'm sitting in my car on the side of the road, and red and blue lights flash through the back window, reflecting in all the mirrors and stinging my eyes every time they hit them.

I'd almost made it all the way to my house in Eureka, which means one thing.

Fuck.

Closing my eyes, I see her face so clearly, pretty hazel eyes wet with tears, wavy red hair stuck to her cheeks and the sides of her neck. Mascara flecks under her eyes.

She was exhausted and weak from childbirth, and she was the most beautiful thing I'd ever seen. I wanted to pull her into my arms, both of them. Baby Ryan, with his tiny fists waving and his little face so perfectly hers.

A Little Luck

He sneezed, and I was a goner.

It was a mistake.

I shouldn't have gone there tonight, but I couldn't stay away. I had to see her. I needed her to know she'd been on my mind every second since Britt texted me. I had to make sure she was taken care of—even if it meant breaking the law.

Even if I haven't had a sober day since the night he died.

Even if I've kept my distance in an effort to absolve my sin; the sin of wanting her so much, I found it hard to mourn my best friend's death.

The tall, dark silhouette walks slowly to where I'm sitting, and my fists tighten on the steering wheel. What is he doing out here at this time of night? He's supposed to be at home with his family, leaving shit like this to the state troopers.

Although, to be honest, I'd rather deal with him than them.

His dark brow lowers over steely blue eyes, and he stops at the driver's side window of my car. My oldest brother Aiden Stone, sheriff of our small town, glowers at me from the driver's side of my car. The muscle in his jaw moves back and forth as he shakes his head, exhaling slowly.

"What the fuck, Adam?" Disgust and impatience permeate his tone.

Anger tightens my jaw. After Dad died, he appointed himself surrogate father, but what the hell does he know about my life? He's always had everything handed to him on a platter. Captain fucking America.

"Piper had a little boy tonight."

Lifting his square chin, he looks out across the empty field. A slow moment passes, and he rubs a hand over his mouth before speaking.

"How're they doing?"

"Good. She's strong. He's perfect." Roughness enters my tone. "He looks just like her with Rex's dark hair."

Even after nine months, saying my dead best friend's name

cuts like a knife. It cuts almost as deep as loving the girl he left behind.

If anything happens to me, you'll look after her... Rex said the words to me the night he died, before any of us knew she was pregnant, before his motorcycle slammed into a tree on the side of the highway, killing him in an instant, the coroner said.

As the words came out, my insides froze wondering if my wish was strong enough to cause something like that.

"I can't ignore this." Aiden's voice is angry now. "You're my brother, but it's been nine months of looking the other way. There have to be consequences."

He thinks I'm afraid of the consequences. He doesn't know I welcome them, anything to assuage the guilt. "Okay."

"I'll drive you home. You can pick up your car tomorrow."

"Tomorrow." I nod, thinking how one day is like all the rest. Nothing makes sense anymore... except her.

I blew it tonight, and when tomorrow comes, I find myself sitting across the desk from Aiden in his office at the courthouse.

I'd barely made it through my door last night, when I passed out on the couch, and he was at my house first thing this morning, dragging my ass to pick up my car and then to face whatever consequences I'm sure he sat up all night planning.

He studies the legal pad in front of him, looking just like our dad, whose job he inherited.

Shifting in my chair, I want to be out on the ocean, riding the waves. I want to lean back on the board, close my eyes, and let the ocean carry me away from all this death and loss and pain and regret.

"Community service." My brother's voice pulls me to attention. "We have a contract with a state mental health professional. You're going to see her for as long as she says, and you're joining the Navy."

"The fuck?" I sit straighter in the uncomfortable wooden chair. "I'm no jarhead."

"No, you're not." He gives me his former-Marine glare. "But they'll figure out what to do with you. They'll get you straight."

"You can't make me join the military."

"I can put your ass in jail. This is the second time I've caught you driving under the influence. Do you know the penalty for that?"

"It's only my first time on the record." If he even filed the paperwork.

"I could make a case for it being your second offense." His jaw is tight. "I have the power to throw the book at you, and don't think I'm not considering it. Mom's pleading might've worked with Dad, but I'm not letting you get away with breaking the law… or wasting your life."

He adds the last part under his breath, and my fists tighten. I'm ready to flip a table. "You're not my dad, asshole."

"No, I'm not." We're both on our feet, facing each other, square jaws tight. "But I'm the sheriff here, and you don't have a say in the matter. It's decided."

At six-two, he's a half-inch taller than me, which pisses me off even more. People say we look alike with brown hair and blue eyes, but I see nothing of myself in him. Aiden's had a stick up his ass since I was a kid.

"You've been waiting for this day."

His lips tighten, but he only shakes his head. "I love you, brother. You can't see it now, but this is the best thing. It's the only thing that's going to save you from yourself. I don't want to pull your dead body out of a ditch next time."

I'd argue with him if I could, but my grip is slipping. Rage is in my chest, but I know he's right. I've lost control, and I can't keep going this way.

The one thing I care about… now two… won't have me if I don't get my shit straight, and I don't blame her.

She was right to kick me out.

It's time I got help.

Chapter 1

Piper

Present day, eight years later

"I'VE NEVER PLANNED A WEDDING IN MY LIFE." PANIC TIGHTENS my lungs as I blink rapidly from Britt to Cass, who's on stage, singing "It's All Coming Back to Me Now" by Céline Dion.

We're at El Rio, the one and only restaurant in Eureka, where Cass's fiancé Alex Stone (yes, that would be Aiden and Adam Stone's middle brother) has convinced the owner to have Thursday night karaoke just so he can hear her sing on stage.

As the richest man in town, Alex Stone gets away with shit like that.

Don't get me wrong, Cass has a beautiful voice, which I can only assume she inherited from her mom, Crystal Gayle Dixon.

Crystal pretty much abandoned her daughters, Cass and Cass's little sister Jemima, when they were babies to pursue a singing career in Branson. She left them in Eureka with their

Aunt Carol, then years later, we learned she died alone in a motel room.

Before all that, however, she was best friends with my doomsday-prepper mom and Gwen, the tarot-reading, psychic.

It's the common link my best friends and I share—messy moms and dead dads—and it bonds us in a way only we can understand.

It makes us like sisters… Where one sister, *me*, is completely freaking out right now.

"I cannot be responsible for ruining Cass's big day," I cry. "You know how shitty my luck is. I'm totally cursed, and nobody wants a cursed person planning their wedding."

"You are not cursed!" Britt holds a plastic cup of ice water against the side of her neck, a faint green hue tingeing her skin.

"The universe would not agree. I don't even plan Ryan's birthday parties."

"Who does?" Her chin pulls back with a frown, and Aiden walks up to hand her a ginger ale.

"Mom, believe it or not. She's actually pretty good at planning little-boy parties."

"Maybe she can help you… Oh, God." Britt exhales heavily, before sliding to the end of the booth fast. "This morning sickness is worse than a curse."

She takes off, practically sprinting for the restroom before I can say, 'At least it'll be gone in a few months.' I can't seem to shake the dark cloud hanging over my head.

Cass frowns, watching us from the stage where she's singing. Aiden and I go after Britt, but she's too fast. The door slams, and we're outside the locked, single serve restroom while heaving noises echo from inside.

My nose squinches, and I look up at Aiden. "Is this all the time?"

He nods, frustrated helplessness lining his handsome face. "She's down to crackers and ginger ale for every meal."

Aiden Stone is six-foot-two inches of pure muscle. He's

always, *always* in control, and as town sheriff and the eldest of the Stone brothers, I'm pretty sure he's never had a helpless day in his entire life. Until now.

I, on the other hand, am an excellent actress.

"They say morning sickness means you'll have a boy." I do my best to lighten the mood—it's what I do. "Or maybe it means the baby has a lot of hair? Shit. Maybe it's red hair."

"If that's the case, she's having a bright red sasquatch."

My brows shoot up, and I snort a laugh. Humor is not something one usually gets from Aiden Stone. "Good one."

Leaning against the wall, I look to where Cass is finishing her song and Alex is standing in the front row beaming at her. They're so in love, and Cass is such a good friend. Their wedding has to be perfect—not cursed.

Britt originally volunteered to plan the whole thing because Cass planned her wedding to Aiden. Then the vomiting started.

"I'm not sure we want Mom taking over." I sigh as we wait. "Little boy parties are nothing like weddings."

Cass steps off the stage straight into Alex's arms. He kisses the tip of her nose, and the two of them walk hand in hand to the booth where we were all sitting. The lock snaps on the bathroom door, and Britt emerges. Her eyes are watery, and her lipstick is gone.

Aiden pulls her gently to his side, kissing the top of her blonde head. "Ready to go home?"

She gives him a pitiful smile and a nod, and I scratch the side of my cheek. She's not going to let me out of this wedding deal, and now *I* feel queasy. Everything Cass does for us is perfect, and I can't be the one to let her down on her big day.

The front door opens, and Adam enters the restaurant. His longish hair swirls in the breeze, and his eyes immediately find mine. My stomach squeezes at the sight of him in loose, faded jeans and a short-sleeved navy sweater. His muscles stretch the fabric, and light glints off his square jaw.

For five years he was off flying planes with the Navy, and

when he came back, he was even hotter than when he left. He was also healthier and very different, in some ways.

Now he's more focused on helping others as opposed to breaking the law, and he wastes no time coming to where we stand, giving me a hug, and catching Britt by the chin.

"Uh oh." His eyes narrow. "I recognize that face. My little sister tossed her cookies."

"Don't be mean." Britt pouts, but Adam pulls her into a hug, rubbing her back.

"One of the ladies at the food pantry gave me a box of her special ginger tea. I'll drive you home, and we can pick it up on the way."

"That sounds really good, but you just got here." Britt's voice is weak, but she'd let him do it.

We've all been friends since middle school, and now that she's married to Aiden, they're basically siblings.

"It takes less than five minutes to get anywhere in Eureka," Adam replies. "I'll be back before the next person finishes singing."

Aiden grips his shoulder. "I've got her. Just tell me where it is, and I'll get it on the way home."

The two of them walk to the door, and I head over to where Alex and Cass are canoodling in the booth we all abandoned. I expected it to be a slow night, but the place is filling up fast.

Doug, Aiden's ancient deputy, takes the stage to do his rendition of Bruce Springsteen's song "I'm Goin' Down."

It's kind of a silly song, but Doug sings it when he's in the dunking booth every year at the annual Founder's Day celebration. It's become his theme song, and he really gets into it.

I'm hanging back, not wanting to interrupt Alex and Cass's love fest, when an arm slips around my waist from behind. My chest jumps, and my pussy clenches when Adam's lips graze the shell of my ear.

"Oy, with the PDAs, already." He gives me a wink, his tone teasing. "Who knew my brothers could be so affectionate?"

I step to the side, doing my best to reestablish the control I try to maintain with him, although, lately, I'm trying to remember why I still need it. He's changed so much from the Adam who left eight years ago.

Still, my baggage unfortunately remains stubbornly the same. I've survived too much, and I've been burned too badly for my past to loosen its ironclad hold on my heart.

I used to imagine how my life would've been different if only Adam had stepped forward that day so long ago instead of Rex. I would pretend he was my handsome knight, and if only we weren't so loyal, we might be together now. I might not be broken.

When he left, I realized I was using him as an excuse not to act. I had to learn to save myself. Fate might have removed Rex, but I'm still learning to trust my instincts and to hear my inner voice.

Clearing my throat, I put these thoughts aside for my next therapy session.

Focusing on his brother, I arch an eyebrow. "Aiden was unexpected, but I had a feeling Alex was just looking for someone to lavish with affection. He's so sweet with his daughter."

"Women's intuition?" Adam grins like he doesn't believe me.

Crossing my arms, I lift my chin. "I'm a newswoman. It's my job to sniff out the truth."

"What else are you sniffing?" He leans closer, and I swallow hard.

Plucking at his sweater, I frown. "You've been cooking."

"That's a miss." He waves to the bartender and orders a Corona and a Modelo before reaching for my bottle and taking a long drink.

"Hey!" I reach for my drink.

"I just ordered you another. We'll share this one." He hands me the bottle, and I take a sip.

"If you weren't cooking, why do you smell like shrimp and grits?"

"I was teaching one of the kids down at the community center how to make it."

"So, I was close."

"Close, but no cigar. Now back to this situation." Adam nods to where his middle brother is gazing besottedly at my best friend. "You expected Alex to act like *that*?"

"Definitely. Didn't you see how he was looking at her at Britt's wedding? When they danced together?"

"They were pretending to be engaged. They fooled us all."

"I wasn't fooled. Men are terrible at hiding their feelings."

As opposed to me, the master.

My therapist says it's a self-preservation technique, similar to laughing or making jokes when I'm truly terrified.

"Are we?" His eyebrow arches, and so much weight is in his question, I shift uneasily.

He's so damn gorgeous, and that dimple in his cheek pushes it all over the edge. I've allowed myself to thread my fingers in his messy brown hair before. I've even allowed a kiss, but it's playing with fire. I won't promise him more than I can deliver.

When he left, he was as messed up as me. No explanation—he just showed up at my door the day after I got home from the hospital, telling me he was off for basic training.

I'd set up my little house in the old shack behind the newspaper office, which I'd inherited from Ned Farmer, the longtime publisher of the *Eureka Gazette*.

Without even meeting my eyes, Adam said goodbye, and asked me to send him pictures of Ryan.

"I'm sorry I won't be here for the big moments." His voice was rough, and his eyes stayed focused on my chin. "I'd still like to see them, if you'll think of me every now and then."

My heart hammered in my chest. "I'll think of you."

How could I not?

With that, he turned and walked away, but I kept my promise. I texted him videos of Ryan's first word, either *Mama* or

Martha—Mom thinks he said her name first, even though I never call her Martha. *How could he know that word?* I'd objected.

I sent him a video of Ryan's first steps on the front lawn outside the newspaper office. He got the full report of Ryan's potty-training escapades, including my mother's instruction to "pee behind a tree" if he couldn't hold it.

I strongly discouraged that directive. Especially when he started kindergarten, and his teacher sent a note home about it. Mom turned it into some statement on governmental control of our children, but I told her he can't be whipping it out in public, even if he is only five.

Then Adam came back and got to work. He built houses, started a food bank, organized supply drives for the waterfront ministry…

Alex has grown their family's distillery so much that all the brothers and their mother are essentially millionaires, but instead of using wealth as an excuse to spend every day on a surfboard like he used to, Adam has become a leader in outreach groups along the coast.

Occasionally, he even flies doctors to Guatemala or Nicaragua to perform cleft palate surgeries for needy children or fit them with prescription glasses, and when he's not being freaking Jesus, he's keeping his nieces and nephews, teaching them to do what he does.

I'd say he's trying to make up for something, but he really seems to enjoy it. He's trying so hard, and I love the model he's setting for Ryan.

He's like a father figure to my son, and my inner voice is cautiously telling my heart to relax, lower the walls. Trust him.

"Is Ryan at my mom's?" Adam's voice is lower, and he's so close, energy seems to move between us with every heartbeat.

"Yeah, Owen said they're going to sleep outside on the trampoline."

His head lifts, and he exhales a laugh. "I'm sure Pinky's there, too."

"And Crimson."

Aiden's son Owen and Ryan are the same age, and they've been best friends since they could walk. Alex's daughter Penelope, nicknamed "Pinky" by her cousin, does her best to keep up with the boys along with her little friend Crimson. She's undeterred by the fact they're three years younger than the boys.

"Mom can't stand an empty house."

The bartender reappears with our drinks, and Adam passes me a fresh Modelo, taking a long sip of his Corona.

"You clearly got your saintly tendencies from your mom, which is lucky for me." I tap the neck of my Modelo against his beer. "I can't afford a babysitter, and I don't like Ryan spending too much time hearing about the apocalypse and conspiracy theories."

"At least we have somewhere to go if the world ever does come to an end." Adam teases, and I cringe.

Everyone knows my mom's a prepper—a *survivalist*, as she corrects us. I'm just glad that's the extent of her crazy. As Britt likes to say, it could be worse.

Although, I'm not sure if having a tarot reader for a mom and a former magician for a grandmother like Britt does is worse than a doomsday prepper.

Mom's not just waiting for the world to end, she's got her suspicious eyes on everyone.

"Are you two going to stand there talking or are you joining us?" Alex calls to us from the booth, and we walk around to sit across from them. "Now tell my beautiful bride how incredible her voice is."

Adam cuts his eyes at me, and I snort a laugh.

"Oh, stop it." Cass playfully pushes Alex's arm. "You're embarrassing me, and just listen to Doug—he's killing it!"

"That might be the easiest song ever written," Alex gripes. "And the most repetitive."

We all glance to where the sixty-something-year-old deputy

is pumping his elbows and doing a little shuffle-step to the fading strains of the song.

Adam laughs, clapping and giving him a loud, taxi-hailing whistle.

"I never could whistle like that." I frown, and he tries to show me how you curl your bottom lip and arch your tongue.

Alex waves him away, explaining it's much easier if you use your thumb and middle finger. Cass and I only exchange a look and start to laugh.

"I'm never going to learn to do it," I confess.

Up next is Terra Belle's sister Liberty, who gets a big response singing "Before He Cheats" by Carrie Underwood.

"I have to hand it to you, Alex," I lean forward, shouting over the music. "I didn't expect karaoke night to be such a hit."

"I have a knack for knowing things." He lifts his chin, and Adam throws the lime from his beer at his brother.

"Cut the shit. We all know you bought out the restaurant in case nobody showed up tonight."

Cass's jaw drops. "You did not! This was all for me?"

"Tell me, Miss Dixon," I adopt an old-timey news reporter's voice. "What's it like to be marrying the richest man in town?"

"Don't print that." Alex points at me.

My eyes squint, and I pretend to consider his request. "Are you attempting to suppress the free flow of information? Typical billionaire behavior."

"Piper…" His voice is warning, and I start to laugh.

"I think I can leave that part out of my review. How's this for a headline, '*Qué Sorpresa!* Karaoke Night is a Hit!'"

"Your drinks are on me." Alex holds up his hand, and we air-high-five across the table.

The rest of the night continues with more silly songs. Adam sings "Monster Mash," since it's getting closer to Halloween, and the entire restaurant is on their feet singing along.

When he returns to the booth, he loops his arm across the

back of my seat. It's not exactly a hug, but the back of my head is against his shoulder.

"That was very unexpected." I wink at him.

"Everybody loves holiday music."

Later, when Liberty sings "And So It Goes," by Billy Joel, he presses his cheek to my head, and a flush of warmth moves through my chest. It sends my thoughts down a rabbit hole.

For five years, I've worked hard, building a life with my son and doing my best to keep the *Eureka Gazette* running and even growing in an age where local papers are dying.

Now the *Gazette* is a true community staple, and I'm a small business owner. I couldn't have done it without my mom's help, and then Adam's. He's always treated Ryan like his son, almost like he adopted him that night in the hospital so long ago.

My eyes rise to meet his, and my heart melts a little more. I'm still a little broken and a lot guarded, but I'm working on it.

"I don't know about you two, but I'm ready to call it a night." Alex stands, signing off on the check. "Let me know if you need to get into the distillery. I heard Britt say she's passing the wedding planning on to you."

Cass's eyes go wide. "You're not planning my wedding! You don't even plan Ryan's birthday parties!"

"Britt didn't know that." My nose wrinkles. "But we're working out the details."

"No." Cass holds up a hand. "I'll hire a professional planner. You are not getting stuck doing this on top of everything else you have going on."

"Hang on, just wait a minute." I catch her hand. "I didn't say I *couldn't* do it. I just said I'll need some help *doing* it."

What am I saying? Adam's expression is somewhere between shock and amusement, but I turn away from him quickly.

Cass takes care of all of us all the time, and Britt would never forgive me if I let a stranger who doesn't even know her come in and try to take over planning her wedding.

"I don't want you in over your head." We're out the door,

and my friend hugs me close. "It's not worth it to me to be a burden to my friends."

"You are never a burden. Your wedding is going to be amazing, and I'll find a good helper. Maybe Mom can pitch in."

Her brows crinkle. "Just as long as it's not bomb-shelter-chic. That might work for little boys, but not weddings."

"I would never do that to you. Don't give it a second thought." I squeeze her before Alex takes her hand, leading her to his waiting Tesla.

Adam catches my hand, pulling me in the opposite direction. "Come on, overachiever. I'll walk you home, and we can discuss this."

Turning to face him, with the full moon overhead and his blue eyes steady and confident, it feels as dangerous as pretending I can plan a wedding in a month.

But his hand holds mine, strong and warm, and I follow him the short distance down Main Street, past Gwen's tarot studio, to my empty house.

Chapter 2

Adam

PIPER'S PLACE IS ONLY A FEW BLOCKS FROM EL RIO. RYAN IS AT MY mom's, and after three years of playing around, keeping things loose, tonight, I'm going to shoot my shot.

I'm guessing she knows, especially after bragging about how men are terrible at hiding their feelings. I've always been her friend. I've kissed her before, which she casually shut down with a joke about too much alcohol.

This time, I'm not letting it go at that.

I'm not the same guy who showed up in her hospital room all those years ago, fucked-up and useless, and I think we're both ready for something real. I know I am, and if she still won't let me in, then…

Who the fuck am I kidding? I'll wait as long as it takes for Piper Jackson. Hell, I've already done as much up to now.

Still, the thought's been growing in my mind like that damn fungus in *The Last of Us*. Aiden gave me the push I needed, and like a killer wave or a risky flight, I have to see it through.

I was wrapping up my shift at the food bank when he texted me,

Aiden: Meet us at El Rio's at nine. Karaoke.

I can honestly say, of all the messages I expected to get from my oldest brother, *Meet me at karaoke night* wasn't one of them. Especially, since I know Britt has been missing work lately because of morning sickness.

Herve is doing karaoke?

Herve Garcia is the owner of El Rio, and while he's nice as hell, I don't think of him as the kind of open-minded business owner who would close his modest restaurant for karaoke in a town the size of Eureka.

Aiden: It's for Cass. Alex bought out the place and wants us there.

That explains it.

Why didn't he do it at the distillery?

Aiden: He wants it to be low-key. Doesn't want her to know.

I really can't get over what a romantic Alex has become since Cass entered his life. He was always such a closed-off tight-ass in his Armani suits and Italian leather loafers.

Out of my two older brothers, he was the one I figured would be single for the rest of his life—mostly because he wouldn't deal with the messiness of another woman. Not to mention his daughter Pinky, who is such a headstrong little tornado, I wasn't sure any woman would be able to handle her.

Then along came Cass…

I'll be there. Just closing up the food bank.

I don't expect another text from Aiden, but a moment passes, and the words appear out of nowhere.

Aiden: I'm really proud of you, bro. You've come a long way.

It's the closest we've ever come to discussing what happened that night. The night he appointed himself judge, jury, and sentencer in my case, sending me away to the military to get my shit straight.

Pausing a beat, I think about what I want to say to him. I've thought about it so many times when I was off in country, calculating all the things I was missing.

I'd think about it every time Piper sent me a video of Ryan saying a word, his little face as serious as hers. When he took his first step, so focused and intentional—just like her… All the big moments in his life, and I was far, far away.

What did I want to say to him now?

> Thank you.

As much as I hated him for it, without Aiden, would I even be here, at the edge of possibly deserving a second chance?

Gray dots float, and a cheeky reply is my reward.

Aiden: Whatever happened to your idea of becoming a pastor? Realized you'd have to clean up that mouth?

"Fuck you," I chuckle under my breath, but I deserve that.

Before he met Britt, when I was freshly back from being overseas and still pretty raw, I'd give him shit for all the things he claimed he no longer believed, including God and love and happily ever after.

I knew all it would take was a sassy little bombshell to blast him out of that bullshit. I didn't expect it to be my old buddy Britt, but I like it. She's really good for him.

> That life isn't for me. Too many things I want to do.

Piper tops the list of things I want to do, and a sly grin curls my cheeks.

> Doesn't mean I can't do good in my community. Make up for all the other shit I've done.

Aiden: I've created a monster.

It was the conversation that brought me to El Rio tonight. It gave me the courage to think I've made it past my old mistakes, past the night she told me to leave, and that I might actually deserve her.

"You are brave." Piper's voice is soft, and it pulls me from my thoughts.

"What?"

"A new sign." She nods at the freshly painted, thin white plank of wood with royal blue lettering.

"How the hell…?" I look up and down the sidewalk lining the town square. "We were all inside, and we didn't see a thing."

Her eyes narrow, and she looks up at me. "You were the last one to arrive. Did you do it?"

My brow rises, and I press a palm against my chest. "Me?" I start to laugh, which I know sounds suspicious.

"Of all the possible suspects, you definitely fit the bill." I really love when she goes all Veronica Mars on me. "You live alone. You're free to do whatever you want whenever you want, and you're very inspirational."

Catching her hand in mine, I pull her closer to my chest. "You think I'm inspirational?"

Her full lip slips beneath her front teeth, and warmth tightens my stomach. I want this so much, and her response tonight is the most encouragement she's ever given me.

She shakes her head, pushing out of my embrace. "You know what I mean."

"I'm not sure I do."

She takes off, walking in the direction of her small house. Picking up the pace, I'm practically jogging to keep up with her.

"Piper, slow down."

"I should say as much to you." We're not far from the tiny shack, and she stumbles onto the front porch, exhaling a laugh as she stops at the door.

I jog up the steps as well, stopping when I'm in front of her, caging her against the wooden barrier with my arms.

"Don't run from me." My voice is low, hungry.

We're both breathing fast, and her mouth is tantalizingly close to mine.

"Then don't chase me."

"Let me catch you." Even I heard the crack in my voice, the break of someone on the edge, not ready to walk away but not able to keep going.

"I can't do that."

"Why not?"

"You know why not. I can't play with Ryan's life. He has to have stability. He's already lost so much."

That's not it, and I won't let her use him to push me away again. "I've been here for him every day since he started kindergarten. I'm one of the most stable things in his life."

"It's true." She tries to pull away, but I hold her arms.

Her chin lifts, and her hair falls away from her face. The moonlight sets her ivory skin aglow, and I've dreamed of this. I've waited for this. Now, it's here.

"I want to kiss you."

"Adam," she sighs heavily. "I don't think it's a good idea."

"Are you worried what people will say?" I'm teasing, and her eyes roll to the side.

"I'm pretty sure our friends already think we're sleeping together."

"Hmm…" I like the sound of that. Leaning down, I lightly follow the line of her hair with my nose, stopping just above her ear. "We can keep it off the record."

A shiver moves through her, and her fingers curl against the fabric of my shirt. "I don't care about what they say. It's just… It's that you…"

Her eyes lower, and she doesn't finish. I'm not sure what she doesn't want to say to me. Is it what I've done? What I haven't done? What else can I do?

Clearing my throat, I stop teasing. I want her to know I'm

serious. "Everything I've done has been for you. When I went away, since I've been back. All of it."

"I know." She nods. "So much has changed. You're different now."

"I'm not entirely different." I slide a lock of hair off her cheek, and her pretty eyes rise to mine. "I want you, Piper. For real this time. I want to spend the night."

She swallows audibly, and her response aches my stomach. "Don't say that. Not now."

"If not now, when?"

Her chin drops, and her brow furrows. My jaw tightens, and I feel the beat of her heart through her breath, in her body so close to mine.

I should apologize. I don't want to pressure her.

Swallowing the intense frustration in my throat, I force the words. "I'm sorry. I'm not trying to push you, but it's been three years. If it's never going to happen for us, I need you to tell me."

Her hand rises, and slim fingers rest lightly against my lips.

"Don't apologize." Her voice trembles, and her eyes, smoky gold with intense green, meet mine. "There's just so much… and I know you've been patient. I'm so grateful for all you've done for Ryan and me. It hurts me to think I might never get past…"

Her chin drops and my heart drops along with it, but before I can reply, she rises to meet my lips. Her fingers clutch at my shirt, pulling me closer, and I grasp her waist.

Our mouths open, and when our tongues slide together, my body comes alive. My fucking dick jumps in my jeans. It's not the first time we've stolen a moment, but I want more than kisses tonight.

I slide my fingers into her hair, curling them against her scalp. My thumb traces a line down her cheek, and I suck her bottom lip into my mouth.

Her back is to the door, and I press my body against hers, moving my teeth to her jaw, cupping her breasts in my hands through her shirt.

She's precious and fine. She tastes like sweetness and honey and years of unrequited longing. Decades of desire crash through me like water over a dam, like fucking Niagara Falls, pulling me down.

I cover her mouth with mine again, tasting her tongue. A whimper slips from her throat, and it prompts a groan from mine. I lift her off her feet, and her legs go around my waist. Rocking her against my erection is tormenting pleasure mixed with pain. I could fuck her right here on this front porch, but what I really want is to take her inside and make love to her.

I want to have her sweet and savoring, then rough and raw. I want to make love to her all night and into the morning. I want to discover every part of her body that makes her moan.

Her hands grip my shoulders, but she turns her face, pushing against me. "Wait… Slow down."

Stepping back, I lower her to her feet, but desire burns hot in my veins. We're both breathing fast, but her head is shaking no.

"Why?" Lust thickens my voice. "What's the matter?"

"I can't, Adam."

You can… It's a primitive protest firing back in my brain. It's completely inappropriate and wrong, but I can't help myself. Frustration grinds my teeth as I struggle against the words trying to spill out of me.

Somehow, I manage to keep my tone gentle. "What else can I do to prove myself?"

She pulls away, killing me so thoroughly, it's like she's taken out a knife and carved a hole in my chest.

"I'm sorry," is all she says.

Staggering back, I scrub my fingers over my forehead. A loose laugh rattles in my chest, and I have to go. I can't do this anymore. I've shown my hand. I laid it all at her feet, and I'm still not enough.

"Okay." Turning, I start to walk away, then I pick up speed.

I can't stay here, and I'm practically jogging away from her in the direction I came.

"Adam…" she calls after me. "Wait! You don't understand."

No, I don't understand, and at this point, I don't think I ever will.

Adrenaline surges in my veins, and I slow to a walk, heading in the direction of my mother's house.

I got a text last week from a number I haven't seen in eight years. It was followed by an email that I dismissed without a thought.

Now I'm giving it a thought.

When I came back to Eureka, I had only one thing on my mind—earning Piper's love, proving to her I'd changed, and showing her I could be the man she and Ryan needed me to be.

Returning to the circuit was not in my plans, but after tonight, I'm rethinking my decision. Checking my phone, it's almost eleven.

The lights are off at Mom's house, and I hesitate. I can't wake the boys, but I don't want to disappear without talking to him.

I'm standing in the driveway contemplating my options when the soft noise of laughter quirks my ears. A flashlight draws my attention to the backyard, and I trot around to see four little bodies all sitting inside the net surrounding the large trampoline.

"Where's my golden arm?" Owen's voice is wavering and spooky, and I know that scary story.

Inside the netting, I see Pinky and Crimson clutching each other, and Ryan is sitting beside his friend flicking the flashlight off and on.

I can't resist. Creeping up beside the round structure, I say loudly, "I have it!"

Four screams ring out so loudly, my ears crackle. Britt's bloodhound lets out a loud barking-howl, and Ryan throws the flashlight in the air.

It bounces off the trampoline behind them, and Owen yells, "Uncle Adam!"

Pinky is on her feet, charging to the split in the net. "I have to go!"

Holding out my hands, I catch her under her arms, lowering her to the ground. "You okay, P?"

She doesn't answer, and Crimson pats my shoulder fast. I put her on her feet, and she races after her friend into the house.

"She peed her pants." Ryan is at the side of the trampoline doing his best not to laugh.

"Dang, I'm sorry." I hold his arm as he hops down. "I thought it would be funny."

"Oh, it was funny all right." Owen snorts, and he climbs to the ground beside me, too. "What are you doing here?"

"I actually wanted to stop by and talk to… you." I point to Ryan, but now that I'm here, I realize how much time I've spent with both the boys these last years.

Only Ryan doesn't have a dad.

I lower to a squat, and he puts his hand on my shoulder. "What's up?"

He's almost nine, and he's already starting to seem more like a little man.

I rest my hand on his waist. "A friend of mine is taking a trip, and he asked me to go with him. It's something I need to do, so I'm going to go."

"Where is it?" His expression is worried, but he does his best to act mature.

It reminds me he'll be hitting puberty soon, and I want to be here for him, for the questions and the unexpected changes he won't want to talk about with his mom.

Looking down, I try to think about how to phrase this so it doesn't seem like I'm running away. I'm not running away. I just need time to get a handle on my feelings for Piper. I need distance so I can compartmentalize them and be a better friend to them.

"Moloka'i." He squints, and I continue. "It's one of the Hawaiian Islands."

Understanding flushes his cheeks, and his small hand curls on my shoulder. "That's pretty far. How long will you be gone?"

Pain twists in my chest, but I have to do this. "I don't know. I'm leaving early tomorrow, but I'll be back for Uncle Alex's wedding."

"That's not 'til Halloween!" Owen's voice is louder, and I remember being their age and how it always seemed like the holidays would never come.

"I think with school and all, it'll go by fast." I hope it will.

Ryan studies me with wide green eyes. "Are you okay?"

Pulling him into a hug, I pat his back. "I will be."

His arms tighten around my neck, and his little-boy voice is a whisper. "I'll miss you."

It's a punch in the gut, but I clear my throat, giving him another firm squeeze before letting him go. "Don't worry. I'll be back, and I'll text you while I'm there. Okay?"

He nods, putting on a brave face. "Okay."

I might not be what Piper needs, and she might not be able to forgive me for the past. But I'll figure out a way to live with it. What I know for certain is I won't let this little guy down again.

Chapter 3

Piper

"He's gone." I'm sitting on the tan leather couch in Dr. Cole's office in Oakville, and the pressure in my chest has only grown heavier in the last three days.

Adam left Eureka Saturday morning, and this time, he didn't say goodbye.

Correction—he didn't say goodbye *to me*.

Apparently, he stopped by his mother's house and told Ryan he was leaving, and then he went to Alex's to let them know he'd be back for the wedding. It was only my house he skipped.

Not that I blame him.

"How does that make you feel?" Drew Cole sits behind a large mahogany desk studying me with calm blue eyes.

A few years ago, a wire story came across my desk about Drew, as she prefers to be called, and her work with paranoid patients, specifically a man who helped track down a murder suspect using the framework of the Nixon-Watergate scandal.

The story fascinated me, and when I visited her to discuss

my mother's condition, we went down the rabbit hole of all the shit I've been hiding for fifteen years.

She saw straight through me, which was unexpected, but apparently she's dealt with trauma in her past as well. Twice a month I make the drive to Oakville, which is far enough away not to raise questions but close enough that I can squeeze in visits during Ryan's activities.

Her question hangs in the air, and my throat tightens as I consider my answer.

"I feel guilty." Looking down at my hands, I clench them into fists. "I feel angry. Really, really angry."

"With whom are you angry?" Drew is about my age, and with her shiny blonde hair, clear blue eyes, and straight white teeth, she looks like someone who has always had a privileged life.

Through my journalistic research, however, I learned her mother died when she was a little girl, her father was a debilitating alcoholic, and her older brother was killed by an IED in Afghanistan.

Just goes to show, you can never tell by looking at a person the demons they've had to fight.

"I'm angry at myself. I'm angry at Rex for doing this to me. He's gone, but even in death, he's ruining my life."

"He can only ruin it if you let him." A black Mont Blanc pen in her hand, and her expression is calm. "Tell me what happened. What events preceded Adam leaving?"

Inhaling slowly, I confess. "He wanted to spend the night with me. I wanted him to spend the night with me, and when he kissed me this time, it was different."

Heat floods my stomach when I remember that kiss. Years of waiting and longing unleashed in one overwhelming, consuming touch. He was hard against my stomach, and my pussy was so wet. I was ready to let him inside my walls.

"You're blushing." A gentle smile lifts her cheeks.

Pushing off my knees, I exhale a bitter laugh. "I've been joking that it's been so long since I've had sex, my hymen grew back."

"You know that isn't possible, right?"

"Yeah, I know." My voice turns quiet. "He's been back three years. Three years doing everything right. Treating me like a queen, devoting himself to my son… and his niece and nephew. He's been amazing. He's been a perfect—saint."

"Do you love him?"

I'm nodding before I even speak. "So much."

Somehow I'm able to tell her things I've never been able to tell my mom or Britt and Cass or even Adam.

"But he still doesn't know. If I'd let him spend the night, he would've seen… all of me. The thought of him knowing the truth scared me so bad I couldn't breathe. My insides froze, and I pushed him away."

"Do you think Adam is like Rex?"

"No," I answer fast. "Adam is nothing like Rex."

Drew studies me. "But you're still afraid to trust him. Why?"

Shaking my head, I study my hands in my lap. So many reasons crowd together in my brain, it's too much. I don't know which is the real answer.

"I can't see the forest for the trees." It's a lame attempt at humor.

Drew doesn't let me off the hook. "Relax your mind. Don't let your thoughts overwhelm you. Take them one at a time."

Dropping onto the couch again, I lean my arms on my knees. I take a moment to breathe, to do my best to focus, to feel my brain relaxing.

"Rex wasn't like Rex in the beginning. When we started out, he was playful and thrilling… I wanted to be with him. Just like Adam."

"Have you seen any signs that Adam could turn into Rex?"

Taking a beat, I allow myself to really consider her question. I close my eyes and try to picture him changing the way Rex did. I imagine the little red flags I ignored that only grew into bigger red flags and then into chains.

I can't make it happen in any version of reality. Even on our last night, when Adam bared his soul to me, and I was too afraid to let him in, he would never force me or take out his anger on me… or hurt me.

"Adam would never be like Rex."

It's so quiet, I hear the ticking of her large clock. Lifting my eyes, I meet her warm gaze. "You didn't make Rex hurt you. That was his choice. It wasn't your fault."

Heat warms my eyes. "But I hid it. I covered for him so well, no one ever knew. They never even suspected, and if I told them now… They wouldn't believe it."

"Is that what you think? Are you afraid Adam won't believe you? Are you afraid he'll choose his friend over you?"

A knot is in my throat, twisting all the way down into my chest. *Is that why?* "I don't know."

But if he didn't believe me, or worse, if he thought I caused it somehow, I'd be devastated.

Drew rises from the chair behind her desk and walks around to sit beside me on the couch.

She puts her arm around my shoulders. "You've never given your friends a chance to be your friends completely because you've never shared your truth. Can you tell me why?"

Shame heats my neck. "I'm the smart one, the funny one. I'm not the type of person to stay with someone who abuses me. I do the right thing, and if I can't fix the problem, I leave."

She nods, exhaling a noise of assent. "I think your friends would be more understanding than you give them credit for. Everybody makes mistakes."

"They were his friends, too."

"Are you afraid they'll defend him? Or blame you somehow?"

Fear quivers in my stomach. "What if they do?"

"What if they don't?"

"Then I'm the victim. I'm damaged goods."

"You're a survivor. You're strong, and you're raising a son on your own. You're a small business owner and a leader in your community."

"Oh, God." I scrub my fingers over my forehead. "Even more of a reason to keep it a secret. I don't want the whole town knowing my dirty laundry."

"Hey," she nudges me in the side. "Don't you run the paper? You don't have to make it front page news."

My eyes fall to my hands, and the weight is in my chest again. "I feel like a failure. I let myself be a victim, and now I'm broken. Now I have a wonderful man like Adam wanting to be with me, and I'm too afraid to let him in."

"We'll work through those fears. Remember the children in the basement? They're trying to protect you, but you don't need them anymore. Let them go."

It's her analogy of old, protective behaviors that no longer serve me.

"If it were that easy, I'd have gotten laid Friday night." Another lame attempt at a joke. Drew was the one who told me laughter was my trauma response. "I don't want to be broken and afraid. I want to be with him."

"I know." She squeezes my hand. "We'll get you there."

"The night Rex died, I found out I was pregnant." Blinking up at her, I smile sadly. "Looking at that positive pregnancy test, I knew I'd be tied to him forever."

"How did that make you feel?"

"Terrified." I remembered the blood draining from my face at the sight of that little pink plus sign. "So I wished with all my heart that somehow I could be set free."

A soft bell pings, indicating our time is up. Her eyes hold mine, and she covers my hands with hers. "You didn't cause Rex's death."

"Have I ever told you about my luck?"

"You can tell me about it next time." We both stand, and she gives me a squeeze. "Spoiler alert: I'm not going to believe it's bad. You have a wonderful little boy."

"The exception that proves the rule."

She smiles, stopping at the door. "You're a lucky person, Piper Jackson."

"Maybe if we keep saying it, it'll come true."

"Owen taught Edward to catch a frisbee in his mouth!" Ryan climbs into the twin bed in his small room at the top of the stairs. "Now he can play hide-and-seek and tag *and* frisbee!"

"I could've told you Edward's a pretty cool dog." I hold the blanket as he slides under the covers. "Although I'm not sure how fair it is to play hide-and-seek with a bloodhound."

"Owen said he sleeps at the foot of his bed every single night."

"That's an upgrade." I tuck the blankets all around my son and down his sides. "I remember when he had to sleep on Britt's crummy little couch."

Ryan's voice is thoughtful. "Do you think I might get a dog one day?"

My nose wrinkles. "Dogs are a lot of work. They need walking and food and vet appointments."

Which means vet bills…

He nods, looking down at his hands. "I know. I was just wondering. I can play with Edward for now."

A brand-new layer of guilt joins the gang already in my chest. Ryan's dark hair and eyes are just like his father's, but everything else about him is all me, from his curious mind to his innocent thoughtfulness. He deserves every good thing he wants. I'm just as poor as a church mouse without even a church.

"You're a great kid, you know that?" He smiles, and I lean down to kiss his forehead. "Is there anything you want to talk to me about?"

When he was a toddler, I anxiously watched him for any signs of unreasonable anger or uncontrolled impatience. What I learned is he's patient and good, and when Adam came back, our lives almost seemed perfect.

Ryan hasn't said anything about Adam's departure, but they were so close, he has to be thinking about it.

His brow furrows, and I brace myself for what he might say. "We were talking about fossils in science class today, and Ms. Taylor said chickens are the closest living relatives to the T-Rex! Can you believe that?"

Not what I expected. "I guess we'd better keep our eyes on Holly Magee's chickens."

"She said they eat mice and rats." His brown eyes are wide. "I thought they only ate corn and gravel."

"Me too." I put his book on the nightstand. "And here I thought alligators and crocodiles were the closest we had to dinosaurs."

"Yeah." He looks down, and I don't want to rush him.

"Is that all you wanted to talk about?"

His lips pucker, and he frowns like he's thinking. I trace my finger across his forehead, moving his hair behind his ear. I've tucked him in tight as a burrito, and even though he's eight, I can still see him as my little baby swaddled in the clear plastic crib.

I can also still see Adam smiling down at him, and my heart aches. I remember his words, *You look just like her...*

He finally shrugs, shaking his head. "I can't think of anything else."

"Okay." I lean down to give him one more squeeze. "Get some sleep—and know you can always talk to me if you need to, about anything."

"I know." He nods before turning onto his side. "Night, Mom."

I pull his door almost closed and switch off the light in the half bath across the hall. Hesitating, I hear a faint hissing noise. Stepping into the tiny room, I lean closer to the sink, then to the toilet, trying to detect the source. *Shit*, I can't tell, and the last thing I need is to have to call a plumber. More bills...

Walking slowly down the stairs, I try to think. Cass is pretty good at mechanical stuff, but I'd hate to bug her with her wedding coming up. If things were different, I'd call Adam to help me. Now that he's gone, I'm starting to realize he helped me with everything—not just my son.

Scrubbing my fingers over my forehead, I go into my bedroom. My conversation with Drew is on my mind, and I pull my T-shirt over my head. *You've never given them the chance to be your friends completely…*

I go into the bathroom and remove my bra, cupping my hand over my breast and turning to the side. Silver scars line my upper rib cage, leading to larger, darker pink ones. Closing my eyes, I remember him pressing me to the wall, a small knife in his hand.

You love them looking at you, don't you? Anger and alcohol were hot on his breath, and my eyes squeezed shut. *You think about them touching you. Is it because you want something new?*

I was so confused. At that time, I didn't want anyone but Rex.

Yes, I felt pretty in my new bikini. I felt sexy, and I guess I did like being noticed. It was a new experience for me, but I didn't want to be with anyone else.

It was the first cut. The first time he said he'd make it so I couldn't show them my body. The first time I believed it was my fault, and it would stop if I could somehow make him feel more secure.

He dropped to his knees and buried his face between my legs as I trembled, doing my best to catch the blood running down the side of my body. Doing my best not to cry as he manipulated my emotions, as he made me orgasm.

After that night, I tried to tease him. I said he was looking at a girl on the beach, too. I had hoped it would make him see he had nothing to worry about.

My plan worked, but it also backfired. He used that moment to say I was just like him. We were no different, and I was jealous like he was. Didn't I see it?

Only, I wasn't a danger to him. I didn't have the strength to hold him down with my forearm against his neck. I couldn't pin him to the wall and scar his body so he'd be embarrassed for others to see him in a swimsuit.

I didn't tell him he'd only be attractive to me now because I'd marked him, because I'd made him mine. I couldn't hurt him that way… and I didn't want to hurt him that way. I didn't want to control him.

Crawling beneath the blankets on my bed, I curl my knees to my chest. I wrap my palms over the scars under my arms, the stripes on my inner thighs. I don't want to be his anymore.

Closing my eyes, I imagine taking Adam's hands and putting them over my damaged places. I imagine him being able to look at me without judgment. I imagine him loving me in spite of the past, in spite of me not being the person I pretend to be.

An ache is in my chest, and I wonder if he could know the truth and still want me. Could he accept it or would it be too much?

I remember his soft lips, his possessive kisses. I remember threading my fingers in his hair and wanting him so badly. My phone is in my hand, and I pull up our old chat.

My thumbs move slowly,

> I miss you.

Wincing, I delete the letters and try again.

> I hope you're finding what you're looking for out there.

No, I don't.

I delete those words and try again. Drew would ask, what do I really want to say to him?

> I love you. Please come back.

My nose heats, and I tap the delete arrow thirty times, counting each letter as it disappears.

Closing my eyes, I do my best to sleep. I do my best to keep breathing, to keep trying to be strong. Maybe I wasn't then, but I'm learning to be now.

Chapter 4

Adam

SAPPHIRE BLUE WATERS CRASH ON VOLCANO-BLACK SANDS. A LONE bolder stands like a sentry guarding the beaches of the island that's been removed from the map.

I flew us in on a Cessna jet out of Los Angeles, as seats on passenger jets are impossible to get—even for residents. Eighteen hours later, we're closing in on the small, emerald island.

"Moloka'i." A dreamy note is in Max's voice as he gazes down on the remote Hawaiian island of less than ten thousand full-time residents. "It's called 'the forgotten island,' but the truth is, they *asked* to be taken off the map."

My eyes trace the verdant cliffs, shaded by clouds passing in front of the sun. The sweet scent of hibiscus floats up to us on the mist from the waterfalls. "These cliffs are amazing."

"I grew up coming here. Tallest cliffs in the world."

"It's perfect."

A forgotten island is exactly where I want to be after Piper's rejection. I want to be isolated, working my ass off, doing whatever it takes to get over her.

I want to stay here until she doesn't fill my mind every time I close my eyes. Until I can sleep without seeing her silky auburn hair falling in waves over her shoulders or her bright green eyes just waiting to crack a joke. Until I can dream without feeling her full lips touching mine.

I don't know how long it'll take. Maybe it'll never happen, but I have to figure out a way to co-exist with her in Eureka for Ryan's sake. I've invested too much time to leave him, and fuck it, I love that little guy.

We touch down on a short airstrip on the top of a small hill. The wind blows in the palm trees, and the tall bamboo sways like a curtain. Giant succulents give the place a prehistoric vibe, and it's so green, it's unreal. It's like I'm looking at the world through a filter.

"Not gonna lie." Max slaps me on the shoulder before climbing out of the small plane. "Becoming a pilot might be the coolest thing you've ever done."

He reaches into the back to grab his pack and his surfboard while I kill the engine and set the brakes. The landing crew blocks the wheels as we step out onto the tarmac.

I chuckle. "When they told me I could learn to fly, I was way less pissed at my brother for shipping me off to the Navy."

"That was fucked-up, man. He blackmailed your ass."

"I don't know." I toss my canvas duffel over my shoulder. "Looking at it from this side of the journey, I think it was for the best. I wasn't going to come out of that tailspin, and I wasn't any good to anybody that way."

"Losing Rex hit us all pretty hard."

Nodding, I don't want to think about my friend dying the way he did. I don't want to think about the sliver of relief I felt—which I tried to drink away, smoke away, surf away…

All for her.

"Hey, you still cooking?" Max punches me on the shoulder.

"Aunt Sheila will let us stay for free, but she expects us to provide all our meals."

"You tell Aunt Sheila I'll cook every dinner while we're here, and she's going to love it."

"Sounds good!" Max nods, pulling his bag higher over his shoulder. "I'll make breakfast. I'm a wizard with eggs."

Starting when we were seniors in high school until I left for the Navy, Max and I were part of a team of local cater-waiters serving fancy parties around Hilton Head and Kiawah Island. Max was from Fireside, so he also worked jobs there.

I only did it when I needed the money, and once Alex turned Stone Cold into a million-dollar bourbon brand, I never had to work again. But sitting on my ass was the last thing I wanted to do.

I liked being with my buddies, and when we weren't walking around in three-piece suits holding silver trays of crudités in our hands, we were on the ocean.

Max got into the World Surf League, and he started traveling. He was on his way back to Fireside from a competition in Sydney when he texted me about coming with him to Moloka'i to check on his great-aunt Sheila.

He promised me it wouldn't be like our old days of drugs and partying. He's gotten more serious about the sport now that he's competing for real money. He's here to hone his skills, while I'm here hoping for an exorcism—if that's what you call it when you're trying to get someone you love out of your blood.

Max drives an old-school beige Jeep from the tiny airport to Aunt Sheila's home. It's a one-level, three-bedroom cinder block house with slatted windows and a hammock in the front yard. She's not home when we park in the yard, so we hop out and drop our bags into the guest rooms.

"You're not going to believe the waves here, bro." Max's eyes dance with excitement. "Let's get out there before the jet lag hits us."

We're going to be messed up for days traveling from South

Carolina to Hawaii, but I know the only way to get ahead of the time change is to dive right into it.

"I don't have a board."

"I got you."

He leads me out to the small shed behind the house, opens the door, and goes inside. While I wait out in the yard under the palm trees, I look up to see a small red bird with a hooked beak sitting on the branch of a tree.

He lets out a long whistling noise that reminds me of the finches we have around Mom's over-planted yard back home. She has a hibiscus bush my dad got for her on their first and only trip to Hawaii. It's my first time to visit the islands myself.

"Here you go." He hands me a waterlogged, gray longboard.

"What the fuck is this?"

He only laughs, taking off down the hillside. "You can make it work. I've seen you surf."

The funny little bird is gone, and a joy rises in my chest. I remember why I spent so much time out on the ocean after my life fell apart. I learned as a teenager how healing the waves can be.

My grandfather died when I was thirteen, then a year later we lost our dad. Aiden stepped up to fill the gap, but he was seven years older than me and a Marine. Then he took over the sheriff's position, and I pretty much decided we had nothing in common.

Then I met Rex, and he led me out to the water. It's hard to describe to anyone who's never surfed, but when you're on the waves, riding that silky curl, it's like the whole world fades away. Nothing matters as you become one with nature.

The salt life fit easily with me, and we developed a community of friends around our shared love of the ocean. It didn't hurt that a bunch of pretty girls started showing up in bikinis to watch us practice.

Out of the whole pile of females, it was a sassy redhead who caught my eye. She was quiet and smart. She wasn't interested in our joking around. She wanted to see our skill, and I wanted to impress her.

Rex was the one who charged up to her first. He was never one to spend a lot of time thinking about first impressions.

"What are you waiting for?" Max yells at me, as he jogs into the ice-cold Pacific. "An engraved invitation?"

Shaking my head, I run right after him, leaving all those thoughts of the past on the sand at the edge of the water. I'm not here to rehash old memories. I'm here to close the book on those days, to grow, and to learn to move forward.

"Who's making Huli Huli chicken?" A creaky voice calls from inside Aunt Sheila's little house, heading to where I'm standing outside at a brick fire pit.

Bright red chicken sections are arranged on the grate over hot coals, and a squat little lady with long, gray-and-black hair braided on each side of her head makes her way slowly to the back door of the house.

Max hops up and jogs over to her, taking her arm and giving her a hug. "Aunt Sheila, I want you to meet one of my oldest friends."

She's wearing a long, loose hunter-green dress with lots of beads and leather jewelry, and I notice right away the cane in her hand. Her eyes travel over my head into the trees behind me.

Aunt Sheila is blind.

A grin lifts her heavily lined cheeks, and she motions in my direction. "Your oldest friend smells like a good cook."

The chicken is all set, and I put the pair of tongs I'm holding down to go to her. "Hi, Aunt Sheila." I take the hand she holds out. "I'm Adam Stone."

"Adam Stone." She nods, like she's making a decision. "A good, strong name. It's nice to meet you, Adam. Have you spent a lot of time in the islands?"

"No, ma'am. It's my first time visiting, but my parents came here before I was born."

"To Moloka'i?"

"No, they went to see Pearl Harbor."

"Ah." She lifts her chin. "They visited Oahu. I've heard the museum there is beautiful."

"Everything here is beautiful." Max walks out, carrying a platter with a round loaf of golden bread, a plate of green beans, and a sliced pineapple.

I grab the beans and the pineapple off the platter and arrange them beside the chicken on the grill. "Want the bread toasted?"

"You know it." Max uses a large knife to cut it into thick pieces.

"I love a man who knows how to cook." Sheila pulls out the sturdy bamboo chair from in front of the small outdoor table and takes a pipe from the pocket of her dress. "How long are you boys planning to stay?"

"Depends on how long you'll put up with us." Max takes a chair across from his aunt and pours three shot glasses of Oke, or Hawaiian moonshine.

"You know I love my favorite nephew." She winks in his direction.

"I'm your only nephew." He puts a glass in her hand. "Cheers—to good times with good friends."

I step over and take the small glass, clinking it against theirs. "Thanks for letting me stay with you here."

"You're welcome in my home. Moloka'i is called 'the friendly island' for a reason."

Returning to the grill, I remove the food, arranging the pieces on plates and setting them at each of our places, starting with Aunt Sheila. Max takes care of the utensils, and he pours glasses of white wine for each of us.

For a few minutes, we eat in pleasant silence—except for my friend's groaning over how good everything tastes. Surfing works up our appetites, and the jet lag is hitting me hard. Still, I'm doing my best to stay awake as long as I can.

"This was good." Aunt Sheila nods, sitting back in her chair. "For someone who has never visited the island, it's very good."

"Thanks. I actually read the recipe in a magazine while we were waiting on the plane and decided to try it."

"That's right. You're the pilot." She lifts her chin, sliding her chair back and standing. "Let me show you our island."

She holds out a hand, and I glance at Max, who's on his feet as well.

"Sure—let's do it." I put my napkin beside my plate.

Aunt Sheila is incredibly sure-footed for a blind person. Using her cane, she guides us to a low fence at the back of her small yard. We pass through a rickety gate to a path that goes straight up the side of a hill.

Palms and small flowering shrubs surround us, and when we reach the top, it opens to a breathtaking view of the green mountains and the shore below.

"It's breathtaking." My voice is hushed, and Sheila chuckles.

"It's the least developed and the least disturbed by tourism of the islands."

"I noticed there aren't any big resorts. Max said there's not even regular jet service."

"We have to hop over to Maui if we need to go anywhere."

It reminds me of Eureka. "What do people do for work?"

"The usual." She seems a bit defensive. "We have jobs in the service industry, in retail, and in local government."

"Doesn't sound like much for an entire island. Unemployment must be high."

"We have what we need, and we're not interested in being overrun with outsiders like the other islands."

"Sounds like I'm right at home." I glance at Max, and he lifts his chin knowingly.

"Tell me, Mr. Stone, what do you do that allows you to stay with me for an indefinite period of time?"

"It's more the result of not taking a vacation in three years. They begged me to go."

"I doubt that." She winks. "But who are they?"

"I work in the service industry. I help run local food banks, fly doctors on medical missions, that sort of thing."

Her blank eyes brighten. "We could use a good pilot here, should you decide to stay. Families often need to get to the mainland to visit relatives or have surgeries or go to school."

"My brother's getting married in a month, so I'll have to go back for that. Otherwise…" Sliding my hands into my pockets, I look out over the island. "I'm glad to help any way I can."

Stepping closer, she touches my face lightly with her fingertips. She starts with my forehead, going down to my cheeks, then my jaw.

Her brow lowers as if she's disappointed, and I exhale a laugh. "Something wrong?"

"You're very handsome."

"Is that a bad thing?"

"I don't know." She turns and starts down the path to her house. "I guess we'll find out."

Chapter 5

Piper

"Really, Drake? A dog for mayor?" Cass's disgusted voice cuts through the small crowd of Eureka residents gathered in front of the gazebo in the middle of town square.

Drake Redford, her douchey ex-boyfriend turned mega real-estate developer, stands beside Harold Waters, owner of the Popcorn Palace out on the old Beach Road.

Harold is wearing a white T-shirt with "Bo for Mayor" on it in red, white, and blue, and standing between the two men is a friendly yellow lab with his tongue hanging out.

One of Harold's employees is walking through the crowd passing out popcorn balls decorated with the stickers of the dog candidate.

"Bo is excited and eager to try new things." Drake ignores my friend's protest. "He's pro-business and willing to listen to the citizens."

"Does he comply with the pooper-scooper ordinance?" Terra Belle quips from the middle of the crowd.

I press my lips together, making a note in my steno pad. I record everything for my articles on my phone, but I make notes of things I want to be sure and remember in my write-up. This is going to be front-page news in the Sunday edition of the *Eureka Gazette*.

Looking around, I estimate a crowd of at least twenty-five has gathered. Alex Stone is standing beside Cass with a furious expression on his face and his daughter Pinky on his hip.

"Have a popcorn ball, Terra." Harold gestures to one of his employees, who extends the basket to her.

"How do I know it's not dog food?" Terra is one of the original Eureka residents, and she's never afraid to speak her mind.

She also never ventures out in public without her Dolly Parton-style wig and bright red lipstick. Her niece Julia stands between her and Alex holding her daughter Crimson's hand.

Pinky Stone's little hand pops up. "Do they have apples with peanut butter in them? *That's* dog food."

Alex and Cass exchange a glance, and for a moment, Alex's frown softens to a warm smile. An inside joke, I'll wager.

"They're caramel, salt, and butter, little lady. Give one a try." Harold smiles at the kindergartener.

"You've made your point, Redford." Aiden steps forward, waving to the crowd. "Let's break it up now."

"We have a right to hold a public forum in the town square, Sheriff." Drake straightens, extending his hand like a traveling salesman. "Redford Park would transform Eureka. How many times have you needed a place for guests or relatives to stay and come up empty-handed?"

Studying the crowd, I see heads nodding, and I worry for Britt's grandmother, the longstanding mayor of Eureka.

"The days of putting up invisible barriers to growth are over," he continues. "Eureka residents are tired of a mayor who is anti-business and in the pocket of the richest citizens in the community."

I cover my mouth so I don't laugh out loud. As a member

of the press, I have to be more professional than that, but *is he kidding?*

Drake clearly knows nothing about Eureka, or he'd know about the historic beef between Edna Brewer, Britt's former-magician-turned-mayor grandmother, and Andrew Stone, late patriarch of the by-the-book Stone family.

Aiden's dad almost retired as sheriff when Edna was elected the first time, but she agreed not to bring anything magical to the courthouse if he'd agree to stay on as sheriff.

As far as I know, she always kept that promise, and they maintained a fragile peace, even after Aiden took his father's place as sheriff.

It wasn't until Britt joined the force as a forensic photographer that the two families finally made true peace—mostly because Aiden and Britt started sleeping together, which had its own set of complications.

Still, the enmity between the Stones and the Brewer-Baileys is as much a part of Eureka's history as Myrtle the Pig or Terra Belle's Pickle Patch.

"Are you referring to *my* pocket?" Alex's jaw is so tight, I'm worried he might crack a molar, and I'm really glad he's holding his daughter.

I know he's been itching to punch Drake in the face for a while, and while that would totally make a great story—complete with pictures, of course—I know Alex wouldn't appreciate that shade of limelight.

Drake seems to sense his nose is in danger, and he quickly wraps up his speech. "So when you go to the polls next month, think Go and vote Bo."

The crowd slowly disperses. I catch sight of a strange man in a khaki trench coat as I walk with Britt back to the courthouse.

"Hey, who's that?" I nod towards the fellow, who has kind of an old-school Columbo look about him.

She squints in his direction, then shakes her head. "Probably a tourist up from one of the beach towns."

"He's kind of messy and overdressed for a tourist, don't you think?"

"Maybe he's a movie scout?"

The odd man turns and walks in the direction of the Star Parlor, so I decide to let it go.

"I always knew Drake Redford was a dick, but I had no idea he'd go this far." We stop at the concrete steps leading up to the building, and I turn over the trifold flier with a picture of Bo in a stars-and-stripes circle on the cover.

When I got the email through the paper's tip line from Drake, I figured he'd be suggesting a new site for the giant resort and golf course he's determined to build here.

I had no idea he was staging a direct challenge to Britt's grandmother.

"What does it even mean to run a *dog* for mayor?" Britt's face is pale, but her voice is strong. Her barfing seems to have subsided this afternoon. "A dog can't be mayor."

"I think it's more a protest option since your grandmother's opposing his development."

Scrolling through my notes, I try to decide how I'm going to finesse his points in my story. I can't leave out Drake's big speech about Edna being anti-business, and it's true she and Alex are allied in opposing the resort. It doesn't mean she's in Alex's pocket.

"I can't believe Harold Waters is letting him exploit Bo this way. We've been so nice and supportive of Harold since he moved here from Chicago." My friend's usually sunny disposition is all feistiness today.

"Tell me about it. I've always given him free coverage anytime he does anything at the Popcorn Palace."

"Gran just wants to keep Eureka like it is. If tourists want to stay at a big resort, go to Disney in Hilton Head. If they want to golf, go to freakin' Kiawah!"

Edna emerges from the courthouse where her office is located, and I jump to attention, holding out my phone. "Any comment on Bo the Dog, Madame Mayor?"

Inhaling deeply, Britt's grandmother shakes her head. "No, Piper. I won't dignify any of this with a comment."

"I understand." I tuck my phone into my pocket again.

Drake has been nothing but trouble since he came to Eureka for Britt and Aiden's wedding. The only good thing to come out of it was he pushed Alex and Cass together, even if it was through a fake-engagement scam.

Edna heads to her Lincoln Town Car parked in the lot, and I put my arm around her granddaughter's shoulders. It's mid-October, which means we're only a few weeks away from the election and even closer to the wedding.

"I'm glad you're feeling better." I give her a nudge. "Does this mean you'll be able to help me finish up the wedding? I've got the caterer booked and the florist, but I have no idea who to get for entertainment. Would Cass prefer a DJ or a live band? And how can we ever top her snickerdoodle cake?"

Britt slides a hand across her forehead. "I have the name of a baker in Oceanside I can give you, but I think I might've overdone it today."

"Do you need something? Ginger ale? Barf bag?"

"I just need to let this wave of nausea pass." She waves a handful of Bo fliers in front of her face like a fan, and I wait until she's able to start moving again.

It's a crisp fall day, sunny, with clear blue skies, and Halloween decorations are all over town. Across the street, Gwen has her tarot studio decorated in neon purple, black, and orange. *The Nightmare Before Christmas* figures, skeletons, and ghosts are scattered throughout the town square and in the gazebo.

Even the courthouse has an orange and black garland around the door.

"I can grab Owen when I pick up Ryan from school if you want."

"Aiden told him to come here as soon as he gets out." Her

brow furrows. "I'll be glad when Adam finally comes home. He's been gone too long."

My stomach twists at her statement, and I can't argue—it's been a long three weeks. "We probably relied on him too much when he was here."

"Adam is family." Britt shakes her head. "He liked spending time with the boys. He's one of the few people who can handle Pinky, and he was practically a father to Ryan."

Swallowing the ache in my throat, I force a smile. "It's true. He's always been such a good friend to us."

"Have you heard from him?"

"No." My voice is quiet. "I'm sure he's too busy to think about us."

"That doesn't sound like him at all. Did something happen? Maybe somebody said something."

"He talked to Alex the night he left." That part still hurts, and I'm ready to end this conversation. I've been doing my best to get past the emotional spiral I went down the last time I thought too much about Adam. "Anyway, I'd better get moving if I'm going to get this story in the Sunday edition."

She makes some comment about deflecting, but I hustle away from her questions and how much I miss him. Our last night is stuck on replay in my mind, and I'm doing my best not to obsess over how it could've gone differently—or if I'll ever get the chance to try again.

***

"What's happening here?" Mom points at the large desktop computer holding the layout for Sunday's paper. "You don't have a single headline on the entire front page!"

"I've got to get this story right before I send it to the printer." My hair is twisted up on my head with a pencil, and I'm giving the Dog-Mayor story a final read-through.

It's a sensitive one, and everyone's going to read it.

"How much time do you have?" Mom walks over to where I'm chewing my thumbnail and staring at my laptop.

"Twenty minutes."

"You're going to finish that story and fill in all these headlines in twenty minutes?"

"I know." My heart beats faster, and I make a quick edit. "I put them off because I suck at writing headlines. They're always too long or too much information—"

"Let me do it. I'm great at headlines. I can make them short and exciting. Like this one about Myrtle the Pig versus Terra Belle... I'll handle it."

My fingers are on the keyboard, and I study my mom in her denim overalls, plaid shirt, and long, graying hair plaited in a single braid down her back. I've never paid much attention to her writing skills, but when my eyes hit the clock, I don't have much of a choice.

"Okay, give it a shot." I nod, returning to the screen. "I trust you."

She grins, stretching her arms in front of her before grabbing the mouse and clicking on the empty space above the first story. "I won't let you down, Chief!"

My nose wrinkles, and I shake my head. I really could use some help around here. Occasionally Adam would proofread the stories, but I'm it when it comes to reporting, photographing, editing, and these last three weeks have been hectic with Drake kicking up trouble and the wedding plans taking up all my free time.

The warning bell dings as I finish reading my story. "Got one for the forum Drake did this afternoon?"

"Where he announced a dog for mayor?" Mom's voice is as disgusted as Cass's. "I'll take care of it."

I hit save, and we zip the files and email them to Stew just as the clock strikes four.

"Made it!" I hold up my hand, and she slaps it. "Thanks for your help."

My mother smiles proudly. "I'd say we make a pretty good team."

Nodding, I think about this potential new angle to our relationship. For most of my life, she's either been embarrassing or confusing to me. I've only ever known her as reclusive and suspicious, but she has friends. She gets out when she wants to.

She simply marches to the beat of her own drum—a drum that believes the government is tracking us and no one can be trusted, which is odd, considering her best friend is the mayor's daughter Gwen. Although, I guess Edna's magician past makes her different from the usual politician.

Hell, Eureka is a *different* small town.

"I really appreciate your help, Mom." And I mean it. "Maybe you can do it again next time?"

The *Gazette* is published biweekly with editions on Wednesdays and Sundays, and unless there's breaking news, we wrap up the Sunday edition on Friday evening.

"I'd love to."

"Hey, Mom! Check it out!" Ryan's voice is loud, and we both turn to see my son charging into the office with a solid black cat over his shoulder. "I named him Fudge! He followed me all the way home from school! Can I keep him? Can I, Mom? Cats aren't a lot of work, and I can teach him to do tricks—"

"Ahh…" My teeth clench, and I look to my mother for help. "I don't know, babe. Cats don't really do tricks."

"That's what Miss Britt said about Edward, but Owen taught him to race and to catch a frisbee. I bet I could teach Fudge to do something."

"You could teach him to chase the mice out of my cellar." My mom reaches out to ruffle his dark hair.

"But Edward's a dog," I try to resist. "Dogs are easier to train than cats, and what if he belongs to somebody? We can't steal another person's cat."

"He's not anybody's cat! We don't know anybody who has a black cat."

"We can't possibly know that, Ryan. We don't know everybody in town." It's a funny statement, considering I remember a time when we did know everybody in Eureka.

"If you let him stay outside, he can come and go as he pleases." Mom scratches the cat's neck, and the animal starts to purr. "He seems like a good guy, and black cats are good luck in some cultures."

"In that case, Fudge will have his work cut out for him." I frown, knowing I'm losing this battle.

"He'll bring us all kinds of good luck. You'll see, Mom!" Ryan is talking loudly, and I decide to go with Mom's option.

"He'll stay outside, and we'll give him a few days to see if he doesn't leave before making any commitments."

Ryan tosses the cat over his shoulder again with a little hoot, and the three of us head out the door.

Being on good terms with Mom makes me happier than I expect, and I loop my arm through hers. "Want to have dinner with us? We'll probably just have hamburgers, but you're welcome to join us."

She smiles at me. "I'd love to have dinner with you."

For the first time in a long time, we feel like a family. The suspicion and disapproval have left her expression. She's almost like someone I could talk to about my problems.

Fall is setting in, and the nights are growing cooler. Mom builds a small fire in the chiminea, and I turn three hamburger patties on the small charcoal grill.

My house only has two bedrooms, which doesn't work for overnight guests, but it's perfect for Ryan and me. We've lived here since he was a baby, and it's all we need. If anything breaks, I figure out how to fix it, and it's right behind the newspaper office. I could stagger into work in my pajamas if I wanted to.

I have never done that.

"Look at him!" Ryan has a feather on a small fishing pole, and he's using it to taunt Fudge and entertain us. "Look how high he can jump!"

He swings the feather, and Fudge does a triple back axle in the air. Mom cheers, and I shake my head as I drop potato sticks into the air fryer.

"That's pretty good. Maybe cats can learn tricks."

"I can't wait for Uncle Adam to see him!" Ryan yells, and my stomach pinches.

"Have you heard from Adam?" Mom's eyes are on me, studying my expression.

Controlling my face, I make my voice light. "I haven't."

I don't know why everyone keeps asking me this today. I need to get back in to see Drew. It's starting to hurt again.

"That's odd. He was so involved with Ryan... with all the kids. He had them playing tee ball, working in the community garden. Something must have happened for him to withdraw that way."

"He's flying people back and forth to the mainland from Moloka'i!" Ryan walks into the kitchen. "He sent me a picture last week, see?"

He hands his phone to my mother, and I watch stunned. "Adam sent you a video?"

"Yeah, we text every day. You don't?" Ryan's brow is furrowed, and he seems genuinely confused.

I'm genuinely hurt.

"I guess I thought he wanted space." My voice is quiet, and I feel my mother's eyes on me again.

Looks like I showed my hand just then. *Good work, Piper.*

"Dinner's ready," I announce brightly.

"I'll set our places at the picnic table!" Ryan grabs napkins and utensils and charges out the door. "Uncle Adam said being a good helper makes people glad to have you around."

"Everyone must love having Adam Stone around, then." Mom's voice has a note, but I don't let the conversation lag.

"Three cheeseburgers…" I put slices of cheese on the hot patties before plating them along with the buns, and handing them to my mom.

She takes them as I grab the big bowl of fries, and Fudge follows us outside. Ryan pours him a bowl of dry cat food, and we all take our seats around the small table. Purple and orange twinkle lights are strung along the top of our fence. An oversized jack-o-lantern is on the side of the house, and I've got a flattened, fabric witch tacked to a tree.

Ryan is on his knees, bobbing side to side as he dips his fries in ketchup before eating them. Mom cuts her burger in half, and I dive into mine. Half of my burger is gone when I lean back in my chair checking out Fudge lying long and shiny on the grass, watching us with bright yellow eyes.

"You think a mysterious black cat showing up at Halloween is good luck?" I squint at the satisfied-looking feline.

"Absolutely." Mom nods, taking a sip of her beer. "The Scottish people believe black cats bring good fortune."

"We're not Scottish."

"We can still believe."

I'm starting to laugh when a strange creaking sound from inside the house draws my attention. It's a low groaning, almost like the noise of an old-timey pirate ship out on the ocean. I'm about to make a crack about Scottish pirates when it gets louder.

It's followed by what sounds like a firehose going off in the house. Through the window, I see water spraying from the ceiling inside, and Ryan jumps to his feet, sending Fudge dashing off into the darkness.

"It's raining in the house!" he yells.

My stomach drops, and I run for the door as my mom lets out a loud yell, "Oh! Oh, no!"

I crash through the door into the kitchen, diving under the sink where the main water line shut-off valve is located.

Everything seems to slip into slow motion as the upstairs toilet crashes through the ceiling of my living room and lands on the floor with water raining all around it.

Chapter 6

Adam

"Hard to believe you're headed home already." Max sits back in the low planter's chair in the large backyard of Sheila's small house. "The time has flown."

"More like *I* have flown," I joke, leaning against the thick palm tree and looking up at the grassy path leading to the cliffs overhead.

After showing me the island and learning I was "the pilot," Sheila put me to work flying local residents pretty much everywhere they needed to go from the small airstrip. Some had medical reasons to get to the big island. Some had to take care of school or work issues.

Occasionally, I'd even taken the small passenger jet to San Francisco or Oakland for residents to visit family or see their grandchildren born or attend weddings.

The only charge was the cost of fuel, and if they couldn't pay it, Sheila had "a fund."

Never once did I regret it. To be honest, I really threw

myself into the work. I used it to drown out the feelings of frustration and anger. I used it to give her space.

I kept in touch with Ryan and Owen and my brothers, and from what I can tell, not much has changed in Eureka. I don't know what I'll find when I get back home, but I'm doing my best to keep my emotions neutral.

It's fucking bullshit, because I think about her all the time. I've started and deleted so many text messages, but I can't send them.

I have to move on, and the only way that's going to happen is by training myself not to need to hear her voice, or her thoughts, or her funny comments.

"What time are you leaving tomorrow?" Aunt Sheila walks out to the backyard, hardly using her cane to guide her steps.

"Before dawn. It'll take me two days to get there, since I'm going back in time."

"Your family will be glad to see you." She sits at the table, removing the cork from the bottle of Oke. "Here's to homecomings."

Sitting across from her, I wait as she pours an inch of the clear liquor into two small glasses. We clink and shoot it, and I wince.

"It's nothing like Stone Cold premium."

The lines on her face lift with her smile. "Is that your brother's bourbon?"

"Best in the world."

"Let's take a walk on your last night." She rises slowly from her chair, and I reach out to hold her arm. "Max, you coming?"

"I'm good." My friend has his phone out, and I'm pretty sure he's keeping up with a pretty surfer he met last week.

I follow his aunt out the small gate and up the worn path to the top of the hill. As many times as we've walked up here over the past several weeks, it still takes my breath away.

"Have you always been blind?"

"I started losing my eyesight when I was eighteen." Her

expression sobers. "At first, I was terrified. Then I got angry. I wanted to lash out at everyone, God in particular. Then I fell into a black depression."

"I think I can understand that."

"When I finally made peace with it, I decided to make the most of every day I could see. I did my best to prepare. I made modifications to my house, my phone, my computer... pretty much everything I needed."

"Are you able to see anything? Lights, shapes..."

"I'm in complete darkness now." She smiles in my direction. "I get the best sleep of my life, and I'm not bothered by all this social media everyone talks about."

"I can't imagine you'd be the type to worry much about social media if you could see."

"You never know what gets people. It's what you can't see that tells you what you need to know."

I can't argue with her. "I'm glad to know I was wrong."

Her head tilts to the side. "About me and social media?"

That makes me laugh. "No, I was thinking what a tragedy it is that you live in this beautiful place, in paradise, and you can't see it."

"The tragedy is to have perfect vision and not be able to see what's right in front of you."

"I'm not sure what you mean."

"What are you running from, Adam Stone?"

Her question hits me right in the gut, but I do my best to play it off. "What makes you think I'm running from something?"

"You're young, rich, and handsome... and you've spent the last four weeks on the most remote Hawaiian island with an old blind lady and her nephew flying people all over the place. If Max were gay, I'd understand, but as it is..."

"Wait... Max isn't gay?" That makes her laugh, but she's not letting me off the hook.

"What's your story? I told you mine."

We take a seat on the soft grass, and I look out across the glowing green cliffs to the water crashing on the beach below.

"My first solo flight with the Navy changed how I saw things. Looking down on the tiny fields, the lines of rivers like veins in a body, I realized how connected we are. How inescapable our paths are."

"Yet you're still trying to escape your path."

"How could you know that?"

"I'm an old woman who lives on an island. No one who looks like you comes here and dedicates his life to the poor unless he's running from something or someone."

"You can't see me."

"I've seen you." I don't even ask how that's possible. "What's her name?"

The pressure in my chest tightens, and I exhale the tension of evoking her presence. "Piper Jackson."

She nods. "Musical, fluid, an old soul, like you."

"We had a connection from the first time we met, like we'd always known each other."

Her smile widens. "She's your constant. Do you believe in past lives?"

"No."

"You don't have to believe it for it to be true. Two particles once associated are eternally connected, across the universe, across time. The two are inseparable; neither makes sense without the other. It's quantum physics, entanglement."

"I've heard of it." As a surfer, I've met all kinds of people with all kinds of crazy beliefs. The one thing true in her words is *constant*. "The first time I saw her, I knew I was in trouble." I exhale a soft laugh. "She was so pretty. She was delicate like a honeysuckle flower… but my best friend asked her out first."

"Such a dumb rule." I watch her dig the small pipe from her pocket, and I've come to recognize it's something she does when she's impatient.

"It's still the rule. Rex was my best friend, and she was his girl." Looking down, a dry ache is in my throat. "Then he died, and I kind of fell apart. She needed me, and I let her down. So she sent me away."

"That's when you came here?"

"That's when I joined the Navy. I went away for five years and got my shit together. I grew up and learned how to be a real man."

"Oh, shit." Sheila's eyes widen. "She married someone else while you were gone?"

"No." I shake my head. "Nothing that dramatic. Piper only has one man in her life now—her son Ryan. I've accepted that truth, so I've closed the book and moved on."

"So you say." She takes a puff from her pipe. "What I hear is a beautiful young woman, a single mom, who you've been in love with since you were teenagers waited five years for you to come back, and you never made a move? What the fuck, Adam?"

That forces a laugh from me. "You heard wrong. I made a move, but she shut me down. She wants stability for her son, and I have a history of being a fuckup."

"And I thought you were smart." She takes a little puff off the pipe. "Sounds like you need a little fire in your belly."

Frustration flares in my chest. "I love her, and I respect her boundaries. I want to be with her, but the days of men storming in and taking what they want are over."

"Maybe you should bring them back." She arches an eyebrow at me. "Have you kissed her?"

"Yes."

"How'd it go?"

"Pretty damn good. What's your point?"

"My point is when you know, you know." She straightens her skirt. "Do you know?"

Looking down at my hands, *I know*. "Yes."

"Do one thing for me when you're back home, and don't come back here unless you've done it." I look up at her, as if she can see me. "Have her tell you straight-out why you can't be together. If she has a reason, I want you to get it and tell me when you come back. If she doesn't, I don't expect to see you here again."

I want to tell her she's from another generation. Things are different now, and these days men wait for a solid yes, not a shaky no. Instead, I pocket my response.

I'd actually like to hear what Piper might say if I tell her this old woman's assignment for me. "You'll see me here again."

My last night in Sheila's small house, I lie on my back with the slatted windows open. A breeze filters through the room carrying the scents of hibiscus, plumeria, and coconut. It's different from Eureka, where pine trees line the shore, and the ocean is too far away to hear.

Turning onto my side, I think how in forty-eight hours, more or less, I'll see her again.

I think about how the ache in my belly hasn't subsided. In fact, it's only gotten worse. I look at my phone, and I see all the texts between me and my brothers. Every day, I've communicated with Ryan. They've sent me videos and updates but none offered me a glimpse of her, and I ache to see her face, her pretty smile, the freckles on her nose.

Her name sits there silent on my list, haunting me like a memory I can't let go.

Rolling onto my back, I'm quiet as sleep creeps over me, and with it comes the dreams I can't escape every night. I might tell Sheila times have changed, but my inner caveman is alive and hungry.

Every night, I cover her mouth with kisses. Thick red hair spills around us in waves, and my hands are dark against the pale-ivory of her skin. I'm strong and hard, and she's soft and willing. Our mouths collide, tongues entwine, and she moans, pulling me closer to her.

Her legs part, and her body opens to me. I inhale deeply her scent of honeysuckle and fresh ocean air. Tracing my lips from her waist up her sides to her breasts, I lose myself in her beautiful body.

Piper never showed off like the other girls at the beach in our surfing days. I only saw her a few times in a bikini. Still, the sight was imprinted on my mind, soft curves and a flat stomach. She's classic, with small breasts and full hips, like something from an old painting.

Maybe that's why she always covered herself in filmy, floral cover-ups. All I know is it made her even more tantalizing to me, like a present to be unwrapped.

How I still want to unwrap her. I want to lay her back on the sand, look down on her, devour her, make her moan my name like it's the most delicious thing she's ever tasted.

Every night in my dreams, it's what I do when I'm with her. We're together, and she whispers the words my body aches to hear. *More…*

Chapter 7

Piper

"It's my luck, as usual." I'm standing at the door to Britt and Aiden's house.

"You should've seen it! The toilet came straight through the living room ceiling." Ryan has his backpack on his shoulder and Fudge in his arms.

Owen is beside him with wide eyes. "Sounds like *good* luck nobody was on that toilet when it happened!"

Britt covers her smile with her hand, and clearly she's getting over her morning sickness—or her around-the-clock sickness. I haven't seen her laugh in weeks.

"I'd offer to let you take the guest room, but Aunt Pearl is here for the wedding."

"It's okay. I appreciate y'all keeping Ryan. I can stay at the apartment in town until we get someone to fix the house."

"Ryan is no trouble at all. I don't know about this cat…"

"Oh, Fudge." My nose wrinkles, and I hear it as soon as I say it. "Just leave him outside. He'll be okay."

Britt shakes her head, handing me the keys to the building that houses her mother's Star Parlor as well as the upstairs studio apartment where she lived before she married Aiden. "You can stay as long as you need to. We'll figure everything out tomorrow."

"Thanks." I give her a hug and head for town.

Britt, Cass, and I have spent many nights in that old apartment having girls' nights, bachelorette parties, and sleepovers. It was the one place we could go when all of our mothers or grumpy old aunts were driving us crazy, and I know it well.

Walking up the short street in the dark, I use the key Britt gave me to unlock the glass front door. The entrance to her mother's tarot studio is immediately to the left, and a flight of stairs leads to the apartment.

It's late, and I'm tired. I slide my fingers over the door to the Star Parlor, where Britt's extra key is hidden, then I jog up the stairs and quickly unlock the door, ready to head inside and crash.

I've just got the door open when a low, gravelly voice stops me in my tracks. "Not one more step. I have a gun, and it's pointed at your liver."

"Don't shoot!" I yell, throwing up my hands.

The light switches on, and I drop all my stuff. A stout, older man stands in front of me in nothing but a T-shirt and thin, cotton boxer shorts. His light brown hair is messy, and his thick brow lowers over small, squinty eyes.

It only takes a second for me to realize it's the Columbo guy from the town forum.

"What are you doing here?" He's flustered and irritated, and I'm pretty much the same.

"I'm spending the night here!" Or at least, that was the plan. "I'm friends with Britt Bailey... I mean, Stone! She said I could stay here. Who are you?"

The click of a gun uncocking helps me relax a tiny bit. I'm

not thrilled this guy is packing, but he exhales a noise and walks over to put the gun in a holster hanging on the bedpost.

"Well, this is a fine mess," he grumbles, going into the bathroom.

"Are you a cop?"

He returns in one of Britt's old robes, and now he's standing across the room from me wearing pink terry cloth with bright yellow flowers on the pockets.

"I'm a private detective. The nice lady downstairs said this apartment was empty. She rented it to me for the month."

My shoulders drop. "Just my luck again."

"What's that supposed to mean?"

"I had a plumbing disaster at my house, and we had to shut off the water. Britt said I could stay here until we get it fixed."

"Well, there's only one bed, and I already paid for it," he growls. "You know, that fella might be a jerk running a dog for mayor, but he has a point. There aren't any places to stay in this town if you don't know somebody."

"It's true." I nod, trying to think. "Are you working with Aiden?"

I'm a little miffed I don't know about this guy, considering I'm friends with Britt and publisher of the newspaper of record. Of course, if he is working with Aiden, that's probably why I don't know about it. Aiden is more tight-lipped than a politician. *What kind of secrets are they keeping?*

"I don't know Sheriff Stone. I'm here on a private matter."

My eyebrow arches, and I study him closer. "I don't suppose you'd mind showing me some identification—so I know you're really who you say you are."

His eyes narrow, but he walks to the couch, picking up his tan coat and pulling out a wallet. He shows me a card that looks like a driver's license, only with "Private Investigator State of Florida" across the top.

"What brings you here from Florida, Marshall Gregg?" I glance up at him.

"That's none of your business, Miss… And you are?"

"Piper Jackson." I stick out my hand. "Publisher of the *Eureka Gazette*."

"Oh, yeah. I've seen it around. Didn't know they still had local papers."

"Most places don't." I walk to the door and pick up my bags. "I've worked hard to keep ours alive. You'd be surprised how much is lost when the only news outlets are run by national corporations."

"I wouldn't be surprised." He watches me, and with all the short sentences, I feel like I'm in one of those old movies. "Where will you stay?"

"I'll figure it out." Before I close the door, I hesitate. "Would you be interested in talking to me? I'd like to hear more about what you do."

"Got any back issues of that paper?" I nod, and he mirrors my action. "I'll drop by."

When I reach the bottom of the stairs, I put the spare key above the Star Parlor door. Then I pull out my phone and shoot Britt a text.

> Surprise—a strange man is renting your apt.

Britt: What the hell? Who?

> Marshall Gregg, PI.

Britt: PI!?

A few seconds pass, and I walk out to my waiting car trying to decide what to do. I could stay with my mother, but if there's any way to avoid that setup, I'll do it. I'd even be willing to sleep at my place with no water.

My phone lights up, and Britt's back.

Britt: Aiden verified he's legit, but no idea why he's here.

> Maybe he's after Drake.

I think about what he said about Drake running a dog for mayor.

She replies with a laughing emoji, then,

> **Britt**: Aiden said to crash at Adam's place. He's not due back til the wedding. Do you know the code for the door?

My breath catches, and I stare at my phone trying to get my heartbeat to calm.

Of course, I know the code, but I don't know if I can actually sleep in Adam's bed. Sitting in my car in front of the courthouse square, I weigh my options: my place with no water, Mom's crazy house, or Adam's empty one.

The answer is obvious. The question is can I handle it?

In the dim light, I see my fingers tremble as I text back.

> Tell Aiden thanks. I know it.

> **Britt**: We've got a lot to talk about tomorrow.

> Meet me at the distillery.

No matter what's happening, Cass's wedding is only a week away, and I won't be the one to let her down. I toss my phone onto the passenger's seat of my car and drive the short distance to Adam's one-bedroom cottage, down the street from his mother's rambling old home.

I'm sure his brothers have been checking on the place while he's been away, but it's strange being here without him. For whatever reason, I don't park in the driveway. Instead, I leave my car on the road, grabbing my bag and locking the door.

The cool breeze blows the scent of pine straw around me as I follow the sidewalk to the house. Going around back, a yellow light flickers warmly from the antique lamppost behind a trickling fountain. A keypad is beside the door, and I quickly type in his father's birthday.

The lock slides open, and I step inside the dim house. Amber night-lights lead down the hall to his bedroom, and when I inhale, my stomach tightens at his scent still faint in the air, sandalwood and cedar.

Can I do this?

I suppose I could sleep on the couch and avoid being in his bed. Only…

Slipping out of my shoes at the door, my feet are quiet on the soft pine floors. I go to the kitchen to get a glass of water, and I notice a picture of Ryan and me on the refrigerator. It's from a few years ago, when Ryan was in second grade.

I'm holding him, and he's standing on a skateboard. Adam was teaching him, and my heart squeezes. I trace a finger down the image, thinking of him looking at this photo every morning, having his coffee. *I miss you…*

Swallowing back the longing, I take the glass of water and walk to the room where he sleeps. His California king-sized bed is neatly made with a dark gray comforter and plaid flannel sheets. It's enormous, and I realize I'll be lost in this bed.

Placing my bag behind the door, I glance at the clock to see it's after eleven. The toilet came crashing down after dinner, then we spent an hour cleaning up and trying to find someone to come all the way out to Eureka on a Friday night.

No luck there, but I wasn't surprised. When have I ever been lucky?

Everyone is finally settled, and exhaustion is hitting me hard. I step over to a leather armchair and strip out of my jeans and shirt. I unfasten my bra, and hesitate in front of his dresser.

Pulling my lip between my teeth, I open the top drawer and look inside. His warm scent is stronger in his folded clothes, this time mixed with a fresh linen scent. I slide my fingers over tank tops, socks, and T-shirts.

Taking out a white tee, I pull it over my naked torso, then walk to his king-sized bed, pulling back the blankets at one corner. I don't disturb the entire bed. I slip carefully between the sheets, pulling a soft pillow to my cheek.

Of course, I picked the side he must sleep on, because I'm

surrounded in a cocoon of Adam. Closing my eyes, it's like I'm lying in his arms, and I reach for another pillow, hugging it to my chest.

Pressing my face into it, I inhale more of him, rubbing my cheek side to side, pretending it's his chest, his shirt. With my eyes tightly shut, I wrap my legs around the long pillow and pretend.

He wraps strong arms around my waist. His full lips touch the side of my neck, and a shiver tingles down my arms. Calloused palms glide over my waist, moving around to the small of my back, and a heartbeat is in my pussy.

Sucking my lip into my mouth, I relive our last kiss, intense and passionate. I thread my fingers in his hair and pull him closer. I tell him I love him, and he rolls me onto my back, pinning me to the mattress.

Plunging deep inside, he drives harder, faster, giving us both what we've wanted so long. My thighs tighten around the pillow, and I rock my hips against it. It's not enough, so I slide my hand between them and massage, circling faster as I imagine him above me, thrusting and moaning.

I'm in the middle of the bed now, rubbing my clit. I imagine him turning me over, plunging in from behind. I feel his muscled stomach quivering, the lines in his throat shifting with a swallow. Heat and wetness flood my core, and with a shudder, I come to the fantasy of his body thrusting against mine, finishing deep inside me.

Chapter 8

Adam

I'M ASLEEP IN THE BACKSEAT OF THE CAR WHEN THE RIDE-SHARE PULLS into my driveway. My flight arrived after midnight, and I didn't want to bother my brothers or anyone else to pick me up at the airport in Savannah. Still, I couldn't keep my eyes open for the long drive to Eureka.

I've been flying all day, taking the small jet to San Francisco, where I caught a commercial flight cross-country. Now I'm finally home. I thank the driver as I step out, hustling up to the front door and quickly typing in the code.

Aiden has been stopping by a few times a week to bring in the mail and make sure nothing is broken or out of place while I've been gone.

I don't even switch on the lights, leaving my bag in the living room and heading straight for my bedroom. The amber lights in the hall are enough to help guide me to my fully dark bedroom.

I go into the bathroom and brush my teeth. I splash warm water on my face and dry it with a towel. Stripping off my shirt, I drop it along with my jeans on the floor. I could use a shower, but I'll wait until morning. No one's expecting me home this early, so I can unpack, do laundry, take care of everything after I sleep.

Returning to the pitch-black room, I rub a hand over my face. Pulling the blankets aside, I slip into my oversized bed. I consider checking the thermostat, because it's not as cool as I expected it to be as I stretch out under the sheets.

I grab my pillow and pull it under my head before instantly dropping into a dead sleep. Consciousness is gone, but the humid breeze carrying Hawaiian scents is also gone. I know I'm home because it's cold and quiet.

Still, my dreams are so intense, I could swear she's here with me. I smell her honeysuckle fragrance on my pillows, in my bed, and my body lights up with desire.

Will I always be tormented by dreams of her?

My cock hardens, and I groan, moving farther into the center of my bed. Reaching out, I touch her body. She's here, and I bury my face in her soft hair. Through the thick curtains of sleep, I kiss her warm skin. I wrap my arms around her waist and pull her back firmly against my chest.

The dream is so real, I don't want to wake up. I feel her skin against my face, and I slide my lips down the column of her neck, pressing a kiss to the top of her shoulder.

"I only want to love you." My voice breaks with exhaustion, but Sheila's command is in the front of my mind. "I want to give you a home and keep you safe. Why won't you let me?"

It's an aching plea from the depth of my soul.

"Because I'm afraid." Her soft voice snaps my eyes open.

What the fuck? Electricity shoots through my body, and I'm wide awake, lying in my own bed in my own house, with Piper in my arms. I'm not dreaming. I'm holding her. Her arms are over mine, and her fingers curl against my forearms. She's not pushing me away. She's pulling me closer.

"What are you doing in my bed?" I'm sure she can feel my heart beating fast against her back, my erection against her ass.

The energy of lust burns beneath my skin.

"I didn't have anywhere else to go." Her voice is soft, barely above a whisper. "Aiden said I could sleep here."

"Where's Ryan?" As much as I love that little boy, please God, don't say he's here, too.

"He's spending the night with Owen."

Relief washes through me at her answer. The reality of what's happening is the next wave that hits me.

I'm completely nude, and I'm very aware she's only wearing a thin cotton tee that smells like one of mine. I don't understand what's happening or why she's here, but she's talking.

She answered my question.

"What are you afraid of?"

"I need to tell you my truth, but I'm afraid you won't understand. Or if you do, I'm afraid it'll change the way you feel about me."

My lips graze her shoulder as I speak. "I can't think of a single thing you could say that would change how I feel about you."

She turns her face, pressing her lips to my temple. "Don't say anything tonight. Don't ask me anything. Just love me."

A pain is in my chest, because I have so much to say. I want to tell her I love her, and I want her to say she loves me, too.

Instead, I lift my chin, covering her mouth with mine. Her lips part, and my tongue slides inside to curl with hers. My fingers curl in the thin cotton shirt, bunching it higher until my hand finds the warm skin of her stomach. A noise breaks from her throat, and my dick aches with need.

Sliding my hand lower, I guide my fingers beneath the elastic of her panties, continuing down until I find the place between her thighs that's hot and slippery.

"Fuck, Piper. Is this a yes?" My fingers graze her clit, and her head falls back against my shoulder.

She nods, her voice low and husky. "Yes, *please*."

Placing a kiss on the back of her neck, I touch her skin with my tongue, inhaling her scent of honey and flowers. Her shoulder rises, and I move my lips lower, between her shoulder blades, placing another kiss against her warm skin.

Her arms are bent at her sides, and I slide her panties off her hips, down her smooth legs, before rolling her onto her back and lifting her thighs, opening her so I can put my face between them.

"Oh, fuck!" She gasps as I trace my tongue hungrily up and down her clit. "Adam… it's been too long. I'm going to come."

I know how long it's been, because I've waited just as long. Tonight I plan to make up for all that time, and I'm only getting started. She said please, and her pleasure is my goal.

Wrapping my arms around her legs, I pull her closer to my mouth, dragging my tongue all over her cunt, nibbling and pulling, licking hard and fast. She grunts and bucks against my face, moaning louder as her belly begins to quiver.

I don't let up. Her breath hitches, and she digs in her heels, riding my face as I stay with her. Her voice cracks in a ragged cry, and she arches off the bed. Her hands fly to my shoulders, one is in my hair, as she shudders and bucks, coming on my face.

Her body is still trembling as I make my way higher, kissing her belly before stopping at her breasts. Lifting them in my hands, I trace my tongue all over her hardened nipple before pulling it into my mouth.

I'm feasting on her body when her fingers close around my shaft, and my mind blanks.

"Fuck," I groan as her hand moves up and down quickly, moistened by the precum dripping from my cock.

Her hand pumps faster, and I'm lost in sensation, doing my best not to come all over her stomach. She pushes against my shoulder, and I roll onto my back, allowing her to straddle my waist. She's still moving her hand, working me faster as her mouth covers mine. Her lips part, and our tongues curl together.

I groan deeply as her hand between our legs tugs and works my cock. My hands are on her ass, and I lift my hips off the bed as she slides my shaft into her pussy, hot and wet.

"Piper…" My eyes squeeze shut, and pleasure blankets my mind.

I'm fully inside her, balls deep, and she's on her knees riding me. Low groans vibrate from my chest as she leans forward above me. Her breasts bounce at my chin, and I pull a nipple into my mouth, sucking hard, making her moan.

She's so fucking tight around my dick. I'm primal, thrusting into her faster as I grip her ass. My finger traces between her butt cheeks before slipping into that tight little hole as well, giving her a lift.

"Oh, fuck," she yells, jerking her body up and down on my cock before leaning closer to kiss me again.

Her insides pull and massage me, and I can't hold out any longer. "I'm coming," I groan, and she slips off me, returning her hand between our legs and gripping my shaft.

She continues jerking me off as I come. Deep groans vibrate from my stomach, and my muscles tighten. My dick responds to every stroke. Hot liquid shoots onto her arm, her legs, our stomachs.

"I'm not on the pill," she gasps against my mouth, sucking my lips with hers again.

"Jesus," I gasp, sliding my palms over her ass, trying to get my bearings from that orgasm.

Her legs are on each side of me, and I reach up to move her thick hair away from her face, holding it behind her neck in my hands. I need some light in this room. I want to see every emotion that crosses her face.

"I have condoms."

"I didn't want to wait." She leans down, and we're kissing again. Her lips slide to my ear, and she whispers, "I want you behind me, thrusting so hard I see stars."

"I'll fuck you til you can't walk if you want me to."

"Okay."

We're speaking in soft, furtive whispers, and all the pillows are off the bed. I sit up, switching on the lamp and opening the drawer where I hope I have enough condoms. I don't have a box, but God knows I held onto some in the hopes I might one day be here with her.

She's on her knees beside me, and I pull her naked body against my chest as I search the drawer. I need to feel her skin against mine in case something happens and she disappears.

Her lips are on my neck, and she traces her tongue along my skin. "Salty," she whispers with a soft laugh.

My fingers land on square foil, and I grab it out. She puts her fingers on my cheeks, looking into my eyes. Her gorgeous, green-hazel eyes shine, and I swallow the emotion in my throat. She's happy. She's here with me.

"It's like a dream." She's still whispering.

"It doesn't have to be."

Her eyes flicker down, and her fingers slide over my lips. My stomach tightens, and I don't want to break this spell.

"Come with me." Lifting her into my arms, I carry her into the bathroom.

I waste no time finding a washcloth, dampening it, and cleaning us both. I'm still holding her as I carry her to the bed again.

Placing her on the soft sheets, I tear open the condom and set it on the bedside table. She climbs onto her knees, and when I turn, our faces are on the same level.

She's so beautiful in the dim lamplight. Reaching up with both hands, I move her hair back, wanting to tell what's on my mind, but not wanting to push her away.

Her pretty eyes move from my face to my hair. She curls her fingers in the sides and whispers, "I missed you."

I missed her every single day, but I don't say that yet. She asked me not to earlier, and I'm not sure if it's safe. So I only smile, placing a hand on her waist and pulling her body to mine. Her cheek rests against my chest, and her head is tucked under my chin. Closing my eyes, I listen to our hearts beating in time. *I want this always.*

My stomach is tight, and I'm still thinking about her fantasy of me behind her. But I'm carefully following her lead. I want this to be the first step of many, many more. I want us to reach the point where I can tell her my fantasies as well.

But tonight, I'll do whatever it takes to keep my beautiful girl right here, secure in my arms and warm in my bed.

Sensing my hesitation, she lifts her lips to kiss my jaw. My hand is on her neck, and I cover her mouth with mine. I worry I'm being too aggressive, but again, I'm gratified when she kisses me back, her fingers curling against my shoulders, pulling me closer.

We slide lower in the bed, and I turn her body so her back is to my chest again. Her breathing picks up, and my lips are behind her ear. I kiss the back of her neck, and she exhales a soft sigh that registers straight to my dick.

Grabbing the condom, I quickly roll it on before pulling her ass to my pelvis. My hand moves around front, between her legs, and I circle my fingers over her clit, sliding them up and down and teasing her wetness.

Her hand threads in the side of my hair, and she pulls gently. She arches her back, inhaling deeply so her beautiful tits rise. Covering them with my hand, I gently tease her, pulling the hard tips with my fingers.

I've never seen her body naked, and I'm like a man discovering a new world. I want to make her come, but I also want to explore every part of her. I want to trace my lips down the curve of her hips, slide my fingers over the swell of her breasts. I want to memorize every inch of her flesh.

Her lips part, and I can't help myself. "You're so beautiful."

It's a low groan against her shoulder, and I'm looking down, watching her move like a wave under my touch.

I kiss her neck, pulling the skin between my teeth, and she moans, grinding her ass against my cock. I can't take much more. Reaching between us, I slide closer to her entrance.

Her hand fumbles behind to grasp me, and my eyes squeeze shut with a groan. She pulls me into her, and I roll us so that she's on her stomach. I'm propped on my forearms, and on instinct I start to thrust rapidly.

Her ass rises to meet me, and she's rocking back, matching my eagerness with her own. We're desperate, moving faster as the overwhelming sensation controls our bodies.

I gasp and groan. She grunts and moans, and together, we chase our release. Sweat slicks our bodies, causing them to slide together. I'm breathing hard, and I can't stop. Pleasure snakes up my legs, radiating in my pelvis, driving me relentlessly.

I have to claim her.

"Oh, God…" Her voice goes high, and her body jerks as if touched by electricity.

Her insides clench and pull, and I feel as she orgasms all around me. I can't stop. She's gripping and squeezing my cock, and I fly over the edge. Holding her steady, I press my forehead to her shoulder as the waves overtake me, pushing me down and turning me around.

A deep groan aches through my throat, and I'm still coming. I didn't think it was possible, but I can't get enough of her. I'm spent and satisfied and so fucking happy.

Rolling onto my side, I reach between us, quickly disposing of the condom before pulling her into my arms and holding her tight to my chest. Her cheek is at my neck, and we're sweaty and breathing hard.

Her fingers cling to my shoulder, and I feel the lift of her smile against my skin. I also feel the warmth of a tear. I don't speak. I only cup her face in my hand, kissing her temple, kissing the line of her hair, kissing the top of her head as calm settles around us.

I'll take her pain. I'll wait for her to tell me her secrets. I'll hold my words and my questions until she's ready for them—if she's ever ready for them.

All I want is to be here and never be apart again.

Chapter 9

Piper

"Something's different about you." Britt stands beside me in the industrial kitchen behind the tasting room at Stone Cold distillery.

"What are you talking about? I'm just like I always am." I frown like I'm so confused.

How could I be different? It's not like your brother-in-law fucked my brains out all night.

The thought almost makes me goofy-grin, so I quickly take out my laptop and set it on the metal table in front of us. Then I open all the spreadsheets I've used to prepare for Cass's wedding.

Spreadsheets are very good for killing joy.

When I opened my eyes this morning, the first thing I saw was Adam's gorgeous face beside me in the bed. My heart jumped to my throat, and happiness squeezed my chest.

He wasn't crowding me. He simply had his palm flat against my waist, almost like he was making sure I was still there as he slept.

I lingered a moment to study his perfect profile in the morning light. His features were relaxed, from his closed eyes, down his straight nose, to his sexy square jaw with the faintest scruff on his cheeks—a scruff that was thrillingly delicious against my inner thighs.

A hum buzzed in my insides at the memory of so many orgasms. My fingers curled with wanting to thread through his dark hair, messy against his neck.

Last night, all my fantasies came true. Almost ten years of longing and desire and emotions and... *love.*

I wanted to kiss his full lips. I wanted to wake him and make love one more time... But as fast as the thrill surged through me, the fear crept right up behind it. I have to tell him the truth now, and it terrifies me.

So I carefully slipped away without waking him. I got dressed as quickly as I could, called Britt, and asked her to meet me here for breakfast, coffee, ginger tea, whatever she wanted, and to go over all the wedding plans.

"You kind of have this relaxed aura going on." She waves her fingers in a swirly motion around my face, and I force a laugh.

"I think you're the one with the aura. That baby is finally cooperating, and you can see clearly now."

"Shew, tell me about it." She leans back, resting a hand on her growing midsection. "Lord knows this baby tried to kill me. Speaking of, would you fix me a ginger tea?"

"Of course!" I'm on my way to the coffee maker, noticing a distinct ache between my legs every time I move. It's amazing.

A smile curls my lips, and her voice cuts through the echoey, metal space.

"See, that's what I'm talking about." Her eagle eyes are on me again. "Your cheeks are all pink. What's going on?"

Turning my back, I chew my lip, racking my brains as I pour my coffee and drop her ginger tea bag into a mug of boiling water.

"Oh, I know!" Clearing the surprise from my tone, I turn

to her, tilting my head side to side. "I'm trying out this new vitamin C serum. Is it making my complexion more radiant?"

She squints at me, taking the cup of tea and settling onto her chair. "I guess."

I direct us back to the wedding planning. "So I've got the caterer lined up and the florist... The staff here knows how to set up all the tables and the chairs. Cass provided a guest list, as did Alex. I think it's the same one Aiden used..."

She scans everything I've done, nodding and sipping her tea. "I don't know what you were worried about. Everything looks great to me." She smiles in her trademark, sunny way. "It's exactly what I would've done."

"The scary part is going to be the twenty-four hours before—making sure everything gets here and gets set up like it's supposed to and nothing is broken."

"Nothing will be broken. These guys do weddings all the time. They know what they're doing. It's only us who do it once, or in this case, twice a year."

"Yeah, but you know how my luck goes."

Her nose wrinkles. "I think you're being too glass-half-empty about your luck. Owen was right. It was lucky nobody was sitting on the toilet when it came crashing through the ceiling yesterday."

"That's a pretty low bar for luck." I quickly type a reply to the email from the florist verifying the delivery date for the flowers. "I still need to find a plumber... and I guess a contractor to do the repairs. We still have nowhere to live until the water's back on."

"Ryan is fine with us—"

"What are you getting repaired?" Alex enters the kitchen, and we straighten.

Britt jumps off her stool, and my heart leaps to my throat when Adam appears behind his brother, looking like the sunrise over the ocean. *Gorgeous.*

"Adam! You're a week early!" Britt squeals, running to hug him. "Piper, did you know Adam was home?"

"Ahh, well… I'll be darned." My heart beats so fast, I'm having trouble breathing. "Hey, you!"

His blue eyes land on mine, and I blink away fast, subtly shaking my head in a *no—not yet* way. In the darkness of his bedroom with the pain of missing him overriding any fear, I could forget everything and hold him.

Here in broad daylight, all I feel is nerves.

"Look at you, Mamma." Adam's voice by contrast is relaxed and confident. "You're really showing."

"And not barfing… oh no, Piper!" Britt rushes to where I'm standing. "Your face is all red. That serum must be irritating your skin. Vitamin C can cause irritation, you know."

I put my hands on my cheeks, turning to the sink. "I'm sure you're right. I should've done a patch test."

"Here, get some cool water." She takes a towel from the counter and switches on the tap.

"What's this about?" Alex laughs, stepping up to where I'm pressing a damp cloth to my face and pretending to be allergic to a serum I don't even own.

Britt slides her hand into the crook of his arm. "We're working on your wedding plans, and you should see what Piper has done. It's going to be so beautiful."

"You know, I can afford a wedding planner to help with this." Alex leans in, giving me a little nudge with his elbow. "You're a busy lady."

"No!" Britt cries. "Nobody knows Cass as well as we do. We'll have all the things she loves. Just let us handle it."

Alex holds up both hands. "I'm just trying to make your life easier."

Adam hangs back watching me, knowing full well I'm not having an allergic reaction. I'm blushing because I'm remembering every way he touched me last night, and my whole body is on fire. I'm buzzing with satisfaction and magnetism and hunger.

He looks so good standing there in faded jeans and a long-sleeved henley. His dark hair brushes the top of his collar, and the dark fabric stretches over his broad shoulders. His blue eyes are full of promise, and I want *more*.

Everything that happened last night was so good. Even if I was guarded, not letting him see all of me, carefully taking the pleasure we both wanted while hiding my pain. We were like two puzzle pieces finally snapping together, and I don't regret a moment of it.

Only one thing remains, and standing here in the light of day looking at him, all the old questions echo in my mind. What will he say? What will I do if he doesn't say what I hope he'll say?

Drew says my past wasn't my fault, and nothing I could've done would've changed Rex's behavior. She says I'm not a failure because I couldn't fix him.

My fingers tighten around my phone, and I wish I could text her. But it's Saturday, and I don't have another meeting with her for a week.

What would she tell me? *I've never given them a chance to be my friends completely… I don't give them enough credit for wanting to be there for me…*

But this is too soon. I'm not prepared, and how would I even bring it up? Would I blurt it out on a Saturday morning at the distillery when Adam has just arrived back in town and we're supposed to be working on wedding plans?

Read the room, Piper.

"Speaking of life, where are we going to put you now?" Britt turns to me, then Adam. "Piper had a plumbing disaster, so we stowed her at your house last night. You two must've just missed each other this morning."

I feel like I'm going to be sick, but I smile through it. "I'm sure I can sleep at my place tonight."

"With no water?" Britt's eyes widen in horror.

"She can stay at my place. I don't mind." The smile in Adam's voice tickles my stomach.

"But you only have one bed." My friend's brow furrows. "I hate to say it, but Drake Redford has a point about accommodations in Eureka."

"Don't even go there." A growl is in Alex's tone. "He's running a dog against your grandmother for mayor."

"What the hell?" Adam laughs, and I bite my lip. "What did I miss?"

"A lot." Britt pulls out her phone. "You might be sorry you came back early."

"Not a chance." His eyes land on mine, and my stomach flips.

"We need to find out who that man is in my apartment." Britt is texting fast. "I can't believe Mom would rent out my place without asking me."

Both our phones buzz at the same time, and I pull mine out of my pocket to see a shouty-caps text from Cass.

Cass: WHERE ARE YOU?

"Oh, shit!" Britt jumps to her feet, grabbing my arm. "We're supposed to meet Cass at the bridal shop in Rockville at ten! We'll have to sort out your problems later."

She makes it sound so simple. "You drive, and I'll text her we're on the way."

I follow Britt out to her old orange truck, leaving Adam standing in the kitchen with his brother watching me go.

"Is it bad luck to buy a used wedding gown?" Cass turns side to side on a round platform in front of full-length, tri-fold mirrors. "Because I kind of love this one."

She's wearing a beautiful, floor-length lace dress with long, sheer sleeves that end in French cuffs with pearl buttons.

"I'd do it if I loved the dress, which surely means it's bad luck." I shrug, inspecting the price tag on a sleeveless, tulle-skirted number reminiscent of *Sex and the City*. "This is cute, and it's only eighty bucks."

"You're not buying a used wedding gown!" Britt yells from across the boutique. "I'm sure the clerk can find a similar gown brand-new."

"Absolutely!" The store clerk reaches behind the desk, pulling out an enormous binder. "I'm certain I saw one just like that by Oscar de la Renta…"

She has a pencil behind her ear, and her stick-straight, blonde hair is cinched tight in a French twist on the back of her head. I'm pretty sure everything she owns is designer.

Cass looks at me with huge eyes, mouthing, *Oscar de la Renta?*

"I can't afford that!" She calls to Britt. "I'm only a poor kindergarten teacher."

"You're not even that yet," I mutter, looking at the small selection of resale dresses. "If the dress was returned *before* the wedding, does that make it unlucky?"

"Yes, that's even worse." Britt marches over, carrying an armload of dresses. "I have several here with sleeves you might like. These are all in your price range, and they're brand-new. Come on."

We follow her into a dressing room the size of my bedroom, and my phone buzzes with a text. Glancing down, I see it's from Adam.

> **Adam:** Sorry if I irritated your skin. Was it my sunny personality?

He includes a winky emoji, and I bite my lip to keep from grinning like a freshly fucked goof.

Instead, I quickly type back,

> Not sure she'd have gone for Vitamin D skin care.

> **Adam:** The all-natural facial?

I almost snort, but I feel Britt's eyes on me as she unzips the gown Cass is wearing.

"I like this one because it reminds me of a leotard." Cass slides the sheer sleeves down her long arms, and I clear my throat, quickly re-engaging with the dress hunt before I'm busted.

"Oh! You want a dancer-inspired gown? I saw a used one with a tulle skirt—want me to grab it?"

"No!" Britt snaps, and I want to pat myself on the back for effectively distracting her.

Cass shakes her long, dark hair, rolling her blue eyes at our friend. She was a dancer for a while when we were in school, and she taught baby ballet lessons, which is where she first met Alex.

"I like this one." I hold up a strapless dress with a sheer overlay scattered with lily of the valley embroidery. "It'll show off your shoulders."

"Alex will pay for your dress." Britt takes the gown from me and hands it to our friend.

"I don't want him to pay for my dress. He's already got me living in his house rent-free."

"That's because you're still Pinky's nanny," I argue.

"I'm her future stepmom." Cass shakes her head. "And anyway, Patricia keeps her most of the time now because I'm taking classes at the college."

"Pinky's also in kindergarten now, so it's not really like she needs a nanny." Britt hands her a new dress to try.

Cass gestures to me. "Piper understands where I'm coming from."

"I don't know what your living situation has to do with anything," Britt fusses, taking out a dress with sleeves. "You can't move out because Piper has more urgent housing needs, and you'll be married in a week."

"I'm still not letting him buy my dress." Cass takes the new gown from Britt, frowning at me. "Why do you have urgent housing needs? What did I miss?"

I quickly fill her in on my plumbing disaster. "Now I'm basically homeless. Or should I say *un-housed*?"

"Adam said you can keep staying at his place." Britt arches an eyebrow in a way that tells me she wasn't completely oblivious to our vibes at the distillery. "You should take him up on it. It's a golden opportunity to test those waters, and he was looking mighty fine this morning. Don't tell me you didn't notice."

My throat tightens, and I'm all ready to deflect when Cass steps between us.

"Help me with this." Her back is to Britt, who finishes zipping her up, and when she turns to the mirrors, we all three gasp at the same time.

"It's the one!" Cass whispers.

My eyes heat, and when I look at Britt, we both start to laugh as tears drop onto our cheeks.

Cass turns slowly side to side, and her face flushes as well. "I don't believe it."

"It's like it was made for you!" Britt coos.

The bodice is smooth, white silk with long, matching sleeves ending in a row of ten tiny buttons on each arm. The skirt is a full flounce, and she's elegant and dancer-esque and perfect.

Britt grabs the price tag and winces. "Put it on your personal credit card, and in two weeks, it'll be community property."

Cass's expression is worried, but I hold up a hand. "Think of it as a wedding gift to Alex. You can't rob him of seeing you walking down the aisle in that dress. He's going to pop a boner in front of his entire family."

Cass covers her face with both hands and nods her head. "Okay, I can live with that."

"You are strong." We're standing on the sidewalk in front of the Star Parlor, and a new sign is nailed above the door.

"Adam's back, and the signs are back." Britt presses her lips together. "You can't tell me the two aren't connected. Plus they're all motivational, which is his whole vibe now."

Chewing my lip, I think back to the conversation he and I had about the sign outside El Rio after karaoke night. He didn't deny it.

"But what about the one on the ball field?" Cass argues. "He couldn't have done that one and taught Pinky to hit a homer at the same time."

"Which one was it?" I pull out my phone to where I've been keeping track of all the messages and the dates, searching for a pattern of some sort.

"It was the one from *Field of Dreams*."

"Right. Dreams do come true."

Britt holds up her arms. "It's like I said, we'll have to mark the date of when the last one appears then check the obituaries."

"Morbid!" Cass cries.

The glass door in front of us opens, and a disheveled little man in a tan trench coat stumbles out onto the sidewalk.

"Ladies, I apologize." He holds up both hands. "I do my best to be normal."

"Mr. Gregg." I step forward to extend a hand. "You might not remember me—"

"It was only last night. I'm not that old." He points a thick finger at me. "Piper Jackson, editor of the local paper. I never forget a face."

He looks like he never brushes his hair either. He's as bushy and messy as he was the last time I saw him—only now he's wearing clothes.

"I'm Britt Stone. My husband is Sheriff Aiden Stone."

"Oh, yeah." He cocks an eyebrow, inspecting my friend. "You're the forensic investigator."

"Photographer," Britt corrects him. "But I usually end up doing investigations. I heard you're an investigator as well."

He rocks back on his heels inspecting the three of us. "What are you, like Charlie's Angels or something?"

The three of us look at each other. "Only Britt is in law enforcement," Cass answers.

Britt isn't letting him off the hook. "What exactly are you looking for in our little town, Mr. Gregg?"

"Well, I'll tell you, Mrs. Stone. I'm looking for a missing person. My client believes she might be somewhere in this area."

My ears perk up, and Britt and I exchange a glance.

"Is it a kidnapping case?" I ask. "Or more like a runaway situation?"

"I'm not at liberty to say." He smiles, and his eyes become tiny slits. "I don't want to put anyone in danger."

"In danger!" Cass's eyes go wide, and I'm about to elbow her in the ribs to be cool when a voice yells from behind us.

"Cass?" It's a voice I haven't heard in years. "Is that you, Cassidy? I'll be damned. I didn't think it would be this easy to find you!"

"I should have her on my team," Marshall jokes.

Cass's face lights, and she spins around to where a girl about her height with long blonde hair, wavy bangs, and bold red lips is trotting towards us. Her eyes are thickly made up, and when she smiles, she looks just like…

"Taylor Swift?" Marshall's voice is loud, and I'm honestly surprised he even knows that name.

"Jemima!" Cass hands me the hanging bag holding her dress and runs to her little sister on the sidewalk with her arms spread wide.

Jemima flies straight into her arms and for a minute the two of them jump around, hugging and laughing.

"When did you get in town?" Cass cries.

"Just now!" her sister answers, a pronounced country twang accenting her words. "I thought I'd have to go to Aunt Carol's to find you. Thank God that didn't happen."

We're all walking slowly to where they're having their reunion when Jemima sees us. "Britt! Jinx! Oh my God! You haven't changed a bit!"

"They've changed a little." Cass leans her dark head closer

to her sister's blonde one. "Britt's got a baby bump, and Gwen won't let us call Piper Jinx anymore. She says it's bad luck."

"Like that ever changed anything." I give Cass's sister a hug. "Good to see you, twerp."

"Ha-ha, I'm taller than you are now." She puts her arm around my shoulder and gives me a squeeze. "I thought Jinx was a fun nickname."

"Apparently it perpetuates bad juju."

"How are the wedding plans going?" She looks around. "Where are all the boys? I'm ready to see some good-looking men."

"No offense taken!" Marshall volunteers in a loud bark.

"Oh!" Jemima yelps. "I'm sorry, I didn't see you there!"

"It's all right." He waves and nods. "I was just enjoying the show. I take it you're…"

"My little sister," Cass volunteers easily. "She's here for the wedding. Otherwise, she's in Branson working as a Taylor Swift impersonator."

"I didn't know that was a thing." He nods. "You make a lot of money doing that?"

"Not as much as you'd expect… and the Swifties are a nightmare. If I get one little thing wrong, holy toledo…" Jemima groans. "Which is why I'm here to stay. It's time I started doing something normal. Who's going to help me find a real job? Jinx, are you still running the paper?"

I blink up at her. "Yeah, but we don't get a lot of want ads these days, if that's what you're thinking."

"Maybe I should just marry one of the Stone brothers. There's one left, isn't there? That's what I'll do. I'll marry Adam Stone."

"Who am I marrying?" Adam walks up, studying me with naughty blue eyes, and heat rises around my collar.

Ryan is with him, holding Fudge over his shoulder.

"Me, you handsome devil. How have you been?" Jemima

gives Adam's arm a squeeze, and I'm shocked by a sudden blaze of anger in my chest.

A sudden, *Get your hands off my man* that almost flies from my lips.

Ryan's eyes are wide, and everything feels too close and too crowded at the same time.

"Are you Taylor Swift?" His little-boy voice is awed.

"I wish!" Jemima cries. "Then I'd do whatever the hell I wanted to do!"

Ryan's big eyes fly to mine, and I wrinkle my nose at him.

"Oh, sorry." Jemima covers her red-velvet mouth with her hand. "You're big enough to repeat stuff, aren't you?"

"He's actually big enough to know *not* to repeat stuff." I hug my son to my side, doing my best to tamp down the green-eyed monster in my chest. I remind myself that I like Cass's little sister, and she's a total tease anyway. "What have you guys been up to today?"

"Uncle Adam came home, and I showed him all the tricks Fudge can do—he did a double backflip trying to catch his feather, and he ate half a lizard on the patio. It was really gross… Then he chased a squirrel up a tree, and Owen's gran said he could stay at her house any time because the squirrels keep digging up her bulbs, and—"

"Whoa, take a breath, buddy!" I tweak his little nose. "It sounds like you've had a busy morning!"

"He's a good cat." Adam slides his hand down Fudge's shiny black coat, and the cat rewards him with a little nip. Adam laughs, and the two have a playful boxing match, which delights Ryan even more.

I smile watching Adam and my son together, so relaxed and comfortable. They're so close, and Ryan is always so content when Adam's around.

"Not much time for hanging signs," Cass mutters in my ear.

"Where's Owen?" Britt looks from Ryan to Adam.

A Little Luck

"He stayed with Aiden," Adam answers, and I wonder if his voice has always sounded so sexy.

"We're on our way to the Popcorn Palace to see if Harold knows any good vets for cats," my son announces. "Cats aren't as easy as dogs, you know."

"You'll do no such thing!" Britt steps forward, catching Ryan's shoulder. "Cass can help us with Fudge."

Cass's smile is more of a wince. "I only do flea dips, and I don't have any of my cat gear anymore. I donated it after the last bout of mites."

"Wait, I'm confused." Adam's brow furrows. "Why can't we take Fudge to the president of the kennel club, who knows all things pets in town?"

"It's Harold's dog running for mayor!" Britt's eyes are wide, and Marshall clears his throat.

It's when we all notice him standing on the periphery of our group listening intently.

"Hey, friend." Adam stands straighter, towering over the small detective. "We haven't met."

"Sorry, friend." Marshall's voice is surprisingly sarcastic, considering Adam is a head and shoulders taller than him with attractive muscles on full display. "I gather you're Adam Stone, the sheriff's brother?"

"That's right. And you are?"

"Marshall Gregg." He shakes Adam's hand. "Private investigator. I'm just in town, getting to know the place."

"You're getting to know Eureka?" Adam's eyes narrow. "Why?"

Britt steps up beside him. "He's working on a missing person's case—a female—but he won't tell us if it's a kidnapping victim or a runaway. It could be a murder for all we know."

"I don't think it's a murder." Marshall shakes his head. "At least I hope not."

"Do you have a photo?" Adam is all helpful now. "Eureka

is growing, but I can't think of any new, single women in town. At least not for years."

He glances at Cass and Jemima, and I don't like how it bugs me that he's keeping track of the new single women in town.

"It's more of a cold case file, but that's as much as I can say." Marshall holds up a hand. "If you'll just go about your business as usual, I'll do my best to stay out of the way."

We all hesitate, but Adam puts his hand on my son's shoulder. "We've got to take care of Fudge before the movie tonight."

"Oh, yeah! It's Headless Horseman night. My favorite!" Cass loops her arm through her sister's and takes the wedding dress from me. "Come on, Jemma. I'll get you settled in at Alex's place, and you have to meet Pinky. She's going to love having Taylor Swift staying at our house."

"I'm not Taylor Swift," Jemima protests. "Those days are over."

Adam's eyes linger on mine, and I hold his gaze a little too long. Luckily no one seems to notice, except maybe Marshall, who's watching everything with an eagle eye. Britt is on her phone, and I can't help wondering about this cold case.

A missing single mother from years ago? How has this never been in the paper? Marshall Gregg isn't getting off that easily, at least not where I'm concerned.

Chapter 10

Adam

ICHABOD CRANE'S GIANT NOSE DOMINATES THE CINEMA-SIZED SILVER screen erected in the courthouse square in front of the gazebo. Piper sits on a blanket in the front row beside Cass, who has Pinky on her lap singing every word to the classic Disney song.

The whole town is out for the monthly Movies in the Park, and of course, this night is Halloween themed. They're starting with *The Legend of Sleepy Hollow* to be followed by *Hocus Pocus*.

Off to the side, Ryan is with Owen and the other boys running from Edward and pretending to be the headless horseman.

I'm standing along the periphery with the other men, dads mostly. Their arms are crossed over their chests, and they form a kind of protective wall around their most valued possessions. I feel the emotion, even if I'm not technically a bio-dad.

Ryan and I spent the afternoon searching for a vet to give his new cat a physical and shots, then we headed over to Piper's little house to inspect the damage. The house is almost 100 years old, so a busted pipe is only the start of her worries.

Still, it can be replaced with PVC, and I have a contractor all set to give us an estimate on Monday.

It leaves two days of her without a place to live—at least a place with running water.

When I woke this morning fully satisfied but alone in my bed, the only thing on my mind was finding her. Our night was incredible, better than I'd dreamed. It pretty much sealed the deal on my feelings, but her "no words, no questions" policy means I still have a ways to go before she's convinced.

We're closer than we've ever been, and I'll abide by her ground rules to get us where I know we're supposed to be. She and Ryan are my family, and I'll fight to have them, even if it's a cold war against an unknown enemy.

A surge of kid-squealing and laughter erupts as the skinny cartoon character shoves his head under his horse's saddle. I can't help a grin. As a kid, I totally related to the terrified school teacher outrunning his horse on a dark night in the woods.

"It's what I like about small towns." A gravelly voice is at my side, and I glance over to see Marshall Gregg crossing his arms over his chest beside me. "Traditions like this bring everybody together and help people get to know one another."

His words are approving, but his eyes survey the seated crowd like he's looking for something.

"You know, I grew up in Eureka." I lower my arms, putting my hands in my back pockets, doing my best to appear approachable. "I run the outreach programs here and in Hilton Head and Kiawah. I might be able to help you with your case if you tell me more about it."

He shifts his position, narrowing his eyes at me and seeming to consider it. Finally, after a few moments, I apparently pass the test, and he lowers his arms as well.

"My missing person is an abuse survivor. A female with a kid."

Anger twists in my stomach, but I shake my head. "I don't know anyone who fits that description—at least not in Eureka."

"Well, you'd be surprised. From what I understand, she's pretty good at hiding. She's been doing it for a long time."

I don't like the sound of that. "You have no idea who it could be? Who hired you?"

"A family member." Marshall exhales, looking down at his tattered boots. "She wants to help her find justice, come out of hiding."

"I can understand that." I glance over to where Aiden has his eyes on Britt.

Right next to him is Alex, watching Cass and Pinky.

"You should talk to Aiden. He doesn't appear to be subtle, but you'd be surprised. He can keep a secret, and Britt can track down clues like you wouldn't believe."

"Nah," Marshall shakes his head. "I don't want to bring in law enforcement at this point. It could tip her off and make her run again."

"I understand." I nod, thinking. "I have an idea for where we could start asking questions. You're staying in the loft above the Star Parlor?"

"I am for now." He nods towards the front of the square. "Unless your girlfriend there has her friend kick me out."

"My girlfriend?" I frown, unsure what he means. "Piper's not my girlfriend."

"Oh, sure, you might have all these other folks fooled, but my job is watching people." Marshall winks, pointing his finger at me. "I see the way you look at her. You're standing here with all the other dads watching over her and her kid."

Exhaling a laugh, I run my hand over my mouth. "I confess, I wasn't convinced, but you might be a pretty good detective after all."

"Been at it forty years. Haven't lost a case yet."

"That's a pretty good track record."

Laughter and squealing break out from the audience, and we both look up to see Fudge on the partition in front of the movie screen. He's right in the middle, walking back and forth, and he looks like he's ready to jump.

"Oh, Fudge!" Ryan yells, running to get him, and I laugh, waving to Marshall.

"I'd better help out before they tear the screen down. I'll be in touch."

"Fudge is a movie star!" Ryan's voice is loud, and he has the black cat slung over his shoulder. "He saw Thackery, and he thought it was his brother."

"He almost brought down the house." Piper slides her hand down Fudge's shiny back. "I'm just glad Adam was there."

Warmth fills my chest, and I want to slide my hand over hers. I want to thread our fingers and tell her I'll always be there when she needs me.

"He wanted to get those Sanderson sisters." Ryan gives the cat a hug. "They're mean."

"They're witches!" Pinky dances around his shoulder, cautiously petting Fudge's head. "Black cats love witches."

"Not those witches," Ryan argues.

"That was a good save, bro." Aiden has his arms around Britt's shoulders, like I want to do with Piper.

We're all standing around, saying goodnight while the kids wind themselves down from a night of overstimulation, and I want to pull her into a hug, my mind drifting to what I hope is coming later at home, behind closed doors.

"Does Edward like cats?" Owen looks up at Britt, whose hand rests on her baby bump.

"I don't think Edward knows what to make of Fudge, but he doesn't seem to mind him."

"Edward knows a good cat when he sees one." Ryan turns so Fudge is facing Edward, and we all tense.

The bloodhound only turns his head towards the road leading to Aiden's house.

"Okay, that's enough excitement for one night." Piper steps cautiously between the dog and the cat. "I think it's time we turned in. The humans and the animals are tired."

I know I'm tired as hell between the jet lag and not sleeping last night, but I wouldn't change a thing.

"Cats are nocturnal!" Ryan's voice is still loud.

"I'm afraid my son is nocturnal." Piper's worried eyes meet Britt's. "Want me to take him off your hands?"

"Of course not, but wait... Where are you staying tonight?" Britt straightens, as if she just realized we never solved that problem.

My chest tightens. I've given her an open invitation to stay with me, which she hasn't taken.

I'm about to repeat it, when Piper replies, "Gwen said I could crash at the Star Parlor. She said there's a cot in the back room."

My lips part, but Britt is the first to speak. "That old cot she got from the surplus store? It's canvas stretched over a wooden frame! You can't sleep on that."

"You're welcome to my garage apartment." Alex is holding Cass's hand in both of his.

"I thought that was 'Cass's room.'" Piper does air quotes while tilting her head in Pinky's direction.

"Mama Cass sleeps in Daddy's bed now." Pinky pets Fudge with more confidence, and his eyes close with each stroke of her hand. "They're about to be married."

"We got busted," Cass explains.

"What about Jemima?" Piper looks around for Cass's sister.

I've never really thought about how big Alex's house is, but now I'm mentally cursing him for having so many spare bedrooms.

"She's staying in the guest room down the hall from Pinky."

"Taylor Swift is staying at my house." Pinky nods at the boys. "I don't need a cat."

We all glance at Alex and Cass, who crashes her head against her palm. "We're trying to have a baby, not a cat."

"I'll be fine." Piper jumps in to save them. "I don't really want to be that far from town anyway—in case a story breaks."

"Oh, sure," Britt complains. "Eureka's a hotbed of breaking news."

"A lot's been happening lately." Piper shrugs. "Now we have those wild pigs to worry about."

"Wild pigs?" Pinky's eyes widen. "Do they know karate?"

"You'll have to read your Sunday paper to find out." Piper tugs on one of Pinky's strawberry blonde pigtails. "Holly thinks Myrtle got knocked up by one."

"What's knocked up?" My niece's nose wrinkles.

"It's the opposite of being a virgin," Owen yells, like he just solved a riddle.

I stand by my position *Hocus Pocus* should be rated PG-13.

"Okay, that does it." Alex swoops his daughter onto his hip and steps forward to give Piper a hug. "Barbara Walters is fine staying at the Star Parlor."

"Who's Barbara Walters?" Pinky is still going.

"Night, babe." Cass gives her a hug as does Britt.

Ryan and Owen have already taken off on foot for Aiden's house with the pets in tow, and it doesn't take long before Piper and I are left facing each other on the sidewalk across from Gwen's tarot studio.

She's wearing a thick cream sweater in the cool night, and she crosses one arm over her waist, looking up at me with round, green-hazel eyes. Her red hair hangs in silky waves around her cheeks, and I'm drawn to her like the ocean to the moon.

The air is thick with electricity, and I step closer. "Sleep in my bed tonight."

Thickness is in my voice, and heat is in my groin. Her lip goes between her teeth as her chin lifts, and she looks up at me.

Reaching out, I place my thumb on that soft lip, pulling it out of her mouth and wanting to kiss her. The undeniable attraction draws us closer, my lips grow heavier...

Say yes.

"Lovely night for a movie." The scratchy, masculine voice breaks the spell, causing Piper to jump away from me.

"Marshall, holy shit!" She exhales a little laugh. "You scared me."

"I'm sorry." He holds up his hands before slapping them down at his sides. "I was headed to my door, and I didn't want to intrude."

I give him an *F* for that assignment. But when I look around, he does basically have to walk through us to get inside. My stomach is tight when she steps back, putting her hand on her chest and shaking her head.

"I'm your downstairs neighbor this evening." Her hand goes into the crook of his arm, and she starts for the door with him. "'Night, Adam."

Marshall looks back at me with a grimace, and I push him away with a wave, shaking my head as I turn to walk the short distance to my own place.

"Goodnight." The word is lost in the cool breeze carrying her away from me.

As tired as I am, I'm lying on my back in the middle of my bed unable to sleep. All around me is her honeysuckle scent and the memories of her body. I viscerally remember her over me, under me, her hands on my cock... and I groan, lifting my phone from the nightstand again.

It's after midnight. I've been lying awake for more than an hour. I wish I hadn't showered this morning, because I crave the scent of her on my skin.

I'm about to roll over when a loud noise from the back

patio causes me to sit straight up in bed. It sounds like someone knocked over a shovel or banged into the side of my house. I imagine it could be an animal, since apparently Eureka has wild pigs now.

Throwing aside the blanket, I swing my legs out of the bed when I hear the back door latch open. I'm on my feet as it closes solidly, and my mind races through my options. I have a baseball bat in the closet. My gun safe is in the kitchen…

The bedroom door opens slowly, and I step back, lifting my fists in case I have to fight. Adrenaline surges in my veins, although I'm actually more curious than scared. Despite what Piper said on the square, nothing ever happens in Eureka.

As soon as I see her, I straighten, dropping my hands and catching my breath. "What are you doing here?"

"I couldn't sleep." Piper stands in my doorway in front of me, still in that cream sweater, but her jeans have been replaced with fuzzy beige pajama pants. "I'm sorry—did I wake you?"

Her eyes are so big in the yellow lights from the hall, and I don't waste a moment going to her and pulling her to my chest.

"No." It's all I get out before leaning down to cover her mouth with mine.

Her lips part, and our tongues collide. She tastes like mint and fresh water, and I lift her off her feet in one fluid motion. Her legs are around my waist, and I carry her to the bed. She sits on the edge as I reach down to lift the sweater over her head, leaving her in a delicate white lace bra that only covers the bottom half of her small breasts.

It provides a teasing glimpse of her nipples and her dark pink areolas, and my dick is instantly hard. "We're leaving this on for now."

I lie her back on the soft sheets and reach behind my neck to pull my shirt over my head. Her eyes race down my bare torso, and her tongue slips out to draw her bottom lip into her mouth as she watches me.

"Keep looking at me like that, and I'm going to have to fuck you hard." I can't keep the hunger out of my tone.

I'm gratified that her pretty eyes shine, and a grin curls her lips. "Promise?"

Yes. Reaching down, I catch the sides of her pants, yanking them off her body along with her underwear. Her legs cross fast, and she turns to the side, away from the light.

"Where do you think you're going?" I reach for her hips to turn her so I can see her body, but she slides off the bed to her knees in front of me.

Her head is at my waist, and her pretty breasts rise in succulent rounds with every inhale. She clutches the front of my boxer briefs, tugging the waistband down and looking up at me with wide eyes.

"It's your turn." Her voice is soft, and I help her stretch my underwear over my erection.

It pops out, nearly bouncing off her lips, and I lean down, cupping her face in my hands. "I'm not keeping score. I want you to have everything you want. I want you to be so happy you never want to leave."

"I want this." She leans forward, sliding out her tongue and softly licking the base of my shaft.

My stomach jumps, and I groan, catching the bedpost so I don't collapse. "Piper..."

Her eyes hold mine as she moves higher, licking her tongue up and down the sides of my hard dick before reaching the tip.

Her warm tongue flickers all around the edges, and my knees weaken.

"Fuck, that's good," I hiss, hypnotized by the sight of her.

Catching my hips, she turns me, pushing me back onto the bed before rising between my thighs. I prop up on my elbows, straining for what she might do next.

My shaft is wet from her mouth, and she puts her hand around it, fingers almost touching as she pumps it quickly up and down. It thickens, getting straighter until it's pointing directly at her mouth, and I exhale a deep groan.

With her eyes fixed on mine, she slips her tongue out again carefully, barely touching my tip. Then she curls it teasingly, flattening her tongue and sliding it back and forth under the base like a lollipop.

"Fuck, Piper…" My ass tightens with each stroke, and precum leaks onto her lips. "You're fucking killing me."

She only smiles, licking my tip once more before pulling it fully into her mouth and sucking hungrily. Pleasure floods my pelvis, and my head drops back with a deep moan. She's moving faster, sliding her hand up and down my shaft to meet her bobbing head, and high-pitched grunts come from her throat.

My hand involuntarily rises, clutching the side of her head, and my fingers curl in her soft hair. It's too much, and I fight my instinct to grip harder and thrust my hips faster.

Her hand circles my base as she continues sucking deeper, deeper. Her head lowers, and her lips get closer to my stomach. I'm exhaling heavily, words slipping from my lips on hot breaths as the top of my dick draws ever closer to the back of her throat.

When I feel her lips touching my stomach, my hips rise off the mattress with a guttural groan. She's swallowing my cock, and I'm seeing stars.

My eyes squeeze tighter, and I'm completely at her mercy. I can't move as she feasts, little noises, soft gags and coughing as she pulls me again and again into the back of her throat.

"Piper, fuck…" My voice breaks, and my thighs tremble as I try to hold back. "I'm coming."

Her head tilts to the side, and she holds my hips. Her face lowers all the way to my stomach and stops. She lightly tickles my balls, and I explode, pulsing and jerking as come shoots down her throat.

"Fuuuck…" Every swallow is another stroke, and I swear, I levitate.

My orgasm rips through the soles of my feet, lifting my knees and rocking my hips. It resets my brain.

I groan low and long, paralyzed until her mouth pops off my cock with a soft gasp. I can barely focus as she slides off me, leaning back on her heels and smiling with a satisfied look on her face.

Her lips are swollen, and her eyes are watery. Her breasts rise and fall in that sexy lace bra, and her chin shines with moisture. She's a fucking goddess.

"You're going to have to give me a minute." My voice is a hoarse chuckle. "I might've died."

Her nose wrinkles, and she exhales a laugh, sliding forward onto my chest. Her hands are on my pecs, and the feel of her bare stomach warm against mine has my body coming to life again.

She leans forward, kissing my lips, and I slide my tongue out to meet hers. Our lips pull each other's, and our tongues curl together. We're both breathing hard. Her legs straddle my waist, and with every movement, I'm very aware of her warm, bare pussy sliding up and down my dick.

"Thank you for being so good to my son…" Her voice is a tad deeper, slightly husky, like swallowing my cock made her wet, and I'm definitely awake now. "And to me."

I slide my hands up her back, rolling us so I'm above her, braced on my elbows. "You never have to thank me for taking care of you and Ryan. Not ever."

She blinks away from my gaze, and her cheeks flush. "You say it like…"

"Like you belong to me." It's not a question. It's a statement of fact, and her body tenses.

Her immediate reaction almost breaks me, but I lower my forehead to her chest and summon all my strength to lighten my confession. "After that blowjob, I'm your fucking slave."

"Oh my god," she laughs, but her body relaxes, which helps me relax. She's not going to run. "You've had blowjobs before."

Never from her, and not since Rex was killed and Ryan was born. I haven't wanted another woman near me since I became her self-appointed protector.

"I've never felt like this before." It's the God's honest truth.

Sleeping with her, coming with her—all of it is completion.

"Well..." She looks around like she's trying to find a response. "You're welcome, then."

I huff a laugh that makes her laugh, and I stretch higher, covering her mouth with mine. My hands are on her cheeks, and I'm ready for her now. I'm ready to fuck her senseless, over and over again like we did last night.

Dragging my lips to her cheek, I nibble the side of her jaw. "You'd better get ready, because I'm about to return the favor... many times."

Her back arches as I move lower, down her chest to her round breasts in that sexy bra.

"You made me come so much last night." Her voice is breathless.

With my nose, I shove down the lace on one side and circle my tongue over a hardening nipple. "I'm about to do it again." Kissing across her chest, I do the same on the other side. "I really like this bra. You have to wear it all night."

"It's not really comfortable to sleep in."

"Okay then, just til I've finished fucking you."

Her eyes close, and she shakes her head. But she's smiling.

Her expression is light, and it's the first time I've seen her look so free, not like there's something holding her back. I don't know why this secret place—us together, here in my bed where no one knows—makes a difference, but I plan to take full advantage.

She switches off the lamp, plunging us into pitch blackness, but I grab my phone, turning on the patio light, which casts soft beams through the blinds.

"I want to see your face." Leaning down again, I kiss her

lips, sliding my tongue against hers before moving my kisses to her cheek then to hear ear. "I want to see you come for me."

Holding my cheeks, she sits up in the bed, moving her body closer to mine. "I like to feel your skin against mine."

Looping my hand around her back, I hold her so our stomachs are touching. Her arms wrap around my neck, and our mouths slide together again. Her lips part, and our tongues curl as a soft moan slips from her throat.

I'm so fucking hard, and I reach into the nightstand to get a condom from the drawer. I had a hard time with Ryan at my side nonstop today, but I managed to grab a sleeve at the grocery store when he was looking for cat food.

Tearing one off, I quickly remove it from the foil, and while I do, she turns, getting on all fours and wagging her ass up at me. My cock jumps in my hand.

"Fuck, Piper, what are you doing to me?"

"Making you hard, I hope."

Catching her hips, I line up my cock and drive balls deep into her before leaning over her back so my lips are at her ear. "You make me fucking titanium."

"Rub my clit." Her voice is a throaty whisper, and my hand slides between her thighs.

I massage my fingers through her wetness, sliding them up and down as I thrust hard and fast into her pussy.

Closing my eyes, I'm lost in the sensation of her body all around me. My chest is against her back. My arm is beside hers as I brace myself on the mattress. We rock together, panting and sweating. My fingers circle fast over her clit, and she turns her face to meet my mouth.

Our tongues collide, and her soft gasps turn to deep *Oh*s. Her ass bucks against my pelvis, meeting my thrusts, and I'm able to hold on a little longer, thanks to that mind-altering blow job. Still, I'm too close, too fast.

I fucking love this woman. Being with her, holding her, joining my body with hers is all I've wanted for so long. I'm hanging by a thread when I feel her pussy start to squeeze and spasm around my cock.

"Adam," she gasps. "I'm coming."

I strain to find her mouth, and we hold the kiss as little noises ripple from her throat. Her back shudders against my chest, and I groan as I hold, as my orgasm pulses through me.

Collapsing forward onto the bed, I roll us to the side, wrapping my arms around her waist and holding her securely. I never want to let her go.

I release her only to dispose of the condom, then she's in my arms again, tight against my chest. Her fingers trace over my arms, and sleep presses against my eyes. I don't want to miss a moment of her with me, but I'm going on two nights of no sleep.

The calm that comes with having her here with me is impossible to fight. I'm losing the battle when I hear a soft little snore come from her, and it makes me smile.

I want to be the one to wake first in the morning. There's something I have to do before she opens her eyes.

Chapter 11

Piper

THE SUN STREAMS THROUGH THE BLINDS WHEN I OPEN MY EYES, AND for a moment, I'm confused. I'm snug and warm in Adam's giant bed, but I'm alone.

Holding the blanket to my chest, I sit up in only my lace bra, which I didn't end up removing after all. I was wiped after another round of mind-blowing orgasms, and my hymen is good and gone.

My nose wrinkles with a grin, and I lean back against the pillow trying to think what happens now. God, I need to talk to Drew.

The sound of the front door opening and closing has me in a panic. Who could that be? Aiden? Alex? I can't be caught here. My eyes fly around the room. Where the hell are my pants and my underwear? Last I remember, Adam yanked them off me when he dropped me onto the bed.

I'm about to dive under the covers when he walks into the

room carrying a breakfast tray with a folded newspaper, a pot of coffee, two cups, and a small white paper bag.

"You okay?" He gives me a playful frown as he puts the tray on the bed.

"Of course." I straighten, wishing I had a mirror to check my hair, my eyes, or at least something to drink to wash away the morning breath. "Do I look okay?"

"You look like you're having a panic attack." He lifts the pot of coffee and pours me a cup.

"I thought somebody was here, and I'm not really dressed…" The blanket is under my arms as I look around. "Where are all my clothes?"

He leans closer, kissing my bare shoulder in a way that sends warmth racing to my belly before sitting beside me on the bed. "I would never leave you unprotected."

A cup of coffee is in my hand, and I take a careful sip, studying the gorgeous man watching me. We got so close last night. I've never felt so safe and so free, and now he's saying he'll protect me?

My voice is quiet. "Can I get a shirt or something to put on?"

"I don't know." His voice is naughty. "You know I love that bra."

Heat rises in my cheeks, and I don't even know myself right now. I'm always the one with the snappy comeback. I'm the smart one. Men don't throw me off balance—except for him.

I'm about to say please when he jumps off the bed and walks to his dresser. It's the same one I rifled through on my first night here, alone in his bedroom, searching for anything that would smell like him. I missed him so much that night, and we've been together every night since.

"Is this okay?" He pulls out a dark green, long-sleeved Henley.

"It's perfect." I sit higher in the bed, but when the blanket drops, my insides freeze.

I look down to see my upper rib cage is exposed. He's at my

side, and I snatch the garment, turning quickly away as I pull it over my head as fast as I can.

"Don't spill the tray." He chuckles, leaning forward to catch our breakfast. "You know we had sex last night, right?"

"I know." A nervous laugh rattles my chest.

He's studying me curiously, and I hold up my arms. "It's so big."

"That's what she said," he teases, straightening everything while I roll up the sleeves.

I dip my nose into the collar inhaling deeply his warm sandalwood and citrus scent. That was a close call, but he didn't see anything. I'm still safe.

Climbing onto the bed beside me, he lifts the small paper bag. "Special delivery."

I squint-smile up at him before unrolling the top. "What is this?" When I look inside, my heart melts, and a real smile splits my cheeks. "You did not…"

I take out the peanut butter-Oreo cupcake with chocolate frosting on top. We discovered them a long time ago at a small, local grocery between Eureka and Kiawah—back when we were in high school, when we lived at the beach all summer long watching the guys surf. The store owner's wife makes them, and I could never get enough.

"Not too much peanut butter to overwhelm the chocolate." He smiles. "It's your favorite."

You're my favorite.

I take a bite of the delicious pastry, closing my eyes as deliciousness fills my mouth. "Mmph… so good."

Our eyes meet, and I want to tell him so much. Instead, I take the mini Oreo off the top and bite half of it, holding out the other half to him.

"You sure?" he teases, opening his mouth as I slip it past straight white teeth onto his tongue.

"How were you able to get over there and back before I woke up?"

"I was very focused." He lifts the paper off the tray. "Now, what the hell is in this paper? You really sold it last night, I gotta say."

"That's my job." I can't help a laugh. Between the cupcake and him my stomach is a fizzy bubble of happiness. "Everybody thinks Eureka is this sleepy, quiet town where nothing ever happens, and they're wrong."

"That's what my mom always says." He holds the paper folded in half and reads aloud from above the fold. "'Bo the Dog Makes a Nutritious Snack'" His curious blue eyes meet mine, and a brow arches. "Interesting take on the mayor's race. What's this? 'Red Tape Holds Up Church Bell'?"

The smile melts right off my face, and my fizzy bubble of happiness explodes. "What the hell?"

His eyes brim with laughter as he returns to the stories below the fold. "'Enraged Pig Injures Pickler with Hoe'… 'Sheriff to Run Down Jaywalkers'… Aiden's going to love that."

"Give it to me!" I snatch the paper from him, scanning the front page as cold realization creeps up my neck. "Mom!" I shriek.

Adam leans on the pillow beside me. "You've gotten very creative with your headlines while I was gone."

"Oh, no." I bury my face in newsprint wanting to die.

He rubs my shoulder. "What happened? Did you try AI or something?"

Slamming the publication down, I fall back against the headboard. "Mom said she'd help me. I was drowning in work and Ryan and wedding planning, and this dog-mayor thing happened late on Friday and I wanted to get it in today's edition, because it's our highest circulation…" I drop my face with a wail. "It never occurred to me to check after her."

"I didn't realize your mom had such a great sense of humor." He continues reading. "'Tornado hits cemetery; No survivors.'"

"Oh my Goooood!" I jerk the blanket over my head and

curl into the fetal position. "I've worked so hard for the *Gazette* to be taken seriously, and now this!"

The sound of the tray being moved off the bed precedes Adam sliding under the covers behind me. His large body curls around mine, and he wraps a muscled arm over my waist, resting his chin on my shoulder.

"I bet nobody notices." His voice is warm, but it has the opposite effect.

"Are you saying nobody reads the paper?"

"Not at all!" He gives me a little squeeze. "I mean I don't think they'll read it *that* closely."

"You don't think Harold is going to notice a headline calling his dog a nutritious snack?"

I can hear him swallowing his laughter before answering. "Maybe he'll think you're saying Bo is hot… in a health-conscious way."

"I've got to get to the office." I push out of his arms, all the way out of the bed, pacing his room trying to find my pants as my phone starts buzzing. "All the subscription issues have been delivered. Maybe it's not too late to get the rest off the newsstand. Where did you get this?"

He's sitting up in the bed watching me with that panty-melting grin on his face. "I picked it up at the Pack-n-Save when I got the coffee."

"I'll never be able to get them all down, but I can try." I stop pacing to face him. "Where are my pants?"

He steps out of the bed and grabs my fuzzy, beige PJ pants off the chair behind the door. "These right here on the chair?"

Shaking my head, I take them from him, quickly pulling them over my hips. "Would you check on Ryan for me? Bring him to the office if Britt and Aiden need a break."

"I don't think they ever need a break. Two little boys are better than one, don't you know?"

"Still…" I'm on my way out the door, striding down the hall when he catches my hand.

"Hey." His blue eyes turn serious. "I want this—what's happening here. Okay?"

Nodding, I look down, swallowing my fears. "We need to talk."

The tip line phone is ringing when I walk into the empty newspaper office, and my phone is still buzzing. What I wouldn't give for a staff right now, and I think about Jemima's question. Maybe she could be my office assistant.

Britt's text is my first order of business.

> **Britt**: Aiden would like you to reassure the public he won't be running down jaywalkers with his truck.

She includes a laugh-crying emoji, but shame burns my cheeks.

> Mom helped me with the headlines.

I include a sobbing emoji and hit send as I snatch up the phone.

"*Eureka Gazette*, Piper speaking." I use my best, upbeat tone despite the cringe in my chest.

"I didn't expect you to answer." A huffy male voice is on the line, and I'm pretty sure I know who it is.

"Who were you expecting to answer?"

"I expected to leave a voicemail. It's Harold Waters. I don't like my dog being referred to as food. It's cruel and disgusting and weird."

"It's none of that, actually." My voice cracks, and I feel like I might throw up. "It's simply a misplaced modifier… Bad grammar!"

"Either way, it definitely crossed a line, and I wonder if it's because you're in the pocket of the mayor. Everyone knows you and Britt Stone are best friends. Are you attempting to slur Bo's reputation?"

"How dare you!" I go from nauseated to pissed at him for attacking my ethics. "I've always provided fair and balanced coverage of every issue in this town, as you well know. Why, I can't even count the number of times I've given your business free coverage in my paper. To think you'd accuse me of being biased."

My throat tightens, and I worry I'm not being entirely professional. Swallowing the rest of my tirade, I simply state the truth. "I had outside help with the headlines for this issue. I won't make that mistake again."

"Were you using artificial intelligence?"

Why does everyone keep asking me that? "No, but maybe I should have."

The office desktop lights up, and I see a string of emails filling the general inbox. Some are outraged, some are laugh-crying emojis, one is from my old high school English teacher. I can only imagine she's all prepared to give me a refresher course.

A shuffling noise behind me causes me to look up, and I see the culprit herself entering the room, waving a paper over her head with a huge smile on her face.

"Thanks for calling, Harold." I put down the phone, and my mother races up to give me a hug.

"Isn't it thrilling?" Her eyes are so bright. "I just read the front page, and the headlines are so exciting! They made me want to subscribe."

I let it pass that my own mother is not even a subscriber. "Are you serious right now? I'm putting out fires left and right because of those headlines."

I don't say *because of you*, since clearly she was trying to help me.

Lesson learned.

"What do you mean? They make the town sound exciting

and fun. Big things are happening in Eureka, and you're covering them with style."

"Harold Waters doesn't think it's stylish for his dog to be called food, and Aiden doesn't think it's exciting to run down jaywalkers in his truck." Dropping into my chair, I rest my face on my hand. "I haven't even heard from the new pastor yet. Probably because he's in church."

"I bet he'll appreciate it. Did you see the church sign today?" My brow furrows, and I glance up at her. "'Forbidden fruit leads to many jams.' That's pretty good, yes?"

"You should ask him for a job." I push out of my chair. "I'm switching the phone to voicemail. We'll just have to ride it out."

Mom claps her hands. "You'll ride it all the way to the bank. I bet you get a ton of new business after this issue."

Exhaling deeply, I shake my head. "I'll get a ton of something, I'm sure. Letters to the editor, most likely."

"That's a good thing! It shows you the readers are engaged."

Thumbing through my story ideas, I think about what needs to be done for Wednesday's edition. A profile of the new pastor would be nice—if he'll speak to me—along with an interview with the outgoing pastor, Dr. Shepherd, whose last act before retiring will be officiating Alex and Cass's wedding.

Two new businesses opened in the strip mall by the Popcorn Palace, and a new veterinarian has moved to the county. I wonder if he's the one who helped Adam and Ryan with Fudge. I feel so disconnected from my son since our plumbing disaster.

"What are you doing today?" My phone buzzes, and I look down to see a text from Britt.

Britt: Aiden says to come for dinner.
Don't worry about the headlines.

I start my reply when Mom answers, "I figured I'd work on my canning for the winter. You can never have too many vegetables."

A forlorn tone is in her voice, and even though I'm still

annoyed with her, the thought of her spending all Sunday in her apocalypse cellar is just sad.

Amending my reply to Britt, I quickly ask,

> Is there room for Mom to join?

Britt's answer is equally quick.

Britt: Of course! Come when you're ready.

"Your vegetables can wait. Britt just invited us to have dinner with her and Aiden. I'm sure Gwen will be there." I give Mom's arm a brief tug. "Come on, Geraldo, let's go hang out with my son."

Frowning, she shakes her dark-brown head. "You don't even know who Geraldo Rivera is."

"I was a journalism major in college, Mom. I know who Geraldo is."

"He was exciting, too." Her lips twist. "Or maybe his mustache was exciting."

Taking out my key, I lock up the office. "He was a kook, and you're never writing headlines for me again."

She only holds up a dismissive hand, walking ahead of me. "Suit yourself."

With the setting sun, Britt and Aiden's back patio glows with twinkle lights, white-sheet ghosts, and oversized skeletons. Fudge walks along the railing between them all like he's the star of Halloween.

"We can make a salt circle to keep away evil spirits!" Pinky grabs the white plastic bottle off the picnic table and runs to where the boys are throwing a frisbee with Edward.

"Pinky, come back with the salt!" Cass calls after her, placing a basket of French fries on the table beside the ketchup.

"You've definitely got your hands full with that one."

Jemima sits with her velvet-red lips curled, holding a bottle of Abita Amber.

"Don't disparage my baby!" Cass argues.

"I never knew a kid so obsessed with Miss Piggy," Jemima groans. "She was in my bed this morning making me watch *The Muppets Haunted Mansion*. I didn't even know that was a thing!"

"At least she's not karate chopping anymore," Britt laughs from where she's standing with Aiden at the grill, and Cass makes a face at her. "What's the word on those wild hogs? I saw your story about the one in Terra's pickle patch. Glad she only suffered a sprain."

"Terra was pretty pissed. It ate half her pickle crop." I grab a beer from the cooler. "Luckily, it was a young pig, or she might've been hurt worse. Holly thinks one of the big ones impregnated Myrtle."

"I thought they were cucumbers when they were still on the vine." Jemima frowns at me.

"It's what Terra calls her farm." I take a seat across from her. "By the way, I have a job for you if you're looking. I wasn't sure what you meant when you asked me the other day—"

"I am!" Jemima sits straighter. "I'm not sure I can top those headlines, but I can write a decent story, and I'm great at getting the scoop from people."

Twisting my lips, I hadn't considered hiring her as a reporter. "I was mostly looking for someone to help me answer phones, open the mail, and keep things organized."

"I worked at a hair salon in Branson answering phones. It was crazy-busy with all the old ladies trying to coax Dolly Parton styles out of their Tweety Bird hair. I told them it's all wigs."

"Our very own Katharine Graham." The warm male voice heats my insides, and Adam takes a seat beside me at the table. "All the fires put out at the office?"

They might be put out at the office, but fire is rising inside my thighs. I do my best not to blush with everyone looking at me.

Adopting a professional tone, I give the low-down. "Harold said he was 'offended and disgusted,' and apparently, I'm in the mayor's pocket because Britt and I are friends."

"What!" Britt yells from Aiden's side. "He's got a lot of nerve. He's in Drake Redford's pocket if you ask me. We should picket the Popcorn Palace."

"Don't start all that," Aiden grumbles. "Nobody's voting for a dog."

"Gram wouldn't even come to lunch today, she's so upset." Britt walks over to where we're sitting. "She really liked that headline, though."

"I knew she would," Mom calls from where she's sitting beside Gwen near the chiminea.

"Of course, you did," I mutter, taking another sip of my beer.

"So Adam, interesting that you're back in town the same night the signs mysteriously reappear." Britt arches an eyebrow at him. "Care to comment on your whereabouts two nights ago?"

His eyes flicker briefly to mine, and my breath catches. I stand, going to the porch railing so my back is to everyone while I pretend to watch the boys playing with the dog. I know exactly where Adam was two nights ago, and thankfully, the twilight obscures my blush.

"There was a new sign?" His tone is all innocence. "What did it say?"

I notice Mom watching us curiously, and I look away quickly. Last thing I need is her seeing me all flustered.

"Mom! Mom!" Ryan runs to where I'm standing, wrapping his arm around my waist. "Did you see Edward catch the frisbee? He jumped almost as high as Fudge does when he's chasing his feather! Where is Fudge?"

The older my little boy gets, the less he likes public displays of affection, so I take advantage of them any time he wants to hug me.

I put my hand on his back, giving him a firm squeeze. "Fudge is a pretty cool cat."

"He's sticking around. I guess that means he wants to live with us, don't you think?"

Sliding my hand in the side of his dark hair, my chest pinches with love. "Maybe, but it's pretty early."

"You'll see—he wants to be with us. There he is!" He jumps away, running to where Fudge is lying on the railing now and scooping him up and over his shoulder. "Did you hear that, boy? You can stay with us as long as you want!"

Ryan runs out to where Owen is playing tug-of-war with Britt's dog for the frisbee. I hold my breath, amazed Fudge is so relaxed. He doesn't seem to mind my son dragging him all over the place.

"He's a good cat." Adam walks up beside me. "I kept waiting for him to scratch or bite us at the vet's office, but he never did."

"Yeah, he's pretty great." I blink up, swallowing my heart back down. "I never thanked you for helping out with that."

"I told you, you don't have to thank me." His voice is low, and the twinkle lights cast an orange glow over his scruffy, square jaw.

It reminds me how incredible our secret trysts have been, our stolen nights in his bed with his cheeks teasing my inner thighs.

"I was thinking I should do a story on the new vet… so people know he's there." It's a lame attempt to cool the rising tension between us. "What's his name? Henry something?"

"Anderson. I'll introduce you to him if you want. He's organizing a feline rescue program, so he'd probably like the publicity."

"Sounds like your kind of guy."

"Not yours?" A smile curls his lips, and I blink a few times to restart my brain.

Since we've had sex, I seem to have lost all my sassy, cool collectedness. "There's only one guy in my life."

"Right." He lifts his chin towards the yard where Ryan is playing then straightens, putting his hands in his pockets. "The contractor will be at your house tomorrow morning. Want me to meet him with you? I know you can handle it, but—"

"That would be great." I want to reach out and touch his arm, tell him I meant to say *two*. There are two guys in my life now, but the moment has passed and it would be awkward.

"I need to get in there and see the damage. I cleaned up as much as I could that night."

"From what I could tell, it's not too bad. You caught it pretty quick."

The air is thick with words needing to be spoken. I know he wants to know what I'm thinking. I know he's wondering if I'll be in his bed tonight and what these last few nights mean.

With the contractor coming to fix my little house, we don't have much time left. I need to tell him everything, but my stomach twists at the thought of damaging what we have with my ugly truth.

"Who's ready to eat?" Britt calls out, and I give him a tentative smile.

"Thank—" I start, but he puts his finger lightly to my lips before moving it away quickly.

"Me! Me! Me!" Ryan runs past us, this time without Fudge on his shoulder.

Owen and Pinky are right behind him. Adam turns to follow them, and I look out at the red, orange, and yellow leaves.

I see the cat sitting in the middle of the fall colors, watching me with his curious, yellow eyes, and I think about what my mom said. I wonder if he's trying to give me good luck.

I wonder if it's possible to change what I am.

Adam is sitting up in bed, shirtless and with a Kindle in his hand when I enter his bedroom. The lamplight deepens the shadows in the lines of muscles on his arms, the lines across his stomach. He's absolutely mouth-watering.

When he hears me, he glances up, and the hunger in his eyes matches how I'm feeling, and a deep ache is in my core. I'm already wet and ready for him. It's almost enough to cancel out the tendrils of fear that are never far behind me.

Last night, I almost didn't turn away in time. My stomach drops at the thought of him seeing my ugly scars, at the thought of him recoiling and then finding out how they got there, but my soul is so tired of hiding. I'm ready to tell him everything.

"You okay?" His voice is soft, and I realize my troubled thoughts are all on my face.

Quickly relaxing my expression, I smile and close the space between us, climbing into the bed in my soft gray pants and long-sleeved tee.

"I'm much better now that I'm with you." Putting my hand on his bare chest, I kiss his full lips.

He's so gorgeous and so wonderful with my son and so good to me. I never want to lose this. I want to stay here forever, safe with my gorgeous protector.

Large hands span my waist pulling me to sit on his lap in a straddle. "Let's see what's under here today." He lifts my shirt, and my stomach tenses.

In this position, facing the lamp, if I lift my arms, he'll see my scars. Exhaling a shaky laugh, I dive off him, onto my back in the bed and shimmy out of my shirt in a way that covers my damaged sides.

His brow quirks, and he rolls over on top of me in that way that I love, resting on his elbows and holding me down with his delicious weight.

Lowering his face, he kisses the side of my neck, sending electricity skittering through my stomach. I laugh and wrap my arms around his neck.

Deep blue eyes hold mine for a moment, and I know he has questions. He doesn't ask them. He only lowers his mouth to mine, pushing my lips apart and sweeping his tongue inside to curl with mine.

My breath rises in my chest, and my arms tighten as our lips part. His kisses are demanding, devouring, and delicious. With my eyes closed, I'm guided by the pressure of his mouth on mine, the teasing sweep of his tongue igniting a fire in my core.

A soft sigh escapes on a breath when he lifts his face to smile down at me again.

"I think you're the most beautiful woman I've ever seen." His voice is low, and my eyebrows lift.

Blinking fast, I hold back the tears his unexpected compliment provokes. "I feel the same way about you."

Closing my eyes again, I lift from the bed to press my mouth to his, kissing him with all the love beating in my veins. He has no idea, but even saying what he did only makes me want to trust him even more. He's become everything to me, and I want to give him everything.

Spreading my legs, I do just that.

Chapter 12

Adam

PIPER IS WRAPPED IN MY ARMS, AND I WATCH THE SUNRISE GROW through my open blinds. I usually keep my bedroom in pitch darkness at night with blackout shades drawn and all the doors closed.

Since that first night with Piper, I've been leaving them open. It's the only way she'll let me see her, and I don't want to miss a thing.

I also don't really understand why, and it bothers me. I want to reassure her.

A few times last night, it felt like she was about to tell me something, but ultimately she didn't. Our time alone is limited. These stolen moments won't be an option when she's back in her house with Ryan. I feel like the clock is ticking faster every day.

Sliding my fingers along the line of her red hair, my chest squeezes as I watch her sleep. I want her to be my wife. I want Ryan to be my son. What would she say if I put it all out there and simply proposed? I think she'd say yes.

"Mm…" She inhales, lifting her cheek off my chest and leaving a cool place behind. "Sorry, I slept late. Don't we need to get up and meet the contractor?"

She blinks pretty green-hazel eyes at me, and the ache in my chest melts to warmth. "You didn't sleep late. We've got a half hour."

"That's all?" She's off me in a blink, hustling to the bathroom and switching on the shower. "I can't meet the contractor smelling like sex."

Swinging my feet off the bed, I walk to the bathroom where she's inside the stall. "It's true. I should get in there with you."

"No!" she squeals, holding the shower door shut. "You'll slow me down, and I've got to get to work right after we meet him. Wednesday's edition is due at the printer by five."

I put my hands on my hips, smiling as I watch her through the frosted glass doors. "I'll get the coffee going then. Leave me some hot water."

"We'll have to replace this line all the way to the tie in down there." Chuck Claus shoves a thick pencil behind his ear. "With the new toilet, replacing the floor and repairing the ceiling… You're looking at about four thousand."

"Dollars?" Piper's voice breaks, and her wide green eyes turn to me. "I can't afford that."

She's so adorable in a black tank top and jeans, with her thick red hair piled on her head in a messy bun. Her full lips are a rosy pink shade, and I'd really like to kiss her, tell her I'll take care of the repairs.

And her.

And Ryan.

Instead, I put my hand on her shoulder. "I'll loan you the money, and you can pay me back."

Her slim brow furrows, and she shakes her head. "I can't let you do that. It's too much."

"It's what I do, Piper." I give her what I hope is a reassuring smile. "Remember? Community outreach?"

"Still, those programs have paperwork and applications…"

"That are simply for record keeping." I can't believe she's arguing with me about this. "Everybody gets the help they need, and you need your house fixed."

Although, I'd be happy for her to continue staying at my place indefinitely.

Chuck waits, looking down and around awkwardly.

Finally, I let him off the hook. "How soon do you think you can get it done?"

He hops to attention. "We're not too busy at this time of year. I could fit her in towards the end of the week. Would that work?"

"No!" Piper's voice goes high. "Cass's wedding is this weekend. It's a crazy week. I can't possibly—"

"I could also get started next week if that works better?" Chuck is a quick study.

I pat him on the shoulder, signing off on the work order. "Next week is great. Thanks for coming out."

He steps out of the mess of broken beams and damp floor. Piper is across the room picking up scattered items from the shattered bureau. It looks like papers and a few keepsake items.

"Was anything ruined?" I make my way over to where she's squatting beside what looks like a box of old pictures.

"I don't think so…" All at once I see a group of photos of what looks like her in only underwear.

"What's this? Boudoir shots?"

"Oh!" She grabs them so fast, I can't really make out anything.

I'm about to tease her, but she seems genuinely upset. She's blinking fast like she might cry, and I reach for her arm.

"Hey, are you okay?" Why would she cry about pictures of her in her underwear? "What were those?"

"It's nothing… something old." Her fingers tremble as she shoves the photographs into her notebook.

It's the third time she's acted this way, and although we said no questions, I can't hold back this time.

"It can't be nothing *and* something." Her eyes don't meet mine, so I touch her chin, lifting it. "Are you ashamed of your body?"

Strain lines her expression, and she's tense, almost like she's trapped. It makes me feel like an ass. I want her to feel safe, not threatened, so I release her at once.

Gentling my tone, I don't pressure her. "I know having a baby changes things, but not to me. I meant what I said last night. Nothing can change how beautiful you are in my eyes."

"Adam…" She exhales a sigh, stepping closer and placing her hand on mine.

Her notebook is clutched to her chest, and she chews her bottom lip, hesitating. She's so vulnerable. She's about to tell me something, and I'm ready. I want whatever this thing is out in the open. I've felt it so strongly over the last few days, every time we're together, and I do my best to ease her fears while also bracing for it.

"You see… back when we were in school… well… this thing happened—was happening. I never said anything to anyone because…"

A loud, brisk knock on the door cuts off her words.

"Hi guys! I'm not interrupting anything, am I?" It's Jemima's cheerful voice, and I swallow the growl rising in my throat. "I went to the paper office, but it was locked. Dang, it's a mess in here! Did you meet with the contractor? Is his name Santa Claus?"

Jemima giggles, and I feel like I can see Piper's invisible shield of practiced professionalism snap back in place. I'm frustrated she didn't get to finish that sentence. *What was happening? What did she never say?*

"I'm sorry." Piper turns to her. "What time is it?"

"It's after nine, chief!" Jemima does a little salute. "You didn't say what time I should be here this morning, but I figured the news never sleeps, right?"

"It's after nine? Holy shit, we're late." Piper still clutches that notebook to her chest as she hurries to where Jemima's waiting at the door. "The answer is yes, I was meeting with the contractor—*Chuck* Claus. I guess it went longer than I expected."

"Understandable." Jemima looks up at the hole in the ceiling. "What happened?"

"I bought a hundred-year-old house is what happened." Piper puts her hand on Cass's sister's arm. "I got a heck of a deal, though."

"It's what you'd call a fixer-upper?"

The two head to the newspaper office leaving me standing in the wreckage trying to figure out what I missed so long ago.

"So you think these fellas might know something?" Marshall is in the passenger's seat of my old Jetta.

The windows are down, and his short brown hair blows around his temples. It's not as cool today, and the scent of rain hangs in the air. He's dressed as usual in his tattered trench coat, white shirt and tie, but I'm more casual in loose jeans and a long-sleeved tee.

I'm driving us out to the old Jones place. Bull and Raif Jones are the "usual suspects" when it comes to crime in Eureka, and while it might not be entirely fair that anytime anything goes wrong, everyone in town points to them as the reason, they don't do anything to downplay their reputations.

"Bull Jones has connections with certain groups around the waterfront," I explain. "If anyone was hiding out or on the run, I expect he'd know about it."

"Are they like the Teamsters?" Marshall squints at me with one eye. "I do my best to avoid those guys."

"I don't think so. I don't think they're that organized."

They're more like a loose band of thugs and ex-cons, but I've somehow gotten invested in Marshall's case, and now I want to know as well whatever happened to…

"What's this missing person's name?" I glance at him as I turn onto the narrow dirt road leading to the Jones property.

They're technically outside of Eureka, in the unincorporated part of the county. It's one of the few reasons Aiden doesn't bother them—unless they come into town.

Marshall shifts in his seat. "I'd rather not have too much information out there until I at least know her whereabouts."

"I don't know what you're worried about with me."

"You're sleeping with the editor of the paper."

It's my turn to squint one eye at him. "How did you know that?"

"I caught her slipping out last night, so I followed her straight to your place. It wasn't hard to put two and two together. I'm not that old, and you're both attractive young people."

I turn into the short driveway leading to a rusty, double-wide trailer where the brothers live with Thad, their father. He's as rough as they are.

Ratty lawn chairs are arranged around a small fire pit behind a tree. A few tractor tires have flower beds planted in the centers, as if someone has taken an interest in fixing up the place, but whoever it was didn't make it very far.

An El Camino is on cinder blocks by a small shed where a motorcycle is parked. Something smaller is under a tarp, probably an ATV. A pile of trash is growing beside an overflowing garbage can, and on the porch are a few scrappy-looking hound dogs.

I put the car in park, and as we exit the vehicle, the door opens. I'm surprised by the man who steps out onto the dusty porch.

"Adam Stone? What the hell are you doing in this neck of the woods?" Willie "Bender" Cartwright is an old friend of my late pop's, and he likes to drop in and drink bourbon with Alex when he's in town.

He's an old-school tastemaker with longish gray hair and a

beard. He's usually smoking a cigar, and he reminds me of the cowboy version of Jeff Bridges. He's plugged into the luxury liquor and tobacco world, but his past is shady. Still, I'm surprised to see him at the Jones residence.

"I could say the same to you," I reply. "Does Alex know you're in town?"

"I came for the wedding, so he knows I'm on my way." He puts a cigar between his teeth and sets a bottle of Stone Cold special reserve bourbon on the porch railing. It's Alex's most expensive and sought-after product. "Care for a snort?"

"It's a little early for me." I stop midway between the car and the porch, and one of the dogs hops down and walks over to sniff my leg. It has one blue eye and one brown eye. "Is Bull or Raif around?"

"They're coming." Ben's boots make hollow thumps as he walks down the steps to where we're standing in the yard. "You must be Marshall Gregg. I heard you were in town looking for Rosie McClure."

My eyebrows rise, and I glance at Marshall. His eyes are narrow, and he's sizing up my old friend. "How'd you know that, Mr. *Bender*, is it?"

"Willie Cartwright, but folks call me Bender or Ben, if I'm lucky." He sticks out a weathered hand. "I used to drink too much."

I drop my face, doing my best not to grin at the flat way Ben puts his past indiscretions out there. I guess his attitude is there's no point in hiding what everybody knows.

The door opens, and Raif walks out onto the porch in jeans and an unbuttoned short-sleeved shirt. "Hey, Adam. What are you doing here? Something happen in town?"

His chest is bare, and he looks like he just rolled out of bed. He walks down the steps to where we're standing, reaching down to pet the dog's head.

"No, nothing like that. We were just looking for someone, and I thought you guys might have heard something." I glance at Marshall, wanting him to take the lead.

"I'm starting to think your friend here has some ideas." Marshall is mellow, but I can tell he's annoyed by Ben.

Ben isn't bothered. "No ideas here. I knew Rosie, but that's about all."

"When's the last time you saw her?"

"Hmm…" Bender slides his hand down his mustache and beard. "Couldn't say."

"But she was in this area?" Marshall clarifies.

"Yep. Right here in Eureka." Bender takes the top off the bottle of Stone Cold and pours an inch into a skinny glass. "Sure you won't try some? It's the best in the country. Hell, in the world, I'd wager."

"No, thanks." Marshall seems done here, and I'm more confused than when we arrived.

"I have an idea," Raif pipes up, and we all look at him.

"What's that?" Bender clears his throat and spits before sipping the bourbon.

"I saw that story about the hog attacking Terra Belle in her pickle patch," Raif points to the edge of the yard where two burn barrels are located, and where the sand-filled grass fades into palmettos and palm trees. "We had a hog rooting around in the woods a few nights ago. They're getting out of control with no natural predators here."

"It's true." I wonder if he's going to tell me it dug up human remains.

"I shot it and dressed it. The meat wasn't too bad. That's when I got my idea." Raif's smarter than people think, but I'm not sure he understands why we're here. "I could kill the motherfuckers, find a local processor, and sell them as free-range pork. I bet folks would buy it. Market it with Terra's pickles or whatever."

We're quiet a minute, and Marshall glances at me as if I might connect the dots.

Bender looks up at the trees, rubbing his chin. "It's an interesting idea. Don't think it's what these fellas are looking for, but there might be a market for it in the city."

Raif exhales a short laugh, glancing down at his bare feet. "Maybe I'll be the next Eureka millionaire."

It's a half-cocky, half-humble brag, but I'm impressed he actually has ambition. I'm starting to think he might be the one planting flowers in the tires, and it makes me want to root for him.

"Stranger things have happened." I glance over at Marshall. "Ready to head back to town?"

The door slams open on the trailer, and Bull Jones storms out onto the porch in a stained white tank and jeans. "What the fuck you doing here, Stone? Somebody's pumpkin patch get raided? Chickens missing? You think we don't have anything better to do than teenage pranks?"

Bull is a big guy with tattoos on his neck and a silver scar slicing his bottom lip. We're the same height, but he's a bit thicker than I am. He's a lot meaner, too, but I straighten to my full height.

"Actually, my friend here is working on a missing person's case. We'd hoped you might have some information on her whereabouts."

"I haven't seen any missing women in town. Neither have you, Raif."

I don't have to tell him his reply makes him look even more suspicious.

Bender cuts in. "I'd be surprised if Bull or Raif had seen her. It's been, what, twenty years since Rosie took off?"

"Give or take a few years," Marshall answers, taking out a card and handing it to Raif. "Let me know if you think of anything. Good luck with your pig project."

I hold Bull's stare a beat longer, mostly because I don't like bullies. "See you at the wedding, Ben. I'll let Alex know you're in town."

"Tell him I'll be over this afternoon if he has time for a visit, what with the wedding and all."

"I'm sure he'll make time."

With that, I turn and head for the car where Marshall's waiting. The three of them stand in the yard, watching as we drive away. Bull has his hands at his sides, and he's snorting like he's trying to live up to his nickname. Raif actually smiles and waves, and Bender pours another shot of bourbon like nothing happened.

"You're looking for someone who's been missing twenty years?" I glance at Marshall as we head back down the skinny sand and dirt road.

"Something like that."

"Is she dead?"

"No, but we're meant to think she is."

Propping my arm on the door, I shake my head. "It would've been helpful to know we were searching for someone older."

"I never said I was looking for a young woman." He rolls a small cigar in his fingers. "Rosie McClure faked her death when she ran away. She made it look like her car skidded in the rain and went off a bridge taking her and her child with it. The only problem was no bodies were ever found."

"You don't think they were swept away by the current?"

"Not anymore. In my research on the area, the name she's been hiding under popped up at a hospital about ten years ago." He takes out a phone and taps a few times on the face. "It's a common name, so it wasn't much of a lead, more a hunch really. Until your friend back there confirmed it."

"He confirmed she'd been here. Not that she's still here."

"She is, though." He looks out the window. "And I'm going to find her."

Chapter 13

Piper

"You're sleeping with him, but he still doesn't know?" Drew's tone is calm, but a painful knot is in my throat. "How are you managing that?"

We're having a quick, FaceTime check-in, and I know she can read my expression as clearly as I can read hers.

"At first it was dark. Then I was able to turn away, so he didn't see." I think of how close we almost got that second night, until I dropped to my knees in front of him.

"How does that make you feel?"

Like a liar.

"I was going to tell him today. I was about to say the words, when we were interrupted by my new employee."

My heart beats faster, and my breath catches when I think of him seeing those pictures. It was the one time I mustered the courage to document what Rex had done to me. I stood in front of the mirror and photographed all my scars, thinking I'd go to someone… not Aiden, of course… but someone who could help me, and tell them how he hurt me, how he cut my body in places that wouldn't show.

Then I started thinking about the consequences and all the different ways it could go wrong. I thought about baring my soul to strangers when I hadn't even told my best friends. My mother didn't even know.

It would be a matter of my word against his with people I'd never met, which again raised the possibility they wouldn't believe me. And if they did believe me, what then? Did I want him to go to jail? Did I want to press charges?

Would I go to court and face a lengthy, public trial where I'd be asked a bunch of embarrassing questions?

It wasn't what I wanted. I only wanted it to stop.

I wanted to be free.

"Do you think work is the best place to have that conversation?" Her question is neutral, not accusatory.

"We were at my house, but my house is right behind the newspaper office, so she went there to find me." I think about Jemima flirting with Adam, and my lips twist.

"What's wrong?" Drew studies me through the screen.

I feel my cheeks heat, and I shake my head. "It's my friend's little sister. She came back for the wedding, but I think she's planning to stay."

"You gave her a job?"

"She asked if I had anything she could do…"

"But?"

A knot is in my throat, and I'm a little embarrassed to confess. "She's been flirting with Adam."

Drew's quiet a moment, watching me. "How does that make you feel?"

Pressing my fingers to my hot face, I confess. "Jealous. *Really* jealous, and I'm so ashamed. Jemima's just young and playful, but it makes me so angry. Then it terrifies me."

Her brow furrows. "Why?"

"Rex would get that way. He said he cut me because he

was jealous, so no one would want me… He said I was the same way."

She's quiet again, and I wish we were in her office. Talking on my phone feels too intimate, like I have nowhere to hide, and all my emotions are plain on my face.

"Did you ever hurt Rex physically?" Her blue eyes are serious.

"No!" I shake my head. "I never touched him except to push him away when he was hurting me."

"Do you want to hurt Adam physically? Or your friend's sister?"

I start to see where she's going with this, and I shake my head again. "I can't imagine hurting someone that way."

"Everyone feels jealous sometimes, Piper. It's a normal human emotion. Abuse is not."

Blinking down, I don't understand why this makes me want to cry. "I know."

"You didn't make Rex do what he did to you. He made that choice."

I know she's right, but sometimes my mind tries to tell me I'm wrong. "These past few nights, in the dark with Adam, I could pretend I wasn't damaged or scarred. I was free."

"That's good." Drew's voice is kind, and I glance up to see her gentle smile.

"I'm afraid when I tell him the truth, when he sees my scars, things will change."

"They might." She nods. "You might be freer than you've ever been. You're no longer hiding, and the real you is no longer trapped in the past."

"Could I be that lucky?" I huff a laugh, a hint of sarcasm in my tone.

"You don't have to mask your feelings with jokes. It's okay to feel afraid."

"But it's what I do." She was the one who diagnosed my coping mechanism. "If I didn't laugh, I'd cry."

"It's okay to cry."

"I don't want to cry about the past anymore. I want to laugh at what bad luck I have. It can't hurt me if I laugh at it."

"The truth will give you freedom, Piper, and maybe Adam can change your luck."

It's an interesting thought I hadn't considered before. In all my years of hiding, I never considered my luck could change, or someone would ever get close enough again to change it.

We finish up, and for a moment in my office, I sit, holding my phone and turning her words over in my mind.

"We need briefs on the grand opening of Heaven Scent and The Human Bean." I'm going through the notes on my phone with Jemima, who sits at a small desk in front of me in the main newsroom.

"And those are…?" Her blue eyes are wide and curious.

"Heaven Scent is an aromatherapy store, but I think they also have candles and body products." I imagine the whole place smelling like patchouli. "The Human Bean is a coffee shop. Basically, a mom-and-pop Starbucks."

"That's handy having them right there together like that."

"How so?"

"If you smell a lot of different fragrances, after a while you stop being able to smell anything. Sniffing coffee beans resets your nose. Haven't you ever noticed how in perfume stores they have those little glass boxes of coffee beans?"

"No." I continue down my list of notes. "We should also do a short profile on Henry Anderson. He's the new veterinarian in Seamist. Something like where he came from, what his plans are, that sort of thing."

"*This* is who you replaced me with?" Mom stalks into the newsroom wearing her usual overalls with her long hair braided down her back. "Isn't she overexposed enough?"

"Excuse me..." I put both hands on my hips. "I didn't *replace* you with anybody. You were never on staff."

She stops in front of Jemima's desk. "Shouldn't you be at a football game or writing songs about your ex-boyfriends?"

Jemima looks from her to me totally confused, until understanding breaks across her face—almost like she's used to dealing with crazy people, which she probably is, considering we have the messy mom connection.

"Sorry, Ms. Jackson, I'm not really Taylor Swift." Then her face lights. "Hey, that was almost a song! I am for real..."

Mom is still scowling. "Is it one of your new ones? Or are you re-recording another album?"

"Ma, this is not Taylor Swift. It's Jemima Dixon. Cass's little sister?"

My mother's brows tighten, and she studies my new reporter a minute longer. Then she breaks into a smile and throws out her arms.

"Oh my goodness, of *course* I remember Jemima!" She gives her a tight squeeze. "Well, haven't you grown into a beautiful young woman? And to think you were just a little bitty thing the last time I saw you with your mom. She and I were best friends, you know."

"I do know!" Jemima hugs my mom back like nothing ever happened. "I also know you're the famous headline provocateur."

"I don't know what that means." Mom looks from her to me.

"Those hilarious headlines you wrote! They're all over the internet." Jemima taps quickly on her phone before turning it to where we can see. "You're a viral sensation. Check out this article on the *Denver Gazette* website. 'Small-town publisher has a way with words,'" Jemima reads. "Piper Jackson doesn't need AI to create a buzz in Eureka, South Carolina..."

Mom's face pales, and she waves her hand. "Tell them to stop. Take that down!"

"If only it were that easy." I cringe at the thought of my name spanning the globe as the author of those headlines.

My luck hasn't changed yet.

"That can't be everywhere." Mom acts like she's seen a ghost.

"And yet it is," I deadpan. "Behold the power of the internet."

"I think you're both taking this the wrong way," Jemima argues. "It's a good thing. You're famous, and I bet you get a lot of new subscribers!"

"That's just what Mom said."

"I have to go." Mom hurries out of the office, but I exhale heavily.

"This is how history is written. I'll be forevermore the person who published those headlines."

Jemima's nose wrinkles, and she starts to laugh. "At least you're famous for something funny."

"Is it funny, though?"

The door opens again, and my heart jumps when Adam enters the room. A smile curls his handsome face when he sees us laughing.

"Glad to see everybody's smiling." His low voice is so attractive, and Jemima walks over to where he's standing at the front counter.

"Hey, handsome! Do you have breaking news to report?"

She blinks her eyes at him, puckering her velvet-red lips as she speaks, and I think about what Drew said about jealous feelings being normal.

Is it normal to want to assign her a story in Alaska?

As if I have a budget for travel.

"Actually, it's possible I do." Adam straightens, placing his large hands on the counter.

Jemima's eyebrows lift, and she glances over her shoulder at me.

I walk to where they're standing, curious now. "Let's hear it."

"Raif Jones has a pretty interesting solution to the wild hog situation." He pauses as if for dramatic effect. "He wants to break into the free-range pork market."

My brow furrows. "What is that supposed to mean?"

"Who's Raif Jones?" Jemima's nose wrinkles.

"Town bad boy. You'd love him."

"Is he as hot as you are?" Her voice is sultry.

"Nobody is," he quips.

"You can say that again." She puts her elbows on the countertop, batting her lashes, and I fight the urge to pull her hair.

"Can we get back to the breaking news, please?" An edge is in my tone, and I don't even care.

Adam's eyes narrow, and I know he caught that. Thankfully, he continues his story without calling me out.

"He shot one of the pigs on his property and decided to have it for dinner. He claims it's pretty good, and now he has the idea he'll hunt them, partner with a local butcher, and sell the meat to specialty stores as free-range pork. He even floated the idea of combining it with Terra's pickles."

Twisting my lips, I evaluate the newsworthiness of this solution. "It's not the worst idea I've ever heard."

"I was pretty stoked to discover Raif Jones had ambitions beyond riding his motorcycle and racing dogs."

"People used to say that about me." Jemima's voice is solemn, and for a split second, I'm lost.

"Which part?"

"Not having ambition." She nods, as if empathizing with our local outlaw. "That's when I got the idea of proving them wrong by impersonating Taylor Swift. I would've made a lot of money, too, if her fans weren't so overprotective."

It's the second time she's mentioned the fans, and my journalistic nose tells me there could be a story there.

"Want to keep proving them wrong by seeing what you can do with that strip mall story? It's over by the Popcorn Palace, and I think Harold would be more receptive to you getting to know his neighbors than me."

"Okay." She glances at Adam, poking his arm with her finger. "I wonder if I could catch a ride with this handsome fellow?"

My annoyance flares, but I tamp it down. I have no reason to be jealous of Adam or mad at Jemima, and even if I did, I haven't given anyone any reason to think we're together—not that I don't want us to be.

"Sure, I can give you a ride." He gives me a wink. "I'll see you in a little while."

"I'll be over here investing in pork bellies."

Jemima blinks at me. "Is that a thing?"

"Not anymore."

Adam doesn't miss a beat. "Wednesday's headline: 'Jones Sends Pork Bellies to Hog Heaven.'"

"No." I throw up my hands, wrinkling my nose. "That's terrible."

"I'll workshop it."

Jemima tilts her head. "I don't think Martha has to worry. You're not replacing her in the headline department."

"Hold that thought." He winks at her. "I'll come up with something better."

The two of them head out to Adam's waiting car, and I hang at the counter watching them. I think about jealousy and change and the truth.

Then I think about luck.

Chapter 14

Adam

> Wild Hogs Can't Be Broken?

'M STILL DOING MY BEST TO TOP MARTHA'S HEADLINES.

I know how much Piper hates writing them, so the whole time her cub reporter interviewed Pearl and Bill, proprietors of the Human Bean Coffee Shop, and Frangelica *No Last Name*, the owner of Heaven Scent, I sent her ideas.

I only took a break to drive us back to town.

> Sell the Farm, These Beans Are Magic.

Piper: The paper can't attribute supernatural powers to coffee.

> I know plenty of people who'd disagree with you.

Piper: Find me the study to back it up, and I'll print it.

> How about, Frangelica's Knocking on Heaven's door?

Piper: Sounds like she's dead.

I only hope I've made her smile. When she's on a deadline, I'm not convinced she breathes or even moves from her chair, and I want my girl staying healthy.

"We have to convince Piper to hire Martha." Jemima steps out of the car, flicking her hair over her shoulder. "She's the headline provocateur."

"That's not a position." I'm pretty sure Piper would murder her mom if they were around each other that much.

Martha can be a lot to take.

"Well, it's a doggy dog world, and you are not cut out for the job." Jemima pulls open the glass door of the *Eureka Gazette* with an air of entitlement.

I do a double take before hopping out to follow her into the building. "What did you just say?"

"How'd it go? Got something for me?" Piper meets us at the counter, moving fast, and warmth tightens my chest.

Always.

Her red hair is twisted into a bun on top of her head, and a pencil is shoved through the mess. A smear of black is on her cheek—possibly ink—and I can't stop a grin sliding across my lips. She's adorable, and very serious about her job, which makes me smother my sudden boyfriend urges, like the one to pull her into my arms and cover those pillow lips with kisses.

"Frangelica claims she's originally from Italy, but I'd recognize that accent anywhere. It's straight Tennessee." Jemima swipes her finger across her phone. "Bill says they roast their own coffee beans on-site, but if that were true, it would smell like coffee, and the only scent I picked up was banana nut muffin. They're importing those beans, although I don't understand why he'd lie about that…" She gasps, eyes widening. "Unless they're not fair-trade beans?"

Piper's cheeks are turning pinker with every word, and it's

not because she's embarrassed this time. I know that look—she's pissed, and my protective instinct starts to rise.

Glancing at the clock, I see it's getting close to four, which means tomorrow's edition is due at the printer in an hour.

"This isn't a gossip rag, Jemima." Her voice is on that razor's edge of shouting. "Did you find out anything about where they're from? What they hope to bring to the community? Why they chose this area?"

Jemima's brow furrows, and she's completely confused. "Clearly they hope to bring coffee and handmade bath products to the community, and they chose Eureka, because who wouldn't? It's beautiful, it's way cheaper than Kiawah or Hilton Head, and you still have access to the elite clientele. It's a win-win-win! But who wants to read that? Readers want gossip."

Piper cuts her eyes to me, and I shrug. "It's a doggy-dog world. We only live in it."

It's her turn to be confused. "Who are you? Snoop? It's 'dog *eat* dog world.'"

"Ew!" Jemima cries. "Why would they *eat* each other? That's disgusting."

"We don't have time for this. Type up what you've got. Lead with something catchy, a detail or something about the business or them, then fill in the details with the most important up top. And no conjecture about fair trade beans or clandestine Tennessee natives!"

"Oh-kay, gah!" Jemima hops over to the waiting laptop, and I follow Piper into her office, closing the door behind me.

"You'd better double-check whatever she writes before you send it to the printer."

"Trust me, I learned that lesson." She throws the words offhand before stopping in place and squinting up at me. "Why do you say that?"

"She's been tossing out all sorts of interesting phrases all afternoon."

She rounds her desk. "Whatever she said, it can't possibly be worse than your headlines."

"Do you know what a myth is?"

"A folk story that explains some phenomenon—"

"A female moth. How about quesadilla?"

"Cheesy Mexican dish?"

"What day is it?"

She hesitates. "I don't understand. You know what day it is."

"She thinks *quesadilla* is Spanish for 'What day is it.'" Piper drops into her chair, and I rub my hand over my mouth to hide my laughter. "I had to warn you. I know bad grammar is one of your pet peas."

I didn't think her eyes could get any narrower and still be open. "Pet *pea*?"

"Forewarned is forearmed, and I mean, if you think about it, a *pet pea* is cuter than a *pet peeve*."

"You think she's cute?" Again, that edge is in her voice, and I'm not sure... *Is it possible Piper's jealous?*

"She has her moments."

Rolling her eyes, she types on her computer. "What are they teaching kids in school these days, anyway..."

"Do you think Jemima graduated high school?" I glance out the glass door into the newsroom where she's typing quickly.

"Is it four-thirty? I've got to call Stew and see if he'll give me more time. I am literally drowning."

The panic in her voice triggers my protective urges. Placing both hands on the desk, I lean closer, looking at the papers spread all around.

"How can I help? Caption writing? Do you need something proofed? Headlines?"

"No more headlines!"

"Mom! Mom!" Ryan yells from outside the door, and her back straightens.

I meet her pretty green eyes and smile. "*That's* what I can do."

"No, it's okay." She stands, rounding the desk and placing her hand on my bicep. "I want to talk to him. We've been so separated since the toilet fell through the roof."

Another thing I can take off her plate.

"Hey, honey!" She bends down to hug him as he dashes into the room, giving her a rough squeeze in return. "How was your day today?"

"Fudge followed me to school this morning, and I thought he was going to leave while I was there, but when I got out for recess, he was still sitting by the fence waiting so I played with him some more…" He pauses to gasp a breath. "And then, when we went to lunch, he was *still there*, and when we got out of school, he was waiting for me!" Ryan's voice goes loud. "He waited for me all day!"

"You're kidding!" Piper's voice rises as she rakes her fingers through his bangs, pushing them off his forehead. "I've never heard of a cat doing something like that before."

"That means we *have* to keep him now, doesn't it, Mom?"

Her lips press into a smile, and she slides a thumb across his cheek. "I guess we have to if he's waiting for you to get out of school every day."

"I don't know if he'll do it every day, but he did it today!" Turning to me, he slides a small hand into mine. "What do you think, Uncle Adam?"

I think I love everything about what's happening right now, except the part where he calls me *uncle*. It started when he was little, because it's what Owen and Pinky call me… since I'm their actual uncle.

Only, when it comes to Piper and Ryan, I want way more than that.

"I think he's a great cat, and if he's waiting for you at school, I like him even more." Taking his hand, I meet her eyes. "What if I take this guy to grab a slushie at the Pack-n-Save then walk over to Aiden's?"

"That would be great." The gratitude in her eyes is all I

need, although I don't want her to thank me for taking care of Ryan. "I'll stop by and tell you goodnight when I'm done here, okay?"

"Okay! Love you, Mom!" He takes off into the newsroom and out the door, where I assume the black cat is waiting.

Piper blinks up at me, and the warmth in her gaze is enough. She'll be sleeping with me tonight.

Ryan's lips are blue from his slushie, and Fudge is over his shoulder. We're walking in the direction of the courthouse where my brother is most likely finishing up his day alongside Britt. Owen is probably there with them, and Edward the dog is likely there as well.

I think about having the same thing with Piper and Ryan. Wrapping up a day at the community center or at the waterfront mission, picking up Ryan from school, and meeting her at the newspaper office. Fudge would most likely be hanging around, maybe he'd be the resident news cat. Then we'd all head home together.

"Uncle Adam?" A worried look is on Ryan's face when he glances up at me, and concern pricks my chest. "Can I ask you something?"

"You can ask me anything." I give him a reassuring smile.

"It's kind of embarrassing." He gets quiet.

"Here." Nudging his arm, I lead us to one of the benches lining the square alongside the gazebo. "Want to have a seat and talk about it?"

He nods, following me and putting Fudge on the ground before climbing onto the bench and bending his knee so he can face me. The way he moves hits me with nostalgia when I realize he's turning into a little man.

I remember the videos Piper would send me when I was overseas in the Navy—his first birthday, and the way he looked at everyone with wide eyes and an even wider smile as they sang to him; his first steps, staggering and stomping faster to his cheering mom with the biggest smile on his face.

I remember his first day of kindergarten, and how he ran straight to Owen and the two of them walked into Mrs. Priddy's class like they were ready to take on the world. Piper, by contrast, was ready to cry all the tears. I took her straight to El Rio, and we drowned her sorrows in mimosas.

I remember the night he was born, and seeing him so tiny with those big eyes watching me, I loved him like he was mine as much as hers. Even if it's not true, I want it to be.

"Did something happen at school?" It's been a while since I was in fourth grade, so I'm not sure what might be embarrassing him.

"We were at gym class, and one of the boys said something I didn't understand."

My concern turns to worry, but I hold my expression steady. "Okay."

He doesn't meet my eyes, and his fingers tug on his shoelaces nervously. "It was one of the big boys…"

I can tell whatever happened is really bothering him, and I hope I can make better progress with his problems than I do with his mother's.

"You don't have to be embarrassed. I was your age once, too, remember? And I've got two big brothers."

He nods, still not meeting my eyes. "He said…" Ryan clears his throat, and his voice gets a little quieter. "He said looking at Sadie Sink made his dick hard. I don't know why he said that, but sometimes it happens to me, and I don't know why it happens either."

His face is bright red, and I scrub my fingers over my lips, remembering how indelicately my older brothers handled the "boner" discussion when I was his age. I plan to do better than that.

"Is Sadie Sink one of the girls at your school?"

He shakes his head no. His eyes are still fixed on his shoelaces, and his face is still blazing. "She's that girl on *Stranger Things*."

"Gotcha." I nod, racking my brain for the most age-appropriate way to explain this. "So, when that happens, it's called an erection, and it's totally normal. Nothing to worry about. It means you're getting older, and sometimes blood rushes to your penis. That makes it get hard like that, but when the blood leaves, it'll go down again."

"Why does it happen when he looks at Sadie Sink?" His brow wrinkles, and he finally meets my eyes.

"Does it happen when *you* look at Sadie Sink?" He shakes his head no, and I put my hand on his shoulder, giving him a little side-hug. "When it does, ask me again, and we'll talk some more about it, okay? In the meantime, just know it's part of being a guy. You're totally normal."

He still seems conflicted, but his face is less red than it was a minute ago. "Why does it do that all by itself? It's embarrassing."

Welcome to the world of being a guy. "It's all biology, I'm afraid. You can try changing positions or going for a walk. Maybe wear a long shirt?"

He frowns up at me, and with a blue-lined slushy mouth, it's hard to believe we're already here, having this discussion.

"Does it happen to you?" His brow furrows.

Not when I see Sadie Sink. But I keep my tone sincere. "Yeah, but when it happens to me, it's different because I'm a grown-up."

"It's not blood rushing to your penis?"

"It's still that, but when you're older, it happens for a different reason. It has more to do with making babies."

His lips twist, but he nods, sliding off the bench to stand in front of me. "Am I going to get hair down there, too?"

"Yep, and under your arms and on your chest and your face." I pat his shoulder, and stand as well. "You'll be having a lot of changes in the next few years, but don't worry. I'll be here if you want to talk about it."

We start to walk again, and he puts his small hand in mine. "I wish you were my dad."

My throat tightens, and I stop walking. He looks up at me worried for a beat, but I take a knee, pulling him into a hug.

"Me too, buddy." His arms are around my shoulders, and when I feel the tension leave his body, I hug him a little tighter. "Me too."

Grouper filets sizzle in a pan of olive oil, surrounded by roasted red peppers, onions, celery, and cherry tomatoes. My conversation with Ryan is on my mind.

I think I handled it pretty well. It was the first of what I hope will be many trusted conversations between us. I imagine him getting older, me getting older, and us being friends in a way I never had with my dad, who died when I was fourteen.

I'll need to tell Piper what happened, and I hope it makes her see what I already know—we should be a real family. The thought of proposing crosses my mind once more.

I cut up a baguette of French bread to toast in the oven, and a bowl of steaming white rice with pine nuts and lemon wedges cools on the counter. I glance at the clock, and it's almost eight. I'm sure she went by Aiden's to tell Ryan goodnight.

The thought of them together here, tucking him into bed in this house makes me smile. I can convert the study I never use into a bedroom, and I'm sure Mom will let me have my old bed until I can replace it with a new one. One he can pick out himself.

Another warm smile curls my lips when she walks through my door.

"Honey, you're home," I tease.

"It smells delicious in here!" I love the sound of her voice, and I quickly remove the fish from the pan, plate it, and return the vegetables to the fire.

I continue stirring them over low heat to finish cooking them. "There's wine in the fridge. Did you make your deadline?"

"Sure did." She goes to the refrigerator and takes out a bottle of Sancerre. "I like having Jemima on staff, but I'm going to have to bring in more money somehow if I'm going to be able to pay her and keep the lights on."

"Hazards of owning your own business." I meet her eyes. "Did you…?"

"Proofread her stories? Definitely, and I have to say, Jemima Dixon has a way with words."

I chuckle, cutting the fire and dividing the vegetables between our two plates. "In more ways than one?"

Placing the pan in the sink, I reach for a wineglass. I'm midway through pouring, when I realize she's watching me with that half-frown on her face.

"What is it?"

"In what way is Jemima Dixon interesting to you?"

The tone in her voice puts me on the defense. "Are you suggesting I have an inappropriate interest in Cass's little sister?"

"She's obviously very interested in you." Her eyebrow arches, and her voice adopts a tone I've never heard before. Definitely jealous. "Do you have a thing for Taylor Swift impersonators? Do you want to fuck her?"

I have no idea where this is coming from, but jealous Piper is kind of hot. I put my wine glass down and switch off the oven. Then I close the space between us, putting both hands on the counter on either side of my girl and caging her between them.

Using my height to my advantage, I look down on her, answering flatly. "No."

To her credit, she doesn't back down. Her chin lifts, and she blinks those green eyes up at me. "How do I know?"

Leaning closer, I slide my nose along her cheek before speaking low in her ear. "Because I only want to fuck you."

Her breath catches, and she fists my chest as if she'll push me away. I'm not going anywhere. "Are you jealous, Piper?"

"No." Her tone is a little too bossy.

She's a little too defiant, and I confess, I can't believe after all I've said and done she actually believes I'd want someone else. It almost makes me laugh. *Almost*.

"Feeling a little possessive?" My voice is low, and I slide my lips along the side of her neck.

A shiver moves down her body, and she tries to push me away. "I'm not doing this."

But she's not going anywhere.

Catching her hands in mine, I hold her steady. "Repeat after me: You're mine."

Her eyes narrow, and she twists her hands out of my grip. "You're mine? Prove it."

With pleasure.

I grab her hips in both hands and pull her pelvis against mine before leaning down to seal my lips over hers. My erection is hard against her belly, and I reach back to cup her ass in both hands.

Moving my lips to her cheek, I bite the tip of her earlobe. "I told you I'm your slave. My cock is for you, Piper Jackson, not some little girl who doesn't know who she is yet."

She's breathing fast, and I reach for the top of her jeans, unbuttoning them and doing my best to push them down her hips. Her hands cover mine, and she shoves them down before reaching for the waistband of my pants.

My jeans are loose and much easier to remove. I'm also not wearing underwear.

Her fingers wrap around my cock, and she slides her hand up and down the hardened shaft. "This cock?"

I exhale a groan, threading my fingers in her hair and pulling her head back so she can see my eyes. "I want to fuck you every minute of the day. Whenever I see you, I imagine all the ways I could bend you over your desk or pull you into the backseat of my car or sneak you into a closet."

"Every minute?" She fists my shirt, shoving it higher.

Our mouths seal again, and she sucks my bottom lip between her teeth. She bites me gently before pulling my tongue into her mouth.

"This fucking minute." It's a low growl. My dick is hard as a rock, and it's weeping for her warm, wet pussy. "Now turn around and show me that cunt."

I push her forward onto the bar, and she lifts her ass, looking over her shoulder at me. Using two fingers, I test her wetness, sliding them forward over her clit then higher, dipping into her entrance.

"Oh, God," she moans, and I grin, sliding my fingers over her clit again.

"You're ready for me."

"Yes…"

It only takes a second to line up my cock and drive hard and deep into her core. "Fuck," I groan, holding steady as I catch my breath.

"Oh, fuck," she grunts, and she starts to move.

Her ass bucks against my pelvis, and my hand snakes around her waist, going between her legs and rubbing her clit fast and firm.

I'm so fucking turned on, I'm going to come fast, and her inner walls are already spasming and pulling me, milking my cock.

"So fucking hot," she gasps.

"Dammit, Piper." My head is on fire, and primal instinct takes over.

One hand grips her hip, and I thrust fast and ragged, crazed like it's our first time together, and I can't get enough of her sweet body. My other hand circles her clit, and her elbows give way. She lies on her stomach, and I fuck her hard and fast, driven by the growing orgasm tightening my balls and causing my stomach to quiver.

The bar squeaks as it slides over the floor, and she rises onto her toes with every hard thrust. Her moans are loud, and her knuckles white as she grips the edges of the wood. A shuddering groan rasps from my throat, and I'm coming. I pull out quick as the orgasm pulses, coating her back with come.

My hand is still between her legs working her clit, and I lean forward, breathing hard.

Her phone buzzes, and we both look over to see a text from Britt on the face.

> **Britt**: If you don't fuck Adam Stone, this week, I will never forgive you.

A short laugh jerks from her throat. "She has no idea."

"I'm not finished with you," I growl, biting the side of her ear. "One orgasm down. One to go."

Taking a knee, I turn her, putting her leg over my shoulder and replacing my hand with my face. My mouth covers her pussy, and my tongue is on her clit, circling and teasing.

"Oh, God, oh…" She gasps, her knees jerking as her inner thighs tremble against my jaw.

Bracing one hand under her ass, I slide my other fingers inside her, feeling her squeezing as she comes, pulling my hair and moaning and rocking in time with my tongue on her clit.

Her wails start to subside, and I slow, easing my movements to soothing as we both gasp for breath, as she lowers to sit on my lap on the floor.

"Jesus…" Her forehead rests against my shoulder, and I hold her, sliding my fingers gently along the back of her neck.

We're both naked from the waist down. We're still in the kitchen, our glasses of wine on the bar above us. The dinner I cooked is getting cold, but that's why God invented microwaves.

Catching her upper arms, I lift her to standing, then I lift her into my arms, kicking off my jeans and heading for the bedroom.

"What about our dinner?" A sassy grin curls her lips.

"It's not going anywhere."

But we are.

Chapter 15

Piper

"OH, FUCK! FUCK... FUCK..." MY STOMACH QUIVERS, AND I CAN'T stop coming.

Adam's face is between my thighs again, and with every swipe of his tongue, his scruffy jaw scraping my sensitive skin, my mind blanks.

Rising over me, he rolls on a condom before sinking into my clenching insides. He's so big, every time it takes a minute to stretch, to hold. He looks down at where our bodies are joined, and wonder is on his face, like he can't get enough of watching us come together

I need to feel him moving inside me. I buck my hips, and his blue eyes hold mine. "My greedy girl."

A cocky smile curls his lips before he lowers his head to seal his mouth to mine. Our tongues meet and stroke, lips pulling and chasing. I'm on my fourth orgasm of the night, and he's fucking me like he's about to break the bed.

My fingers curl against his shoulders, and I pull harder. I

want to meld his body with mine, join us in every way. I love the feel of his body, tense with need. I love the feel of his muscles quivering as he comes.

It isn't long before his mouth breaks away. A bead of sweat traces his cheek, and I lick it, tasting the salt on my tongue. He's focused, eyes closed, jaw clenched. His muscles flex, and a thrilling moan rips through his throat.

He holds above me, pulsing and finishing. I wrap my legs around his waist and hold him closer, never wanting to let him go.

He smells like soap and sweat and sex, and he lifts his chin, sliding a large palm over my forehead, moving my hair away from my face, and looking into my eyes.

We don't speak. We only look at each other a moment like we're trying to believe this is really happening. Maybe we should've done this three nights ago, but it's the first time it all feels different, like we've turned a corner.

"Say it." His voice is rough, and a hint of a smile teases the corner of his mouth.

My lips press together briefly, and my own voice is hoarse from crying out his name. "You're mine."

Leaning down, he kisses my cheek, my nose, my lips. "You're mine."

He has no idea how true those words are, lying here, secure beneath his warm, strong body. I'm his, and I'll never be anyone else's.

"I can't believe how good this is." We're sitting in the bed with the tray again, only this time it holds glasses of wine and plates of pan-seared grouper and fall vegetables. "I can only fry hamburgers and scramble eggs. Oh, and I can grill cheese."

He takes a bite of the flaky fish. "The caterer was always

overbooked and understaffed, so I was constantly pulled into the kitchen. Then, I don't know, I guess I liked doing it."

"You can do all the cooking at my house."

He glances at me briefly before taking a sip of wine. "I'll do the cooking. And whatever else you need doing."

Setting my clean plate on the nightstand, I take my glass of wine and lean into his chest. "I like the sound of that."

We're both naked from the waist down, and I'm still in the black tank top I wore to work, although I stripped my bra off between our second and third round of orgasms.

He puts his plate aside as well, turning to face me in the bed. We're both propped on pillows, and he reaches out to cup the side of my head, sliding his thumb above my brow.

"Are we talking about the future now?" His voice is quiet, and his eyes track the movement of his thumb over my skin.

Reaching out, I put my hand on his cheek. "Cass's wedding is in three days. Can we talk about it after that?"

His eyes flicker to mine, and I love him so much. I just want to have him this way a little bit longer… just in case everything changes when he knows the whole story.

Even though I believe Drew, and I really do think it's going to work out, that tiny sliver of glass, that shard of fear is still lodged in my heart.

"You didn't really think I wanted to be with Jemima, did you?" He's not smiling, and embarrassment heats my cheeks.

"She's so flirty, and you're so flirty, and I don't know."

"Piper." The disappointment in his tone pinches my stomach. "You can't be serious."

"I don't know." My shoulders rise. "I'm as surprised by it as you are. I've never thought of myself as a jealous person."

His brow lowers, and he studies me for a moment. "I guess I'd rather you care than not care, but you never have to be jealous about me."

My lip goes between my teeth, and I have the strong desire to pull the blanket over my head. "I'm sorry?"

"Don't apologize." He turns to rest his back against the headboard again. "I want you to tell me what's on your mind."

"I know." Soon I'm going to tell him everything, and I pray he's true to his word.

"Your son asked me about boners today."

"What?" The sudden declaration snaps me out of my fear.

"One of the older kids is getting boners for a girl on Netflix, so naturally he told everyone."

"Everyone?"

"All the boys."

"My poor baby." I frown, putting my hands on my cheeks. "What did you say?"

"For starters, he's not a baby anymore." He grins, and that dimple pierces his sexy cheek. "I think I handled it pretty well. You'll be comforted to know Ryan is not getting boners for little girls on Netflix… yet."

"I can't even think about that." Leaning forward, I rest my forehead against his chest. "What would I do without you?"

"I gave you six weeks to figure it out."

Sitting up again, I can't tell if he's joking or not. "We never talked about Hawaii. What was it like?"

He exhales, turning to face me. "It was beautiful."

Scooting closer in the bed, I rest my cheek against his chest and wrap my arm around his waist. He shifts to allow me to hold him, and my stomach is tense. I want to know about his time away, but I don't want him to leave me again.

What else can I do to prove myself? His last words haunted me every night he was gone. Only one thing is left.

"Ryan said you were flying people back and forth to the mainland."

"Mostly, I just took them to the big island and back. It was part of an outreach for needy families."

My heart squeezes. He's so good. "How did you find out about that?"

"Max's great aunt was one of the coordinators." The

impatience leaves his tone, and he grows more thoughtful. "She was a neat old lady. Totally blind and very wise."

"She was blind?"

"Yeah, but you'd never know it from the way she marched all over the place. She lived near the top of a cliff."

"It sounds beautiful. Did you surf much?" I remember watching him on the water, riding the waves.

He made it look so easy, and he was always so focused and beautiful doing it.

"I went out with Max a few times, usually in the evening after work. I would sit on the board and watch the sun set. The colors were amber and gold and green. It reminded me of your eyes."

Tucking my chin, I reach down for the hem of his shirt and slide my hand under it, so I can trace my fingers over his warm skin. His hand moves from my hair down to my waist.

"Flying the plane into Moloka'i, the curve of the islands rising out of the water was like the curve of your hip in my bed." His palm slides to my hip. His face is against the top of my head, and he inhales. "The scent of plumeria isn't quite the same as honeysuckle, but it's similar."

"All of Hawaii reminded you of me?" My voice is quiet. "When you never texted, I thought you'd decided to forget me."

"I went away to try. I thought I would leave this place and put you out of my head, but I should have known the truth. Everything beautiful in the world reminds me of you. I see your face whenever I close my eyes."

Tears fill my eyes, and an ache is in my throat. "Adam..."

My tears dampen his shirt, and he lifts my chin with his fingers. "I didn't mean to make you cry. I wanted you to know the truth."

I don't have words, so I stretch higher in the bed and press my mouth to his. He rolls me onto my back, and our lips part. Our tongues slide together, and I open my body to him. We might not be talking about the future, but it's coming.

Chapter 16

Adam

"If she was on the run with a child, wouldn't she need food?" I grunt, lifting a box of peanut butter out of the back of the van. "There might be a record of her here."

"Not a chance." Marshall stands back watching me unload donations at the food bank behind the church.

Today he's not wearing his usual trench coat—only slacks and a blazer over a rumpled white shirt. As usual, I'm in jeans and a tee. It rained overnight, but the air is still humid and warm. Fall weather on the coast is completely unpredictable. One day it's cool and crisp, the next it's hot and sticky.

"You send their applications for food to the government?" He motions to the clipboards hanging on the wall at the pickup line.

"Only if they have Medicaid or emergency assistance. We get reimbursed for those."

I pass the cardboard box to a college kid helping us restock the shelves. The last Wednesday of every month, we get huge donations from local supermarkets. They clear out items past the "sell by" date, but almost everything will last another month. Produce, not so much.

"That would be too risky." He rolls a small cigar in his fingers, and I pull out a flat of collard greens.

"Tell Mrs. Andrews she'll need to hand all these out by Friday," I say to the kid who takes it from me. "They won't last through the weekend."

She nods, placing the dark green, leafy vegetables in a shopping cart and wheeling them through the back door.

"How long you been doing this kind of thing?" Marshall nods at the white Chevy cargo van stacked full of boxes.

"About four years. Since I got out of the Navy." I drag another flat of produce out the back. This time it's packaged fruit, which will last a bit longer.

"Will you be here all day?"

Wiping my forehead against my shoulder, I stop and inspect the near-empty vehicle. "I could probably take a break. You need help with something?"

"Thought you might show me around town. Give me the grand tour."

Dusting my hands off, I decide they've got enough kids, and the vans are almost empty. "Technically, I'm still on vacation, but I know this is a busy day for them. Figured I'd come and help out."

"You're a real do-gooder."

"You make it sound like a bad thing." I grab a paper napkin off the lunch table and wave to the pastor's wife to let her know I'm leaving. "You don't have to be a do-gooder to help out in your community. You just have to care."

"Don't know a lot of guys your age with the time or the inclination is all."

"Technically, it's my job." I wipe the sweat from my face and toss the paper in the trash. "And I spent enough time doing bad. Let's say I'm trying to balance the scales."

"Tell me something bad you've done." He stops at my car, but I wave for him to follow me.

"We don't have to drive. The town was designed to be walkable." I point past the storefronts lining the grassy, rectangular park. "The courthouse and the church anchor the main square, and the neighborhoods form an arch behind them."

"Very French."

"It's not a wheel, but it's similar."

We take off in the direction of the oldest neighborhood in town, where my family has always lived. It's directly behind the courthouse, which stands at the west end of the square facing east, towards the ocean.

Crepe myrtle trees line the sidewalks, along with black, wrought-iron street lights. The trees are tall with thick trunks, and it's clear they've been around a while. In the autumn, the afternoon sunlight is more golden, and I realize as beautiful as Moloka'i is, I like living in Eureka.

"My great-grandparents on both sides were town founders. The distillery was my grandfather's hobby, and when he died, Alex took it over and turned it into what it is today."

"Stone Cold." He nods, lighting the cigar. "Did that have something to do with your troubled past?"

"Nah, Alex was still in California when I was fucking up." We're walking in the direction of my parents' large house. "When my dad died, I didn't practice 'healthy coping strategies' to quote our family therapist, and our mom wasn't emotionally prepared to deal with me."

"Understandable."

"This is where I grew up." I gesture to my mom's house.

It's a sprawling white farmhouse surrounded by flowering bushes and trees. An ancient live oak with thick branches reaching all the way to the ground is where we took all our prom, homecoming, you-name-it photos growing up.

A bright red hibiscus bush brought all the way from Hawaii grows at one corner of the wraparound porch. Palmettos and

Yucca plants grow in front of the lattice covering the crawl space beneath the porch, and the scent of sweet olive laces the air.

"So what, you spray-painted houses? Tipped cows? Stole cars?"

Wincing, I look down at my feet as we continue walking, following the road further away from the town center.

"It was mostly alcohol and drugs. The problem is, when you mix the two, you don't always make good choices, and I made a lot of bad choices." We're approaching another large house; this one is more of an antebellum style with a porch clearly added later. "This is Britt's mom's home."

That gets his attention. "Gwen Bailey? She was married to the escape artist who died."

"Lars," I answer. "My dad worked that case for years. He never felt right about it, and Gwen was determined he didn't take it seriously. It caused a lot of bad blood between our families."

"Why wouldn't your father have taken it seriously?"

"Dad was never a fan of Lars's stunts, and Gwen thought he blamed Lars for what happened." I think about our family history. "He almost resigned when Edna was elected mayor."

"But he changed his mind?" He says it like he already knows the story.

"Yeah."

I watch as he walks up the drive, studying the exterior of Gwen's house. Unlike my mom, Gwen cultivates roses, and several large bushes grow around the perimeter. The scent is distinct and unusual—just like everything Gwen does.

"Did she always live alone after her husband died?"

"As far as I can remember—other than Britt, of course."

He walks a short distance up the driveway, inspecting the crawl space beneath the porch. "How long has she been here?"

My eyebrow arches. "You think Gwen might know something?"

He straightens and looks up at the two chimneys on each side of the structure. "I was just thinking, a widow with a little girl and a big house. Maybe somebody stayed with her at some point."

"We can ask her if you'd like. She's probably at the Star Parlor, but she's always down for a good mystery."

"I'll talk to her when I get back to town." He returns to where I'm waiting on the sidewalk.

"What's that little house down there?" He nods to one of the smallest homes in this older part of town.

I know the place well, although I'm not sure it's considered part of the neighborhood. For a long time it sat empty, and I think it was once a carriage house back in the day.

"That's Martha Jackson's place. It's where Piper grew up."

"Has Martha always lived there?" One of his eyes narrows like he's winking at me, and I realize it's a twitch he tries to hide behind the cigar smoke.

"No, they moved here when we were kids, and Cass came a year later with her mom." I remember those days so well. "Crystal didn't last the summer, but they were all good friends until she left."

"They?"

"Gwen, Martha, and Crystal." I don't know why I never realized the three mothers were close before their daughters were.

"Did they live together?"

"Cass's mom stayed with her sister Charlotte on the other side of town."

He nods, continuing in the direction of Martha's old place. "So Crystal had family here, but Martha didn't?"

"She had Gwen." I shrug. "When you're a kid, you don't think much about your friends' parents. They're part of the scenery, the constants."

Using that word reminds me of my last talk with Sheila. Piper and I clicked from the first day we met, and I would think about her even when we were apart. *She's your constant…*

"You don't seem to know much about them when you grow up either."

"Sorry?" His question pulls me out of my memory of Sheila.

"You don't seem to know the people right here in front of you."

Catching him by the shoulder, I need to stop this déjà vu loop. "I know Martha, but she's always kept to herself. She doesn't like being questioned about her life."

"Sounds like her daughter got it honest."

"Piper's not Martha." Although I can't argue with him—there is a similarity there. "We can walk to the paper office and ask her about it if you want."

"Why does she live in a shack in this nice part of town? It's like she's hiding."

"She'd probably say she is."

"She would?" Marshall's getting excited, and I hate to burst his bubble.

"Martha's a prepper, or a *survivalist* as she calls it."

His bushy brows lower. "One of those people who believe the world's about to end?"

"Yep, and while that house doesn't look like much, you should see her cellar." I remember all the times we sneaked underground to marvel at her doomsday stockpile. "She's been working on it since they moved here. It has rifles, a crank radio, walkie-talkies, hydroponic gardens, sun lamps, and enough food and fuel to last, hell, probably a year."

He doesn't move for several seconds, studying the cedar-plank structure hidden behind pine trees and scrub brush. "A whole year?"

"I'm just guessing, but probably." We continue walking, following the circle that will take us back to town by way of the newspaper office.

"A survivalist..." Marshall scratches his chin, and I can't tell if he's confused or impressed.

I've always thought it was impressive, but Piper always hated her mom's obsession when we were growing up.

"It's kind of embarrassing to Piper, so maybe don't ask too

many questions. Martha is more interested in talking about it than Piper is."

"Isn't that always the way?" His chuckle morphs into a cough, and he finishes off his cigar. "The kooks always want to tell you all their wild ideas."

"You know those things will kill you." I nod towards the stogie in his hand.

"Eh, being alive will kill you."

I can't really argue with him. We're approaching the *Gazette* office, and Piper's small house sits in the bushes behind it. "You recognize this place?"

"Toilet through the roof." He nods.

"It was the original newspaper publisher's home, built back in 1922, just before the *Gazette* was founded."

"It's in pretty good shape to be so old—and in this climate."

"It's on the historical register."

Ryan was just starting kindergarten when I helped her move here. It was the summer I came back from the Navy, and I had one objective—proving to Piper I'd changed. For so long, nothing I did seemed to matter, and now this weekend, it feels like everything has happened so fast.

Have her tell you straight-out why you can't be together... Shelia's words haunt my mind. I haven't asked her, and we're still not together. Even with all our stolen moments and hot-as-fuck sex, she's still holding back. She's still hiding something. She said after the wedding, but will it change then? Or is this my last week in Eureka?

"Thanks for the tour." Marshall touches his head like a salute.

"You're not coming inside?"

"I think I got what I need. Maybe you should do the same."

Again, I can't argue. "Let me know if you think of anything else."

When I enter the office, Jemima hops up and walks to the

counter to meet me. "Hiya, handsome. Got some breaking news?"

Today her blonde hair is twisted up in a bun, and her bangs rest on her thick, black eyelashes. She's still doing the Taylor Swift thing, but I hold back on the teasing.

"Does the wedding tomorrow count?"

"Everybody knows that's coming." Leaning forward on the counter, she drops her voice, looking side to side. "I've got a feeling something's coming with Drake Redford. He hasn't done anything since he pulled that dog-for-mayor stunt, and he's a total disrupter."

"The dog-for-mayor stunt was only last week." Piper breezes up beside her, placing a stack of papers on the counter.

The sound of her voice perks up my insides. I haven't seen her since I left her in bed this morning, tangled in my sheets with her red hair spilling over my pillow. Now she's all business in a black turtleneck with that pretty hair in a high ponytail. Her eyes are more amber than green today, and when she looks up at me, I want to pull her to my chest and kiss her.

Walking around with Marshall, it really hit me how difficult growing up with Martha must've been. I was so wrapped up in losing my dad and all my shit, it didn't occur to me she was doing her best to have a normal life, while her mom was doing her best to stockpile for the end of the world.

I guess in her own way, Martha was being a good mom, thinking she was protecting her daughter. Maybe if I'd paid better attention, things might be different? Is it possible Rex gave her the security she needed?

She must've been afraid to find out she was pregnant at twenty. Alone with no job and a crazy mom, I understand why she needed stability, someone to trust. I'm pretty sure I spent the entire nine months of her pregnancy high. Shit, I want to kick my own ass right about now. No wonder it took her five years to give me a second chance.

Watching her working hard, doing what she does

best—surviving, making a life for her son, doing the impossible, publishing a newspaper *today*?

I don't just want to be the guy who has always loved her. I want to be the man who lifts her up when she's tired of being strong. I want to be the rock holding her steady in the storm.

The door behind me opens, and Jemima straightens, blue eyes blinking wide as her red-velvet smile. "Hey there, welcome to the *Gazette*."

"Hey…" A hesitant male voice answers behind me, and I know who it is.

Turning, I frown, reaching out to shake his hand. "Hey, Raif, what's up?"

Piper stops what she's doing and walks over as well. The Jones brothers don't just show up in town without a reason, and they definitely don't go to places like the newspaper office or the courthouse or, God forbid, church.

"Did something happen?" Piper's voice is all business.

"Ah, no." He exhales a laugh, looking down at his beat-up tan work boots.

He's wearing a white tee and jeans, but he's pulled a plaid shirt over the top, covering the tattoos on his arms. His long hair is brushed, and he seems to have made an effort to look nice.

"Obviously, he has breaking news." Jemima has a grin on her face.

"The breaking news is me." Raif winks up at her, and I never noticed he had a dimple in his cheek.

"It certainly is." Jemima is not shy. "Has anyone ever told you you look like a young James Dean?"

"Young James Dean is the only one we had," Piper mutters under her breath, moving her starstruck assistant to the side. "Have you done something, Raif? Need to report anything?"

"Not yet, but I'm planning on starting a business, and I want to let people know about it." He straightens, smacking the counter. "Want to do a story?"

"Is this about the wild hogs?" Jemima's getting excited. "I'll interview you. I think it sounds like a great idea. All those rich people in Kiawah and Hilton Head are all about their free-range meats. Let's give it to them."

"That's what I thought."

Piper looks from him to her to me. I lift my eyebrows, and she nods. "Okay, see what you can do with it. If it's any good, I'll put it in the Sunday edition."

Jemima grabs her phone, walking around the counter to take his arm. "Right this way—we can talk in the conference room."

He goes with her to the smaller office beside Piper's. He looks at her in a way I recognize all too well. His lips curl into a smile, and he looks at her like he's seeing his future.

"How do you feel about the name Outlaw Pork?" she asks, closing the door.

"I like your red lipstick," is the last thing we hear him say.

Piper turns to me. "I've created a monster."

"I think she arrived that way. She's kind of a natural at news, though."

"If you call gossip news." Piper shoves a pen behind her ear and looks up at me. "We're scheduling all the stories for Sunday today, and Stew said he'd do the print run on Saturday so we can get the wedding photos in the Sunday edition."

"Smart having the wedding on a Friday."

"It was my idea—before I knew I'd be planning the whole thing as well as covering it for the paper."

"I think no matter what you do, my brother is going to be too infatuated with his bride to worry about it."

I would be if it were Piper.

"Cass will be the same way," she exhales heavily. "I'm probably putting too much pressure on myself to make it perfect."

"You love your friend."

"And tomorrow night's the bachelorette." She leans against the counter. "Are you getting together with the guys? Are y'all planning something crazy?"

"If by crazy you mean sitting around the distillery listening to music and shooting the shit while we drink my brother's expensive bourbon."

"We're meeting at the Star Parlor since Gwen rented Britt's old apartment." Her lips twist. "It'll be our first girls' night with no watermelon margaritas."

"Does this mean we're growing up?" I catch the end of her long ponytail, sliding the soft hair back and forth between my fingers.

"Heaven forbid," she scoffs, and I exhale a laugh. "We still know how to party and have fun—it's just all these babies." Her eyes land on the clock, and she does a little jump. "Shit, and I've got to finish this story."

"I'll pick up the little man." Catching her cheeks gently in my fingers, I lean down to trace a ghost of a kiss across her pink lips.

Her breath catches, and she blinks up at me. Lust is in her eyes, and my dick twitches.

Stepping forward, I put my hands on each side of her on the countertop. "Just think if you hadn't hired that assistant what we might do right now."

She touches my waist, moving closer, and my muscles tense. "If I hadn't hired her, we might not have christened your kitchen bar last night."

A naughty smile is on her lips, and my dick is fully hard. "This office needs some updating. Blackout shades for your office, or curtains at the very least."

"Are you offering to help me with that?"

"Yes, ma'am." I nip the side of her jaw before pushing away and heading to the door. "I'll take care of all your needs."

Chapter 17

Piper

A HUGE SMILE IS ON MY LIPS, AND I NEED A FRESH PAIR OF UNDERWEAR. I don't know how I'm supposed to finish this feature on the new pastor with nothing but dirty thoughts of Adam Stone in my head.

Glancing to the smaller office, I see Jemima sitting in her short skirt with her legs crossed in Raif's direction. He's leaned back in the chair watching her, and I've never seen the town bad boy look completely helpless.

I shake my head and start for my office when the door opens. "Excuse me, I wonder if you might help me."

"Grand Central today," I mutter under my breath, turning to see an older man on the other side of the counter.

He's dressed in pressed jeans and a charcoal blazer over a white shirt. His dark hair is touched with gray, and he's got a scruffy beard on his chin. He could be a wealthy tourist up from one of the beach resorts, possibly searching for the distillery, but when our eyes meet, my skin bristles.

"I can try." My tone is neutral.

"I'm looking for someone." His gaze reminds me of a predatory bird, and I think of a T-Rex chicken—and I hope Adam has Ryan and they're on the way to the house.

"If you'd like to file a missing person's report, the sheriff's office is at the courthouse."

He smiles, but it doesn't reach his cold eyes, which are fixed on me. "I'd rather not involve the authorities. It's a delicate matter."

I don't go to the counter. Instead, I keep a distance between us. "Who are you looking for?"

"Rosie McClure." As he says the name, he studies me, almost like he's looking for any reaction I might have.

I don't recognize the name. "Is it your child? Grandchild?"

"My wife." Again, the flatness in his tone doesn't feel like he's worried.

It feels like he's hunting.

"Did you say Rosie McClure?" Raif walks up to the counter beside me, and I have to do a double-take.

His voice is low and challenging, and he's no longer helpless. He stands up straight, making him taller than I realized. His blue eyes are focused, too, and I realize he can hold his own in a fight. Of course, he can.

It hits me that Raif Jones might be the most dangerous of the Jones boys. Bull is an in-your-face asshole. He's ugly with neck tattoos and a bad attitude, but Raif is polite. He's disarmingly handsome, and sometimes he even approaches sweet.

Right now, he's looking at this stranger like he's ready to kick his ass. His muscles flex against the sleeves of his overshirt, and the muscle in his square jaw moves. To his credit, the stranger squares his stance, preparing to defend himself if necessary.

I'm confused as fuck. "Do you know who he's talking about?"

Raif's eyes don't leave the man's. "It's the second time I've heard that name this week."

"The second time?" The man's voice is quiet surprise. "When was the first?"

Raif ignores his question. "You said she's your wife, so your name's McClure?"

The man's jaw flexes, and I'm concerned by the rising tension in the room. Jemima walks slowly to my side and holds my arm. Her eyes are wide, and she looks from Raif to the man.

Stepping closer slowly, I interject. "I can assure you, sir, no one by that name lives in Eureka. As publisher of this paper, it's my job to know, and unless she's just relocated, she's not here."

He blinks from Raif to Jemima to me, the intensity still in his gaze. Jemima's fingers tighten on my arm, and for the first time in my entire life, I can honestly say I'm glad Raif Jones is here.

"You'd better keep on moving." Raif's voice is almost a growl. "We don't like your kind around here."

"What's your name?" The man's voice is low like a threat.

"Raif Jones." Raif's shoulders seem to broaden, and I guess with a brother like Bull, it's hard to be afraid of anybody.

"Tell me, Raif Jones. Have you ever lost something that belonged to you?"

"Sure, I've lost lots of things, but people don't belong to people."

"I see you've never been in love."

Raif's brow lowers, and he takes a step closer. "That ain't love."

The journalist in me instantly wants to know more about Raif Jones's story, but the man at the counter demands all our attention.

He takes a step back, lifting the fingers of his left hand as if doing a low wave. "I'm sorry to have bothered you."

He turns and leaves as abruptly as he arrived, and the three of us exhale at the same time.

"What the fuck was that?" I turn to them with wide eyes.

"One word…" Jemima sounds almost excited. "*Swoon!*"

"What?" I shake my head. "You did not think—"

She trots over to where Raif is coming down from what I now see was him preparing to fight.

"You liked that guy?" He gives her a quizzical look.

"No, dummy, you! Those were some seriously swoony protector-vibes you were giving off just then. Too bad Adam wasn't here. You could've been like the wonder-twin superhero hotties."

"Where do you think he's going?" My thumbs fly over my phone face as I text Adam.

> Do you have Ryan?

Gray dots float, and his response is quick. It's a picture of the two of them smiling, holding up skateboards and peace signs.

> **Adam:** Headed to the park to get some exercise.

The picture makes me smile. My shoulders relax, knowing my son is safe with him.

> Have fun!

The clock is bearing down on me, and I decide a weird man asking about a woman I've never heard of isn't my problem. My problem is getting the Sunday edition to bed before I have to lock into wedding mode.

"I'll take care of that guy," Raif mutters. "Don't worry."

"What about Protector Pork instead of Outlaw?" Jemima's still flirting, and he glances back, giving her his old, reluctant smile.

"You're the expert." He swings his hand up and points at her like a gun. "I'll see you around, Princess."

"I'm no princess," she teases.

"Good thing, because I'm no prince."

"Having the time of your life!" Britt, Cass, and I sing at the top of our lungs, and I'm dancing on the couch with a cup of virgin watermelon margarita in my hand.

Except I'm the only dancing queen. Britt sits on the gold velvet sofa in the Star Parlor with her cup balanced on her baby bump, wearing a headband that reads "Let's Go Girls."

I have the "Drunk AF" headband *again*, and this time Cass is wearing the "Same Penis Forever" sash across her chest.

"I'd call that headband false advertising," Britt's bare feet are propped on the small coffee table in front of the fireplace. "None of us are drunk as fuck, and it sucks."

"Don't rain on my bachelorette party!" Cass sifts through the rotating box of supplies. "Too bad they only gave us one bumper sticker."

She's also wearing the *Bride* headband and the necklace that reads *Engaged AF*.

"I nearly lost it when I saw that 'I pooped today' bumper sticker on the back of Alex's car!" Britt cries, and I almost shoot my sip of margarita through my nose.

"You guys are so crazy!" I laugh, and I wonder if it's possible to get drunk on virgin margaritas. "Who knew Alex Stone, Mr. Uptight Billionaire, had a sense of humor?"

"He's got a lot more than that." Cass waggles her eyebrows, and her lips curl into a naughty grin.

"Why do I feel like I'm hearing things I shouldn't know now that I'm his sister?" Britt frowns, scratching her stomach like a peasant. "It's like ew, nobody wants to know that about their brother."

"You're not his real sister." Cass gives her shoulder a shove, but I'm less inclined to pursue the matter.

I've been dodging questions from them about shacking up with Adam all week, and I'm not sure Cass's bachelorette part is the right time to spill my guts. It feels like stealing the spotlight.

"What are those guys doing tonight?" I ask, hoping to change the direction of the conversation.

"It's like second verse, same as the first," Britt answers. "They're all at the distillery."

"Should we have done something more exciting?" I bite the side of my thumb feeling like the worst party planner ever. "Did y'all want to go to New Orleans or to the beach or something?"

"In my condition?" Britt points both hands at her pregnant

belly. "I'm not getting into a bathing suit, and I wouldn't have any fun in New Orleans."

"Yeah, I'm fine being vanilla." Cass snuggles in beside me, holding up three penis straws. "This was the photo that sent Alex over the edge."

She drops the three straws into our glasses and pulls out her phone. "Now, take a sip, you two. It's Adam's turn to get a boner for Piper."

"I'm sure his brothers will love that," I deadpan, but it's all an act.

My lady bits tingle at the memory of Adam's response to that blow job a few days ago and everything that came after it.

"Suck it, Piper!" Britt orders, and I snort a laugh.

"Rude!" Still I lean forward, puckering my lips around the tip of the penis straw beside Britt who's doing the same.

Cass leans forward to do the same as she holds up her phone to snap the selfie. Then, with a few taps of her fingers, she sends it to Alex, I guess. It doesn't take long before all of our phones light up with the photo.

"You started a group text!" Britt claps.

"We'll all be related once Adam and Piper stop dancing around the truth." Cass scoops up the remote. "What's our movie for tonight? *Practical Magic* in honor of Halloween?"

"You're the bride, so you get to choose." Britt rests her head on Cass's shoulder. "I expect I'll fall asleep in five minutes anyway. All I want to do is sleep now that I'm not barfing anymore."

"You are not sleeping through my bachelorette!" Cass lifts her shoulder, giving her a nudge. "You already dumped all the planning on poor Piper."

"I'm not so poor!" Not sure why this makes me feel defensive all of a sudden. "I think the wedding is going to be gorgeous, even if I did plan it."

I still can't believe nothing's blown up yet. Maybe Adam is my good luck charm.

"I'm sure it will be amazing." Cass puts her arm around my shoulder as we watch the opening scene of the movie.

The curse is cast, and as I watch the mother of our main characters fall in love with their dad, my mind drifts to last night with Adam.

When I stopped by Aiden's on my way home, Ryan couldn't stop talking about learning to do a 50/50 on his skateboard.

He had to explain to me a 50/50 is when you do a jump and slide the middle of the board across a flat surface before hitting the ground again.

"Next I'm going to try a 180 and then a 360, and Uncle Adam said it won't be long before I'll be going for the 900 just like Tony Hawk!" He was talking loud and fast like he does when he's excited, and I just laughed and hugged him.

When I got home, I went straight into Adam's arms, hugging him so tightly. It wasn't long before his mouth met mine, and we were fumbling our way to his bedroom. The light was dim, and I managed to keep my top on halfway again.

Even if he does accept my past and respond beautifully, like I dream he will, every time I'm naked, he'll be confronted with the scars on my body.

He'll know I'm damaged, and even if he doesn't want to, he'll either think I'm ugly or he'll pity me. Both scenarios make me cringe so hard, I almost want to forget the whole thing.

Except…

I really do want to be with Adam. I've never feared how starting a relationship might change our friendship. I've only ever feared how the truth might change it.

But if I ever want us to be anything more, I have to overcome that fear.

Drew keeps telling me to give my friends the chance to be my friends for real, and I glance at Britt and Cass snuggled up with their eyes on the flatscreen television.

"Mom says they're like the Fireside Ladies." Britt shoves a handful of popcorn into her mouth. "She got them to put a protective spell over the town against Drake Redford's development plans."

"Maybe it's working," I joke. "I haven't seen him around since Bo announced his candidacy."

She shoves me with her foot. "Are you taunting the spirit world? According to Mom, the spirits revealed the truth about how my dad died."

"I believe it." Cass nods slowly, then her expression morphs to curiosity. "We never did that whole blood sister thing. Why not?"

I've had enough cutting, I think stepping out of the tangle of my best friends' limbs on the couch. I don't say it out loud. Instead, I go to the kitchen to refill our shared bowl of popcorn.

While I wait for the air popper, I walk to the living room to watch Sandra Bullock hiding under the covers as her little girls try to comfort her, as her sister returns to her side.

Cass and Britt lean against each other sniffing as the tragedy plays out onscreen. Only, it's not over, of course. It's only getting started.

"I think the point of this movie is that sisters can save you from dying of a broken heart." Cass's voice is wobbly.

"Speaking of sisters, what's Jemima up to tonight?" I do my best to keep the annoyance out of my tone.

"Is she making you nervous?" Britt slants an eye up at me. "Worried she'll try and steal your man?"

"Oh, she's not interested in Adam." Cass exhales heavily. "As if her life wasn't bad enough, she's obsessed with Raif Jones. She keeps saying he's her James Dean daydream and singing about how they'll never go out of style. The delinquent from the worst family in town is her new crush."

"I wouldn't be so quick to write him off." I think about how he acted in the newspaper office, and I think about what I know. "Sometimes the good guys aren't who they seem to be, so maybe it's true of the so-called bad guys as well."

"Okay, Miss Ecumenical."

The popcorn is done, and I refill our glasses. We all sit and watch as Nicole Kidman makes bad choices and ends up with the abusive Jimmy. My stomach tightens, and I start to feel hot around the neck as they struggle in his car.

The more they fight, the sicker I get, and I don't know why I'm reacting this way. I've watched this movie before. Still, my breath is shallow, and I'm having a hard time keeping my eyes on the screen. The room grows smaller, and my throat grows tighter.

Maybe it's because I've been talking about it so much to Drew. Maybe I've dug all those skeletons out of the hard dirt where I packed them away so long ago.

Or maybe it's because I'm so close to telling Adam, and decades of anxiety are rushing to the surface.

"I hate this part." Britt puts her hands over her face, and Cass hugs her.

Jimmy pulls out the lighter to brand Gillian, and invisible fingernails claw at my throat. I struggle against the phantom sensations, doing my best to regain control, to be cool. But as the fighting onscreen grows more intense, the pain in my temples becomes unbearable.

I have to get up and walk. It's too much…

"Did you like the way he looked at you?" Rex's rough voice cracks like his lips.

His eyes are glazed, and I know he's done something, meth or coke or alcohol or all three. His dark hair slips over his dark eyes, and I can see it's going to be one of those nights.

"Did you want to fuck him?"

"No!" My voice shakes, and the word comes out as more of a strangled gasp. "I only want you."

At that point in our relationship, it was a total lie, but I had to tell it. I had to be convincing.

Tonight, I'm failing.

My stomach muscles tense. My whole body is tight, and I try to pull away from him, to make myself small so I can slip out of his grasp and run away.

It's my recurring dream, running away, being free.

"You are mine." His fingers wrap around my upper arm, and he shoves me against the wall. "You can never leave me, because if you do, what will happen?"

His hand is under my shirt, and the tears coat my cheeks. Little whimpers escape my throat on every breath.

Swallowing my fear, I summon my calm. I want him to stop, not do it tonight. "They'll know I'm yours because you marked me."

"I don't think it's enough for them to see." His hand moves from my arm to my face, grabbing my jaw and slamming my head against the wall. "I think it's time to put it where they'll see it. When they try to touch what's mine."

His hand goes between my legs, and I cry out. But nothing will stop him when he's determined to hurt me.

I'd made some inadvertent look, some errant gaze I don't even remember.

My eyes had lingered too long on a boy at the beach or I'd automatically smiled in response to a greeting, and now I was going to pay for it.

First the pain would come.

Then, he'd see the blood.

Then he'd be overcome with guilt and want to kiss me. He'd want to fuck me, and if I didn't want to touch him, it would start again.

Over and over…

"You okay, Piper?" Cass's voice pulls me out of the darkness.

Exhaling a loud, shaky laugh, I look down to see my feet are on the couch, and I've wrapped my arms around my knees. My cheeks are wet with tears.

In my mind, I left the movie and the loft far, far away and that old, dead demon had resurrected to torment me.

Only I wasn't fighting. I was cowering. As usual.

My whole body trembles, and I drop my feet to the floor. My brain searches frantically for a joke, something to deflect the fact they've caught me in my memories, but for some reason, this time, I can't laugh away the trauma.

Instead, I leave the ornate room and dash out the door on my bare feet. Looking both ways before I cross the empty street, I run to where the vacant gazebo sits, lit by tiny white twinkle lights in the darkness.

A noise behind me tells me I'm not alone. Cass is running to catch up to me, and Britt isn't far behind her, although she can't move as fast.

"Slow down, I'm coming," Britt calls.

I stagger into the small, round space, wrapping my arms over my waist and pacing, struggling to calm my breath, to regain control, to push this past back into the box where I kept it far from the light. Far from where it could hurt me.

"Shh…" Cass wraps her arms around my shoulders, rubbing up and down. "We're here."

Britt waddles up the steps, and the two of them surround me. I'm holding onto myself, and they're holding onto me.

I'm like the little boy with his finger in the dam. If I pull it out, the entire ocean will come crashing in and drown us.

Only, for the first time, I wonder if it might be the reverse. If I might actually be on the other side of the dam, drowning in the ocean while I hold the water in.

Cass puts her chin on my shoulder, and Britt traces her finger along my temple, moving a curl off my face. She hands me a tissue, and I blot my cheeks, my eyes.

"Is this about Adam?" Cass's voice is quiet. "Did he do something? Or not do something?"

"God, no." I shake my head. "He's been nothing but patient and wonderful and good."

He's so good.

He doesn't push. He doesn't ask questions.

He takes what I'll give him, and then he holds me. God, I love how he holds me like I'm the most cherished thing in his world. Like he'd fight all the demons in hell for me.

"What is it then?" Britt's voice is soft. "This is serious."

The truth presses like a cannonball in my chest ready to explode, and Drew's words are in my brain on repeat. *Let them be your friends… Let them be there for you…*

My chin drops, and the fear is so strong, but this time, the pressure of the truth is stronger. "I've never told this to anyone."

"Maybe we should have a seat then." Cass guides us to the wooden bench lining the inside of the gazebo.

Two sets of hands grasp mine, and two sets of concerned eyes hold mine. My eyes lower, and I force myself to say the words I've never said outside of Drew's therapy office.

"Rex… When we were together… He…" Pausing, I inhale calm. "He hurt me. A lot. All the time." The shame tries to bubble up in my throat, to steal my voice, but I swallow it down again. "He would take drugs and drink, and he would get jealous of other guys looking at me or me looking at them. He would fly into a rage, and he would cut me or burn me. He said it was to mark me as his. He said it was to show them I belonged to him, and I could never leave him."

The words spill out of my lips like the water draining out of that hole in the ocean. They diffuse the pressure in my chest, and I realize how long I've needed to let this darkness out of me.

Tears rim my friends' eyes. Britt hiccups a breath, putting her hand over her mouth, and Cass holds my hand tighter in hers.

"How long…" Britt starts. "Was it the whole time?"

Shaking my head, I look out at the purple neon sign of the Star Parlor across the street, from where we came. "It started after high school, when I went to college and he didn't. He got deeper into drugs, and he became someone I didn't know."

"Oh, honey." Cass puts her head on my shoulder. "I wish we'd known. Maybe we could've helped you…"

"I was so embarrassed." My chin drops. "Then I thought I could handle it. I knew him, right? We'd grown up together. I could make it stop." Quiet creeps into my tone. "Then when I realized I couldn't, I was afraid I'd waited too long to say something. When I tried to fight him, he'd tell me, 'See? You're just like I am.' He'd say he was going to tell people I hit him, too… And all I could think was what if they believed him?"

"We would've believed you." Britt's voice is quiet, and she wraps her arms on top of Cass's. "We know you."

"The night I found out I was pregnant, I was so hopeless. I knew I'd never get away from him." It's quiet as I finish the story. "I stood in that bathroom, looking at that pink plus sign, and I begged to be free of him. I begged with all my heart, from the bottom of my soul…" Lifting my eyes, I gaze at the millions of actual stars overhead, and I wonder who answered that desperate cry for help. "It was the night he died."

No one speaks. Two sets of arms hold me, and I realize we're rocking slightly, side to side. I realize the cannonball is gone, and I don't feel like my chest is about to explode. The ocean has drained away, and I'm no longer drowning.

I've spoken my truth to the two people I should've trusted so long ago, and they're still here, holding me together, sharing my pain. Lifting my hands, I hold their arms.

"I just want to be normal. I want to be beautiful like the both of you. I don't want to be scarred and…" I swallow the tears, "ugly."

"You are so beautiful." Britt gently strokes my hair back. "Can you really not see that?"

"No."

Cass lifts her chin. "I've still got connections in the beauty industry. I'll ask about scar revision and what's new. You don't have to see them forever."

Nodding, I blink down, and fresh tears are on my cheeks. "I've made peace with them. They show me I'm strong, and I can survive. But I don't know what someone else will see."

"They'll see a beautiful, strong woman who lived through hell and came out alive."

"Maybe… maybe not." I let the tears fall.

"Oh, honey." Britt hugs me closer. "The right man will love you no matter what. I'm proof of that."

"Yes…" I take the tissue and blot my face. "You have these wonderful men who would give their lives for you. Mine only wanted to hurt me. What's wrong with me?"

"Nothing." Britt tilts her head to the side. "I know a man who would give his life for you. A man who already thinks you're the most beautiful thing on the planet. And he's been to a lot of beautiful places."

Beautiful places… That night in bed when we'd talked about Moloka'i and all the beautiful things he'd seen. *Everything beautiful in the world reminds me of you.*

A smile tugs at my lips, and I can't believe I can smile. "Adam."

"Does he know?" Concern lines Cass's face.

Shaking my head, I twist my fingers. "I don't know how he's going to take it. Rex was his best friend. They were like brothers. If he doesn't—"

"Adam will believe you." Britt is emphatic. "He's in love with you. He has been for so long."

"I'm so afraid of what he'll say." Lowering my chin, I rub my forehead. "What if he doesn't? What if he can't?"

"He can." Cass threads her fingers in mine. "He knows you as well as we do, and if I'm wrong, we're always here for you."

"Thank you for telling us." Britt looks up at me, and my vision blurs with tears.

We're all crying now, but this time it's tears of freedom. My friends' arms surround me, and I look up again at the multitude of stars, as gratitude squeezes my heart. I've made the first step.

I have to believe I can make the next one.

Chapter 18

Adam

"WHAT'S GOING ON WITH YOU AND PIPER?" IT'S THE NIGHT before the wedding, and Aiden is beside me at the bar in Stone Cold. "Don't think I haven't noticed you two eye-fucking each other all week at the house."

The bar is closed, and I've cued up songs on the jukebox. I'm not feeling the 1990s surfer vibes as much as I was a few months ago, when we were celebrating Aiden and Britt's upcoming nuptials.

Tonight, I'm feeling more of the angst. It's a Billy Joel, Bob Dylan, Tyler the Creator kind of night "Don't Think Twice, It's All Right" as opposed to "All the Small Things."

Alex is across from us pouring drinks. "You finally got out of the fucking friend zone? How many times did I tell you not to make friends with the woman you love?"

"Yeah, that sounds like good advice." My brother Alex is trying to act like he didn't pine after Cass for years before finally making a move. "Should you be the bartender at your own bachelor party?"

"I don't mind." We're right back where we were two months ago, and so much has changed. "I thought you went to Moloka'i for a fresh start?"

"I did." I lift the tumbler, and the three of us clink glasses before drinking the amber liquid. It's smoky and smooth with hints of vanilla and roasted nuts. "Then I came home, and she was in my bed."

"You're welcome." Aiden clinks my tumbler with his. "Britt tried to put her everywhere but there."

"You never slept with her before this week?" Alex's eyebrow arches. "And you're giving me shit for building this brand, busting my ass to make a million by the time I was thirty, before getting with Cass?"

"I wasn't sitting around doing nothing." I look at my tumbler, not wanting to give too much away. "We weren't strictly platonic, but no, we never went all the way until I came back."

"Leaving was a smart move." Aiden slides his glass across the polished wood. "It helped her see her feelings more clearly."

"Speaking from personal experience?"

"Yes." He nods, watching as Alex refills his cup. "I had to lose Britt to get my head out of my ass, and I'm not ashamed to admit it."

"I'm really proud of you, bro." I can't resist teasing him. "You've really evolved out of that caveman persona."

"Alex was right, though. You messed up sliding into the friend zone."

"Like I had a choice. We *were* friends. We've been friends since middle school. She was with Rex."

"Best friends are the worst," Alex laughs. "Especially when they beat you to the shot."

I don't want to dwell on the past, so I jump us back to the present. "How's Pinky handling Mamma Cass being out of the house tonight?"

"She's fine now that AJ is staying with us, who we are *not* calling aunt."

"Holy shit…" I almost shoot bourbon through my nose. "I didn't even think of that."

"To be honest, I didn't either, but Cass was prepared."

My head drops forward, and I scrub my fingers over my eyes. "How did Crystal not see that coming when she named her daughter Jemima?"

"Funny you should say that. I asked Cass the same thing." Alex pours us another finger of bourbon. "Apparently, her sister is named after their great-grandmother, and according to Cass, it's a biblical name that means peace or beauty or something."

"She could stick with Aunt Taylor," Aiden jokes.

"That was her first choice." Alex lifts his tumbler and clinks it to ours. "Jemima says she wants to move away from that persona. It's all very suspicious."

Our phones all ping at the same time, and he sets his glass down to check the message. We all check it, and my throat catches when I see the photo of Britt, Cass, and Piper with penis straws in their mouths.

"Damn, those girls," Aiden laughs, and Alex gives him a high-five.

"Put a ring on it."

I'm not feeling as confident as they are. I have too many recent memories to accompany this image, and I'm still not inside the gates enough to be high-fiving my brothers.

"So what's the holdup?" Aiden seems to be reading my mind.

"She's still holding back." I polish off my drink. "If there were anything more I could do, I'd do it."

It's not entirely true. I still haven't taken Sheila's advice and put it to her directly. I've been enjoying the orgasms a little too much to get confrontational, but we're running out of time.

"Is she worried it'll ruin your friendship?" Alex gives me a cocky grin, and I kind of liked him better before Cass, when he was all broody and miserable.

Now he's just a little too full of himself.

"I'm pretty sure she knows nothing could ruin our friendship."

"Just get a ring and fucking get down on your knee." Aiden whips out the impatient, know-it-all big-brother attitude. "If she says no, then you've got your answer, and you can move on, go back to Moloka'i or whatever."

"Break Mom's heart." Alex chuckles, and I shake my head.

As much as I hate to admit it, my brothers are right. We've reached the point where it's either piss or get off the pot. "I plan to."

We didn't say much last night when she got home from seeing Ryan. We had a late dinner, then I took her to bed. We weren't as frantic or angry. It was nice and easy—still in the dark, still only allowing me to see so much, but she said again how we need to talk once the wedding is over.

It's as if everything is on pause until after this damn wedding, but as soon as we send Alex and Cass riding off into the sunset, I'll be ready to find out exactly where we stand.

"Hey, turn that up—it's our song." Alex reaches for the remote above the bar and cranks the volume on "Mr. Brightside."

"That's not your song. Your song is 'Margaret,' 'cause when you know, you know."

A funny smile curves his lips, and he reaches for the special reserve. "It's true, and you know what? You know, and Piper knows, too."

It's late when we finally call it a night. The girls are all sleeping together at Gwen's place, on a mattress on the floor according to another photo from Britt. I see my girl surrounded by the two people she loves most in the world, and my heart warms.

I want to be the one to make her happy, but above all, I want her to *be* happy.

The distillery is about a half mile outside of town, nestled on twenty acres of grassy fields all belonging to our family. Ocean breezes mix with woody straw as the wind pushes cooler air down from the north. The humidity has thinned out. The rain is gone, and a sky full of stars is over our heads.

"It's really peaceful here." We're walking to our vehicles.

"Which is why no one's building a resort and fucking it up," Alex grumbles.

Drake Redford is itching to turn these green fields into green dollar bills to line his pockets and destroy our bucolic small town in the process.

Aiden grips my shoulder as we pause beside his truck. "Spend the night at our place. Ryan's been sleeping in the queen bed in the guest room. There's plenty of room for you there."

"I don't want to crowd him." I rub my fingers over my eyes, sick of being so close and still feeling like an outsider. "I'll just go to my place."

"If you think that little boy doesn't think of you as his dad, you really are dumb."

"Hey, don't spare my feelings," I joke.

"Night, bros." Alex cruises past us on the way to his car. "This time tomorrow, I'll be a married man."

"A married man on a diet," Aiden laughs, and I frown.

"What's that supposed to mean..." The question dies on his lips, and we see the bright orange bumper sticker on the back of Alex's Tesla that reads *Don't park too close. I'm chunky*.

"That girl." Alex's response is somewhere between a laugh and a sigh, and I can't help thinking *Damn, he's got it bad*.

He waves, climbing into his car, and I turn to my brother. "Yeah, I'll do it. I'll spend the night at your place."

I'm pretty sure I won't get any sleep alone in my bed surrounded by the scent of honeysuckle. It'll only be torture missing her, wishing she would walk through my door.

We drive the short distance to Aiden's, and I head to the guest room while he settles up with the babysitter.

Inside, I find Ryan splayed out in the center of the bed like a starfish. Fudge is nestled beside his leg like a dark little guard, and I chuckle, shaking my head as I continue to the en suite bathroom.

After splashing some water on my face, I brush my teeth and strip down to my shorts. I grab a T-shirt out of the bureau and gently move my bed partner to his side. He grumbles a bit in his sleep, and Fudge's ears lay back on his head.

"Keep your fur on, I'm not hurting him," I tease, giving the black cat a scrub around the whiskers. "We're going to be a family, so you'd better get used to me."

I decide it's one of those affirmations, and I crawl under the sheets, pulling the blanket over my shoulder before turning to the opposite side.

As I start to drift, Ryan starts to little-boy snore. It's not too loud, and mostly sounds like a stuffy nose. It reminds me of when he was a baby, and I remember Piper sending me the videos.

My heart expands, and it strengthens my resolve. I decide she has to want more if she sent them to me. She never let me miss a milestone.

Pulling out my phone, I roll onto my back and take a selfie of the two of us, then I send it to her with a text.

> Hope you had fun tonight. I'm crashing with our little man.

She doesn't reply, but it's late. Britt sent that photo of them going to bed almost an hour ago, and I expect they're all either asleep or discussing whatever they talk about when they're together.

For several minutes, I lie awake in the darkness thinking about the next few days and what's coming. Nothing she can say will change how I feel about her. I went away, but even on the other side of the globe, I couldn't escape my feelings for her and my desire for what we should be.

It's time to do what everyone said, what I want to do, and I don't need a fucking affirmation. All I need is a yes.

Chapter 19

Piper

I should've known when the alarm didn't go off it was going to be one of my bad luck days.

"Fuck." I jump up from the palette on the floor where Cass and I are butt to butt and hurry to the bathroom.

Britt's on the couch wearing an eye mask and snoring.

When I come out again, Cass is in the kitchen scratching the ponytail on top of her head. "One thing you can say for virgin margaritas, no hangovers on your wedding day."

She pulls the carafe out of the coffee machine and fills it with water while I jump to pull on my jeans. "You can say that again. I felt like shit at Britt's wedding."

Thinking about that night, I remember sitting at the bar with Adam while he poured me Stone Cold's special reserve, and we complained about the "Cupid Shuffle." It feels like ages ago, but it was only a few months.

"What can I do to help?" She turns, crossing her arms over her chest while the coffee pot gurgles behind her.

"Just show up." I return to the bathroom to brush my teeth. "It's your wedding. You're only supposed to be pampered and have a good time today."

"You've got the florist all set?"

"I'm heading over to meet them now." I spit and straighten, twisting my red hair into a bun on top of my head.

"Did you decide on a DJ or a live band?"

"It's a surprise." I kiss her cheek, and she catches my arm, pulling me back for a hug.

"You're one of the best people I know, Piper Jackson. What happened in the past does not define you. Nothing he did can take away from who you are."

I exhale, pausing in my haste to hug her back. "Thanks, Cass."

"It hurts so much to know you were going through that all alone." I straighten to see her gray-blue eyes are liquid.

Tugging her ponytail, I tease. "Is this you being an empath or are you pregnant now, too?"

"I don't know." She laughs, dabbing her eyes with her fingertips. "What I do know is you deserve every good thing that's coming your way, and everyone who knows you and loves you will believe you and support you."

"Thanks, babe." I step forward for one more brief hug. "Now I've got to get to the distillery."

She puts a travel mug of coffee in my hand, and I dash out to where Adam's old Jetta is waiting. He loaned it to me yesterday when Aiden picked him up for the bachelor party.

Also on my phone when I opened my eyes this morning was a text from him along with a photo that melted my heart. He was in the bed, looking back over his shoulder, and Ryan was passed out with Fudge curled up at his side, that funny cat with his yellow eyes watching over them.

Our little man... My chest squeezes at the words, at the two of them together. They're my whole world wrapped in a blanket, and I want it so much.

Tapping back quickly, I reply.

> Hope you were able to sleep. He expands to fill the space he's given.

I add a laughing emoji and toss the phone onto the passenger's seat before pulling out to make the short drive to the distillery.

It's located a few miles outside of town, down a lonely, two-lane road. I think about what happened to Britt on this road as I cover the distance, and the strange man who showed up at the newspaper office returns to my mind. Something about him felt familiar, like a dark shadow from a dream or a memory too distant to recall.

I have the strangest urge to talk to my mom about him, to see if she knows anything or maybe recognizes the woman's name. Perhaps it's nothing more than his persistent manner and Raif's overprotective response, but even if the person he's searching for isn't in Eureka, I'm curious about who she is and why she left him.

It's probably just my nose for news—or Jemima's rubbing off on me with all her gossipy questions. One thing's for sure, I wouldn't want to meet him in a dark alley alone. His creepy eyes and creepy manner twist my stomach, and I wonder if Raif is right. I wonder if he's not gone, which makes me further wonder what the heck Raif plans to do about it.

Deciding it's not my business, I put away all thoughts of staring bird-eyes and focus on the wedding and happier things. Not the alarm bells ringing quietly in the back of my mind.

***

The distillery rises before me, a set of dark wooden buildings in the middle of an open field, and I pull the Jetta into the empty space next to Alex's reserved parking spot.

Two large vans are waiting, and I hop out, rushing over to

where the men are standing. The biggest one holds an iPad and glares at me impatiently.

"Sorry…" I tap my forehead as he holds the iPad out for me to sign for delivery. "I set my alarm for PM instead of AM, and I didn't even catch it. Have you been waiting long?"

"About five minutes." He doesn't smile, and a bead of sweat slips down the line in my back.

"I'll run inside and unlock the doors to the event space. You can drive around and start unloading back there."

"We know what to do." He's growly, and I'm not sure a five-minute delay warrants this level of annoyance.

The humidity blew away overnight, and it's a clear, blue-sky, cool and sunny fall day. It's the type of day residents in the South dream of, and this guy needs to turn his frown upside down and get in the wedding spirit.

The crunch of tires on gravel is the only warning I get of Alex pulling up in his Tesla. He hops out, and I give him a wave.

"It's like you're sneaking up on us all the time in that thing." I start to tease him when I see the new bumper sticker and quickly add, "Chunky."

A broad smile splits his lips, and he could accurately be described as glowing. "Yeah, I'll get her for that one."

I only laugh. He and Cass have been pranking each other with silly bumper stickers since she started nannying for him over the summer.

It's almost as exciting as the mysterious signs that have been appearing all over town for the last few years. We never know what they'll say, but at least with Alex and Cass, we know who's doing it.

A few cars and a white truck pull into the parking lot, and the extra staff pile out. They'll help set up the round tables and chairs for the guests, the platform for the live band Alex helped me find, and the long tables to hold the chafing dishes and platters of food.

"I'd better get inside." The words are just off my lips, when the florist's van rolls past us, picking up speed. No one is in the driver's seat, and the sliding side door is wide open.

"What the hell?" I turn as it passes.

It's moving faster, and large arrangements of flowers start flying out like grain spilling from a bag. Alex and I are momentarily stunned, watching it blaze across the half-empty parking lot, when all at once a large guy appears, running hard after it.

Sweat traces down his face, and he's yelling, "No, no, NO!"

"Holy shit!" I shove my coffee into Alex's hand and chase after him. "Not the flowers!"

The guy catches up to the side of the van, but when he grabs the driver's side door, it flies open, sending him spinning out across the gravel lot.

I dig my heels in, pumping my legs and doing my best to run faster, but it's too late. The van crashes into the small ditch behind the large Stone Cold sign, and Ficus trees in clay pots crash out onto the curb.

Skidding to a stop, my hands clutch the sides of my hair. My heart pounds so hard in my chest I lean forward to catch my breath, and I'm not sure whether to laugh or cry.

I'm coming down on the side of cry, since it appears half the floral arrangements for the wedding are now smashed to bits in the parking lot or broken on the curb.

"That did not just happen," I groan.

Feet crunch on gravel, and Alex jogs to where I'm standing. "Was that…?"

"All the flowers for your wedding?" I finish his sentence. "God, I hope not."

The big guy is breathing hard, sweat coating his face. "I'm sorry."

He goes to where the van is stuck, climbing inside and attempting to back out of the ravine. The tires only spin, and the original big guy from this morning dashes past us.

"Brett!" He yells in a snarl. "How many times have I told you never to leave the van in neutral?"

My head is light, and I'm pretty sure all the blood has left my face as I walk to where he's standing. "Please tell me you have backup arrangements?"

It's the same guy who glowered at me when I arrived, and he looks at me like I'm a bug he'd like to squash. "What do I look like, a greenhouse?"

"You look like a florist." I'm starting to lose my temper, and he holds up both hands.

Alex is at my side, glaring at the guy and gently touching my arm. "It's okay—I have an idea. Come with me."

Turning to him with panic surging through my chest, I follow him into the distillery. He leads me past the bar, past the kitchen, past rows and rows of barrels, all the way to the back storage area of the building.

"We've got lots of decorations left over from Aiden and Britt's wedding, and last year we decorated for Halloween. Maybe we'll be a little light on flowers, but we can put twinkle lights around the columns and I'm pretty sure I have arches in here somewhere."

"You're not supposed to plan your own wedding!" My voice wobbles, and I'm trying not to cry as I curse my bad luck. This is why I'm not in charge of party planning.

"And vans aren't supposed to fly by and crash into ditches, but that happened." He shrugs, and we start dragging out boxes of fake pine boughs, plastic arches, sparkling ribbons, and so many twinkle lights.

Inside the venue, the catering crew is setting up in the kitchen, and workers are muttering about ghosts and the distillery being haunted.

"The distillery is not haunted." The last thing I need on top of bad luck is a bunch of ghosts.

"The florist guy said he put the van in park," one of the female cater-waiters argues. "Something knocked it into neutral."

"Probably his big ole butt!" Another girl laughs as she carries a chafing dish out to the waiting tables.

She's two steps through the door when she stumbles and falls, sending the silver platters crashing and then sliding across the wooden floors with an ear-splitting, metallic clang.

"That's what you get," a guy mutters as he passes, returning to the kitchen.

I turn wide eyes on Alex. "This isn't happening today."

His brow is lowered as he surveys the scene. "I never considered the place might be haunted, but the old, original structure was here through prohibition. A lot of people were gunned down in those days."

"Why is this the first time I'm hearing about this?" Both hands are on my head, and now I really am freaking out.

"I've only noticed things like flickering lights when I'm alone here at night," he continues, thoughtfully. "I just assumed I was tired or it was old wiring."

"Which is a total fire hazard." I slap my hands against my thighs and go to where the girl is collecting the platters off the floor. "This is just great."

Bending down, I help her pick up the items. Any other time, I'd be intrigued by the possibility of the distillery being haunted. I'd possibly even consider doing a feature story for Halloween.

Not today. Not when I'm tasked with pulling off the most important day of my best friend's life.

"Who plans a wedding in a possibly haunted space on Halloween?" The waiter grumbles as she heads back to the kitchen to wash the serving utensils.

Placing my hand on my forehead, I take a deep breath and pull out my phone. I can't believe what I'm about to do, but I hastily tap out a quick text to Gwen.

> Need you to cast a protective spell over Stone Cold. Lots of random accidents. Alex says could be ghosts.

I hit send, and it only takes a few minutes for her to text back.

Gwen: Alex said that?

> I had to double-check too.

Gwen: Strangely active year. I'll take care of it, then I'll handle our unwelcome guest.

Strangely active year? Unwelcome guest? Uneasiness stretches across my chest, and I wonder if she means the ghost or someone else.

I don't have time to spend wondering. Alex and I return to the storage closet to retrieve more boxes, and I've got to make the most with what we have. The décor will be more *Midsummer Night's Dream* than English Country Garden, but it'll still be magical if I have anything to do with it.

I'm up to my elbows in dusty boxes and coasters when my phone buzzes.

Adam: You good? I'm getting Ryan ready and will be there early if you need anything.

Sitting on my butt on the dusty closet floor, I push my hair off my face and gaze at Adam's text. My good luck charm.

> All good here. Just finishing up. See you soon—thank you!

Adam: I told you not to thank me for taking care of you.

I huff a breath, and a lone tear traces down my dirty cheek. Pushing it away, I shake off the momentary discouragement and drag myself off the floor. I've got this, and after all the shit I've overcome, mischievous ghosts had better get out of my way.

"Drink this." Jemima puts a glass of champagne in my hand while she stands beside Britt, who's arranging my hair. "We're the only ones who can drink, and I think you've earned it after this ridiculous day."

Today, Britt was in charge of Cass, and I took care of all

the rest. Adam took care of Ryan and Owen, and Alex's mom had Pinky. Now we're all in the small dressing room putting the final touches on our glam before it's time to walk out for the ceremony.

"Why was today ridiculous?" Cass frowns, holding up her skirt as she hops over to where I'm in the chair. "I could have a glass of champagne. Nothing's happened for us yet."

"Get that girl a drink!" I hold up my glass. "Everything is fine—we just had a few little hiccups getting started."

She's in her beautiful, dancer-inspired dress, and Britt and I are in matching, sage-green silk and tulle dresses. Britt's is empire waist and strapless, while mine has a V-neck and butterfly sleeves with a deep slit up the front.

"Alex failed to tell us the distillery is haunted." Jemima is in a one-shoulder, floor-length sage green dress that reminds me of a toga or something Julius Caesar's wife would've worn.

Her hair is arranged in a braided updo, and she has long, thin earrings hanging from her ears.

"Haunted!" Cass's eyes widen, and Britt, who's doing her makeup, exhales loudly.

"Be still! You're going to have mascara all over your face."

"Alex didn't say a word about ghosts to me."

"Don't worry." I pat Cass on the shoulder. "We had a meeting of the minds, and no ghost is allowed to break another thing or trip anyone or cause any more mischief."

"Was all of that happening?" Britt's jaw drops.

"I also asked your mom to cast a protective spell, just in case."

She snorts a laugh. "You must've really been scared."

"Not as scared as I was when the florist's van went into the ditch." Peeking out the door, I survey the large space. "I think our backup plan worked out well."

The twinkle lights and pine boughs filled in the gaps left by the missing flowers, and luckily, the workers were able to use the flowers that survived to pull the room together.

"Is that why the parking lot is all messed up behind the sign?" Jemima walks over to where I'm peeking out at the event space. "Oh, no. Guess who just walked in the door?"

Britt and I exchange wide eyes, and she runs over to where we're standing. "Who?"

"Drake Redford just walked in with Harold Waters." Jemima's voice is disappointed. "You don't think they're a couple, do you? Harold is so nice when he's not doing whatever Drake tells him."

"Drake wasn't gay when I dated him, but maybe that was his problem," Cass calls from where she's arranging the line of buttons down the back of her long arms. "Maybe he was in the closet? It certainly would make sense, considering how bad he was in bed."

"Who invited him?" Britt crosses her arms roughly, pacing the small area. "Alex can't stand Drake Redford. They almost came to blows at Pinky's birthday party."

"Don't worry about him." Cass rubs her hands up and down our pregnant friend's arms. "My future husband won't break anything in his precious distillery."

"I hope you're right." Britt looks up at her and her expression melts. "Oh! Are you ready to walk down that aisle and become Mrs. Alex Stone—and more importantly, my sister-in-law?"

"I was born ready!" Cass starts to laugh, and the three of us hug closer.

"Let me in! I want to be a part of this gang." Jemima puts her arms over ours and does her best to hug us.

"Get in here." I pull her closer.

It's the day we've all been waiting for and nothing, not even a crashed florist van or supernatural mischief or uninvited guests is going to bring us down.

Aunt Carol peeks her head in the door. "It's time, girls."

Cass hops over to fetch her bouquet, and we all take our places in line. Adam texted earlier that he and Ryan were here, but Cass wanted us to stay together until after the ceremony.

The four of us join hands for a moment. Cass takes a deep breath, blinking widely, and it's time. Britt leads the three of us, and I wait as she makes her way to the front of the cozy clutch of friends surrounding the old pastor who has joined so many Eurekans in holy matrimony through the years.

Jemima goes next, walking down and taking her place beside our pregnant friend.

Now it's my turn.

"Wait." Cass catches my arm before I step through the door. "Is everything okay? Really?"

Stepping back, I pull her into a hug, giving her what I hope is an encouraging smile. "Yes. We've shined a light on the past and uncovered ghosts in more ways than one, but it's nothing we can't handle. Right?"

Her brow relaxes. "Right. We've got this."

I squeeze her hand. "Are you ready to be a Sadie?"

It's a reference only my Broadway-obsessed bestie would get.

"A married lady?" She smiles. "You bet I am."

Walking down the aisle, with the sun setting outside the windows, I'm delighted by how beautiful having more leaves than flowers can truly be with the right amount of twinkle lights.

The place *is* magical, and I think the naughty ghosts might've been working in Alex's favor. Cass is an empath, after all, and she did assist Gwen for a little while.

Then my eyes land on Adam, and my breath stills. His blue eyes are intense. His dark hair is tied back in a small ponytail, and he's wearing the same gray suit as his brothers. But my entire body tingles with desire.

Beside him, my son is in a little-boy version of the mens' suits and vest, just like Owen. Pinky is in a sage green dress similar to ours, and all of them are watching, waiting for the bride.

Only Adam has his eyes on me, and I feel distinctly, all the way to my bones, that he's been waiting to see me.

When I reach his side, his hand moves to my waist, and

the warmth of his face hovers close to my neck. "You are so beautiful."

Tingles like warm liquid flow down my skin, and the music changes. The Bridal March begins, and everyone stands as Cass emerges from the small dressing room.

She steps out, looking like the supermodel she is, tall, willowy, with long dark hair and dancer poise. I sneak a glance at Alex, and his eyes are fixed on hers like he's seeing his future and he can't wait.

Chapter 20

Adam

"THE WEDDING WAS AS BEAUTIFUL AS OURS," Britt announces from where she sits with Aiden's arm around her shoulders. "Great work, Piper!"

A live band is playing a mix of old and new favorites, and Alex and Cass are on the dance floor surrounded by several of the older guests dancing to the instrumental version of "Fly Me to the Moon."

"Just barely," my girl grouses at my side. "Damn ghosts."

"What ghosts?" Ryan stands at the table beside her eating a dinner roll.

"The distillery is haunted," Jemima tells him, sliding one of the few flowers that survived the van wreck behind her ear. "But the wedding was so magical, the ghosts realized we didn't need them, and they all went and did shots with the angels."

Ryan's whole face wrinkles in disbelief, and he looks at me as if to get affirmation this Taylor Swift lookalike is crazy.

Piper puts her hand on her son's waist. "That's not what happened."

"Don't be humble," Jemima cries. "The wedding *was* magical!"

Piper holds up her hands. "Thank you, and there are no ghosts. It was a joke."

"Cats are good at finding ghosts." Ryan stuffs a big piece of roll into his mouth. "I bet Fudge would've kept those bad ghosts away."

"Fudge would've run away from this place." Piper gives him a hug. "The waitstaff kept tripping and dropping things and making loud noises."

Leaning closer, I whisper in his ear. "I think they were moving too fast, and ghosts were an easy excuse."

Ryan raises his eyebrows, nodding like he knows exactly what I'm talking about. "Ghosts. Pfft." He rolls his eyes.

"Hello, hello, hello, and welcome to the reception." A loud voice on the mic cuts through the music. "We're getting started with the couples' dances! Who's ready to shake a leg and dance like a couple? A couple of what, you say? Well, let's find out, shall we?"

Piper's face wrinkles, and she stands to meet Alex, who's leading Cass off the dance floor. "Who is that?"

Alex glances at the stage. "I don't know. He doesn't seem to be with the band."

"Uncle Alex! Aunt Cass!" Ryan runs up to them. "I told Mom Fudge is great at chasing ghosts! I can bring him and let him chase them all away if you need me to!"

Cass scrubs her fingers in his hair. "You and Fudge are my favorite ghostbusters."

"Might not be a bad idea to have a cat up here." Alex holds her waist. "Better than mouse traps."

"Fudge is great at catching mice, too!" Ryan shouts over the music, and Owen walks over to get in on the action.

"I didn't know we had ghosts in the distillery." Cass looks up at my brother, her voice low and soft. "Or mice."

"Surprise." Alex kisses the tip of her nose, and I'm pretty sure they won't be with us for long.

The emcee comes on the mic to announce the first of the couples' dances. "Ohhhkay, ladies and germs! Let's get started with the daddy-daughter dance. Let's have all the sexy daddies and their hot little daughters on the dance floor right now, and that includes our beautiful bride!"

Piper's jaw drops, and she flashes shocked eyes at Britt, mouthing, "Who is this guy?"

Jemima is on her feet, hustling to the stage, where I assume she'll set the announcer straight.

"Daa-day!" Pinky stomps up in her green tulle dress, grabbing Alex's hand. "You said you'd dance with me, and he just said it's the daddy-daughter dance!"

"Okay, baby." He kisses the top of Cass's shoulder, before allowing Miss Priss to drag him away.

Piper is out of her seat. "I did not approve this guy."

Cass smiles dreamily, going to where Piper and Britt are fuming like two protective mother hens. "It's okay—I seriously don't care."

"I want to know where he came from." Piper watches Jemima speaking to the lead guitarist. "She'd better be telling them to get rid of him."

"It sounds like he's been drinking." Britt's hand is under her bump, and her brow is lowered.

The music takes over, and the band launches into "The Way You Look Tonight" as Pinky climbs onto Alex's feet to dance.

Ryan and Owen take off, running around the perimeter of the event space. I walk over to where Piper still has her arms crossed, sliding my hand along her lower back.

"Pretty sure nobody cares about him." Curling my fingers along her waist, I pull her closer to my side.

Her lips tighten. "Except Cass, and I don't want her day ruined."

"She looks like she's having a great time to me." We glance

at where the bride is dancing with her little sister, holding hands and swinging them side to side while they sing along to the music.

"I'm glad Jemima's here…" The words are just leaving her lips when her entire body tenses. "Oh, fuck."

Drake Redford steps up beside Aiden and Britt, smiling like a Cheshire cat. "Lovely wedding. I heard you planned it?"

He's dressed in a chocolate brown suit with a darker brown sweater under his jacket and matching brown leather sandals. I swear, I hate this guy. Who wears sandals to a wedding?

Britt's frown deepens. "Piper planned the wedding. I had to bow out because of morning sickness."

"I'm sorry to hear that." He looks over at us and nods. "Nice work. Did you have much trouble finding places for the guests to stay?"

Piper's eyes narrow, and she chews her bottom lip. I know Marshall's comment about hotels in Eureka is on her mind, especially in view of her own housing situation, and I step forward ready to shut this guy down.

Cass beats me to the punch. "Are you bothering people again, Drake?" She walks up, holding her sister's hand. "Haven't you done enough dragging poor Bo into your schemes?"

"Hello, Cass." He steps back, surveying her dress. "I wouldn't have called your marriage a scheme, but I guess you'd know better than me."

My jaw tightens as Alex walks straight through the group to where they're standing. "What have I told you about speaking to my wife?"

"Alex…" Drake straightens. "I was merely commenting on how lovely the wedding is. Congratulations."

"That's not how it sounded to me." My brother's fist is tight, and I make my way around the table, doing my best to get to where he's standing.

Aiden is beside him, but the last time Cass's douche of an ex was around—at his daughter's fifth birthday party, no less—Alex almost punched his lights out.

"And now for the mother-of-the-bride dance." The emcee is back at it again. "Can we get all the smokin' hot grandmas on the floor? How about you there? Ready to cut a rug?"

He points to Gwen, who is walking past the stage to where we're standing. She cuts her eyes at him, and he holds up his hands.

"Don't mess with that funky grandma, I'll say."

Piper groans, clutching her forehead. "Make him stop!"

"Brigitte, how are you feeling?" Gwen goes to where Britt is holding her stomach.

"I was doing fine until he showed up." Britt hooks her thumb at Drake.

"I'm not sure you should be on your feet this long." Her mother clutches her forearm as if to check her pulse.

"Ah, Gwen Bailey. I don't think we've met." Drake steps up to Britt's mother. "I heard you sicced the Fireside Ladies on us."

He exhales a laugh, and I'm starting to wonder how this guy is so successful. He's clearly a dumbass—or he really doesn't know how to read a room.

"The Fireside Ladies are a powerful group of women." Gwen's voice is stern. "I wouldn't make fun of them if I were you."

"I heard they're a coven of witches," he counters. "Hey, Cass, didn't you work with this lady? Does that mean you're a witch now, too?"

"Gwen isn't a witch—" Cass starts, but he keeps going.

"It all makes sense." His eyes widen as if to make fun of them. "I finally understand how you bagged Alex Stone. Witchcraft!"

Alex's fist flies so fast, I almost don't even see it. I only hear a loud *crack!*, and Drake flies on his back onto the tabletop, sending plates, glasses, and chairs crashing to the floor. He keeps going as well, sliding across the table to the floor and losing a sandal in the process.

"Fuck!" Alex groans, shaking his hand.

From the sound of it, I'm pretty sure he broke something, but my brother, the groom, is not finished. He lunges for Drake, but Aiden catches him around the waist just in time.

"Let me go, Aiden," Alex growls.

"Nope." Our oldest brother barely restrains him, and I hustle closer to help. "I don't want to have to arrest you on your wedding day."

"Sounds like the party is really getting started now!" Drunk Emcee is on the mic again. "You know, they say it's not a party until somebody loses their pants. Or in this case, their sandal! Tell me, does this guy have some style or what?"

The band quickly exits the stage, taking their instruments with them, and "Party Rock Anthem" blasts through the speakers.

Drake is on his feet, blood running from the corner of his mouth, and I duck just in time to avoid a punch in the face. He staggers forward, almost falling to the ground from the momentum, and I can't help thinking *Fuck, that would've hurt.*

"Get him out of here," Aiden shouts over the music, and I catch Drake around the waist.

"Let's go, asshole."

Drake turns in my arms, pointing back at Alex. "You'll be hearing from my lawyer."

"I can't wait." Alex goes for him again, but Aiden has a better hold on our brother now.

Cass is at their side, and Pinky runs at top speed with both hands up, yelling, "Can I karate chop him, Daddy?"

"No." Gwen reaches down and catches Pinky. "That man said a bad thing, and your father took care of it. It's over now."

I'm wrestling Drake to the exit when the music switches to "Kung Fu Fighting," and I see Drunk Emcee giving us the thumbs up. The kids race to the dance floor and start karate chopping and kicking, and I see Piper sitting at the table with her face in her hands.

I'll take care of her once I'm done with this jerk.

"Let go of me, Adam." Drake throws his arms up once we're outside the door, and I let him go. "I was assaulted."

"You're lucky that's all that happened to you." My hands are on my hips, and I wait as he paces back and forth in the grass in only one sandal.

"Your brother should be arrested, but of course he won't because Aiden's the sheriff."

"My brother's got at least ten witnesses who'll say you provoked him."

"All family and friends."

"It's a wedding, asshole, of course it's family and friends. And in case you're too stupid to notice, you're not welcome here."

"I was invited to this wedding."

Taking a step closer, I look him straight in the eye. "Consider yourself uninvited. Now get moving."

He hesitates, studying me, and I almost wish a bitch would. The pain in his jaw must change his mind, because he backs down.

"You Stones don't own Eureka."

"Never said we did."

I wait as he turns and stalks to his Escalade. When he's good and gone, I head back inside to find Piper.

"This wedding is a disaster, and I wanted it to be so perfect for Cass!" I finally find my girl in Alex's office sitting behind his desk with her head down on her crossed arms. "I wanted to have everything she loves, and instead we have no flowers and fights and drunk emcees…"

I walk around the desk and slide my hand over her shoulder. "Not to go all Jemima on you, but I think you're taking this the wrong way. It's a good thing. No one will ever forget Cass and Alex's wedding."

She only lets out another wail, not taking her head off her arms.

"Come here," I laugh, reaching down and lifting her out of the chair.

Her lips are pouty, and I put my finger under her chin, forcing her pretty amber-green eyes to meet mine. "This wedding was a hugely entertaining success, and even in the face of wrecked vans, clumsy waitstaff, and inappropriate hosts, you pulled it off. You're incredible."

"Don't forget offensive ex-boyfriends."

I wrap my arms around her, chuckling. "Drake claimed he was invited, but even if he was, who goes to their ex-girlfriend's wedding?"

"We reused Britt and Aiden's old guest list," she groans, dropping her head forward against my chest. "Wasn't he on it? I am so cursed."

"You're busy, not cursed." Sliding my hand along the bare skin of her back, I thread my fingers in her hair, looking around my brother's cozy, mahogany-wood and leather office. "I seem to remember Alex and Cass sneaking in here during Aiden's reception. I wonder if that door locks."

Naughty eyes blink up to mine, and she tilts her head to the side. "What are you thinking, Adam Stone?"

"I think you know what I'm thinking." Leaning down, I pull her lips with mine, but she skips back, circling the large desk.

"Hang on." She laughs softly. "I've got kitten breath."

"I didn't notice." Neither did the boner in my pants.

She reaches for her purse, but it falls face down onto the floor. "Dammit!"

"I've got it." I bend down to pick it up, doing my best to keep the contents from spilling out.

I don't succeed, and four small, Polaroid photos spread across the Persian rug. I realize as I collect them, they're the pictures from her damaged house, the ones she scooped up so quickly.

They're lying facing up, and it only takes a blink for me to see what's in them. My stomach churns at the sight, and with every blink, my rage grows hotter.

One is of Piper in her underwear showing her upper rib cage. Another is a photo of the same place, only close-up. The next is of her inner thighs, and the final one is under her arms.

In every photo, ugly dark purple or red marks stripe her skin where she was either cut or burned, I can't tell which. All I know is she was wounded badly, and over a period of time from the look of it.

"Oh!" Her voice is a sharp whisper, and she snatches the photographs from my hand, clutching them to her chest.

My brow is lowered, but I hold it back. I'm not sure what I'm seeing, and clearly, there's something here I don't know.

"What are those?" Swallowing the burn in my throat, I nod at them. "Did you… do that to yourself?"

"No!" Her eyes blink wider, and the anger I'm barely holding down turns into an inferno in my chest.

My fists clench, and murder is on my mind.

When I speak, I don't recognize my own voice. "Who. Did. This?"

Her fingers tremble, and the thought of someone hurting her that way is more than I can handle. Stepping forward, I put my hands on her arms, struggling for control.

"Tell me, Piper." It's no good. I still sound like I'm on the edge of murder. "Who did this to you?"

"It's what I need to tell you." She's so quiet. I watch her return the photos to her purse. "I didn't know how to tell you… or anyone when it happened, so I didn't. But keeping the secret pushed me further away from you all."

I can't take much more of this. "Who did it, Piper?"

She inhales slowly, and her eyes don't meet mine.

With one word, she stops my heart. "Rex."

Chapter 21

Piper

THE ROOM FALLS SILENT WHEN I SAY HIS NAME.

Adam stands in front of me, and he's so angry. My chest is so tight, I can't breathe, and my stomach twists so hard, I'm afraid I'll vomit.

I can't read his body language.

His fists are balled, and his jaw is clenched. He's clearly holding himself back, but I can't tell if he's on my side. I can't tell if he believes me, and for the love of God, I don't want to cry.

I don't want pity. I want to know what he's thinking.

When he finally speaks, it's hoarse and broken. "Rex did that to you?" I nod, and he swallows. "When?"

Fear grips me, and I'm not sure I can do this.

I *have* to do this.

"In college." My voice trembles. "He would smoke… meth… and he would say things. He was jealous."

Adam stands so straight in his gray suit with the sage-green tie that matches my elegant dress, and it all feels wrong. We're too formal, too distant. Space yawns between us, and I want to be away from here. I want to run away and hide.

"Jealous?" Adam pushes the sides of his hair behind his ears with both hands and lifts his chin to look at the ceiling. "He did this because he was fucking *jealous*?"

He's not shouting, but I feel his rage. It's barely contained, and I don't know what to do.

"Yes."

Silence.

I can't bear the silence.

"I was afraid to tell anyone." My eyes fix on the floor. "I didn't know what would happen if I did. So I tried to make it stop."

"How long?"

"Until he died."

It's so quiet. A clock on the bookshelf ticks as loud as a hammer, and my brain counts every beat, *five… four… three… two…*

"Why didn't I know?" He exhales the words, and my heart pinches and curls in on itself.

He doesn't believe it.

"I'm sorry." The tears are fighting their way back to my eyes, and I hiccup a breath.

It seems to pull him from wherever he is, because he looks at me. His blue eyes are broken. They hold all the same emotions I felt the first time it happened to me—stunned disbelief, confusion, loss—but they also hold something else: *Rage*.

He takes a step closer and hesitates. "Can I touch you?"

It hurts, but I nod. "Yes."

In a sweep, I'm in his arms. He holds me close, strong and tight, inhaling at my hair, sliding his face along the top of my head. I feel him tremble, and I don't know what he's thinking. I can't tell anything about how this is affecting him.

He and Rex were friends as long as I knew them. They were like brothers…

Now I'm the one outside his walls.

Large hands cup my face, and he kisses my damp cheeks, first one then the other. Then he pulls me to him again. He's breathing deeply, and I almost hear him… groaning?

His arms wrap around me once more, holding me so tightly to his body, it's almost like he's moving through this pain with me.

Lifting my hands, I hold his arms, closing my eyes and feeling his strength. Turning his face, he kisses my hands, clasping them in his before meeting my eyes.

His are so tormented. "Are you okay now?"

"I'm getting there." Blinking fast, I force a tentative smile. "I've done a lot of therapy."

"That's good." He nods, sliding his thumbs across my cheeks. "Thank you for telling me."

His tone cramps my stomach. It's still too formal, too distant. I don't want him to thank me. Honestly, I don't know what I want him to do.

"Are *you* okay?" I ask, studying his expression.

When our eyes meet, I see it. He's not okay.

"I think… I have to…" He taps his forehead. "I have to do something."

His last words trail off, and he steps away. Hesitating, his eyes move from mine, down my body, lingering at my legs, then up again slower, lingering on my torso. It's like he's reminding himself where the wounds are, like he sees my scars through my dress.

His eyes tighten, and he steps to me once more, cupping my cheeks and kissing me. Then he turns and leaves.

"Best thing you can do after a party is hire a cleanup crew." Britt stands across the bar from me, whipping up raw eggs, cheese, onions, and mushrooms in a bowl. "Nobody's drunk or tired or hungover. They come in fresh, probably just woke up from a nap, and they clean it all up."

I'm sitting across from her holding onto a mug of coffee for dear life.

Adam left. He walked out of Alex's office, and he never came back. He didn't say a word to anyone. Aiden said he tossed his tie, hopped in his car, and drove away.

Not a text, not a word, only he had to do something.

Britt took my hand and told me to sleep here, so I curled up with my son in the guest bedroom and studied the picture Adam sent me last night. The three of them, curled in this bed. Only this time it's me with Ryan and Fudge.

"How'd you sleep?" She's watching me like I'm a time bomb… ticking.

"Good." I nod, taking a long sip of coffee. "Ryan stayed on his side of the bed, and Fudge stayed right next to him the whole time."

"I can't get over that cat. It's like he came to this town specifically for that boy."

"Or we started feeding a stray cat, and he knows a good deal when he finds it."

Looking down at my phone, I want to shake it. I want to yell at it to vibrate. I want to yell at him to talk to me.

"Have you heard anything?" Her voice is quiet, and I shake my head.

"Not a word."

"So text him." She's quietly urging. "It doesn't have to be weird. Ask him when he'll be back."

"No." I stare at the black screen as the crack in my heart slowly grows deeper. "I have to let him do this."

"Do what? Run away?"

"I don't know." I don't know, but it hurts like hell.

I don't know how I expected him to react, and I guess I got part of what I wanted when I told him. He pulled me into his arms. He held me and hugged me and wanted to know if I was okay…

Then he left.

What if I had said I wasn't okay? Would he still have left?

"Hey, aren't you tired?" Aiden enters the room. "I can make breakfast."

He's dressed in low-slung, gray sweats and a tee, and he's scratching his stomach looking for all it's worth like his brother.

The crack in my heart pierces deeper.

"Hey, handsome. I'm visiting with my girl." Britt leans her head back for a kiss, and I need space.

"Mom wasn't at the wedding." It's like I just realized it.

I was so distracted by all the things, I forgot that I noticed at some point in the evening. Probably when Gwen joined us, which was right before Alex punched Drake in the face.

"That's right!" Britt frowns at me. "Gosh, so much happened last night, it was hard to keep up with everything."

"Tell me about it." Aiden exhales a laugh, grabbing a mug from the cabinet. "Good thing I was off duty."

"You wouldn't have arrested your brother." She elbows her husband in the side.

"No, but I'd have had to do something."

Britt pours the egg mixture into a hot skillet and looks up at me. "When's the last time you heard from her?"

My throat tightens, and I try to think. "She was at the newspaper office fussing with Jemima… Last week?"

Am I that shitty of a daughter?

"To be fair, you were running a paper, dealing with a contractor, planning a wedding, and sneaking around with Adam all week."

Aiden laughs through his nose as he sips his coffee, and I glare at her. "Thanks."

"Do you really think you're that sneaky? It was clear after years of pent-up sexual need, you both were getting lucky."

Her words pull me up short. *Getting lucky...* but I don't have time to dwell on them.

"I'd better check on her." Grabbing my hoodie off the rack, I head for the door. "I won't be gone long."

"I'll have breakfast ready when you get back."

Aiden's big house is the first one on the street. It's near his mother's and all the other original founders of Eureka's grand homes. Gwen and her late husband bought an older one at the end of the road when we were kids, and she's been fixing it up ever since.

My mother's house is the only one that's very clearly ancient. It's tall and narrow, hidden behind trees, and she's never cared a minute for fixing it up. All of her attention has always been on her work underground.

Shoving my hands into the pockets of my hoodie, I walk up the sidewalk. It's a chilly morning, and like always when I visit here, all my old feelings of embarrassment from high school creep up my shoulders, making me want to sink even further into my jacket.

My mother and this place and everything about my life was always so intensely cringey to me growing up. None of my friends cared, but oh, how I did.

Looking back, I wonder if that's why I allowed Rex to treat me the way he did. Did I believe I somehow didn't deserve better?

Dry twigs crunch under my boots, and saplings have sprung up all the way to the front door. It's not a new phenomenon. The front walk has never been swept or weeded or cleared, and if it weren't for the cedar planks lining the dark-green exterior, it probably would've rotted away years ago.

The lights are off inside, and it looks like no one is home. I'm not fooled by this. My mother has always lived as if she were in hiding, and whenever I asked about it, she'd give me some paranoid answer. *Never be too easy to find*, or some such nonsense.

Lord knows, we have to stay hidden from the zombies.

Cupping my hands around the window, I peer inside. The living room is empty, so I try the front door. It's locked, and I don't have my key.

I walk around to the back where her old green truck is parked under the carport.

The house is the shape of a small box with equally small, square windows. It's rumored to have been the carriage house of a much larger mansion that burned to the ground years and years ago, before the Stones and the Brewers and the Belles and the rest of the original families founded Eureka.

"Mom?" I call, opening the dark-green wooden door.

I expect to find her in her elaborate cellar canning vegetables or listening to her CB radio for important updates from the network.

To be honest, I was kind-of relieved when I grew up and discovered there was a vast network of doomsday preppers in the world. I'd spent most of my childhood thinking my mother was mentally ill. Then I found out she's the okay kind of paranoid, because who knows? An incurable virus could break out or zombies could attack or civilization could completely fall apart one day.

I mean, to her credit, things have gotten pretty unpredictable in the last few years.

"Mom?" My voice is louder, and I go to the narrow door beside the refrigerator.

If you'd never been here, you'd think it's simply a broom closet or a pantry—extra storage. Having grown up in this house, I know it's a portal to another world.

Pulling the door open, I yell to the underground. "Mom, are you down there?"

Still no answer, and a sliver of worry filters through my chest.

Jogging down the steps, I flick on the light. Dim yellow bulbs illuminate a long corridor that curves around and down the farther it goes. To my right is a cabinet holding an assortment of rifles, gas masks, walkie-talkies, and a satellite phone for easy grabbing.

Rows of shelves stretch along both walls holding industrial-sized cans of beans and tomato sauce. Giant cans of lard sit on top shelves, and there's so much toilet paper.

"Mom?" I pick up an unusual-looking radio, which I'm sure is specially designed for the end of the world. "Are you down here?"

I don't really like this place. It might make my mother feel safe, but it makes me claustrophobic. If I weren't afraid she might have fallen or had some sort of accident, I'd come back later with the boys and let them search for her. They *love* running around Grandma Martha's hideout.

Taking a deep breath, I pick up the pace and stride all the way down and around and around, to the very end of her bunker. All the way to the stacked metal beds with scratchy green, Army-surplus wool blankets tucked tightly over thin mattresses.

The place is empty. I even look under the beds to be sure.

Confident she's not here, I hustle out of this nightmare, all the way back to the surface where normal humans live.

Only now I'm worried. *Where is she?*

I pull out my phone and send Britt a quick text.

> She's not at her house.

Britt: That's weird. Need Aiden's help?

Twisting my lips, I think about it.

> Not yet. I'll check with your mom then Carol.

Britt: Keep me posted!

If Gwen doesn't know where she is, and Cass's aunt hasn't heard from her, I'll bring the sheriff in on this. I can't help thinking what a great time for Adam to go MIA.

My chest pinches at the thought of him. He hugged me,

kissed my cheek, and left without any explanation. I want to cry, but my insides are too confused. Instead, I'm quietly waiting.

Gravel crunches under my feet as I approach Gwen's rambling farmhouse. It's all decked out with Halloween decorations, and unlike my mother's house, her yard is neatly mowed.

Several rose bushes line the front walk, and they fill the air with their clean, sweet perfume. It's so Gwen to have rose bushes leading to her house. *Magical.*

I walk up the driveway, past a large picture window overlooking the street, to the kitchen entrance in the back. Gwen is always in the kitchen brewing up tea or some other concoction.

She's not a witch, but she doesn't fight the appearance too hard.

"Gwen?" I jog up the steps, tapping on the screen door before opening it. "Have you seen my mom…"

The question dies on my lips when I realize she's not alone.

"Piper." She stands, fixing serious hazel eyes on me. "Have you met Ethan McClure?"

My heart beats faster, and I see Old Bird Eyes sitting at the small table in Gwen's kitchen. A deck of arcana cards is in front of him, and in addition to a reading, they're sharing what looks like either banana bread or carrot cake and tea.

"Yes." I take a cautious step inside, easing the screen door closed behind me. "He's searching for someone."

Ethan stands, and he's in a different tweed suit. His dark hair is pushed back from his face, but a piece is caught on his cheek, in his beard.

"Piper Jackson, publisher of the *Eureka Gazette.*" He says the words like he's reading my byline. "We met the other day."

My eyes flicker to Gwen's, and she's deadly calm.

"I wasn't sure if you girls were finished at the Star Parlor, so I invited him here for a reading." She smiles like she's in complete control of the situation, and she walks to the table where her cards are waiting. "The spirits never let me down."

"Would you like to join us?" Ethan watches me in that too-intense way. "There's plenty for three."

"Oh, no. Piper can't have any of the breakfast bread." Gwen looks at Ethan. "It has walnuts in it, and she's very allergic."

I'm not allergic to walnuts, but I'm not stupid enough to correct her.

"It's okay. I was just… ah…" I'm thinking fast. "I spent the night with Britt, and we thought you might like to walk down and have breakfast with us. But I guess not."

"Thank you for the invitation. Tell Brigitte I'll stop by this afternoon and check on her." She smiles, turning her attention briefly to Ethan. "My daughter is expecting. Now, if that's all…"

Her hand is on my elbow, and she leads me to the front door, which is down a long hall, past the living room and the stairwell, away from the kitchen.

My eyes lock on hers when we reach the door, and I silently mouth, *Are you okay?*

Her expression is fixed, and she practically shoves me out the front door, speaking barely above a whisper. "The other place." Her voice rises just as fast. "See you this afternoon."

The door closes in my face, and I turn, looking out at the old country road.

My heart beats faster, and I think about what she said.

What other place?

Chapter 22

Adam

Tybee Island is a barrier island on the north Georgia coast about thirty minutes outside of Savannah. It takes me less than two hours to drive from Eureka to where my ex-best friend was laid to rest in his family's plot almost a decade ago.

My jaw grinds the entire drive, and I do my best not to break all land-speed records. I threw my coat in the trunk of my Jetta and changed into a tee when I left the distillery, and now, with the windows down, the briny air pushes against my cheeks, through my hair, drying my eyes.

But it does nothing to cool the anger blazing in my veins. It's like a volcano went off, and I'm burning from the inside out.

When I saw the pictures, and she confirmed what it was, everything crashed down on my head. It was all I could do to hold her, try to comfort her, do my best to ensure she could be as strong as she's always been.

I had to get out of there. I had to get a handle on my feelings, and I had to make this drive.

Every time I close my eyes, I see her wounded body, and I imagine the abuse she suffered right there, with me so close, and I never even knew. God, was I that fucked-up?

All I lived for in those days was escape. I dropped out of college after only two years and did nothing but surf with Rex and Max and the rest of the guys.

We all took drugs, we ran up and down the coastline, we joined the circuit, but we dropped out when they left for Australia or South America or Hawaii.

I didn't care about traveling. I didn't care about anything. I only wanted to kill the pain of losing Pop then losing Dad… And I was in love with her.

I'd stopped pretending it wasn't what it was. I was fucking in love with my best friend's girl. So I did what you do in that situation—I did everything else.

I never dreamed in a million years he would've hurt her.

If I'd known…

I'm pretty familiar with the island, so it only takes a few minutes to find a place to stay. The annual Pirate Fest that happens every October has ended, and the off-season has officially begun.

I park the car and dump my things in the small motel room before walking the few blocks to the shore. The tide is out, and the wet brown sand stretches for what looks like miles. It's not. When the tide changes, it all comes back in a rush.

Just like the fucking past.

I walk in the direction of Mid Beach, striding hard to get the burn out. I know where I'm headed, and I can either walk on the street or I can walk on the shore. I opt for the shore, and after about a mile, I turn and start walking inland.

I cross block after block, getting closer to the tall pine trees, leaving the sand and waves behind me.

The closer I get, I see one of those signs out front, and I wonder who came up with the concept of church signs. This one reads, *Is what you're living for worth dying for?*

I don't even hesitate. Yes.

Yes…

Memory takes me back to that strip of highway nine years ago, the night Aiden stopped me, the night he busted my ass, and I hated him so much for it.

He gave me an ultimatum, and I could've fought him. His case was thin, and he had no evidence. But I was broken. I'd just held newborn Ryan in my arms, and he was so fucking perfect. He was so beautiful.

She was so beautiful.

And she told me to leave.

My brother was right, and I wanted to change for them. I wanted to deserve them.

Continuing past the sign, I go to the back of the church, past another larger building that is either a gym or a fellowship hall or both. I've only been here once before, but I know where to go.

A black wrought-iron gate opens to a field where the pine trees have been strategically cleared and benches placed beneath them to create a pastoral landscape.

It's not a large cemetery. Headstones are situated in neat rows, and cement blocks are on top of the plots to hold them down. I follow two rows and take a right to a lone square in the middle of a space designed for more.

He wasn't supposed to die first, but if he weren't dead, I'm pretty sure I'd kill him.

When I see his name on the headstone, I lean forward, gripping my knees as my chest heaves. Gasping air like a fish out of water, I struggle for control.

So many thoughts are in my head. He was my best friend, he was practically my brother, but those aren't the words that come out.

"You fucking bastard." My voice cracks. "You said you loved her. You said you couldn't live without her. You should've treated her like a queen, like I would've treated her."

The fury burns hotter in my chest, and I drop to my knees.

His name is in my face on that fucking piece of marble, and I lift my fists and beat the ground. Right, left, right… it's not enough.

Reaching out, I grip the headstone in both fists and yell as I try to pull it out of the earth. It doesn't budge, so I turn and kick it. I kick it again and again until I'm bleeding. Until I finally give up and roll to my hands and knees.

Pushing off the ground, I start to pace. I'm filthy and my hands and feet are bleeding, and when I breathe, I wheeze and growl like a wild animal.

"I called you my friend." My eyes are wet with tears. "I loved her, but I let you have her. And you fucking hurt her. You fucking piece of shit. You're lucky I didn't know."

My tears are not for him. They're for the lies. "I grieved you, and you were a monster."

Taking another shaky breath, I straighten. "She's mine now. He's mine now, and if I have anything to do with it, she'll never shed another tear." It's not a realistic promise, but fuck realism. Piper's suffered enough.

"He'll never know what a bastard you were." That's a promise I can keep. "I'm glad you're dead. I only hope it hurt."

Turning, I walk away from the grave. I'll never come here again.

Sitting on a board, staring out at the expanse of deep blue ocean, I wait for peace to come.

The waters off the coast of Tybee Island aren't great for surfing, but it's hurricane season. A guy at the Waves surf shop said they'd been getting one- and two-footers these last few days.

When I was young and life hit us with death after death, the only place I could find peace was on the ocean. For a while, it was just me out there, catching that rush of adrenaline and release as I flew through the thick curls of salt water.

I slept like shit last night. The anger still held me so tight, but this morning I pulled on my swim trunks and came out here.

Beating up his grave didn't do it, and if he were still alive, I know beating him for real would only be temporary satisfaction. The years of therapy I did as part of my deal with Aiden taught me to dig deep and name these feelings. Own them and let them go.

Otherwise, I can't be there for her like she needs me to be.

Seeing her pretty eyes, her loving heart, and knowing what she suffered... Fuck, the darkness is so deep in my chest.

The water swells around me, and I jump to my feet. It's not a strong wave, but it's enough to carry me a good distance. I step off and pick up the board, walking back out and then swimming farther.

I spend the rest of the afternoon doing what I love, until the fire, the ache, the fist in my chest starts to loosen.

Walking the beach, I think about what I need to do when my phone buzzes. My muscles tense, and I think it's her, but when I pull out my phone, it's Aiden.

He always keeps up with me.

Aiden: Where are you?

> Tybee Island. Sitting on a board.

Aiden: Rex's hometown? What's that about?

> Had some things to say.

I stop short of adding *to the bastard*.

What happened is Piper's story, and I don't know who all she's shared it with. From the sound of things, she kept it a secret for a long, long time.

Aiden: You need to come home now. Something's come up.

My chest flashes, and I tap back quickly.

> Is Piper okay?

I should probably text her now. Now that I've calmed my emotions. Now that I have control.

I never, ever want her to think I'm angry with her. I never want her to think I blame her because I wasn't there to help her… Or that I could ever love her any less for what that piece of shit did to her.

Aiden: She's good. And Ryan. But we need you here now.

Nodding, it doesn't take long to reply.

> On my way.

My next text is to her.

> Coming home. See you soon.

I want to add *I love you*, but I'll wait. I've got an errand to run before I get there.

Chapter 23

Piper

I DON'T GO BACK TO BRITT'S HOUSE. INSTEAD, I RETRACE MY STEPS TO Mom's place, tearing through my memories as I go. *The other place...* I think she only mentioned it once, and I dismissed it the same as I did all the rest of her paranoia.

She'd said, "If I'm there, it's too late," or something along those lines. Which I simply interpreted as her braggy way of implying none of us had survived.

The cellar beneath her house was common knowledge, only mindless zombies wouldn't know to look there. But if someone *wasn't* a mindless zombie, if someone knew what he was looking for...

All at once, it makes sense.

Changing course, I break into a run, following the road back to town, back to the Star Parlor. Pushing through the glass doors, I run up the stairs, banging on the door as hard as I can.

"Marshall?" I yell through the wood. "Marshall, it's Piper Jackson!"

I hear a shuffling from inside, and the door jerks open a crack. "Eh, why are you up so early? I thought you had a wedding last night."

"I need to talk to you. It's about Rosie McClure."

His bushy brows lower, and he closes the door to unfasten the chain. "Did your boyfriend tell you about her?"

I'm out of breath from running, but I shake my head. "Adam knows about her?"

"He knows her name." Marshall pulls the jacket over his shoulders.

"I need to know why you're looking for her. Who sent you?"

He hesitates, studying me a moment. "I'm not authorized to—"

"I know, you can't tell me details, but you have to tell me something. It's important."

Seconds like hours tick past as he seems to weigh his options and my level of determination. "A woman was killed by her husband. Her sister is determined to bring him to justice, so she asked me to come here and find Rosie. She hopes Rosie might help her."

"Why would Rosie help her?"

"Rosie was Ethan's first wife. Years ago, she supposedly died in a tragic car accident."

My chest tightens, and it's hard to breathe. "She didn't?"

"Ethan hired a PI, and they discovered she was still alive and living under an assumed name. About nine years ago, she briefly reappeared, but she disappeared again just as quick. I'm trying to find her before he does."

About nine years ago, Mom didn't want me to use our name at the hospital, but I insisted…

"I don't know anyone named Rosie McClure, but I'm pretty sure I know someone who does." He's in Gwen's kitchen, and my heart flashes. "Would you say Ethan McClure is dangerous?"

"So far, he's only dangerous to the women he marries, but I wouldn't get in his way." Marshall puts his hands on his hips.

"If you know something, you'd better tell me. Don't go off trying to stop this guy on your own."

"I wouldn't do that." Not after seeing what he looks like. "But I can't speak for Gwen, and I just saw him at her house. Do you know where she lives?"

"Yeah, your boyfriend gave me the tour last week."

Marshall and I look at each other for a split second before we both start moving fast, heading for the stairs.

"I'll go to Gwen's," he says, charging out the door.

I don't tell him where I'm going. Primarily because I'm starting to realize, I might have been wrong about everything.

I leave the truck on the side of the sandy gravel road and take off on foot into the pine trees, palmettos, and live oaks. I'm a few miles outside of town in the opposite direction of the distillery, away from the ocean.

When we were kids, we heard stories about the old mansion that burned to the ground. Only a foundation and two crumbling brick fireplaces are still standing, and parents would say it was haunted.

They'd tell us the original owners were killed in the fire, and they wandered the place at night, searching for their kids or their pets or whatever the grown-ups thought would keep us away from here.

Even as a teenager, I knew they said it to keep us from playing around the ruins and getting hurt. Mom never joined in the haunted chatter, but one night she said the most dangerous thing out here were snakes.

She said it in such a specific way, I got the feeling she'd encountered one. I asked her about it, and that's when she hit me with her cryptic warning.

"The old fruit cellar behind the second chimney is still in

good condition," she'd said. "It's another place to go if it's too late…"

I can still hear her offhand observation while stacking mason jars in the kitchen. I'd been heading out the door to meet everyone at the beach, and the last thing I cared about was another fallout shelter or secret hideout or whatever. I now realize my mother knew every place to hide in Eureka.

Looking all around, I keep to the tree line as I make my way around the perimeter of what used to be a yard. I'm pretty sure I wasn't followed, but if she really is here, I'd like to be able to say I kept her location secure.

Watching out for hibernating snakes, I cut up in the direction of the second chimney, slowing down as I scan the ground, the old foundation, looking everywhere for a cellar door.

It's so remote and isolated here, my chest unexpectedly twists. I picture her hiding here, alone, and for the first time in my life, I want to cry. For so long she feared this day would come.

My toe hits something on the ground, and I stumble. Catching myself, I turn to see it's the wooden corner of a door in the ground, only the wood is new. It's painted to blend with the scenery, and when I lift the handle, it opens silently.

Steps lead down into a dark pit, and while I know I'll either find it empty or holding my mom, fear tenses my muscles. I take out my phone and turn on the light, holding it down into the hole.

"Mom?" I call in a normal tone. I don't want to yell or surprise her.

When I get no response, I take a deep breath and slowly descend the steps with the light in front of me. Before I step onto the earthen floor, I scan all around for snakes again.

Seeing nothing, I step into the open space. It's completely empty. It smells like damp earth and old ash, and I'm not sure what to think. Light shines in from the overhead entrance, and I go to the walls, shining my light up and down them, looking for another passage or hidden door.

A burlap sack sits beside an old coal chute in the corner, and I walk over to see if it's hiding something. It's not, but an old grate is under the chute.

Dropping to a squat, I thread my fingers in the metal weave and move it away.

"Oh!" I fall back on my ass when the barrel of a rifle appears, followed by the click of a gun cocking. "Mom! Don't shoot—it's me!"

Picking up my phone, I shine the light into the small space to see my mom holding a rifle, glittering eyes focused. I turn my phone so the light illuminates my face, and the gun lowers.

"Piper." She motions me inside the smaller hole. "What are you doing here?"

I crawl inside and sit in front of her. "I could say as much to you. How long have you been down here?"

She turns on an electric lantern, and I see a sleeping bag in the corner, a few jars of food, and a small cooler. Her long hair hangs down her back in a single braid, and she's dressed in Army-green fatigues and a puffer coat.

"How was the wedding? I'm sorry I missed it. Did everyone have a nice time?"

I can't believe she's acting like this isn't completely insane. "Mom! You're underground. Who cares about the wedding?"

"Well, it was a big deal to you and the girls." She shrugs. "And you never liked talking about any of this."

"You never went missing for a week."

"It hasn't been a week."

"Care to fill me in on what's happening?" I lift the lid on the cooler and peek inside to see soft drinks and a yogurt. "Last I checked, there's no flesh-eating fungus or zombies attacking."

She exhales heavily, placing the gun across her lap. "I don't know how to tell you this, Piper, but technically, I'm not a survivalist."

"You're kidding."

"I let you believe what you wanted because I didn't want to frighten you, and well… maybe it was easier that way."

"Mom." I take her hand. "The thought of a zombie apocalypse or an alien invasion or a planet-destroying virus is pretty terrifying to a ten-year-old."

Her slim brow furrows over her pale blue eyes. "I don't think Ryan finds it terrifying."

"Because I told him it was your special, top-secret game. I made it a fun adventure." She exhales a dismissive note, but I'm done with hiding. "What's going on?"

"Your stepfather has come to town." She shakes her head. "Of course, the minute you get comfortable, the minute you think the monster is gone and you could possibly live a normal life, he appears like one of those horror villains, Michael or Jason or the other one."

"Time out." I hold up my hands. "I have a stepfather? Why am I just now hearing about him?"

"You didn't need to hear about him." Her lips are tight. "You were too small to remember, and I chose a different life for us. I chose not to live with a man who was controlling and abusive, and I got us out of there."

An abusive stepfather? *What the hell?* It's like I'm waking from a long dream… And yet, at the same time, I can't help wondering if this sort of thing is hereditary. Are we genetically predisposed to fall for evil men?

"Is your name Rosie McClure?"

"No." She shakes her head. "I put that name away a long time ago. I'm Martha Jackson now. It's on my driver's license, and that's all that matters."

"But who am I?"

"You're Piper Jackson, publisher of the *Eureka Gazette* and mother to Ryan." She lifts her chin as if she's announcing I won a major award.

I exhale, looking down at my hands. What do I do with all of this? "Can you at least tell me what happened?"

Her chin lowers slowly, and she looks down at her hands. Short fingernails, no polish. "I was a young single mother barely making ends meet when Ethan appeared. He was rich... not particularly handsome, but I was more interested in a home, security... I didn't trust my instincts telling me he was dangerous."

"So you did at least pick up on that?"

Lord knows he scared the pants off me.

"The first time he hit me, I said I was leaving." Her eyes hold mine. "The next day, he showed me the suicide note he'd written in my handwriting. He told me if I loved you, I'd never threaten him again. He wouldn't let me shame him. As if a man who beats a woman has any reason to be proud."

My throat knots, and my voice is too tight to speak.

"I knew then what I had to do." She reaches out and clasps my hand. "The only way to get us to safety was to fake our deaths and start all over again."

She says it so simply, like it's as easy as going to the store or running an errand.

"If we'd had family who could help us, maybe that would've made a difference, but we didn't. After that, I made a point never to need a man again. I made a vow to myself, and I kept it."

"I don't remember any of this."

Her expression warms. "You were just a little girl. It was so easy to play a game, hide-and-seek, and we got as far away as we could. We stayed off the grid. I homeschooled you until I found Gwen, and she brought us to Eureka."

"But what about my real dad?"

Blinking down, she smiles briefly. "I'm not sure where he is. I'm not even sure who he is, if I'm being honest." She exhales a little laugh. "It was a crazy summer, and I had several adventures."

"Are you saying you pulled a *Mamma Mia*?" Shaking my head, I rock back on my ass. "Cass is going to love this."

"I don't know what that means."

"It means you're a ho."

"Don't slut shame me!"

"Sorry. Forget it. We'll sort that out later." I look around the small space. "You can't stay down here."

"I have to. Gwen will let me know when it's safe to come out."

Pressing my lips together, I frown. "You're letting Gwen handle it?"

"Of course."

My face falls into my hands, and I exhale a laugh. She's the original version of me, and I know from personal experience telling her to go to the police or even to come out of hiding would be like telling me these things back then.

"You remember Marshall Gregg, the detective? He works for the sister of Ethan's second wife. She's hoping you might help her bring him to justice."

"That doesn't happen." Mom turns the gun on her lap. "Even if they believe you, even if you get a restraining order, do you know how many abusive husbands end up killing their wives?"

I swallow the knot in my throat. "Yes." I do.

"Then you know it won't matter."

I know it too well.

The sound of feet crunching fast over gravel outside makes me jump and almost scream. Mom clutches her hand over my mouth and scoots me behind her.

Lifting the gun, she pulls the hammer back slowly, quietly cocking the gun, and aims it directly at the door. My heart beats so hard, I'm going to vomit, and I curl my fingers in her puffer coat.

Our bodies are so close, and for the first time in a long, long time, I let her protect me.

"Martha?" It's Gwen's voice, and we both exhale loudly.

Mom lowers the gun. "We're here!"

Britt's mom leans her curly brown head down to peer in at us. "He's dead."

My eyes widen. She says it so simply, so matter-of-fact.

"Are you sure?" Mom doesn't move, and my fingers still clutch her for dear life.

"Yes." Gwen straightens, waiting for us to emerge from the hole.

Mom crawls forward to the exit, but I hesitate, trying to process all of this, trying to wrap my brain around what just happened.

"Come out, Piper," Mom orders.

Crawling, I peep my head out and look up at the two of them watching me with impatience. When I'm finally out they return to each other as if I'm not even there.

"How did it happen?" Mom asks.

"Funny story…" Gwen starts for the stairs leading out of this cellar. "Apparently several people were trying to kill him."

"Several?" My voice rises.

Mom takes a step, but then she pauses and leans against the wall. She puts a hand on her chest, and I hurry to her, worried she's having a heart attack or something. But she starts to laugh.

Her eyes squeeze shut, and she bends forward, covering her face with both hands. Her shoulders shake, and she simply stays there. Then she cackles. I'm still reeling and not sure what to do, so I stand beside her, rubbing her back and watching her laugh so hard her eyes water. She's crying with laughter, and I'm a little scared…

It's like instead of descending into a cellar, I actually fell down the rabbit hole into Wonderland and everything is upside down and not what I thought.

At the same time, I get it.

I totally get it.

Gwen waits quietly on the steps, looking down at her feet as my mom lets it all go.

"It's over…" Mom hiccups, standing and pulling me in for a hug, silent tears sliding down her cheeks. "Oh, thank God."

"And everyone else who played a role," Gwen sniffs.

I look up at her. "Who else?"

Gwen's eyebrows rise, and she looks down at her fingernails. "Well, I personally made a delicious breakfast bread filled with Wolfsbane. That youngest Jones boy set a trap for him that's normally used to capture hogs. I have no idea what he was planning to do if he caught him."

"Raif did that?" I whisper.

"He reminds me of a young James Dean." Mom pushes off the wall, walking with her arm around me to where Gwen is still waiting on the steps.

"Ben simply shot him in the chest," Gwen finishes, and we both stop. "He got rough with me at the house, and Ben put an end to it. He's at the courthouse discussing it with Aiden and that detective now. They're figuring out what to call it... self defense, or whatever."

Mom's eyes narrow. "Ben Cartwright spent the night at your house?"

Gwen wraps her sheer silk jacket tighter over her body and continues up the steps. "I'm not discussing it in front of the children."

"Wait... You're sleeping with Bender?" I call after her.

"I have to get to the house and dispose of that banana bread before anyone tries it." She steps into her waiting truck. "I'll have to bury it."

Without another word, she heads down the overgrown drive, leaving the two of us to walk to where I left my car.

"It's good to have friends," Mom says, watching her go.

We slowly walk down the narrow road, and the truth of everything I just learned hits me so hard. I think about what I wanted people to say when I told them about my situation.

"I'm sorry I never knew."

"I'm sorry if you were afraid." She wraps her arm around my shoulders. "I only wanted to protect you."

"I know that now." We stop at the car, and I look up at her. "It happened to me."

Our eyes meet, and hers are so sad. "I know."

"Why didn't you ever say anything?"

"I didn't know how to help you. I only knew my way." Her hand clasps mine, and she lifts it to her chest. "It had to be your decision, but I know what it's like to hide, to be ashamed and to have secrets. In the end, the truth always finds you."

"More like I made a deal with the devil, and now I have bad luck."

"There is no devil, and now you have Adam Stone. That's very lucky."

"I thought you didn't believe in luck."

She winks at me. "I believe you can find a little luck, and if you can't, you can make a little of your own."

Chapter 24

Piper

"These pictures are amazing!" Jemima cries from the front desk where her phone is connected to the big Mac, and she's alternately squealing and laughing. "You've got to see this one!"

After dropping Mom at her house, I came straight to the office. We're overdue to get the wedding photos to Stew so he can print the Sunday edition in time for delivery, and now I've got breaking news to try and slide in under the wire.

Sitting at my desk, I have my phone on speaker on my desktop, calling Aiden to see if he'll make any comment about the shooting at Gwen's.

"I don't have time!" I yell from where I wait at my laptop, chewing my nail. "Pick four or five good ones and write up captions."

She's in my office. "Look at this!"

Her phone is on my desk with a perfect shot of Alex's fist making contact with Drake's face. Cass is in the background with her hands up and her eyes wide. Her mouth is an oval, and I can almost hear her saying *Oh!*

Beside her, Britt is grinning with her nose wrinkled and both fists in the air like she's about to do a cheerleader jump. Gwen holds her waist, and even Drunk Emcee on the stage is doing a fist pump.

I can't help laughing. "That's pretty good, but we can't use it. We're trying not to give Drake's lawyer any more ammo."

"Boo!" She pokes out her red-velvet bottom lip as she stomps to my door. "Who knew a wedding could be so fun? That was the best reception I've ever attended."

"It certainly wasn't boring."

"Did you hear about the shooter at Gwen's this morning?" Jemima turns when she reaches my door. "I heard an intruder broke into the house, and Bender shot him! It's just never a dull moment around here!"

"That's what I'm always saying." The phone connects, and I jump, waving her away.

"Aiden here." His tone is impatient, and I'm pretty sure he knows why I'm calling.

"Hey—on the record, what can you tell me about the shooting at Gwen's?"

"How do you know about that?" he snaps.

"Got it straight from the horse's mouth." My fingers are on my keyboard, and I'm waiting to capture anything he says.

"No comment."

"Aiden!" I practically shout. "The citizens of Eureka have a right to know how a man was killed right here in town—"

"We're still gathering the facts, Piper. I'm not making some half-cocked statement to the press until I have more answers."

"Will you at least verify it was self-defense?"

"No."

"Breaking and entering?"

"Gwen was serving him tea and doing a reading. He didn't break and enter."

"Assault with a deadly weapon?"

"Goodbye, Piper." He disconnects, and I growl under my breath.

"Aiden Stone, you are well-named."

I type up a short brief based on what I know for publication tomorrow. I have to preface it as a rapidly developing story and indicate the facts have not been independently verified. Gwen likes to exaggerate, and she's not the best interpreter of the law.

Everyone will know the whole story by the time the Sunday edition hits the newsstands, but I've got it for the historical record. Not only that, it's a pretty important event for my family.

Quickly hitting save, I upload the revised front page to the news server then hustle out to where Britt is walking through the door with Ryan and Owen and Fudge.

"There you are!" My friend hustles inside. "What a morning!"

"Tell me about it. You won't believe everything that happened after I left your house."

"Oh, trust me, I would." Her eyes are big, and she nods. "Aiden got a call in the middle of buttering the biscuits and had to go to Mom's."

"I hope that's not a euphemism!" I give her a wink.

She pinches my arm. "I wish."

"What's a euphemism?" Ryan walks up and puts his arms around my waist.

I lean down and give him a hug. "It's when you say one thing instead of saying something else."

"Huh?" His nose wrinkles, and I gently boop it.

"Thanks for letting me crash with you and Fudge last night. I didn't want to be by myself."

Ryan picks up the black cat, who hangs in his arms as if he's boneless. "I don't mind, but Fudge thinks it's getting kind of crowded in the bed."

"Oh, does he?" I laugh, scrubbing the cat's cheeks.

Fudge hops onto the counter and trots over to where Jemima is still sorting pictures from the wedding reception.

"Jemima!" I cry. "It's after five! You haven't sent them yet? Stew is literally holding the presses for us right this minute."

"I know!" she whines. "I can't choose between this one of Alex and Cass dancing together or this one of Alex and Cass dancing with Pinky holding their hands."

Hesitating, I look back and forth between the two shots, and she's right. They're both really great.

"Oh, let me see." Britt pushes between us to look.

The first is very *Beauty and the Beast*-vibes with Cass's dress swirling around them, and Alex gazing into her eyes. But the one with Pinky is too cute with her kicking up a foot and the two of them looking down at her with so much love.

"The one with Pinky." I look at Britt, and she's nodding.

"Definitely," she confirms.

Jemima clicks on it and quickly types up a caption. "You really should bring Martha back to write our headlines. She has pizazz."

"I was actually thinking the same thing." After all that happened, I want to spend more time with her. I want to know who she really is, not who I mistook her for all those years.

Fudge flops on the counter in front of me, and I slide my hand down his long, shiny coat thinking about the text I got this morning from Adam.

Anticipation is a low hum buzzing in my stomach, and I keep checking the clock. He didn't say when he'd be back, and since leaving my mom, it feels like I've entered a wormhole where time has slowed to a crawl.

"That's not even the biggest story." Britt leans on the other side of the counter, blue eyes huge.

"There's something bigger than that?" I'm skeptical.

"Maybe not bigger, but equally shocking. Gram said Harold called to tell her Bo has dropped out of the Mayor's race, and he was sorry his dog was a part of Drake's schemes."

"He should be sorry," I grouse.

"*And* Drake Redford just signed a deal with the Ridgeland Town Council to develop a huge tract of land on the other side of the community college."

"You're kidding!"

"I'm not." Britt laughs. "He's taking his resort and going home."

"I wish you'd told me this twenty minutes ago! I might've gotten it in tomorrow's edition."

"I can only move so fast these days." She nods down at her baby bump.

"Although I have to admit, Drake's proposal did highlight the need for more places to stay in Eureka..." My voice fades when I glance out the window, up Main Street in the direction of town square.

Lightness fills my chest, and even though he's several blocks away, I know it's him striding in this direction. Pushing off the desk, I don't even notice the door as I open it and run outside. I vaguely hear Britt laughing, telling my son he won't be crowded tonight.

Outside, the sunshine is brighter. The colors of the flowers are breathtakingly vivid, but my eyes are fixed on his. I'm pulled by a magnetic force. I'm running, tears are on my cheeks, and I can't stop.

People slip past me, but I don't notice them. I only see one person, and he's jogging now, too. A smile breaks across his handsome face, and I hear myself laughing. I'm barely breathing.

My whole body tingles with light and joy and desire, and when I reach him, I don't stop. I do a little jump, and I'm in his arms.

I'm surrounded by his strong embrace, and my legs wrap around his waist. My breasts flatten against his firm chest, and I hold him so tight.

We're cheek to cheek, my lips at his ear, and from the depth of my soul, I sigh, "You're here."

His low voice is a delicious vibration through my body. "I have to be with my girl."

"I have to be with you."

He's standing, holding me, and he lifts his lips to mine, sliding them across my mouth and pulling them with his. Around us, I hear cheers, and when I look up, I see Britt and Jemima in the window waving. Britt's making kissy faces while the boys shake their heads.

"We have some catching up to do." His voice is low, and my panties are melted. "Are you free now?"

"Yes." The paper is done, my son is with my best friend, and all I want to do is spend every minute with him.

"Good. Come with me." Sliding my legs down, I'm tucked under his arm, firmly against his side, and he leads me up the sidewalk in the direction of his house.

"When you told me what happened, I had to go." We're in his bedroom, and he's sitting on the bed with his hands on my waist, looking up at me.

"Oh…" My voice catches, and my heart starts to break. *He doesn't want me.*

I take a step away, and he's on his feet, stopping me and holding my chin with his thumb and index finger. "I couldn't take knowing I'd been so close, and I'd let you be hurt that way. I felt like I was burning from the inside out, and I needed to calm down. I needed to get a grip on my feelings… because I love you so much."

Warmth from his words mends my heart, and I reach up, sliding my palms along his scruffy cheeks. "How could you know? I never told you."

Sitting again, he puts his face against my stomach, his strong arms around my waist. "You are so precious to me." His voice is rough, and I lean down to press my lips to his temple.

"You're the love of my life." I say the words, and he looks up.

He stands, and our kiss immediately turns hungry. Catching the hem of my sweater, he sweeps it over my head.

I start to freeze, wanting to pull the curtains or turn off the lights, but he holds my shoulders, looking into my eyes. "I don't want you to hide from me anymore. I want all of you."

My stomach is tight, but I nod. It's time.

Reaching up, I push the unbuttoned plaid shirt he's wearing off his shoulders, and he shrugs it away. Then he reaches behind his head to remove the T-shirt he's wearing under it, leaving his hair messy around his cheeks, his square jaw, the dimple in his chin.

His gorgeous bare chest is in front of me, muscular and firm, and I lean forward to trace my nose along the top of his pecs, inhaling sandalwood and citrus. I slip out my tongue to taste the salt on his skin.

Large hands circle my waist, moving higher to unfasten my bra. Swallowing my fear, I let the scrap of lace fall to the floor. He cups my breasts, lifting and sliding his thumbs over my hardening nipples.

He moves me back so he can see my body, then sighs. "So beautiful."

I exhale a little noise, crossing my arms, and his eyes darken, meeting mine. Guiding me onto the bed, he lays me on my back, his blue eyes intense and searching for any sign of hesitation.

My insides tremble as he unfastens the button of my jeans, but I help him slide them over my hips and down my legs.

Sitting up, I unbutton his jeans, and they drop to the floor, leaving him standing in front of me, his cock long and thick.

Reaching down, he lifts it in his hand, sliding his fist up and down the shaft, and the space between my thighs heats and grows slippery as I watch him harden.

Licking my lips, I want to pull it into my mouth. I want to turn off the bedside lamp and pretend there's nothing to see here, but he won't allow it.

"Lie back." His blue eyes hold mine, and his square jaw is set.

I do as he says, and he reaches down to slide my lace panties down my thighs. A knot is in my throat, and I wait. I know he sees them now, but I don't know what he'll do.

Dropping to his knees, he slides his palms up the outside of my thighs and leans forward. His eyes are on my legs where the scars are lighter, almost like stretch marks.

He dips his head and places warm lips against my damaged skin.

My stomach squeezes, and I inhale sharply. "Adam…"

It's barely a whisper, and his mouth moves higher to my stomach, following the silvery lines on the outsides of my abdomen, actual stretch marks from carrying Ryan.

He rests his cheek on my side near my hip. "I should've been with you when you were carrying him. I'd have liked to see you naked and pregnant."

Tears shine in my eyes, and I trace the hair off his cheek, behind his ear. "And all stretched out?"

"All full of life."

"There's time…"

Darkness enters his gaze, and it returns to my body. Both of his hands are on each side of my torso. His waist is between my legs, and he moves higher, sliding his arms around my back to hold me.

My breasts are exposed, but his eyes are on the scars lining my ribs, the uglier ones, the fiercer ones. His expression is unreadable to me. Is he sad? Disgusted? Angry?

Lowering his face, he kisses my side, tracing his lips in a way that almost tickles. "This one hurt."

He places his palm over a raised pink keloid, and tears heat my eyes. I can't speak. I can only nod slightly, and the pain in his eyes shatters me. Replacing his hand with his lips, he rests his forehead on my body, holding me.

When he speaks, his voice is thick. "They all hurt."

Curling around him, I hold him. "Not anymore."

After a few moments of breathing together, he only moves his face to the other side and repeats the process of smoothing his lips over my scars, kissing and loving where the pain once was, where healing has replaced the sorrow. Where his love is mending all my hurts.

Rising higher in the bed, he props on his elbows so his fingers are in my hair, tracing my cheeks. "You're so beautiful." His voice is low. "I'll never let anyone hurt you again."

Another rush of tears pools in my eyes, and I lift up to kiss him, holding his jaw until I can't wait any longer. "I love you."

"I love you." So much confidence is in his tone.

Not a single doubt, and it fills me with so much healing warmth.

He kisses my jaw, my neck, my collarbone. His palms cover my scars as his mouth lowers to my breasts, kissing and pulling my nipples, teasing them with his teeth. I moan in response, arching my back, and he rises higher between my thighs.

His pelvis slides against my core, massaging my clit, and I feel his erection, long and hard on my legs. Rocking my hips, I whimper, needing more of him.

Velvet lips trace a line from my breasts to my jaw, and the way he worships me, the feel of his hard body against my soft one, the urgency of our reunion is all too much.

"Please fuck me," I beg, and his mouth covers mine.

His tongue invades my mouth at the same time his cock enters, stretching me, making me break away with a loud moan.

"Fuck…" His head drops against my shoulder, and his hips pick up speed. "It feels so fucking good."

My knees rise, and I rock my pelvis in time with his movements. We're feverish, and I'm so sensitive, orgasm races through my thighs to my core, heating and burning my lower belly.

"Don't stop," I gasp. "I'm so close."

He drives deeper, fucking me harder as if he can't control himself. It grinds my clit, and the faster he moves, he finds a place deep in me I've never felt. My eyes squeeze shut, and sparks ignite behind my lids.

"Oh, God!" I gasp, gripping his tight ass and pushing him further, frantic to help him keep hitting that spot.

He doesn't stop, and with every stroke, I rise higher, my toes curling, my muscles twisting tighter. Delicious heat floods my pussy, until all at once, I burst into a thousand shuddering sparks of light. A high-pitched moan rips from my throat, and I jerk, arching and coming.

In that moment, he holds, and I feel his cock, thick and veined pumping again and again as he groans. His ass tenses beneath my grip, and another flash of orgasm tightens my core. It makes him groan again, and I feel his heart beating so hard against my chest.

We're consumed, holding and loving, riding out the highest of highs. Letting our bodies melt into one until at last we find the shore. We're smiling and panting, teeth colliding as we smile through kisses.

Coming down from a place where my scars don't matter. Where our past is behind us, and what we have is passion and love and a future to create together.

Chapter 25

Adam

Rolling onto my side, I cradle her body in mine, tracing my fingers along her shoulders, loving the feel of her in my arms. "I wanted to kill him," I confess, not meeting her eyes.

"He's dead." I look up, and her face is so relaxed, she actually looks free. "And anyway, I thought you were about peace and love."

"I'm not so peaceful when it comes to you." I've come to accept it about myself now more than ever.

"For the first time, I feel like it's really over."

"It is over." As long as I have anything to do with it.

She cuddles deeper into my embrace, and I only want to hold her, love her, take away all her fear as long as I'm alive. She awakens a protective urge in me that's beyond my ability to control.

Lifting her chin, she looks up at me with those pretty hazel eyes. "Why do you love me so much?"

Gazing down at her, all the reasons crowd together in my

mind. "You're smart and kind. You're funny and a great mom. You're really good at your job, and you're damn sexy in that office. I seriously want to christen your desk."

"Hmm…" Her eyebrow arches. "I think we can make that happen."

"Don't tease me." Dipping my head, I kiss her neck, tracing my lips to her shoulder. "I'm glad you stopped hiding from me. Because you've got perfect tits."

A laugh ripples from her throat as I cover her breast with my mouth, and she's so light and happy, it makes me grin… which results in my teeth raking her taut nipple.

"Oh…" she gasps, pushing my shoulder so I'll roll onto my back.

Her mouth covers mine, and our lips part. Our tongues curl together, and the heat between us reignites. Her fingers thread in mine, sliding our hands above my head on the mattress.

Her body moves against my chest, awakening my senses.

"I was so hurt yesterday when you left." She's breathless, tracing her lips down my chest and pulling my nipple with her teeth, making my cock jump.

"Fuck…" I groan.

"Now I realize it means you're safe." She rises, quickly pressing her mouth to mine again, kissing me sloppy and wet before holding my eyes with her pretty green ones. "When you're angry, you don't hurt me. You walk away until you're not angry anymore."

My brow lowers, and I hold her steady. "I'll never hurt you, Piper. Or Ryan."

She blinks quickly, then leans forward to kiss me again, and I roll her onto her back. Kissing my way down her chest, I want all of her, every part of her gorgeous body.

Her legs part, and I place my palms against her inner thighs, sliding them higher so I can cover her pussy with my mouth. Her body jumps with the first pass of my tongue, and I glance up to see her back arch.

"You're so beautiful." I speak against her inner thigh, kissing the crease before making my way to her clit once more.

With every pass of my tongue, her fingers tighten in my hair. I kiss her slower, gliding my tongue back and forth, circling and sucking, sliding my fingers into her wetness until I feel her thighs begin to tremble.

Looking up once more, she's on her elbows watching me, her eyes glassy. Her legs shake harder, and her head drops back. I curl my fingers, licking faster until she breaks with a sharp jerk. Her stomach quivers and she curls off the bed with a loud moan.

"Oh…" Her hands are in my hair, and I rise up to meet her mouth.

She cups my face, kissing me deeply, pulling my lips with hers as we fall back and I sink my cock into her hot, wet pussy.

"Fuck, Piper," I groan, rocking my hips. "You're so fucking wet."

Her mouth is on my neck, and she bites and pulls the skin with her lips. "You make me come so hard."

She has no idea. Holding her hips, I thrust faster, driven by primal instinct. I'm so fucking turned on by her, it doesn't take long before I'm coming deep, holding my body against hers, getting lost in her.

Her arms are around my neck, and I bury my face in her soft hair, inhaling honeysuckle and sweat. She's in my arms, and it's so damn good.

It's everything I want, but it's not all.

"Look at Fudge!" Ryan runs onto the deck at Aiden's, where the black cat sits on the railing, watching him with his tail curled around his body like something out of one of those Egyptian murals. "He's just waiting to see what we're going to do today, aren't you, boy?"

"We're going to carve a pumpkin, and you're spending the

night tonight after trick-or-treating." I scrub my hand over his head and he hugs me around the waist.

"Are we going to start staying at your house now?"

"Do you want to? I know you like being with Owen."

Ryan's nose wrinkles, and he tilts his head to the side. "I guess that would be okay. If Fudge can come."

"Of course, he can." I laugh. "I wouldn't separate you from your pal Fudge."

My old study made a perfect little boy's room—it was even the right color, navy and brown wood. My old bed from Mom's is set up and made, and next weekend we'll head to the furniture store to let him pick out something he likes.

"Uncle Adam! Mom said I can show you my 180!" I look up to see my nephew running out onto the deck carrying his skateboard. "I just got it last night—watch me!"

"Where's your helmet?" I cross my arms, and he makes a growling sound before stomping over to the patio to pick it up.

Helmet in place, I follow him out to the driveway, and he drops the board. I watch as he pushes off, rising into the air and starting to turn. Just as he reaches the ground, he falls off to the side, and the board shoots into the grass.

"Aw, man!" He follows it to the grass and drops down onto his back. "I had it."

"You gotta work your shoulders!" Ryan runs over and grabs the abandoned board.

I cross my arms, watching as he drops it before pushing off and catching air then flipping his body around along with the skateboard before hitting the concrete and gliding up to Aiden's parked truck.

"It's all in your body." Ryan carries it back to his friend, who's still lying on the grass.

Only now Edward, Britt's bloodhound, is licking him on the forehead.

"I can't do it," Owen groans, pushing Edward away from his face.

"Yeah, you can." I walk over and reach out a hand to him. "It's a tough trick. Most people aren't comfortable skating backwards."

"I did it last night." He grabs my hand, sitting up with his shoulders slumped.

"I believe you." I pull him up and rub his back. "You might get the Pop Shuvit first."

"I almost did a backside 180 last night!" Ryan jumps beside me, holding my hand. "Then I fell on my butt."

I take out my phone. "You know what Tony Hawk says about the backside 180?"

"What?" He blinks his mother's eyes up at me, and I scrub his head, loving him a little more every day.

"He says you have to use The Force to land it."

Both boys snort laughs, and Owen runs up to grab my other hand. "I'm going as Tony Hawk for Halloween this year!"

"Want to spend the night at my place tonight with Ryan? You can practice on my ramp."

"Yeah!" He jumps up and down, and I pull out my phone to let Britt and Aiden know they're off the hook for trick-or-treating.

I'm sure Britt will be relieved.

"Come on. We've got a pumpkin to carve."

Piper was up and out of bed this morning when I opened my eyes, claiming she had to get a head start on the Wednesday edition with Halloween happening and Drake's new deal in Ridgeland.

It gave me enough time to take my special Savannah purchase to Britt's and get her thoughts on sizing and whether she thinks Piper will like it. She cried, but I don't know if it's because she's pregnant and crying over memes these days or if she's really impressed with my selection.

She claims it's the latter, but being pregnant helps.

I plan to have pizzas for the boys and lemon butter Mahi-Mahi with air-fryer broccoli, basmati rice, and a chilled pinot grigio for us when she gets home.

The boys are elbow-deep in pumpkin guts, and I've got my phone out taking pictures to send to the group. Owen and Ryan hold up fistfulls of pumpkin pulp while Fudge sticks his whole head in the carved hole at the top of the gourd like a good cat.

Britt: Uncle of the year!

Britt adds a cheering emoji, and I imagine she's on the couch with her feet up right about now.

Aiden: Tell Owen to cut away from his hand.

Alex: When did you turn into such an old dad?

Aiden: When you were 16.

Our oldest brother grumps, and Britt replies with laughing emojis in her typically sunny way.

Where's the pink tornado tonight?

Cass: Julia has the princesses

She adds a heart-eyes emoji.

Feels like a missed opportunity.

I can't help teasing.

As much as I love my only niece, Alex's daughter is a handful. Cass is the first person she's ever allowed to tell her what to do besides our mom, and I'm pretty sure Mom bribes her with chocolate and ice cream and fingernail polish and whatever works.

Starting a new thread outside the group, I message Piper,

You didn't tell me your mom is Rosie McClure.

Piper: Orgasm brain...

She adds a sly-smile emoji.

A Little Luck

Piper: She's not anymore, tho.

> I missed a lot in 24 hours.

Piper: Eureka is a busy little town. I keep saying that.

> You and my mom.

I chuckle.

> When will you be home? I miss you.

Piper: In time to see my little Jedi and Tony Hawk and kiss my favorite surfer dude.

> Hold off on kissing. I've got ten pounds of candy to give away.

Piper: I love candy.

> That settles it. Lights out and we'll eat candy all year.

She replies with crying-laughing emojis, and

Piper: We'll give it to the kids. Then I'll give you a special treat after the boys go to bed.

I reply with a wooden log and the water spray emojis. Getting serious, I have to let her know.

> The judge ruled Ethan's death justifiable homicide. Marshall left to wrap up his case and let his client know. He asked me to tell you goodbye.

I'm not sure if she'll reply, and I think about all we've learned these past weeks. It feels overwhelming, yet at the same time, it feels like a long time coming.

Piper: He was a good man. I hope we see him again.

> Me too.

A few hours later, the sun is setting, and the streets are glowing and buzzing with orange lights and kids in LED necklaces and bracelets. The boys are all decked out in their Halloween costumes when Piper bursts through the door looking like the best thing I've ever seen.

A long red curl has escaped her low ponytail, and she's wearing a black turtleneck and rust-brown corduroy pants.

"Honey, I'm home," she sighs, walking straight into my arms.

I hug her close to my chest, kissing the tip of her nose. "I've got dinner on the stove and a scotch waiting for you by your favorite recliner."

Her nose wrinkles, and she tilts her head to the side. "Really?"

"No."

She laughs more, bending out of my arms as the boys run into the room and Ryan hugs her around the waist. "Check it out, Mom! We made a Jack o'lantern on a skateboard."

"I love it!" She squeezes him, kissing his head, and my stomach warms.

My family is together like we're supposed to be.

"Come on, Ryan! There's Jimmy!" Owen takes off running out the front door, and Ryan steps back to give me a hug.

"Thanks for helping me with my kickflip."

"You got it, buddy." I give him a squeeze. "I've got pizza waiting when you're ready."

He takes off running into the night, and my eyes meet Piper's. Hers are warm amber, brimming with a shine that echoes my feelings with every heartbeat.

"You're the only dad he's ever known." A wobbly smile curls her lips. "The only dad I ever want him to know."

Stepping forward, I pull her into my arms. "He was mine the night he was born."

I lean down to cover her mouth with mine just as the front door explodes with three little voices crying, "Trick or Treat!"

"Trick or Treat, Uncle Adam!" Pinky stomps up to the front door waving a wand and holding her best friend's hand.

"Oh my goodness!" Piper coos, totally out of character. "Are you... Ariel?"

"She's my favorite princess." Alex's daughter nods, tilting her head to the side. "Who are you?"

"I... ah..." Piper looks down at her black turtleneck and brown pants. "I'm the reporter lady from *Scream 3*."

My niece frowns. "I can't watch that movie. It's for grown-ups." She looks at me and shakes her little pink head as if she's disappointed in my lack of a costume.

I only laugh. "I've got full-sized candy bars for you. How's that?"

Crimson bounces on her toes. "Thank you, Coach Adam!"

I don't give her two candy bars like I want to. I give them each one, and Pinky steps forward to hug me. "It's okay, Uncle Adam. You can dress up next year."

"Thanks, Pink."

They trot off, and I look at Piper. She snorts a laugh, but we don't have time to discuss it. We're mobbed for the next two hours by ravenous little ghouls. When we finally run out of candy, I switch off the lights and close the front door.

"Who knew there were so many little kids in this town?"

"I think they come from all around." She leans closer, putting her hand beside her mouth. "They heard somebody gives out full-sized candy bars."

"Didn't you always want that as a kid?" I shrug. "I did."

The boys come charging in through the back door yelling. "Uncle Aiden gave us eyeball lollipops! Look!" Ryan holds up a cat's eye on a stick.

Piper recoils. "That is disgusting. Looks like something Britt would come up with."

"Ms. Belle made monster Rice Krispie Treats." Owen pulls

out a green square with one eye. "She said they're safe because she doesn't have time to put pins and needles in her snacks."

"Lovely," Piper mutters under her breath. "Oh, what's this?"

"Gran made us caramel pretzel bites, but she said it's special just for us," Owen explains, taking out the bags of white chocolate-dipped caramel pretzels.

"These look amazing." I turn the bag in my hand. "Why didn't she make these for us?"

"You're not a grandkid." Piper elbows me in the side.

"We should have a candy tax on these."

Piper leans down, making big eyes. "Sounds like you'd better run! Take all the candy to your room."

They yell and take off running with their pillowcases full of candy to Ryan's new bedroom.

"You think that's a good idea?" I squint, watching them go. "The one time Mom let me keep my Halloween bag in my room, I ate so much candy I barfed."

"Did you learn anything?" Her lips twist, and she looks up at me.

"Only about eating too much chocolate."

"Sounds like a good lesson, then."

"Maybe…" I'm not sure I agree, but I'm not interested in spending time on it now.

We have a quiet dinner together at the bar. She tells me about the latest on Drake Redford and Harold Waters, who apparently had a falling out at the wedding as a result of Drake calling Cass a witch.

When we're done, we put our plates in the dishwasher and walk back to my bedroom. Before we retire, I follow her to where the boys are in bed eating pizza and watching *Frankenweenie*.

Fudge is right in the middle of them, curled up at the foot of the bed.

"Brush your teeth before you go to sleep." Piper holds out her hand. "And hand over the Halloween bags. I'll put them in the kitchen until tomorrow, then we'll sort out a reasonable amount to have each day."

Ryan starts to whine, but he looks up at me and stops. "Okay, Mom."

I'm not sure what to make of it, but I give him a wink and a thumbs up. If he behaves like a good kid for my benefit, I'm okay with that.

Owen does whatever his friend does, and he hops off the bed, running to the bathroom. "Mama Britt said if I don't brush my teeth, they'll turn black and fall out."

Ryan's eyes widen, and he looks up at Piper. "Is that true?"

"If Britt says it's true, it must be. She's a scientist, so she knows all about rotten and dead things."

He jumps off the bed and runs to the bathroom, and I nod. "That forensic photographer thing must come in pretty handy with little boys."

"She sees dead people," Piper whispers, then calls to them. "Goodnight!"

I take her hand and lead her to the bedroom. It's not long before we're brushed and changed and climbing into bed as well.

I curl my body behind hers, burying my face in her neck and kissing her shoulder. "This is how it ought to be."

She snuggles further down into my arms, turning her cheek so it's pressed to my bicep. "It only took a little time to get here."

"You've always had me whenever you wanted."

"Have I?" She tilts her head up to look at me.

I lean down to kiss her lips. "Yes."

Only one thing is left to do.

Chapter 26

Piper

"I don't like waking up alone." Adam is over me in the bed, strong arms on both sides of me.

We're sweaty and spent, and I can't help a soft laugh. "If you keep giving me orgasms like that, I'll never leave the bed."

"Promise?"

After waking up with a woody at my backside this morning, I couldn't help reaching around and giving it a little tug, which led to burning hot kisses against my shoulders, down the center of my back, over my ass and then between my legs.

Now he's covering my shoulders with post-coital love and making me wonder how long I can put off getting ready for work.

"What are you up to today?" I curl my fingers in his long hair, and he smiles, that sexy dimple piercing his cheek.

"I'll meet with Chuck at your place, then I'll get the boys

to school and let the community center know I'm back for good."

"Not going back to Moloka'i?" I grin, squeezing him with my legs.

"I'll go back." He leans down to kiss the side of my neck. "And I'm taking you and Ryan with me."

My stomach tightens, and I hum with satisfaction. "Okay…"

"How about you? Any progress on the budget situation?"

"Yes!" I grip his rock-hard biceps. "Jemima had the great idea to let parents purchase personal ads for their kids for Halloween. She passed out fliers at the school, and we raised almost five thousand dollars! It's enough to cover her salary for almost three months."

Adam rests his head on his hand, and I step out of the bed. "Sounds like something you could continue through the holidays as well."

"And we can expand it to couples at Valentine's Day and families at any time." I walk to the bathroom. "The only hard part is sorting through all the emails and getting them ready to print."

"I'll make coffee." He walks into the bathroom where I stand naked, about to step into the shower, and he wraps his arms around me, holding my back to his chest facing the mirror and placing his hands on the scars above my waist. "You are so beautiful. I'm going to carry you back to bed."

"No!" I laugh, turning in his arms and cupping his cheeks so I can kiss his soft lips. "I have to get to work."

Large hands cover my ass, and he gives me a squeeze. "You know I have enough money to sponsor whatever you need. Just say the word."

"I like figuring it out. The *Gazette* is my baby, and the town really supports it."

"They support you." He kisses my shoulder, and I'm getting used to my new life pretty fast.

Acceptance, honesty, forgiveness.

Okay, I'm still working on that last one.

The boys are at the bar with their heads together over Adam's iPad laughing. Music plays, and they bounce in their chairs.

"Watch him jump over that pole!" Owen yells.

"He jumped right on that man's shoulder!" Ryan reaches up to scrub Fudge's head. "Think you could do that, boy?"

The cat stands beside them watching me with bright yellow eyes.

"What are you watching?" I walk over to look at the small screen. "Is that…"

"It's Didga, the skateboarding cat!" Ryan grabs my arm, pulling me closer. "Watch him jump over that dog!"

The board rolls between the legs of a giant Rottweiler, and the gray tabby jumps over his back.

"Whaaat?" I squint, looking for signs of computer generation. "Is that a trick?"

"It sure is, and I'm going to teach Fudge how to do it!" Ryan playfully pushes Owen's shoulder. "He can jump over Edward."

"If you can get Edward to stand up long enough." I walk over to get a cup of coffee. "Go brush your teeth. It's almost time for school." Adam is frowning at his phone near the toaster. "Everything okay?"

He slides the device into his pocket fast and smiles. "Hey."

"That wasn't suspicious. What's up?"

"Just Chuck saying he can't start for a few days." He wraps his arm around my shoulders, kissing the top of my head. "Last job went over."

"I'm okay with us being here a little longer. Especially now that you made a place for Ryan."

"Of course. Ryan should be with his family, and I think you should be here permanently."

My breath stills, and I blink up at him, a huge smile fighting to split my cheeks. "But what about my little house?"

"Eureka does have a shortage of rentals, and real estate is a solid investment."

Chewing my lip, I can't stop my smile. "A publisher and a landlord?"

That gets me another, longer kiss. "You're a mogul."

A laugh snorts through my nose. The toaster pops, and the boys run into the room again to grab their Pop-Tarts. Owen has his skateboard in hand, and Ryan has Fudge on his shoulder.

"Look, Uncle Adam, he's doing it!" Fudge stands on Ryan's shoulder for less than half a second before jumping to the floor and running outside. "We'll keep working on it."

Ryan gives me a hug around the waist, and I kiss his head. "Have a good day!"

Both boys run after the cat, and Owen drops his skateboard on the driveway, rolling out to the street.

Adam catches my chin, looking into my eyes before kissing me. "I like this idea a lot."

"Me too." I slide my thumb down his lips, pulling the full bottom one.

He pulls it into his mouth, giving it a suck, and we both catch a breath. "You're trying to make us late."

My body is on fire, but I shake my head, stepping forward to kiss him once more before sending him after the boys. "Tonight."

"I'm going cross-eyed looking at all these photos!" Jemima cries when I walk into the office. "Why did I think this was a good idea?"

"It was a great idea. Let me see." I scoot in beside her at the large desktop computer up front, where she has photo after photo of kids in Halloween costumes. "Look at that one!"

We're laughing and cooing at the images of pumpkins

and marshmallows and Grimaces and Hamburglars and Super Marios…

"There's three hundred of them!" She groans, leaning against the desk. "I thought charging fifteen dollars would scare people away."

"That's okay. We can run them over the next two issues and figure out what we want to do for Thanksgiving. Maybe thankful for grandparents?"

My phone buzzes, and I look down to see a text from Britt.

Britt: Your boyfriend's at it again.

She sends a photo, and I see it's a new sign outside the gazebo in the town square. It's too far away to make out what it says, but I tap a quick reply.

> He was with me all morning.

I don't add that I'm sure, because we were fucking before the sun rose.

Britt: Where was he last night?

> Inside me.

I punctuate it with a sly-grin emoji.

Britt: Whoot! Glad your hymen is good and gone.

> Dr Drew said it couldn't grow back, even after nine years.

"What are you grinning about?" Jemima walks over to where I'm standing at the door to my office. "Sexting with Mr. Stone?"

"Britt still thinks he's the phantom signer… Sign hanger?" I tap the photo and hold it for her to see.

"Oh, yeah! I saw that on the way to work this morning." Her blue eyes drift to past my shoulder as if she's remembering. *"The Truth Will Find You…* What could it mean?"

My eyes widen, and I know.

"Mom!" I shout, shoving my phone in my pocket and heading for the door. "I'll be back in a few minutes."

"Are you bringing Martha back to write headlines?" Jemima calls after me.

I'm out the door before I have time to answer, jogging around the back way, through the short strip of forested road to where her cedar shack is hiding in the saplings.

Only, the closer I get, I see a lot has changed in just a few days. Trees have been cut, and signs of a front walk are starting to emerge. She's no longer hiding, and I'm surprised by how happy it makes me.

It's like we've both been set free from the chrysalis of the past, and we're both emerging as different varieties of butterflies. Hers has pots of rose-bush cuttings on the front porch that look like they came from Gwen's yard.

Following the scent of coffee, I walk around to the back of the house. Everything is different since the last time I was here, frantically searching for her.

Inside, she's dancing around the kitchen humming the tune to "Karma" by Taylor Swift. I can't help a snort.

"Mom?" I call through the door, and she throws up both hands with a loud yelp. "Sorry," I manage through my laughter. "I didn't mean to scare you."

"Piper Ann, what are you doing here?"

It's the first time she's called me that in a while, and I go to where she's standing at the coffee pot to pull her into a hug.

My mind filters through the messages she posted around town… *Follow your path, Open your heart, Trust your instincts, You are brave, You are strong…*

In every one, she was telling me what I needed to hear in a way I might listen.

"Thank you." My voice is thick with unshed tears.

"For what?"

"For doing what you could, even when I made fun of you." Meeting her eyes, I watch hers grow misty. "Even when I pushed you away."

She pats my arms so I'll release her and turns to face the

coffee pot. "Children are supposed to push their parents away. It's how you learn to stand on your own."

"But you were always there."

She drove me to the hospital when Ryan was born. She stood at my side, silently guarding me the whole night. She built this entire, elaborate underground shelter to keep me safe as a little girl. She risked everything, changing her name, faking her death…

"I like what you're doing with the place." I look out the screen door, where bags of mulch sit beside paint supplies in boxes under the carport. "Jemima thinks you should write headlines for us again. I can't pay you, but I could sure use the help."

Turning to me again, a coffee cup in her hand, she grins. "Those were pretty good headlines, you have to admit."

"They were not." I put my hand on the door. "But you have good instincts. I bet if we just moved a few words around, they'd be perfect."

"Perfection is a construct we use to keep ourselves in cages."

"Maybe." I pause to kiss her cheek before I go. "But we're still going to write better headlines. Stop by on Friday, and we can work on the Sunday edition."

"Everything in its time." My cheek rests against Adam's bare chest, and his fingers thread in my long hair.

He slides his hand up my arm, leaning forward to catch my eyes. "What's that?"

"It was one of the signs." All the messages over the last year float through my mind.

"Those signs." He exhales in understanding. "Aiden was not a fan, but I liked them. They were always inspirational."

"They were for me." Lifting my head, I rest my chin on my hand. "Mom did them. She made them all, painted them all, and hung them around town where I'd see them."

"Seriously? She told you that?" He sits higher on the headboard, and I lean beside him, less worried about covering my body with a sheet than I have been in a long time.

His constant affection and compliments make me feel beautiful, confident. *Dreams do come true*… another sign.

"When I found her in that fruit cellar, and she told me about Ethan and running away, she told me 'The truth always finds you.'"

A smile curls his full lips, and he lets out a low, "Ahh… She outed herself? Or did she want you to know?"

"I think maybe she wanted me to know." Scooting closer, I snuggle into his side. "I never really knew my mom. I'm glad I get the chance to make up for it now."

"It's how I feel about you." His fingers thread in my hair again. "All those years, and I never knew… Now I can. Now I can make up for everything I got wrong and show you how much I've always loved you."

"You didn't get much wrong." I turn my face to kiss the warm skin of his chest. "We both were on a journey."

"I'm glad it brought me back to you."

"Me, too."

Sitting up again, he holds my shoulders so I'll face him. "I'm supposed to ask you one thing. I was given an assignment."

It makes me laugh even though I'm frowning. "Okay?"

"I love you. I want to be with you. You have to tell me if there's any reason why we can't be together."

Lifting my chin, I gaze straight into his pretty blue eyes. "I don't have a reason. I want us to be together."

"Then we always will be."

Reaching up, he slides his thumb over my cheek, and I lean forward to meet his kiss. Our lips part, and we slide down into the bed. My core is warm and slippery, and it's not long before he's sliding between my thighs, making us one.

Trust is a tricky thing. It can come so fast, and it can be lost so easily. But if you work really hard, and if you have faith and maybe a little luck, you can find it again.

Just like love.

Epilogue

Adam

"We'll start by replumbing the upstairs, then we'll repair the subfloor and plaster over the hole." Chuck points with his pencil to all the different construction points. "We should be done by Saturday."

"Seriously? It's Thursday." I look around the messy room.

"We'll make up the time, since we're late getting started."

"Oh, don't feel like you need to rush." Piper calls from where she's standing at the front door. "We're all set for now, and I'd rather you take your time and do it right."

"I'll get it done, and you'll be happy with the work." I catch a hint of defensiveness in his tone, and I jump in quickly.

"Thanks, Chuck. I know it'll be great. Just let me know if you need anything."

Heading to the door, I catch Piper's hand with Ryan following behind us. "Once he's done, we'll hire someone to come in and clean, then we can pack it up and put it on the rental market."

Her eyes widen as if she's startled, and I do my best not to take it personally. "Unless you're having second thoughts about staying with me?"

"No… it's just… This was the first house I ever bought. It's the one thing that ever belonged completely to me."

We're at the door to the *Gazette*, and I lean my elbow on the wall beside her cheek.

Bending down, I kiss her lips. "In that case, we'll do whatever you want. I'd never ask you to part ways with your favorite house."

She traces her finger in a circle on the neck of my tee, a little smile curling her lips. "Your house is my favorite house."

"Now you're just being confusing."

We start to laugh, and Ryan exhales a little groan. "I've got to get to school."

He takes off, and I kiss his mom on the lips. "See you tonight."

Jogging to catch up to him, I tap him on the shoulder. "Hey, little man, I want to talk to you about something."

"Like how you're always kissing my mom now?" He rolls his eyes like he's done with it.

A tinge of worry filters through my stomach, and I catch his arm, stopping his progress. "Do you not want me kissing your mom?"

He shrugs, wrinkling his nose and not looking entirely convinced. "I mean, I don't know. It's just… different."

Standing straighter, I put my hands in my back pockets, taking a beat to think before I continue. I'd planned for this to go super smooth, without a hiccup, but Ryan is way bigger than a hiccup.

"Well, that's kind of what I wanted to talk to you about. Your mom and I have been friends for a really long time, since we were just a little older than you are now."

"I know." He watches his feet scuffing the pavement as we walk, getting closer to the school.

"I love your mom. I want to ask her to marry me, but I want you to be happy about it."

He stops, but his eyes are on the road, and he doesn't speak. I squat down so I'm on his level, and I wish we were back near the square. I wish we could take a seat in the gazebo. I'm not sure what's changed since then.

"Hey," I hold his hand. "Are we still friends?"

He doesn't move his head, but his green-hazel eyes, so much like his mom's meet mine. "Yeah. Friends."

My brow furrows, and I'm confused by the way he says it. "Being friends is a good thing, right?"

"I guess. I don't know." He starts to walk, but I hold his arm.

"Tell me what's bothering you." A weight is in my chest, but I ask the obvious question. "Do you not want me to marry your mom?"

His small mouth tightens, and a hint of a tremble is in his chin. "You'll marry Mom, and it'll all be good, right?"

"I hope so."

"Then what happens if you have a baby like Miss Britt? What happens if it's a boy?"

Hesitating, I think about what he's saying. "I think that would be great."

"Because it'll be your real family. You'll have a real son, not a fake one like me."

"Whoa… is that what you think?" Shaking my head, everything in me revolts at the idea. I haven't discussed this with Piper, but I'm not letting him think these things. "Ryan, you've been my little boy since the day you were born. I drove all the way to the hospital just to see you, and when you looked at me with those big, serious eyes, I knew I'd have to step it up if I was going to be the dad you needed me to be. That's why I joined the Navy, but the whole time I was gone, your mom told me everything you did. She sent me videos of your first words, the first time you walked. When you were potty-training, she sent me pictures of your poop…"

"Ew!" His nose wrinkles, but his cheeks are pink. He's doing his best to be a strong little man and not cry.

"I love teaching you to play baseball and skateboarding. Soon we'll learn to surf." Reaching out, I put my hands on his waist. "You'll always be my son, Ryan, and well, I hope you'll let me try and be a good dad. I'll probably mess up sometimes, but I'll do my best."

His mouth turns down at the ends, but he nods. "I'll do my best, too."

"Come here." I pull him into a hug. "You're already the best, and nobody can take your place. And if we do have a new baby and it's a boy, you'll have to help me teach him all our skateboarding tricks and baseball and whatever else we're already doing. Okay?"

I give him a nudge, and he lifts his head, a hint of a smile curling his lips now. "Okay!"

"I'm the youngest, so I can tell you, I always looked up to Uncle Aiden and Uncle Alex. It'll be just like that. You'll be the great big brother, and he'll think you know everything."

"I will know a lot more than a baby does!" Ryan's voice is louder, and the clench of worry in my chest unfurls.

It's all going to work.

"I can't believe Herve is doing this again." Piper's hand is in mine, and we're walking the few blocks from my house to El Rio for another karaoke night.

"He told Alex it was the best business he'd done on a Thursday night in six months." I thread our fingers, thinking about what else is going to make tonight the best. "He's making it a first Thursday of the month thing."

"I guess that's good?" She squints up at me. "Are you going to sing something?"

"Maybe."

"You are?" Her eyes go wide. "You should do 'The Monster Mash' again. Everybody loved it, and Halloween was just Sunday."

"We'll see what happens."

When we reach the restaurant, Liberty Belle is onstage singing "Before He Cheats" again. We walk slowly through the dim room until shouts reach us from the round table in the back.

"Alex and Cass are back in town?" She looks up at me, and I shrug like I had no idea they were going to be here.

I knew they were going to be here.

Jemima hops up and runs to us, giving me a not-so-subtle wink. "You made it!"

She's dressed in a flapper-style gold dress with her blonde hair gathered in a messy bun on her head. Her lashes are full black and her lips are deep red, and I'm worried she's a little too on the nose for her part in the surprise.

"Don't tell me." Piper holds up a finger. "You're going to sing something by Taylor Swift?"

"That's why you're the publisher of the *Gazette*." Jemima boops her nose. "Nothing gets past your cute little nose for news!"

Piper shakes her head, laughing as she scoots into the booth beside Britt. "Can you believe it's been a month since you were dumping the wedding on me and barfing in the bathroom?"

"Ugh, don't remind me!" Britt holds up a ginger ale. "I'm staying on the safe side until this little lady is out."

"Lady!" Cass shrieks. "You're having a girl, and you didn't tell us?"

Britt's blue eyes go comically wide, and her mouth forms the shape of an *O*. "I wasn't supposed to say that."

Aiden starts to chuckle. "I can call off the fire department now—no gender reveal party."

"I wouldn't have set anything on fire!" She pushes his arm. "I'm a responsible member of law enforcement."

"Except when it comes to wedding receptions and babies," he teases.

"And state fairs." She cuts naughty eyes at him, and he leans down to kiss her solidly on the mouth.

"Oooo…" Jemima coos. "There's a story there!"

"Speaking of stories, this is the second time Liberty Belle has sung that song…" Piper tilts her head to the side. "Who cheated?"

"Sounds like a job for an intrepid Gazette reporter." Britt elbows her friend.

"Howdy, partners!" Deputy Doug struts up, pumping his elbows. "Are we ready for fireworks, or do we want to go down?"

He waggles his eyebrows, and Jemima hops up and runs around to my side.

"Are you ready?" She's not whispering very quietly, but Piper doesn't notice. "Looks like everybody's here."

I don't know why a sudden knot is in my throat, but I swallow it down and give her a nod. "Let's do it."

"Okay!" She does a fake fast-clap and skips over to the DJ, giving him the thumbs-up.

Liberty passes her the microphone, and the lights change to warm yellows. The DJ announces her name as Taker Slow singing "Love Story" in the style of Taylor Swift.

The banjo refrain begins, and my heart beats faster. I can't believe I'm nervous.

Jemima inhales an audible breath, and I'd think she was nervous, too until I see Raif Jones walk through the glass front door. He stops just inside the restaurant with his eyes fixed on her like he's starstruck.

Or is he Romeo? Who can say? I'm just listening for my cue. She said it's after the long musical break.

I know this song pretty well from when we were in school, and all the girls would sing it. Jemima insisted we do it this way, because she said it'll be, quote, *The most romantic thing ever!*

My ears quirk when she sings the part about Romeo saving

her, and she waves her hand fast. She is not subtle at all, but it's go time.

"Let's dance." Taking Piper's hand, I help her slide out of the booth.

"What's going on?" Her nose wrinkles. "This isn't really a dance song."

Jemima sings louder, growing more staccato with every word, as if she's guiding me to my part. Piper is on her feet, and my palms are damp. Our entire group is on their feet, and I almost start to laugh. I can't believe I let Jemima talk me into doing it this way, but here goes nothing.

She practically shouts the part about how he knelt to the ground, and I follow orders.

Lowering to one knee in the middle of the dance floor, I pull out the engagement ring I bought in Savannah. I look up at my favorite girl whose hands are over her mouth. Her eyes are wide and shining with tears, and I say it.

"Marry me, Piper."

Jemima continues singing about never being alone, and the whole place is shouting the lyrics along with her. It all happens at once, but as soon as the question leaves my lips, Piper's laughing and nodding.

Her eyes shine, and as I slide the ring on her finger, she drops to her knees as well, wrapping her arms around my neck and kissing me. "Yes, so much yes!"

Our tongues slide together, and I rise to my feet, lifting her off of hers. We're both hugging and smiling and kissing.

The song winds down, and our friends rush around us in a mob.

"If she hadn't said yes, I would've!" It sounds like Terra Belle, and a ripple of laughter floats through the group.

"You two! Let me see that ring!" Cass tugs on my arm, and I turn so Piper can show off the two-carat, square-shaped champagne diamond with white, rectangular baguettes on each side.

It's elegant and her colors, and when I saw it, it seemed exactly perfect for her—which Britt verified.

Martha steps up from where she'd been hidden at Terra and Liberty Belle's table. "Best wishes to my daughter."

"Mom!" Piper turns to hug her. "What are you doing here?"

"I got a tip someone was proposing tonight." She holds out her hand to me. "Congratulations, and I hope you're both very happy."

Taking her hand, I go to where she's standing beside my future wife. "More than I can say."

Her eyes shine, and I agree with Piper. It's time we got to know the real Martha.

"There's my favorite headline writer!" Jemima skips up behind Martha, placing her hands on her shoulders. "Did Piper tell you we miss you, and we want you back?"

"That is not how she put it." Martha smiles at her daughter. "But perhaps we can win her over."

"Yes, we can!" Jemima hugs her again, before turning to where Raif is now lurking at a high-top table in a dimly lit corner. "And I see someone in need of company."

I slide my arm around Piper, leaning closer to her ear. "Ready to get out of here?"

She laughs softly, lifting her chin and blinking dreamy green eyes up at me. "I'm ready when you are, Romeo."

Exhaling a laugh, warmth rises behind my ears. "Jemima helped me plan that."

"No kidding."

"Did you like it?" I give her a cringey smile, but she puts her arms around my neck, rising onto her toes and kissing my lips.

"I loved it so much." She exhales a little laugh. "For all my trauma-laughing and survival skills, I'm just a hopeless romantic at heart."

Hugging my arms around her waist, I lean down to kiss her ear. "You can pack all those other things away. All you need to worry about from now on is the romantic part."

Threading our fingers, I'm ready to head out the door, when an unusually tall, blonde woman in a sparkly purple, bell-bottom pantsuit enters the room.

It only takes me a blink to realize...

"Is that a drag queen?" Excitement is in Cass's tone.

"Monay?" Jemima's voice rings out over the music, and she runs across the room to hug the new arrival.

"Girl! I have been looking everywhere for you!" Monay places her hand on her chest before hugging Jemima, who looks tiny by comparison.

In her white platform boots, she has to be checking in at around six-foot-four.

"Guys! This is Monay Strangely, my absolute favorite Dolly Parton Christmas impersonator from Branson!" Jemima gestures to her friend. "Monay... this is everybody!"

"It's always a *hard*... candy Christmas when I'm in town, if you know what I mean." Monay bats her false lashes and laughs, waving her hand at us like a pageant participant.

"What are you doing here?" Jemima's eyes are as wide as her smile.

Monay's expression turns serious in a blink. "I came to get you, Jem. You've got to come back to Branson with me tonight."

Jemima's face is serious as well, and her voice drops so low, I only barely hear her response. "You know I can't go back there. He's looking for me."

"Dennis sent me to get you, girl. Things are getting hard for us queens, and he can't keep your daughter any more. You've got to come get her or he'll have to turn her over to the feds."

"He can't do that! She'll get lost in the system!"

"Hang on." Cass walks up to where her sister is speaking low and fast, but not low enough that we're all not stunned into silence. "Jemima? Did you leave a daughter in Branson?"

Her sister blinks rapidly, shaking her head. "Yes, but you don't understand. It's more complicated than that."

"It's not complicated." Impatience enters Cass's tone, and

I know being left by their mother is a sore spot with her. "You either have a daughter or you don't."

"You don't know the whole story, Cassidy!" Jemima grabs Monay's arm and starts for the door. "We've got to talk."

The two of them exit the restaurant, leaving the rest of us looking at each other, not knowing what to think.

"You heard her." Martha's no-nonsense voice cuts through the collective confusion. "We don't know the whole story. We'll let her explain it when she's ready."

"She's going to explain it to me now." Cass storms out of the restaurant after her sister.

Alex gives us a wave and takes off after his wife, and I notice Raif leaving cash on the high-top and shoving his hands in his pockets.

He walks over to our group. "Hi, Ms. Martha. Glad to see you're okay."

"Thank you, Raif." Martha doesn't smile. "You'll be around to help me next week?"

"Yes, ma'am." He nods before ambling to the exit as well. "'Night."

"What am I always saying?" Piper turns to me, shaking her head. "It's never a dull moment in Eureka."

I take her left hand, sliding my thumb over her ring finger before lifting it to my lips. "Ready to go now?"

"Yeah." She tucks her hands into the crook of my arm.

"Well, that's one way to end the evening." Britt walks over to give Piper and me a hug. "Best wishes, congratulations, all that stuff. I'm sure we'll find out what in the world is going on with Jemima soon enough. I'm exhausted."

Piper laughs, hugging her friend. "Get some rest, little mamma."

Aiden shakes my hand. "Good work, bro. That was fun."

I shrug. "Piper liked it."

That's all that matters to me.

The babysitter is paid, and Piper is sitting on the foot of my bed tilting her hand back and forth, watching the light glint off her engagement ring.

"It's so beautiful," she coos.

"You're so beautiful." I'm ready to carry her to the shower and get dirty while we get cleaned up when Ryan wanders into the room rubbing his fists over his eyes. "Hey, buddy, you okay?"

"I had a bad dream, and Fudge isn't in the bed." He walks to his mom, and Piper pulls him into a hug, smoothing her hand up and down his little back.

"I'm sorry. What did you dream?"

"Something exploded and there were a bunch of fireworks and I don't know why."

Piper frowns up at me, and I go to where they're sitting, taking his hand. "Come on, I'll take you back to bed."

"I heard Fudge in the litter box," Piper calls after us. "He's probably on his way to your bed now."

The two of us walk to his dark bedroom, and I tuck him under the covers. Sitting on his bedside, I hold his hand, thinking about how much he's still that little baby from so long ago.

"When you were born, I sang a song to you. Want to hear it?"

He nods, and I hum a few notes before singing the chorus of "Beautiful Boy" by John Lennon. Ryan's nose wrinkles, and I break off with a laugh.

"You don't like it?"

"I don't want to be called *beautiful*, Dad."

The burst of warmth provoked by that word hits me harder than I expected. *Damn*, I'm a dad.

"It's not *beautiful* like a girl. It's like how the ocean is beautiful or the passage of time."

His little eyes narrow as he thinks about it. "I guess that's okay. Just don't say it out loud. Or in front of anybody."

I can't help another chuckle. "Okay."

Fudge hops onto the bed between us, appearing like a black surprise.

"Fudge!" Ryan scrubs his face, and the cat stretches his neck and closes his eyes. "Ready to sleep, boy?"

"Think you can go back to sleep now?"

"I think so." He nods. "Thanks, Dad."

"Anytime, son." I lean down and give him a hug. "I love you."

"I love you, too."

Later in bed with Piper curled up in my arms, I think about all we've learned and all the years still to come. "Ryan called me Dad tonight."

She lifts her chin, placing her hand on my jaw. "Was that okay?"

"Yeah." I lean down, pulling her to me. "It was fucking great."

Exhaling a smile, she nuzzles her forehead under my chin. "It's how it's supposed to be."

She speaks the words I've felt so many times, only now I know them to be true.

We've come a long way, and we have more years ahead of us. We've learned things are never what they seem, and people can be all kinds of things you don't expect.

One thing we have for sure is our love, and with that and a little luck, we can face whatever comes our way. Because we'll be doing it together, and together is how we'll stay.

Thank you for reading *A Little Luck*!
Raif & Jemima's marriage of convenience, small-town, forbidden romance *A Little Naughty* is coming March 14, 2024!

Get a New Release Alert: Sign up for my newsletter at https://geni.us/TLMnews and/or text TIALOUISE to 855-902-6387 (*U.S. only*).

Will be available in Kindle Unlimited and on Audio at release.

READ NOW
A LITTLE TASTE is Aiden & Britt's spicy, small-town, single dad, grumpy-sunshine romance. Keep turning for a short sneak peek!

A Little Taste

Special Sneak Peek

Aiden Stone is a **six-foot-two former Marine** with a **permanent scowl**, dark hair, and **dreamy blue eyes.**

He's the oldest of **the Stone brothers**, and his "by the book" family has battled mine for control of **our small town** for generations.

The last thing I should do is **sleep with him.** Or nearly run him down with my truck. Especially since he's sort-of **my new boss**…

It doesn't help that my grandmother (the mayor) is a former magician, and my mom is a psychic (sort-of)… And my dad died in a failed escape-artist attempt (that my mother is convinced was a murder).

Trust me, **I know crazy**, but I'm just plain ole Britt Bailey, Shania Twain-loving, non-magical forensic photographer. Yes, I take pictures of dead things, but I don't see them in my bedroom at night.

I only want to see one thing in my bedroom at night, and when I'm called home to help Sheriff Stone on an investigation, he actually stops frowning for a minute, and **my teenage fantasies get very real.**

It's a terrible idea. We work together, he's **seven years older** than me, he's **a single dad**, he hates all things magic, but *a little taste*, and **we can't say no**.

Until the town crime wave turns personal, putting everything on the line, and we'll need more than a magic bullet to get our happily ever after.

(**A LITTLE TASTE is a small-town, grumpy single-dad romance with a touch of light suspense and lots of tasty spice. No cheating. No cliffhanger.**)

Chapter 1

Aiden

"Yep, he's a goner." Deputy Doug Hally straightens with a groan, holding the squashed cucumber out for my inspection.

I nod grimly, and Terra Belle throws up her arms in distress. "My entire pickle farm is destroyed! Who would do such a thing?"

We're standing in the middle of the two-acre field now riddled with large, circular ruts and damaged fruit still on the vine. The pattern of the tire tracks reminds me of that movie about the aliens making crop circles, but this damage was definitely done by a vehicle of some sort.

"My money's on them no-good Jones boys." My sole deputy tosses the damaged fruit to the side, lowering his brow in a knowing way.

"You think it was Bull and Raif, Dad? Are you going to arrest them? Can I go?" My son Owen blinks up at me, his seven-year-old eyes wide, and I hesitate.

If he weren't here, I'd say this looks more like asshole teenagers who watched that movie and wanted to play a prank. The Jones boys were probably too drunk or high last night to do something this precise, but it's important to me to be a good role model, even when I'm tired.

Placing my hand on Owen's shoulder, I summon my dad, the former sheriff of Eureka's calm wisdom. I think about what he'd have said to me at Owen's age.

"It's not our job to decide who's guilty, son. We have to collect the evidence and make our best determination, then we'll get a judge to issue a warrant."

"Oh, you know it was those Jones boys." Terra drops to a squat, holding up a vine of crushed cuke after cuke—it looks like a sad party favor. "I'm tempted to gather up the rest of these and beat them to death with 'em."

"Now, Terra," Deputy Doug cautions. "Two wrongs don't make a right."

"Yeah, don't go there, Terra," I add. "Then I'd have to arrest you, too."

"So you *are* going to arrest them?" She stands quickly. Her dark hair is tied up in a red handkerchief, and she's wearing faded overalls and from what I can tell, nothing else. "This kind of vandalism can't go unpunished. It's trespassing, destruction of property, murder…"

With every charge she shakes the pickle vine at me, and I stand straighter, rising to my full six-foot-two height and lowering my voice. "Take it easy, Terra."

It's my standard way to diffuse tense situations, and sure enough, Terra deflates.

"What am I going to do about my existing orders?"

"You've got insurance, don't ya?" Doug squints as he walks to where we're standing.

"Of course I do!" she snaps at him, but I let it pass.

She's facing a pretty significant loss, which has her understandably emotional. I have no clue how long it takes to grow a crop of cucumbers, and Terra Belle's Pickle Patch is regionally famous, which I guess might make her a target. Of what, I don't know.

Exhaling slowly, I maintain my calm. "I'll head back to the office and get you a police report to send to the insurance company. Hopefully, that'll get you some money pretty quick." She starts to argue it's not enough, and I nod. "I know you want justice today, but I can't go arresting people without evidence. It'll just get thrown out, and that's not how we do things."

"Well, maybe it should be," she grouses.

I'm tired. I haven't had my first cup of coffee. The call to come out here had me out of bed before the sun even broke the horizon. Now it's climbing higher in the sky, and I'm ready to head to the office and possibly have breakfast.

"Doug, you finish up here, and I'll get Terra's report ready." I'm not sure the correct way to phrase my next question. "Before I go, do you have any enemies or rival... picklers?"

"Oh, I've got plenty of rivals, but no one would stoop to this level." She wipes a tear off her cheek. "Destroying my *babies*."

Pressing my lips together, I nod. I'm not good with tears, especially tears over "baby pickles," which in reality are called *cucumbers*.

"All the same, send me any names that come to mind, and take plenty of pictures. I'll have that report to you by lunchtime."

I whistle to my son, who's holding a squashed fruit with a stick and examining it. He drops it at once and takes off running to my truck. I let Doug drive the cruiser. In this town, I'm fine with a black Silverado and a light on the dash when necessary.

Terra can work this out with her insurance company, and I'll have Doug inspect every teenager in town's vehicle for traces of cucumber vines. It won't take long in Eureka, South Carolina. I'll include the Jones boys to cover all the bases.

We're halfway back to town, the radio playing some old country song. Owen's beside me, buckled in and bouncing Zander, his tattered, stuffed zebra on his legs. "Why would anybody drive a car in Ms. Belle's pickle patch?"

My hand is propped on the top of the steering wheel, and I think about it. "The older I've gotten, the less I understand why people do anything. I guess that's why towns need sheriffs."

"I'm going to be a sheriff when I grow up!" He smiles up at me, pride in his eyes. "Just like my dad."

My stomach tightens, and warmth filters through my chest. I'm generally considered something of a grumpy badass, but this little guy… He's a lot like I was at his age, thinking my dad was the greatest and wanting to grow up to be just like him.

I thought I'd have a chance to work right alongside him, but a heart-attack took him two days after I graduated from college. I've missed him every day since. Especially when life hits hard. Especially when I need advice.

I went from being a student, to being a Marine, to being a sheriff, and now Owen wants to follow in my footsteps.

"You'll be one of the best." I glance at him before returning my eyes to the road.

He sits straighter, lifting his chin, and I almost grin. I had no idea when he was born how much he'd carry me through the dark times.

He was barely old enough to remember his mom when she was killed four years ago on her evening walk. I'd mourned her and pledged to find the person who hit her and drove off without even looking back.

Then a year later, when I'd finally worked up the strength to go through her things, I found a box of love letters from Clive Stevens, who happened to live on the very street where she was hit.

He'd even had the balls to attend her funeral before he moved back to wherever he was from. It never occurred to me to be suspicious of her evening walks, but after that, I pretty much swore off anyone not related to me by blood. They're the only ones you can trust, and even then, it's good to keep your eyes open.

"Do you know what a zorse is?" Owen looks up at me, bouncing Zander on his leg. "It's a cross between a zebra and a horse!"

"Is that so?" I park the truck in front of the courthouse, which houses the mayor's office and our headquarters.

"A group of zebras is called a dazzle. I wonder if a group of zorses would be called a zazzle?"

He looks up at me like I would know. "Forget sheriff, you should be a zebrologist when you grow up."

"That's not a thing!" He groans as he climbs out of the truck, slamming the door and trotting up beside me, slipping his little hand in mine.

It warms my chest, again almost making me smile. I don't smile often, and I definitely don't hold hands, but with Owen, everything is different.

"You can be the first." I scoot him through the glass doors ahead of me, hoping Holly, our secretary and dispatcher, ordered breakfast—or at least has a pot of coffee ready.

"Aiden, I heard you were at Terra Belle's Pickle Patch." I'm met at the door by Edna Brewer, longtime mayor of Eureka, and unfortunately my boss. "My intuition tells me something sinister is afoot."

"Terra would agree with you. She left her house without her wig on."

Edna's dark brown eyes widen. "You saw Terra's real hair?"

"She had a handkerchief around her head, and she was in overalls."

"Only something truly sinister would cause Terra to leave the house in such a state."

"I suspect it's nothing more sinister than teenagers." I start to walk past her, but she pulls me up short with her next words.

"Owen, your father is a good man, despite his lack of faith."

My jaw tightens. We were almost having a nice moment, and she had to go there. "I prefer sticking to the facts when doing my job."

"Magic has never let me down, Sheriff, which is more than I can say of people."

She'll get no arguments from me when it comes to people, however, "Where was magic when Lars needed it?"

Her eyes narrow. "What happened to my son-in-law was a tragic accident, but escapologists are not magicians."

Neither are you. The retort is on the tip of my tongue, but I don't say it. We're fighting old battles, and we only go in circles.

The Brewers and the Stones declared a truce after my father died, and I've done my best to honor it since starting as sheriff—as long as Edna keeps her hocus pocus to herself and out of my work.

Placing my hand on Owen's back, I give him a little pat. "Why don't you run see if Holly got donuts on her way in." He takes off with a little whoop of "Krispy Kreme," and I turn to the mayor. "I apologize for saying that about Lars. It was insensitive."

She lifts her chin. "I accept your apology."

"And I'd appreciate it if you didn't put ideas in my son's head."

"Your son is very bright, Aiden."

"Thank you."

"And children are very sensitive to spiritual things. Owen's fascination with zebras is a clear indicator. They're remnants of a time when the world was shadows and light."

"No." My tone is firm.

She waves her hands. "I'm not trying to start a fight. I simply wanted to let you know I've been monitoring this rise in crime lately, and I think we need to bring in some backup."

My brow furrows. "What does that mean?"

She starts for her office, and I follow. Edna is almost seventy, with silver hair that hangs in a bob to her chin. She's dressed in a white silk blouse and tan pencil skirt with matching pumps, and in this conservative disguise, you'd never know she's a former magician and matriarch of the town's resident band of carnies.

She believes in premonitions and psychics and *vibrations* as much as cold hard facts when making civic decisions. It drove my dad nuts, and it doesn't make me too happy either—particularly when she drags her "psychic" daughter Guinevere into the mix. Gwen is a real space cadet, and sneaky as fuck.

You'd think Edna would be ready to retire by now, but this crazy town keeps voting her back in office every time she runs. If the town of Eureka were a zebra, she'd be the black to my white—and I'm sure she'd say the exact opposite.

"Someone has been nailing messages on telephone poles for a month. Last week, Holly said three of her hens were stolen. Now Terra Belle's prized pickle patch has been demolished. I think we need someone with special training in this type of work."

Heat rises under my collar, and a growl enters my tone. "You're not to call in additional officers without consulting me."

"I'm consulting you now. Doug's pushing sixty, but even if he was younger, you know he isn't up to this type of work. You could use the help."

I'm annoyed she's right. Still, the last thing I need is some new person coming in, getting in my way, asking a bunch of questions—or worse, another kooky mystic reading tea leaves and being totally loyal to Edna.

"Who did you have in mind?"

"That's the best part." She claps, rising to her feet and smiling like she's about to pull a rabbit out of a hat. "My granddaughter Britt has been working in Greenville, training at the crime lab at Clemson. She's got the best possible credentials."

My stomach tightens. "Britt said she wasn't coming back to Eureka."

The last time I saw Edna's granddaughter— at her going away party, which my youngest brother tricked me into attending—she'd said she wanted to define her life outside this town and her family's reputation.

"Oh, poo." Edna waves her hand. "Guinevere will call her. She'll want to be back in her hometown with her best friends and family."

I'm not so sure of that. I'm also not so sure about her working with me. Britt Bailey is too young and too pretty, and on the night of her farewell party, things got a little too blurry on the back porch of her friend's home.

We somehow wound up out there alone, and we started talking about her life in Eureka, my time in the Marines, her dreams, my son. It was the first time I'd seen her as the only sane member of her family.

Our bodies had drifted closer until we were almost touching, and the conversation faded away. She blinked those pretty green eyes up at me, and the starlight shone on the tips of her blonde hair. She smelled like fresh flowers and the ocean, and her pink lips were so full and inviting. It had been so long since I'd lost myself in the depths of a beautiful woman…

Obviously, I'd had too much whiskey.

"I can tell by your pleased expression you like this idea." Edna nods. "I'll have Gwen call her today, and I'll let you know how soon she can get started."

"That wasn't what I was thinking." My expression was *not* pleased. "Is she even old enough to work here?"

"She's twenty-eight, Aiden. Don't be ageist."

Seven years younger than me.

"But this would be her first actual job as a crime scene investigator?"

"She's an experienced forensic photographer. You can get her up to speed on the rest. She's a fast learner." Edna picks up her phone, excitedly tapping on the face. "Trust me, once you have my granddaughter at your side, you'll wonder how you ever survived without her. The vibrations are shifting already."

I'm sure they are, and it's exactly what's putting me on guard.

Read **A LITTLE TASTE** today in Kindle Unlimited, on audiobook, or in paperback.

Books by
TIA LOUISE

THE BE STILL SERIES
A Little Taste, 2023★
A Little Twist, 2023★
A Little Luck, 2023★
A Little Naughty, coming March 14, 2024★
(★Available on Audiobook.)

THE HAMILTOWN HEAT SERIES
Fearless, 2022★
Filthy, 2022★
For Your Eyes Only, 2022
Forbidden, 2023★
(★Available on Audiobook.)

THE TAKING CHANCES SERIES
This Much is True★
Twist of Fate★
Trouble★
(★Available on Audiobook.)

FIGHT FOR LOVE SERIES
Wait for Me★
Boss of Me★
Here with Me★
Reckless Kiss★
(★Available on Audiobook.)

BELIEVE IN LOVE SERIES
Make You Mine
Make Me Yours★
Stay★
(★Available on Audiobook.)

SOUTHERN HEAT SERIES
When We Touch
When We Kiss

THE ONE TO HOLD SERIES
One to Hold (#1 - Derek & Melissa)★
One to Keep (#2 - Patrick & Elaine)★
One to Protect (#3 - Derek & Melissa)★
One to Love (#4 - Kenny & Slayde)
One to Leave (#5 - Stuart & Mariska)
One to Save (#6 - Derek & Melissa)★
One to Chase (#7 - Marcus & Amy)★
One to Take (#8 - Stuart & Mariska)
(★Available on Audiobook.)

THE DIRTY PLAYERS SERIES
PRINCE (#1)★
PLAYER (#2)★
DEALER (#3)
THIEF (#4)
(★Available on Audiobook.)

THE BRIGHT LIGHTS SERIES
Under the Lights (#1)
Under the Stars (#2)
Hit Girl (#3)

COLLABORATIONS
The Last Guy★
The Right Stud
Tangled Up
Save Me
(★Available on Audiobook.)

PARANORMAL ROMANCES
One Immortal (vampires)
One Insatiable (shifters)

GET THREE FREE STORIES!
Sign up for my New Release newsletter and never miss a sale or new release by me!
https://geni.us/TLMnews

Acknowledgments

THANK YOU, reader-friend, for going on this emotional journey with me. I hope I got it right.

Huge thanks and so much love to my husband Mr. TL and my two beautiful daughters, who are my constants.

Thanks so much to my alpha readers Renee McCleary and Leticia Teixeira for your funny notes and highlights, and for helping me cover all my bases.

Huge thanks to my *incredible* betas, Maria Black, Corinne Akers, Amy Reierson, Courtney Anderson, Jennifer Christy, Heather Heaton, and Michelle Mastandrea. You ladies rock!

Thanks to Jaime Ryter for your awesome editing and to Lori Jackson and Kate Farlow for the killer cover designs. Always love to my dear Wander Aguiar for the *perfect* cover images, and the amazing Stacy Blake, who makes my print books *so beautiful*.

Thanks to my fantastic Starfish, to my *mermazing* Mermaids, and to my Veeps for keeping me sane and organized.

Thanks to the incredible Booktokers and Bookstagrammers and ARC readers and edit makers, who help me so incredibly much, specially Jimena, Morgan, Lemmy, Mindie, and so many more—you all mean the world to me!

I can't begin to put into words how much I appreciate the love and support of my author-buds. We're all so slammed, and your support means the world to me, in particular Melanie and Lena for letting me gripe and complain and ask allll the questions…

Again, thank *you* for helping me do what I love.

Stay sexy,

<3 Tia

About the Author

Tia Louise is the *USA Today* best-selling, award-winning author of super-hot and sexy romances. She'll steal your heart, make you laugh, melt your kindle... *and have you begging for more!*

Signed Copies of all books online at:
http://smarturl.it/SignedPBs

Connect with Tia:
Website
Instagram (@AuthorTLouise)
TikTok (@TheTiaLouise)
Pinterest
Bookbub Author Page
Amazon Author Page
Goodreads
Snapchat

** On Facebook? **

Be a Mermaid! Join Tia's Reader Group at
"Tia's Books, Babes & Mermaids"!

www.AuthorTiaLouise.com
allnightreads@gmail.com

Printed in Great Britain
by Amazon